THE FORM ON
THE CIRCULAR PATTERN
JERKED ONCE . . .

. . . its head thrown back, the tendons in its neck standing out like knotted cords.

Then it lay still.

Brown cut power. The machine cycled down.

He walked over to the platform, stood over the being locked into it. It was a few moments before its eyelids fluttered open.

There was intelligence in those eyes. And something else—something that seemed to hold him captive for a moment.

"Brown," said the android. "Isn't it?"

"That's right," said Brown. "And you are . . . ?"

"Captain James T. Kirk—Captain, U.S.S. *Enterprise*." He chuckled. "The improved version."

Look for STAR TREK Fiction from Pocket Books

STAR TREK®

DOUBLE, DOUBLE

MICHAEL JAN FRIEDMAN

POCKET BOOKS

New York   London   Toronto   Sydney   Tokyo

An *Original* Publication of POCKET BOOKS

POCKET BOOKS, a division of Simon & Schuster Inc.
1230 Avenue of the Americas, New York, NY 10020

ISBN: 0-671-66130-2

First Pocket Books printing April 1989

10 9 8 7 6 5 4 3 2 1

POCKET and colophon are trademarks of
Simon & Schuster Inc.

Printed in the U.S.A.

For my son,
Brett David.
May the stars smile
on all his *Enterprises*

Double, double, toil and trouble;
Fire burn, and cauldron bubble.

. . . Stars, hide your fires!
Let not light see my black and deep desires:
The eye wink at the hand! yet let that be,
Which the eye fears, when it is done, to see.

I dare do all that may become a man;
Who dares do more, is none.
                              —Shakespeare,
                              Macbeth

DOUBLE, DOUBLE

Chapter One

BROWN HAD BEEN AWAY a long time.

It had begun as a simple mission of exploration along the Lower Rim, in search of additional ruins. His creator had thought there might be more machines down there. "Wonders," he'd called them, "beyond those we've already seen."

So he'd set out, alone, with what seemed like an ample supply of equipment. But even Doctor Korby could not have predicted the weakness in the cavern wall, or the cave-in. Or the futility of trying to dig himself out, before he decided to search for another way back instead. Or the long darkness after his searchlight batteries had expended all their power.

Now, he was home. He recognized the geometric shape of the sliding door. He heard the familiar hum of the energy generators, noted the familiar light sources of the outer areas.

Home.

He pressed the plate next to the door. With a hiss, it opened. Brown walked into the antechamber.

Usually, there was work going on here. Either Ruk or the other Brown or, sometimes, he himself would be assigned to this place. Repairing pieces of the old machines, or fashioning new ones. But the room was empty.

Where was everyone?

In the main chamber, then. With the machines. Perhaps Doctor Korby was creating somebody new. Yet another Brown? Another Andrea? Or someone else entirely?

The inner door, like the outer, opened with a sharp rush of air.

In the glare of the overhead lighting, the machine shone a bluish gray. It sprawled, filling half the chamber. The indicators on its control console were dark, dormant.

And again, the room was empty.

Brown felt a pang of disorientation—something he had not experienced even in the long months of darkness. He knew that the feeling had not been programmed into him, because he could not put a name to it. Yet it was there nonetheless.

Most curious. But his next move was clear. He had to go on. To find Doctor Korby. To make sure everything was all right.

The next room was the main parlor, where his creator had spent much of his time. Here, the lighting was more subtle. There were wooden tables and chairs, a small computer, rugs on the floor, tapestries on the walls. Ornamentation, in which Doctor Korby had found some sort of stimulation.

"Doctor Korby?" called Brown, though he could see that there was no one here either.

He had not heard his own voice in quite some time. It sounded foreign as it echoed in his ears.

Nor did he use it again, for it only seemed to intensify the feeling of disorientation. Crossing the room, he placed his hand against the control plate.

The door slid aside, revealing the small, stark chamber behind it. Unlike the parlor, it was devoid of ornament— used mostly for storage. And dark.

But not so dark that Brown didn't notice the form on the ground. He reached out, found the light plate where he knew it would be.

And saw, in the ruddy glow of the single overhead, the body of the other Brown. Half his abdomen was torn away, revealing the fused ruin of his internal systems. The damage must have been considerable, for there was no sign of function at all.

Brown knelt by the body, giving the ruined area careful

2

scrutiny. He ran his fingers along the ragged edges of the opening and felt his own lower torso tighten involuntarily.

This had not been an accident, the result of an explosion in one of the machines. Only a tightly concentrated force could have had this effect.

But he knew of no such force.

Was there a connection between what had happened to his counterpart and the disappearance of the others?

It was likely. Highly likely.

The feeling of disorientation began to mount. After all, Brown had not been programmed for such an eventuality.

Perhaps, if he had more information . . .

And then he remembered. Of course—the closed-circuit monitor. He had installed it himself, though it had been Andrea's job to maintain it.

It would have kept a record of all that transpired here. All he needed to do was play it back.

Leaving the other Brown where he'd found him, he turned off the light. The door swished closed behind him.

Brown sat in the chair that had been Doctor Korby's.

He switched off the playback unit. He watched the images on the screen dissolve.

So.

They were gone, all of them. Ruk, who had been created by the Old Ones, who seemed indestructible. Andrea.

Even Doctor Korby himself.

And all because of this human—Captain Kirk. He was the one who had disabled the other Brown. He was the one who had caused the destruction of his own duplicate, who'd forced the creator to obliterate Ruk—and then destroy Andrea along with himself.

All gone, all.

Brown strained to comprehend it.

If the creator was no more, and his purpose was to serve the creator . . . then what purpose was left? Should he tend the machines as Ruk tended them, for time immeasurable, until another creator came to give him instructions?

No. He was not like Ruk. He could not serve another creator.

3

Then what? What could he do?

What would Doctor Korby have *wanted* him to do?

Suddenly, the answer came to him. It had been recorded in his memory banks when he'd heard it on the playback unit.

Can you understand that a human converted into an android can be programmed for the better? Can you imagine how life could be improved if we could do away with jealousy . . . greed . . . hate?

They were the words of the creator himself.

No one need ever die again. No disease, no deformities. Why, even fear can be programmed away and replaced with joy. I'm offering you a practical heaven, a new paradise. . . .

Brown leaned back in the chair.

This had been Doctor Korby's purpose. He was sure of it. And as he continued to scan his memory banks, he recalled something else. Doctor Korby had given him a plan to carry it out—hadn't he?

Could he do it by himself? No. Not even the creator could have done that. He needed someone to serve him—a Ruk, or an Andrea. He needed to make more androids before he could even begin.

But how might he create another android—even one? He did not know enough about the programming process—nor had he been given an aptitude for it.

The other Brown came to mind, but he was beyond repair. Even if his internal organs could have been rendered workable again, his programming would have been wiped clean.

Brown ran the monitor sequences over again in his mind, searching for an answer.

And found one.

The machine's high-pitched whirring became a dull hum as the focal platform slowed its spinning. Long before it came to a halt, Brown knew he had been right.

The machine's template of the human had been preserved. Or at least, the physical data had remained intact, for the being before him was a complete and normal specimen.

But it would be a useless specimen, Brown told himself, if the mental patterns had not also been preserved.

He made the proper connections among the machine's circuits and adjusted the neural output control. Then he activated the appropriate receptors.

The form on the circular pattern jerked once, its head thrown back, the tendons in its neck standing out like knotted cords.

Then it lay still.

Brown cut power. The machine cycled down again into quiescence. Its lights blinked in the proper sequence.

He walked over to the platform, stood over the being locked into it. It was a few moments before its eyelids fluttered open.

There was intelligence in those eyes. And something else—something that seemed to hold him captive for a moment.

"Brown," said the android. "Isn't it?"

"That's right," said Brown. "And you are . . . ?"

"Captain James T. Kirk, Captain, U.S.S. *Enterprise*." He chuckled. "The improved version."

Brown nodded, satisfied. His creation not only looked like the human he'd seen in the playback. He sounded like him—*acted* like him.

"Now," said the *Kirk* android, "how about getting me out of here?" With his eyes alone, he indicated the lock that held him fast to the platform.

The android's tone was mellow, almost charming. But it was a tone that demanded obedience.

Before Brown knew what he was doing, the lock had been opened. He took a step back, giving *Kirk* room in which to move.

Naked, the android glanced around the chamber.

"You know how to shut down the machines, don't you?"

"Of course," said Brown.

"Then I suggest you do so. We won't be needing them for a while."

Brown began to move toward the main power supply, stopped himself. He chided himself for falling so easily into the servitor mode.

He was the master now. He must remember that, he told himself.

"Something wrong?" asked *Kirk.*

"I am not finished with the machines," said Brown.

"Explain yourself," said *Kirk,* stretching.

"You are only the first of the androids I plan to manufacture. It will take a large number of us to carry out Doctor Korby's plan."

Kirk laughed. Derisively, Brown thought.

"One of me is enough," he said. "Or did you expect to populate the galaxy with Jim Kirks—without arousing anyone's suspicion?"

Brown had no answer for that. He had not thought out his scheme quite that far.

"But the creator's plan . . ." he began.

Kirk dismissed him with a wave of his hand. "Do you think you know the creator's mind better than I do? A *Kirk* was to be the instrument with which he saved humanity. My program *is* his plan."

He strode across the room, palmed the plate on the wall. When the door slid open, he stepped through.

Brown hurried after him into the next chamber—one set up as a small bedroom.

"What are you doing?" he asked the android. He had the feeling that matters were spiraling out of control. Out of *his* control.

"I'm getting something to wear," said *Kirk.* "Starship captains don't walk around mother-naked if they don't have to."

He rummaged through the chest of drawers until he found a set of overalls.

"You must understand," said Brown, "that I am in charge here. I created you."

Without looking at him, *Kirk* slipped on the overalls.

"My dear Doctor Brown," he said. *"You* must understand that you're talking to a starship captain. While you are only a faint echo of a second-rate scientist—an analog rather than a duplicate, since the original Doctor Brown was already dead when you were made."

Kirk smoothed out the wrinkles in the overalls against his body.

6

"To put it bluntly," he continued, "I don't think there's any question who's more . . . *qualified* to lead this operation."

Suddenly, he looked up. Brown saw a distinct hardness in his eyes.

"Any objections?"

Brown tried, but he couldn't think of any. He had to admit that what *Kirk* had said was entirely logical.

And what did it matter who led the revolution? As long as Doctor Korby's purposes were carried out.

Mind your own business, Mister Spock. I'm sick of your half-breed interference, do you hear?

Kirk pushed himself away from the computer console. He made a fist with his right hand and pounded it into his left, and the sound it made echoed momentarily in the cavern.

That was it!

It had taken him hours—scrupulous poring over the physical plan of the *Enterprise*, patient introspection of the human Kirk's automatic responses to various stimuli on board. But he'd found it.

The conditioned response to any encounter initiated by the ship's Vulcan first officer. *Mind your own business, Mister Spock. . . .*

How clever. Kirk must have drilled it into himself sometime before the original *Kirk* android's mental patterns had been set. Perhaps even as he lay on the focal platform.

And at some point, the android—suspecting nothing, for he had no reason to—had spoken those words when he visited the *Enterprise*. Of course, it had aroused suspicion in the highly perceptive Vulcan. And *that* was what had led to the landing party later on.

Kirk had had no other way to get word to his ship. It had to be the response he'd planted.

Satisfied, *Kirk* smiled. He would make no such mistake when he took Kirk's place on the *Enterprise*.

For, surely, that was the way to accomplish Doctor Korby's imperatives. From the command chair of the *Enterprise*, he'd have at his disposal everything he needed to spread the seeds of a secret revolution. Power. Prestige.

Wide-ranging transportation. Access to the Federation's communications and data nets.

Impulsively, he called up a cross section of the starship on the screen of his console. It held a certain intrigue for him. A certain attraction.

Control of the *Enterprise* was crucial. *Crucial.* So much so, in fact, that he had difficulty conceiving of any strategy that did not include it.

But first, he needed a way to get off Exo III. Not only for himself, but for the replication machinery as well. That was the other key element—to find a base of operations. A planet with population and raw materials sufficient to fuel large-scale android manufacture.

Of course, there was but one way to obtain transportation. Depressing the intercom button, *Kirk* called for Brown.

The other android appeared in the doorway within moments.

"I have not yet finished cleaning the receptor rods," said Brown.

"How long will it take?" asked *Kirk.*

For just a fraction of a second, Brown seemed to hesitate. A flaw in his programming? *Kirk* filed it away for future reference.

"Perhaps another hour," he said finally. "But there are other maintenance tasks to be performed."

"Leave those for later," said *Kirk.* "When you're finished with the receptor rods, you will build a communications device. The most powerful device you can assemble."

Brown nodded slowly. "It will be done. And you? What will *you* do?"

Kirk narrowed his eyes. "I will spend my time wisely," he answered.

Frowning, the android turned and departed.

Kirk watched the door close behind him. Then he returned his attention to the computer screen, where the *Enterprise* was still displayed in cross section. He punched in a command and it swung about ninety degrees, coming finally to face him.

For a while longer, he studied it.

Chapter Two

Captain's Log Supplemental, Stardate 4925.2:

The meteor swarm we detected will enter T'nufo's atmosphere in less than an hour. When it does, it will devastate the length and breadth of P'othpar Island.

Since there was no other way to get the inhabitants safely to the mainland in time, we have resorted to the use of the *Enterprise*'s transporter unit. Fortunately, there are only two small villages on the island—K'neethra here on the southern tip and Az'roth on the eastern shore.

Nonetheless, the evacuation effort has been a tedious and complicated one. The P'othparans are a quasi-religious group, who long ago isolated themselves from other T'nufans in order to rediscover certain primitive social values. This means, of course, that they have no access to telecommunications—so that we've had to locate each individual dwelling, no matter how distant from the main village, and warn each P'othparan in turn.

To further convolute matters, our translation devices are only programmed for this world's major languages. And with the exception of only one man, Crewman Donald Clifford, none of my people can even come close to the P'othparan tongue.

9

As a result, we've had to enlist the aid of native-culture experts from the provincial university on the mainland. We talk to them and they talk to the P'othparans.

Meanwhile, of course, we are continuing our efforts to prevent the meteors from falling in the first place—though it seems futile at this point. Had the swarm approached from Federation space, and not from beyond the Romulan neutral zone, we might have been able to destroy it long before this. As it is, we'll chip away as best we can—until impact.

JIM KIRK, captain of the U.S.S. *Enterprise*, stood in the ancient village square with the rest of the evac base team. There were half a dozen of his own people and an equal number of the mainlanders, speaking in low voices that showed their fatigue as much as their respect for this place.

Kirk was tired too. Tired and hot. But most of all, he was frustrated.

Beyond the intricately carved stone buildings, beyond the dark humpbacks of the hills, a magnificent red-purple sunset was just beginning to build among the clouds. And somewhere beyond that was the meteor swarm, getting closer with each passing second.

Kirk sensed someone approaching, turned. He recognized the scholar called Lee'dit, the nominal leader of the university contingent.

The T'nufan was born to this climate. After all, the weather on the mainland was nearly as hot and dry as on P'othpar. But his dark bronze skin was every bit as streaked with sweat and dust as that of the humans. And his nerves, like theirs, seemed to be stretched tight as he waited for the last outlying family to be brought in.

Lee'dit indicated the spectacle of the setting sun. "Lovely, isn't it?" he asked Kirk. "The way the clouds catch the light?"

The captain nodded. "Quite lovely."

"You know," said the T'nufan, "a P'othparan seldom sees clouds. He considers them a blessing. A sign that celestial fortune is smiling."

10

Kirk grunted. "Some blessing. To have one's home near obliterated."

Lee'dit shrugged. "It all depends on how you look at it. True, P'othpar may be destroyed—but thanks to your intervention, the P'othparans will survive. Isn't that something of a blessing?"

"*Our* intervention," said the captain. "And I suppose it is, if you want to wax philosophical about it."

"I can tell you," said the T'nufan, "the P'othparans are nothing if not philosophical." With a gesture, he took in the square and the buildings beyond it. "All this means less to them than you might think. The external world, according to their beliefs, is only significant to the extent that it fuels the internal."

"Still," said Kirk, "they haven't exactly looked happy about leaving."

"There's no question," said Lee'dit, "that they will *miss* this place. But if they have to, they'll find another—one that offers them the same degree of insulation from the modern world." He smiled wearily. "Of course, the help we've provided today may encourage a broader cultural dialogue with our province. Did you know, Captain, that as recently as fifty years ago, there was no contact at all. . . ."

Kirk knew a lecture mode when he heard one. He was listening with only one ear when he noticed Clifford headed in their direction.

"Sir," said the crewman, wiping his sunburned forehead with his sleeve, "it's Critelli. He's back."

Kirk followed Clifford's gesture and spotted the small group wending its way down from the hills. Only one of the still-distant figures wore a Starfleet uniform. Another was dressed in the pale robes of the university group, and two more in drab P'othparan tunics.

The captain nodded. "Thank you, Mister Clifford." He flipped open his communicator.

"Kirk to bridge. Come in, Spock."

"Spock here, Captain. I was growing concerned."

"The last of the villagers are just coming in now," said Kirk. "I'm sure Mister Scott will be glad to hear *that*."

"I believe he will," said the Vulcan. "He has been

anything but pleased with the burden we've placed on his energy reserves."

Kirk grunted. "How's Chekov doing at Az'roth?"

"Quite well," said Spock. "In fact, he's being beamed up now—with the last members of his landing party."

"Good." Kirk paused. "And our marksmanship?"

"About as effective as can be expected, Captain. Unfortunately, most of the meteor mass will still be intact when it hits the island."

"Too bad," said Kirk. "I've developed a certain fondness for this place."

"I too regret the loss," said Spock. And Kirk knew he meant it, though he'd never actually seen P'othpar. "But I hope," continued the Vulcan, "that you will not linger to contemplate it."

"Not for long," said the captain. "Kirk out."

It was only then, with his communicator off, that he heard the thin, high-pitched wailing. Turning, Kirk traced it to Critelli's group, which had just come past a rocky outcropping.

Of the two P'othparans, one was an elderly male, who needed Critelli's support to make any progress. The other was a female—younger, perhaps only middle-aged, though she too was being helped down the incline.

It was the female who was responsible for the wailing.

Kirk turned to Lee'dit. "Do you have any idea what that's about?"

The T'nufan shook his head. "None."

"Then perhaps," said Kirk, "we should find out." Before the words were entirely out of his mouth, he'd started across the square.

He met up with Critelli and the others just as they entered the outer circle of the village. The female's cries only sounded louder as they echoed among the stone buildings.

"What's going on here?" asked the captain as Clifford came up behind him.

Critelli shook his head helplessly. "I don't know, sir. Kul'lad says she's just upset about leaving the island." But something in the crewman's voice said that he wasn't completely convinced.

Kirk eyed Kul'lad, the young mainlander who'd been

12

teamed with Critelli. The look in his eyes wasn't hard to read. Kirk had seen slow panic before.

Next, he regarded the female. He saw the agony in her pale, T'nufan eyes. Tears glistened on the bronze of her skin.

And there were fingermarks on her arm—a sign that she'd been dragged against her will.

Finally, he turned to the elderly male. The P'othparan was too winded to speak, but there was grief in his face as well.

"No," said the captain. "I think there's more to it than that." Again, he fixed Kul'lad with his gaze. "Isn't there?"

The mainlander could barely contain his anxiety.

"She's babbling," he said. "Who knows? Perhaps she's mad."

The female's wailing began anew.

"Mister Clifford," said Kirk. "Can you understand what she's saying?"

Clifford listened to the female, trying to pick out the sense in her words. His brow furrowed, drawing down an unruly shock of brown hair. After all, his familiarity with the P'othparan language had been limited to what he could speed-learn en route to T'nufo.

Tentatively, he posed a question. The female's lamentations took on a new intensity.

"Well?" asked Kirk, torn by her misery.

"She's incoherent," said Kul'lad. "And we have no time for this. We must leave—*now*. Before . . ."

Kirk glared at him and he shut up.

"It's her son," said Clifford. "He went up into the . . . the hills early this morning. To hunt . . . some sort of flying lizard."

"It is called *slik't*," said a T'nufan voice.

Kirk glanced over his shoulder at Lee'dit, who had arrived with the last of the base team.

"And it was not the creature itself he was hunting, but its eggs. They are considered a delicacy here."

The female cried out in anguish.

"He hasn't returned yet," added Lee'dit. "Though by now, he should have. And she does not want to leave without him."

"He's probably dead," said Kul'lad. "Do you know how

13

treacherous those hills are?" He looked at Lee'dit beseechingly. "Should we have waited for him—and jeopardized *our* survival?"

The scholar said nothing.

Suddenly, the female let out with a long chain of ululations, and pointed to a pass just west of the village.

"She says," Clifford translated, "that he can be saved. She says he's not so far away. Just up that pass."

Kirk shaded his eyes against the slanting rays of the sun and followed Clifford's gesture. Indeed, there was a passage there between the hills, and it seemed to lead up into them.

"Sir," said Clifford. "I'll go after him."

Kirk looked back at him and saw the resolve in his face. "No," he said. "I need you to finish up here."

"But, sir, there's nothing left to—"

"That's an order, mister."

Clifford stiffened, turned a shade ruddier than the sun had already made him. His eyes narrowed, but he restrained himself from any further protests. "Aye, sir," was all he said.

Kirk glanced once more at the female.

"When you return to the ship," he told Clifford, "inform Mister Spock of my whereabouts."

The crewman's features went slack. "Whereabouts, sir?"

"Whereabouts," confirmed the captain.

And before they could waste any more of what little time was left, he loped off in the direction of the pass.

The forward viewscreen showed the periphery of the meteor swarm, chiseled and defined by the white-hot glare of T'nufo's sun.

Suddenly, a beam of intense, red phaserlight stabbed through the swarm. Found a chunk of rock, obliterated it.

But the rest of the meteors, unaffected, continued to plunge toward their rendezvous with P'othpar.

Lieutenant Hautala, acting as navigator in Chekov's absence, spun around in his seat.

"Mister Spock," he said, "we are now within photon torpedo range."

In the command chair of the *Enterprise,* First Officer Spock punched up a channel to the weapons room.

"Adler here."

"Ready to fire photon torpedoes, Mister Adler."

"Aye, sir."

Spock could hear Adler barking orders to his team.

"Fire," said the first officer.

A moment later, the viewscreen lit up with blue-violet pyrotechnics. When it cleared, there was a gap in the swarm that hadn't been there before. But the vast bulk of the meteor mass remained intact.

Spock leaned back in the captain's seat, his elbows resting on the armrests. He formed a bridge with his fingers and held it out before him.

"Ready to fire again, sir," announced Adler.

"Fire," said Spock.

Again, the screen sizzled with blue fire. And again, the torpedoes had limited effect. The meteors moved inexorably toward their ultimate rendezvous.

Spock sighed—a barely perceptible flaring of his finely shaped nostrils.

"Shall we try it again, sir?" asked the weapons officer.

"I think not," said Spock. "For now, resume phaser barrage. We will try the torpedoes again when the swarm is closer."

"Aye, sir. Adler out."

Spock felt thwarted, helpless, as he watched the phaser fire lance through the meteor configuration. And of all the human feelings he'd inherited from his human mother, he found helplessness the most onerous. Almost, he wished he could trade places with the captain. At least he'd be *doing* something.

There was an abrupt hiss as the door to the turbo lift opened behind him. But Spock didn't have to turn around to know who'd joined them on the bridge. The muttered invective was sufficient identification.

Chief Medical Officer Leonard McCoy was hovering over him a moment later. The Vulcan maintained his scrutiny of the viewscreen.

"Spock," said McCoy, in a voice too low for the rest of the bridge contingent to overhear, "I just got wind of a nasty rumor. I want you to tell me there's no truth to it."

"That would be difficult," said Spock, "not knowing the substance of the rumor."

"Blast it," said McCoy, "you *know* what rumor. Scotty says Jim's left the evac site and headed for the hills—on some wild-goose chase."

"Actually," said the first officer, "the captain's objective is a native youth. I do not believe that geese are among the four thousand three hundred and ninety-four species still extant on T'nufo."

The doctor raised his voice to a harsh whisper. "I'm all for saving lives, Spock. But you know the odds of finding anyone in those hills. How can you let him traipse around down there when there's less than an hour before impact?"

Spock resisted the impulse to correct McCoy's estimate. There were actually thirty-two-point-two-four minutes— ship's time—left before the devastation would begin.

"Need I remind you," he said instead, "that the captain is still the commanding officer of this vessel? I can hardly beam him up against his will. What's more, his decision is perfectly logical. Until the danger posed by the meteors becomes more immediate, why not continue the search? In the worst case, he will only fail to find the youth."

McCoy leaned a little closer, his blue eyes blazing.

"Sure. And because he's a rational being—just like yourself, Mister Spock—he'll accept that failure in plenty of time to beam up. Is that what you're telling me?"

Spock conceded that the doctor had a point there. Finally, he looked at him.

"Very well," he said. "When the time comes, I will remind the captain of the situation."

McCoy sputtered. "When the *time* comes . . . ?"

A couple of heads turned on the bridge. Spock cocked an eyebrow.

The doctor made a sound deep in his throat—one which Spock recognized as a sign of concession among humans.

"All right," McCoy said finally. "I suppose I should be glad I got *that* much out of you." He straightened, taking up a position by Spock's side.

On the forward monitor, yet another phaser beam sliced into the meteor swarm. There was an explosion—pitifully small, in the context of the screen—as it found a mark.

"You need not remain on the bridge," said Spock, "if you have duties awaiting you in sickbay."

"The hell I need not," said the doctor. "I'm waiting here until the *time* comes. To make sure you keep your word."

Spock shrugged. "Suit yourself, Doctor," he said.

Did McCoy honestly think he'd fail to contact the captain —at the appropriate juncture? Or that he hadn't planned to do so all along—even prior to this conversation?

After all, one didn't have to be human to be worried about a friend.

Kirk scrambled up the trail, dislodging pebbles in his haste. The riotous sunset had all but descended behind the ridge to his left, and the sky was turning darker. Soon, there'd be no light but what the stars threw off, for T'nufo had no moons.

But that was the least of his problems. The meteors would start to hit long before the light was gone.

His communicator beeped again, and he whipped it open without breaking stride. "Kirk here," he said, a little hoarse from the dry air and his exertions.

"Captain, y've got t' come aboard!" It was Scotty again— for the third time since he'd left the village. "Y've less than twelve minutes now before impact—surely, y've done all ye could."

Kirk swore beneath his breath. *Less than twelve minutes.*

"Did ye say somethin', sir? A' didna hear ye."

"Have you got a fix on my coordinates?" asked Kirk.

"That a' do," said the chief engineer. "Shall a' beam ye up, then?"

"Not yet," said Kirk, nonetheless grateful for Scotty's preparedness. "I'm not ready to throw in the towel just yet, Mister Scott."

"But, sir . . ."

"Kirk out."

He replaced the communicator on his belt and negotiated a sharp bend in the trail, using his hands to help his progress. As he mounted the turn, he saw that the ground fell away abruptly just beyond it, spilling into a deep, dark ravine.

17

For a moment, he stopped to peer into it. But it was no good—he couldn't see the bottom. And there was no sign of the youth along the long, smooth slopes.

Kirk went on, wondering if Kul'lad had been right. There had been a dozen places like this on the way up, where the P'othparan could have slipped and fallen to his death.

But he still had time left. There was no sense giving up until he had to.

It was the kind of logic even Spock couldn't have argued with.

A dry wind scoured the hills as Kirk pelted along beside the ravine. It seemed to be growing narrower, he noted, and its flanks steeper. After a while, it was almost a sheer drop on either side.

Suddenly, there was a rush of air just behind him, and a thin, high-pitched scream. Kirk threw himself flat against the ground—just as something large and leathery passed over him.

Then the thing was up ahead, gliding on what must have been an updraft from the ravine, gleaming like lapis and emeralds in the dying light.

It was huge, with a wing span nearly twice as long as Kirk was tall. And the hooked talons it carried beneath it were only partly concealed by a long, reptilian tail.

A *slik't,* Kirk told himself. It had to be.

And if it was headed back to its nest, it might lead him to the P'othparan. That is, if the youth had made it this far.

Kirk got up and started after the creature. As if to oblige him, the *slik't* seemed to slow down a bit—just enough for him to keep pace with it if he pushed himself.

Part of Kirk acknowledged the inadvisability of moving so quickly, so near to the ravine. It was the part of him that held things together, that enabled him to make decisions when four hundred thirty lives depended on them.

But another part of him wasn't fazed by the danger. That was the part that couldn't shake the sight of the female's face . . . the agony of her cries. . . .

As the shadows deepened, pooling in the hollows, it became harder and harder to keep track of the *slik't.* Its scaly hide, shielded from direct light, was almost indistinguishable from the patches of scrub that grew out of the hillsides.

How much time was left now? It was difficult to say. He could have called up to the ship, of course, but that would only have slowed him down. When the meteors came, he'd know it.

The *slik't* soared and glided, sinuous, graceful for all its size and deadly capabilities. Kirk felt a burning in his chest as he strained for more oxygen than T'nufo was willing to give him. His legs started to get sore, sore and rubbery, as they felt the deprivation.

There was a broadening of the ledge he traveled, a hooting of the wind in the hills to his left. A further darkening of the sky by a shade.

A turning, a winding of both the ravine and the valley that rose around it—and the *slik't* was lost to his sight around a slope of naked rock.

Kirk surged forward, stumbled on some loose rocks, surged again, and came around the bend—hoping that the creature hadn't finally eluded him.

It hadn't. In fact, it was no longer coursing along on the air currents above the ravine. As he watched, hearing the breath rasp savagely in his throat, feeling his heart pound against his ribs, the *slik't* flung out its massive wings and came to roost.

The creature's nest was situated some twenty feet above the opposite ledge, on a chunk of rock that jutted out from the hillside. There were three or four younglings inside, and they sent up a chorus of piping sounds as soon as the *slik't* began to alight.

Kirk hadn't noticed it before, as he'd been behind the creature the whole time, but it had been carrying a small animal in its beaklike mouth. No sooner had the carcass been deposited in the nest than the younglings began to tear at it.

It was only after a moment that Kirk was able to tear his eyes from that grisly tableau. And that's when he noticed the humanoid form sprawled on the ledge below the nest, surrounded and nearly concealed by the scrub trees.

The P'othparan was sprinkled with loose branches, which he must have grabbed at as he fell. Also, a large rock seemed to lay across one of his legs. Had he dislodged it as he reached for the nest? And managed to somehow get pinned beneath it?

Kirk peered at the youth from across the ravine. There were no signs of blood, though it was hard to tell in the descending gloom. And no movement whatsoever.

The *slik't* screamed and spread its wings suddenly. Kirk looked up and saw that its long narrow head was pointed in his direction. He could barely make out the ruby-colored slits of his eyes, but he had a feeling he knew whom they were trained on.

As he slowly backed away from the brink of the ravine, his communicator beeped. He opened it.

"Kirk here," he said, still breathing hard.

"You've only a minute now before impact, Captain." It was Spock's voice, and Kirk thought he detected a trace of anxiety in his first officer's normally dispassionate tone. "Mister Scott is still waiting in the transporter room."

With Kirk's retreat, the *slik't* had returned to its nest. But it still had a bead on him.

"Spock," he said. "I thought I'd be hearing from you before long."

He turned his attention to the figure on the ledge. Gauged the distance across the ravine, and the space his own ledge would afford him for a running jump. Estimated the time it would take to roll that boulder off the P'othparan.

"Captain?"

"I'm still here," said Kirk. "And I've found the fellow I was looking for, though he's a little worse for wear. Alert Doctor McCoy that we'll need a trauma unit in the transporter room. And tell Mister Scott that there will be two to beam up—but not right away. I need a little more time."

"There's not much time *left*," said Spock. He could almost hear the *Jim* on the end of Spock's plea.

"Give me one minute," said the captain.

"Impact will have begun by then," said the Vulcan.

"But only barely. Kirk out."

He flipped the communicator closed and attached it to his belt again. Then he backed off even farther from the ravine—as far as he could, until he had a slope too steep to climb behind him.

Here goes nothing, he told himself.

And sprinted across the ledge. When he reached the lip of the ravine, he launched himself with his last step. Impenetrable darkness yawned beneath him, like the maw of a leviathan.

Then he was across, scrambling to keep his balance on the gravel that covered much of the ledge. He scraped one knee badly before he came up against the far slope—not more than a few feet from the P'othparan.

Out of the corner of his eye, Kirk saw the *slik't* dart out from its nest—heard the *whoosh* of its wings as it took to the air.

But he couldn't concentrate on that now. In a matter of seconds, he and the youth would be beamed up. And if he couldn't roll the boulder out of the way, it would be beamed up with them—become part of the molecular mix that the transporter had to sort out, a part it wasn't programmed for. Kirk didn't want to take the chance that they'd be integrated with the rock when they materialized.

As he laid his shoulder against the boulder, he caught a glimpse of the P'othparan's face. It was still, so still. Was he too late?

The *slik't* shrieked, stooped as if to slash at Kirk with its talons. But it was used to attacking on open ground, apparently. The sheer size of its wings and the profusion of scrubs kept it from getting too close to the slope.

Kirk threw his weight behind the boulder, pushed. It rocked a little, but that was about it.

The *slik't* shrilled and came at them again, from another angle. A second time, it found the space too difficult to negotiate, and managed only to slash one of the branches as it went by.

Suddenly, Kirk's eyes were drawn past the creature—up to the heavens, where streaks of gold were falling. As he watched, they multiplied, stretched across the darkening sky.

It gave him a new sense of urgency. With all his strength, he heaved at the boulder. Slowly, it began to budge. And a moment later, all at once, it rolled free of the P'othparan.

The youth stirred, murmuring something. Kirk leaned over him, saw the eyelids flutter, and then lie still again.

He gripped the youth's shoulder. "Hang in there," he told

21

him, though he had no way of knowing if the P'othparan could hear him, much less understand the words.

The *slik't* was soaring, preparing to attack a third time, when the first meteor hit. It made a sound like a thunderclap, and the force of it made the ground shudder.

A big one, Kirk remarked to himself.

The second one was less noisy, but the third was as loud and as close as the first. Then they started coming in rapid-fire succession.

It relieved Kirk of one problem. Startled by the sound and the sudden streaks of light, the *slik't* rapidly sought the refuge of its nest, where its younglings were piping frantically.

However, his other problem was growing greater by the moment. So far, none of the meteors had fallen in this particular valley. But for how long would they continue to be spared?

He opened his communicator.

"Scotty?"

The chief engineer's voice was as taut as he'd ever heard it.

"A'm tryin', Captain—a'm givin' it m'best shot. But m'poor transporter's been strained t' th' limit, and she's just nae respondin'—sir!"

The sky was resplendent with meteors now. They exploded among the distant hills every few seconds, sending tremors through the earth.

"How long before you can get it working again?" asked Kirk, ignoring the cold slither of panic in his gut.

Scotty cursed eloquently. "A few minutes, maybe more. She needs t'draw up enough power—"

Abruptly, he was cut off by a wave of static. Kirk made some adjustments in the setting, but it didn't help. The meteor activity must have blocked the signal.

The P'othparan murmured again.

"Don't worry," Kirk told the wan and expressionless face. "It won't be that long. The transporter was working just a little while ago."

He glanced at the streaks of gold in the sky, felt their distant impacts.

"He'll have us up in no time," said the captain. "Scotty always works faster than he thinks."

The youth's mouth worked, but this time nothing came out.

Kirk swallowed. "C'mon, Scotty. *C'mon.*"

Suddenly, there was a tremendous impact high on the slope opposite them. Kirk shielded his eyes from the blinding flash as the meteor shattered the rock of the hillside, producing a rain of fragments. Some of them burned as they plummeted.

Hovering over the P'othparan, Kirk took the brunt of the barrage. Fortunately, all the bigger fragments seemed to miss them—but even the smaller ones hurt like the devil.

For a while, as the dust cleared, there was silence. A space in time free of the terrible explosions, the ground-jarring impacts.

Kirk raised his head, wondering if the storm had somehow passed by the valley. Then he saw what was headed for them.

Instinctively, he ducked.

The meteor hit the slope above them about halfway up, and the whole island seemed to lurch. Fiery death blossomed from the hillside, came cascading toward them.

That's when Kirk felt the tingling he'd been hoping for. And before the blazing rain could claim him, he was kneeling on the transporter platform—with the P'othparan cradled in his arms.

Chapter Three

ON THE STARSHIP *Hood*, the distress call was distinct and unmistakable.

This is Doctor Aaron Brown. Repeat, Doctor Aaron Brown, of the Roger Korby expedition. Do you read me? This is Doctor Aaron Brown. . . .

Communications Officer Alan Paultic swiveled in his seat, to face the command chair and Captain Martinez.

"It's a preset message, sir," said Paultic, "transmitting on several different frequencies. On some kind of loop, so that it repeats continuously." He made some quick calculations. "And it's coming from deep beneath the planet's surface."

Martinez peered at the forward monitor and the blue-white world depicted there. "Return the signal," he said finally. "Pertinent data, Lieutenant Banks?"

Science Officer Banks consulted with his computer terminal. Small, vivid lights flashed on and off, reflected on his dark, flawless skin.

"Its name is Exo III, Captain. Gravity one point one Earthnorm, atmosphere breathable. But the surface temperature is a hundred degrees below zero—which is why, I imagine, the signal's coming from *beneath* the surface."

"So it would seem," commented Martinez, thoughtfully.

Banks' temples worked as he called up another file.

"Doctor Roger Korby. Known as the Pasteur of . . ."

Martinez held up a hand.

"Spare me that particular bio, Lieutenant. I'm quite familiar with Korby's work." He paused. "And Exo III *was* the world he disappeared on, wasn't it?"

"It was, Captain. But that was more than five years ago. Since then, three expeditions have failed to find him. The most recent was that of the *Enterprise*—only a few months ago."

Martinez glared at the viewscreen, as if he could wring some more information out of it. But the blue-white world just hung there, impassive.

"What about this Doctor Brown? Can we confirm that he was part of the expedition?"

Banks keyed in another callcode. The file sprang up on his terminal.

"He was indeed," said the science officer. "Aaron Brown. First accompanied Doctor Korby on Orion excavation, stardate—"

"*Thank* you," said Martinez. "That's quite enough, Lieutenant."

Banks bit his lip and punched the button that would clear his screen.

"Sir?" It was Paultic.

"Yes, Lieutenant?"

"Sir, I've made contact with Doctor Brown."

"Put it up on the screen, please, Paultic."

A moment later, an image coalesced on the monitor. The face they saw was a narrow one, with dark brows and graying temples.

"This is Doctor Aaron Brown," said the man on the screen. He smiled. "Whom do I have the pleasure of addressing?"

"Captain Joaquin Martinez, U.S.S. *Hood*," returned the captain. "What's your situation down there?"

"One of delight," said Brown. "It's been years since we've seen another human face."

"You mean you and Doctor Korby?"

Brown registered sadness.

"I'm afraid," he said, "that Doctor Korby died shortly after our crash landing here." He seemed to hesitate for a moment. "Only I and another of his assistants—Johann Zezel—survived."

Martinez grunted. "I'm sorry to hear about Doctor Korby. I'd admired him for some time."

"So did we all," said Brown.

"Paultic," said the captain, "make arrangements with engineering to have these men beamed up."

"Actually," Brown interjected, "there's more than ourselves to beam up. We've made some . . . fascinating discoveries down here, Captain. You'll no doubt want to take a look at them before we bring them on board."

"Discoveries?" echoed Martinez.

"Yes," said Brown. "Of a *sensitive* nature. I'm sure you understand."

Martinez frowned. "Of course. I'll beam down with a few of my officers as soon as we can get a fix on your coordinates."

Doctor Brown nodded. "Thank you, Captain. We'll be waiting."

The image faded.

"Captain," said Paultic, "Mister Berg says he's established the source of the signal. He's ready to transport."

"Good," said Martinez. "But tell him he'll be beaming down instead of up. A party of three—myself, First Officer Stuart, and Science Officer Banks."

Paultic relayed the information to the transporter room.

For a moment, Martinez just sat there—staring at the dark and featureless viewscreen, massaging the lower portion of his face.

Something bothered him—had, in fact, since they first received the distress call. Something he couldn't quite put his finger on.

It was more than the question of survival. Given sufficient supplies and equipment from their wrecked ship, Brown and—what was his name? Zezel?—could have kept themselves alive, he supposed. Even reconstructed the devices they'd used to send out the signal.

But why hadn't the other expeditions turned them up—

heard the signal? Jim Kirk, captain of the *Enterprise,* was about as thorough as anyone he'd ever known. Why hadn't Kirk discovered them?

Perhaps, he told himself, they'd only recently gotten the communications equipment to work. Yes—that would be it, wouldn't it?

Just in case, however, he had Paultic put him through to security.

"Simmons here, sir."

"Stand by with a landing party, Mister Simmons. Ready to beam down at my request."

"Will do, sir."

"Thank you," said Martinez.

He felt a little better now. Standing, he turned over the conn.

As *Kirk* came into the chamber, Brown was swiveling away from the communications system.

"They are beaming down," said Brown.

"Yes," said *Kirk.* "I heard."

He noticed the expression of concern on Brown's face— the lines that converged at the bridge of his nose.

"Is something wrong?" asked *Kirk.*

"I don't think Martinez was entirely convinced by my performance. I wonder if he suspects . . . something."

Kirk shrugged. "And what if he does? Can he refuse to honor our request, knowing what kinds of 'discoveries' Doctor Korby's teams have unearthed in the past?"

"But if he believes something is amiss, will he not take precautions?"

"Some," conceded *Kirk.* "He'll be armed, for one thing. And he'll probably have a security force ready to beam down at a moment's notice."

"Then perhaps," suggested Brown, "we should alter our plan. If we were to—"

"No," said *Kirk.* The chamber rang with his response. "There will be no alterations. You will do exactly as I've instructed."

Brown looked at him. "Even Doctor Korby did not speak to me in that tone of voice."

27

"Doctor Korby failed," said *Kirk*. *"I* will succeed."

"Doctor Korby was the *creator*," said Brown.

Kirk regarded him, saw the anxiety etched deeply into his face.

It was the wrong time to antagonize Brown. Without him, *Kirk* could accomplish nothing.

"Of course," he agreed. "But his was the mind of a scientist—a philosopher. Not that of a military strategist."

After a moment, Brown relaxed. He seemed to accept the distinction.

"Now, go," said *Kirk*. "Our friends will be transported to the surface momentarily." He smiled. "We don't want to keep them waiting."

Dutifully, Brown stood and crossed the room. A moment later, the door opened and he was gone.

Kirk watched him go, glad once again that he had introduced an obedience protocol into the replication program. It would make matters so much easier.

Science Officer Jamal Banks hated the cold.

His first tour of duty had been in a floating exploration base on the polar seas of Rakatut Two. In a year and eight months, he'd never felt warm enough.

Now they stood just inside a cave—or rather, the outermost of a system of caves—the snow-and-ice terrain of Exo III rising and falling all around them, until it culminated in a hard, serrated ring of mountains. The sky was gray and flat, with only a dim, pinkish disk of a sun to lend any color to the place.

Banks shivered, despite the fact that a transparent barrier protected him from the frigid temperatures outside.

"Well," said Stuart, "what do you think?"

"We'll give them a few more minutes to show up," said the captain. He peered into the half-dark cave. "I'd hate to ask Berg to transport us down there. It'd be pretty tricky, and I've got no desire to become a permanent feature of the rock."

Banks, standing closest to the opening, heard something. A scraping, as of footfalls on a coarse and uneven surface.

"I think they're coming," he said.

Martinez didn't address any response at all to him. And that was fine as far as Banks was concerned. Being ignored, he'd decided a while ago, was far better than being ridiculed and belittled.

He still didn't understand why Martinez disliked him so. He was a good science officer—efficient, dedicated, all he was supposed to be. Yet the captain had had it in for him since he stepped on board the *Hood.*

Somehow, he'd rubbed Martinez the wrong way—right from the beginning. Or was there any truth to Vedra's theory about Banks's predecessor?

No matter. His transfer was about to come through. His friends in Starfleet had told him as much. And when it did, he'd no longer have to put up with Martinez.

The footfalls grew louder, closer. They saw a light flicker, then fill the cave.

A moment later, Doctor Brown appeared. He held his searchlight off to one side, so as not to blind them.

"Gentlemen," he said. He held out his hand to Martinez. "It is so *good* to see you."

Martinez took his hand, shook it.

"We were about to give up hope," he said.

Brown chuckled. "Just imagine what it's like to wait *five years*—and more." He glanced at Stuart and then at Banks. "Will you follow me?"

Stuart fell into line behind Brown, and Martinez came after him. Banks brought up the rear, as he'd fully expected.

The caves turned out to be beautiful, in a way. Brown's searchlight picked out purplish iridescences and quartzlike gleams among the dusky blue surfaces. The stalactites, of which there were many, seemed to glow a sullen red.

"Be careful where you walk," the archaeologist told them. "We're about to skirt the edge of a large pit. Not all the footing here is as solid as it appears."

As if for emphasis, Brown cast his light along the brink. Beyond it, Banks saw, there was nothing but black emptiness. The light couldn't begin to find the bottom.

He swallowed and hugged the opposite wall, keeping as far away from the pit as possible.

Their trek seemed to go on for some time. Banks glanced at his chronometer, saw that they'd been descending for more than an hour. It was no wonder Brown had been a little late.

Shortly thereafter, they began to pass through a series of arches. Banks couldn't get a very good look at them, because Brown held the only light, and he was up ahead. But it was plain that they weren't natural formations.

Nor could Brown and his companion have built them. For one thing, there were too many of the things. For a second, they couldn't have had the equipment.

Where, then, had the arches come from?

Martinez must have been wondering the same thing, because he asked Brown about it.

The archaeologist's voice carried well in the narrow corridor. "It seems, Captain, that they were fabricated by an indigenous race—one which may have lived on the surface before the sun here began to dim. At first, we speculated that the arches gave support to otherwise weak portions of the tunnels. After studying them, however, we've concluded that they are merely decorative."

Only a few minutes later, they came to a diamond-shaped slab of metal, seemingly embedded in the rock. Brown pressed his hand against a small plate to one side of it, and the slab moved—not unlike the doors on the *Hood,* Banks noted.

One by one, they passed inside.

"Nice place you've got here," said Stuart, surveying some sort of parlor. He glanced at Brown with those deep-set, pale green eyes of his. "Another leftover of the previous inhabitants?"

"The structure of the place, yes," said Brown. "But not much else. We were able to salvage a great deal from our ship." He gestured. "That computer, for instance. It controls the ventilation and lighting systems, among other things."

Martinez nodded. "Where's your colleague—Zezel?"

The captain looked uncomfortable down here, Banks observed. Trapped, in a way. And as usual, Stuart only echoed the mood of his superior.

The science officer saw nothing amiss, however. Only some rather interesting architecture.

"He must be in the next room," said Brown. "We should take a peek in there, in any case. That's where you'll find the discoveries to which I referred."

"Good," said Martinez. "Let's have a look."

Brown opened the door to the next chamber, and they followed him through. It hissed closed automatically behind them.

There was no sign of Zezel in there. But what they saw made them forget him for the moment.

"All right," said Martinez. "It's big enough. But what is it?"

Banks recoiled inwardly at his captain's brusqueness. Perhaps later, he could apologize to Doctor Brown.

"What it is," said the archaeologist, unruffled, "is a device for the creation of artificial life-forms."

Banks saw Martinez glance at Stuart.

Brown smiled a thin-lipped smile. "You seem incredulous, Captain. And to be honest, I don't blame you. But this machine *can* create life." He paused. "Perhaps a demonstration would change your mind. I promise you—you won't be disappointed."

The captain grunted. "Sure, go ahead. Demonstrate if you like."

"Thank you," said Brown. He traversed the room and opened a compartment near the wall. With some difficulty, he removed something large and grayish green, carried it over to a circular platform.

Banks felt a dryness in his throat. He had *heard* of instances in which artificial life had been created. Read reports. But to see such a thing, close up . . .

He watched carefully as Brown laid his shapeless burden on the platform, then brought the lock down across it.

The archaeologist looked up. "And now," he said, "I need a volunteer." He fixed his gaze on Martinez. "Captain?"

Martinez smiled. "Sorry. Machines break down. I don't want to be inside this one if that should happen. And I'd prefer not to place my men in that kind of danger either."

Brown looked a little sad. "I assure you," he said, "it's quite safe. We've tested it inside and out."

"I'm sure you have," said the captain. "But it doesn't change my mind."

"Sorry," said a voice. "I'm afraid we must insist."

Banks whirled, saw the figure standing directly behind them, in the shadows of the machine. It took him a moment to realize that it was holding some kind of weapon.

By that time, his fellow officers had gone for their phasers. There was a blast of yellow-white light, jolting Stuart off his feet. Martinez rolled, sending a red stunbeam in the newcomer's direction. But it missed, glancing off the stone wall of the cavern.

As the captain rose to a kneeling position, to get a better bead on his target, there was another, tighter blast—and his phaser went flying out of his hand.

Only then did Banks remember his own weapon. His heart thudding against his ribs, he reached for it.

But just as he drew it out, something clamped around his wrist. Something powerful, for suddenly the bones in it were close to breaking.

Banks screamed with the pain.

His hand opened reflexively and the phaser clattered to the floor. Then, abruptly, he was released. He fell to one knee, clutching his wrist to him like a wounded bird.

And looked up into the expressionless face of Doctor Brown. Through the haze of his pain, Banks wondered where the man could have gotten such strength.

Slowly, with the captain's help, Stuart got to his feet.

"Are you all right?" asked Martinez.

The first officer shrugged. "I've been worse. I guess *he* has a stun setting too."

Martinez glared at the man in the shadows. "Well, Zezel? Aren't you going to tell us what this is about?"

The man stepped clear of the shadows, his weapon still leveled at them. He was a handsome man, Caucasian, medium height and build.

And he looked naggingly familiar.

"Kirk?" whispered Martinez, taking an involuntary step forward. "Jim Kirk?"

The man with the weapon smiled. *Charmingly*, it seemed to Banks.

"Good to see you again, Joaquin. It's a pity it couldn't have been under more cordial circumstances."

Banks remembered now. The cocktail party on Starbase Five. James Kirk, commander of the *Enterprise*. But . . .

"I . . . I don't get it, Jim," said Martinez. "I just don't get it."

"You will," said *Kirk*. "Unless you take your hand away from your communicator."

Martinez frowned, did as he was instructed.

"Now," said *Kirk*, "over toward the platform. Move."

Martinez just stood there, watching his adversary. Hoping he could frustrate him into making a mistake.

Kirk made a quick adjustment in his weapon. "Move," he repeated evenly, training it on Stuart. "Or I'll kill your first officer."

"Don't do it, Captain," said Stuart.

Brown took a couple of steps toward *Kirk*. "If you harm him," he said, "it will make matters that much more difficult."

Kirk glanced at the archaeologist. "I don't need you to tell me that, Doctor." He looked back to Martinez. "Well?"

Reluctantly, the captain moved toward the platform.

Within minutes, Brown had him locked into place alongside the gray-green mass. Martinez struggled against the lock, saw that he'd have no success with it.

"You won't get away with this," he said. "Either of you." He craned his neck to look at *Kirk*. "I don't know what you think you're doing, but Starfleet won't look kindly on it."

"Starfleet," said *Kirk*, "won't know anything about it—until we've already carried out our purpose." He nodded to Brown, who stood now by a control console. The archaeologist pressed a series of buttons.

The platform began to turn.

"You wanted to know what our game was," said *Kirk*, over the growing hum of the machinery. "This will help to educate you."

DOUBLE, DOUBLE

He regarded Stuart, then Banks. His gaze was cold—ever so cold.

"And soon, gentlemen, you'll receive the same education."

The platform speeded up, until Martinez was nothing more than a blur.

Banks began to tremble.

Chapter Four

"How is he?" asked Kirk.

Nurse Christine Chapel stood at the foot of the P'othparan's bunk, consulting the life-support displays on the wall above him. Tall and fair, almost stately in her bearing, she glanced at the captain as he approached.

"He needs a lot of rest," she said. "But the surgery was a complete success. Doctor McCoy says the boy's leg will be as good as new." She scowled in imitation of the chief medical officer. "Maybe better," she rumbled.

Kirk laughed softly, inspecting the P'othparan's face. Some color seemed to have crept back into his cheeks.

"Good," said the captain. "I was a little worried."

The youth stirred then. He moaned, turning his face to one side and back again. Chapel moved to the head of the bunk and, gently, brushed a long strand of golden hair from the boy's eyes.

"I told the authorities on the mainland," said Kirk, "that he'd probably be well enough to beam down in a few days. Any problem with that?"

Chapel shrugged. "Obviously, we'd like to monitor him for a little longer. But he'll be better off in familiar surroundings, no question about it." She looked up at Kirk. "Of course, Doctor McCoy will want to have the final say."

Kirk grunted. "Of course. Why should this matter be any different than countless others?"

Chapel smiled. "Actually, you can get it from the horse's mouth if you care to wait a few minutes. Doctor McCoy said he would stop by to check on our patient—on his way somewhere else, apparently."

Kirk nodded. "I know. I'm the someone he's going there with."

"Oh?"

"Yes. We have a little wager—and we're going to settle it tonight."

Of course, *tonight* was a relative term. But the *Enterprise* ran on a twenty-four-hour clock so as to minimize any disruption of the crew's circadian rhythms.

"What sort of wager?" asked Chapel.

"It has to do with . . . a physical," he admitted.

The nurse frowned, but there was humor in it. "You mean," she asked, "Doctor McCoy has agreed to let you forgo your physical? If you win a *bet?*"

Kirk shrugged. "Not forever, mind you. Just for a while."

"I don't believe it," she said. "I know how you hate physicals, sir—your disregard for your own well-being has assumed epic proportions among the crew. But how did you convince Doctor McCoy to go along with this?"

"It wasn't easy," he agreed. That got a laugh out of her.

There were some people whose laughter was precious, like sea treasure. Christine Chapel was one of those people.

But just as Kirk was starting to enjoy it, he saw tears stand out in her eyes. A moment later, she had to dab at them with her fingers. She reddened, embarrassed.

"Something I said?" he asked, confused.

Chapel took a deep breath, let it out. She looked around sickbay. It was empty, of course, but for the two of them and the sedated P'othparan. The life-support display provided an undertone to the silence.

She turned again, finally, toward Kirk.

"I'm sorry," she told him. "I didn't mean to do that. It's just that . . . I need to thank you, sir. For what you did. Or rather, what you didn't do."

It took Kirk a moment to figure out what she was talking about. When he did, it was *his* turn to be embarrassed.

"That's not necessary," he said.

"I think it is," she insisted.

She removed something from the pocket of her uniform. It was a computer tape, which she popped into a nearby playback device.

"'Captain's log, stardate twenty-seven-twelve point seven. Unfortunately, like the two expeditions that preceded us, we have been unable to turn up any evidence which would point to the survival of Doctor Roger Korby on Exo III. Two of my crewmen, Rayburn and Matthews, were lost in the course of a comprehensive search that took us deep into the planet's subterranean passages, where Korby was believed to have preserved himself.'"

Kirk remembered the words. They were his, of course.

"'My recommendation is that no further searches be conducted, nor personnel placed at risk. We must resign ourselves to the fact that one of our most brilliant and innovative minds is gone, having perished in the pursuit of truth.'"

She stopped the tape and removed it.

Kirk shrugged. "Doctor Korby was a great man, Christine. What happened on Exo III doesn't change that."

"That's the way I've come to think of it also," said Chapel. "But then, I was in love with him."

For a long moment, silence.

"Well," she said finally, "I just wanted you to know how I felt." She paused. "It's important that good deeds get noticed—by someone."

Kirk felt awkard. He didn't know what to say to that.

In the end, it was McCoy who bailed him out, showing up at the entranceway.

"Hah!" said the doctor, striding across sickbay as if he owned it—which wasn't, after all, far from the truth. "I see you're willing to put your money where your mouth is, Captain." He stopped beside the P'othparan, bent over the youth's leg.

"You know," said Kirk, "that I can't resist picking up a gauntlet."

McCoy made a derogatory noise as he inspected the wound.

"That," he said, "I know you can do. It's the triple dip I have my doubts about."

Chapel raised an eyebrow, Spock-like.

"Triple dip, sir?"

Her voice was even, free of the huskiness that had marked it when she'd spoken of Korby.

"Triple dip," he confirmed, glad to see she was herself again.

"Christine," said McCoy, "would you be so good as to get me a new dressing?"

Chapel moved crisply, efficiently.

And Kirk sat, knowing that it would be a few minutes before the doctor finished his ministrations.

He *had* taken a chance in logging that white lie, hadn't he? If anyone in Starfleet found out the truth, his goose was cooked. No—incinerated.

But Korby had deserved a better fate. And if men couldn't show each other a little mercy, of what value were all the Federation's lofty ideals?

Lord knows, he mused, if what happened to Korby ever happened to me, I'd sure as hell be grateful for that kind of mercy.

Besides, he asked himself—what harm could it possibly have done?

By the time they got to the gym, there was a small crowd around the horizontal bar.

"Somehow," said Kirk, "I get the feeling that news of our wager has leaked out. Any idea how that could have happened?"

McCoy smiled angelically. "As my great-aunt Florence used to say, 'The people have a right to know.'"

"Was that the same great-aunt Florence who kept her shades down all the time?"

The doctor harumphed. "Perhaps it was."

As they approached the stainless-steel apparatus, Kirk overheard a muted argument.

"Never," said one of the voices. "Our class champion could barely manage three and a half."

"Aye," said another voice, in a familiar Scottish brogue.

38

"But yer class champion didna have th' advantage of a mature mind in a mature body. It takes more than muscles, laddie."

"A guy his age is lucky to do two. At most."

"Y're daft. Or maybe ye just dinna know th' captain as a' do."

Kirk glanced over his shoulder to see who Scotty was contending with. But there were a number of new crewmembers standing around the chief engineer, and the conversation stopped when they saw him look their way.

Only Scotty himself met Kirk's gaze. He winked—a gesture of encouragement.

The captain couldn't help but smile as he dipped his hands into the tray of chalk powder or as he rubbed the stuff into his palms.

"What are you smirking about?" asked McCoy. "I'm the one who should be smirking."

Kirk approached the apparatus, took up a position just below the bar.

"Don't count your chickens, Bones."

And with that, he leaped up and grabbed the bar. A moment later, he'd swung himself up to a position where his hips rested against it.

Again, he heard the subdued conversation.

"A nifty move, that, if a' say so m'self."

"Not bad," said one of the others. "For a dinosaur."

"A dinosaur, is't? Why . . ."

Kirk cut the distraction short with a well-placed bon mot.

"It's all right, Mister Scott. I'm enjoying my sunset years."

That got a laugh from the crowd.

Kirk took a deep breath, dropped down again so that he hung perpendicular to the floor. After all Scotty's protestations, he told himself, he'd better prove that he *wasn't* a dinosaur.

In four swings, his feet had reached the height of the bar. In two more, they had well exceeded it.

Then, before his arms could grow too tired, he put an extra effort into his foreswing and let go of the bar. A split second later, he tucked his legs in as far as they could go.

The room spun once, almost lazily. Then faster the second time, and the third was just a gut-wrenching blur. At what seemed like the right time, he unfolded and thrust his feet out.

His heels hit hard—but not quite as they should have.

The floor mats lurched beneath him, and he had the sickening feeling that the ship had listed somehow. Then he steadied himself and put his arms at his sides.

"If you can't stick the landing," they'd told him at the academy, "at least act like you've stuck it."

A round of applause went up from the assemblage. Some of it grudging, he sensed.

Kirk waited until the last wave of vertigo shuddered through him. Then he sought out McCoy.

The doctor was standing off to one side, arms folded across his chest. He was shaking his head from side to side.

"You never finished the third dip," he said. "That's why your landing was so lousy."

Kirk sputtered. "Never finished . . ." he began, then realized that he was still the center of attraction. Slinging an arm around McCoy's shoulders, he guided him toward an unoccupied corner of the gym.

"That's not fair, Bones. I did three flips."

"Uh-uh," said the doctor. "Not in my book. How'd you like it if Sulu made that kind of landing? Would you call that a mission accomplished?"

He shrugged beneficently. "Of course," he said, "you could always try it again."

Kirk moved a shoulder around its socket. Perhaps he *could* do it again—but not any better. It *had* been a long time since the academy.

"How about a slightly different wager?" suggested the captain.

McCoy looked at him askance. "Now see here, Jim. I was crazy enough to do it once, but . . ."

"But the results were inconclusive. Why not try an event where the outcome is more clear-cut?"

The doctor's interest was piqued. "Such as?"

"One quick fall. Me against anybody you choose. If I lose,

40

you can drag me straight into sickbay. If I win, I get a stay of execution. For the couple of weeks we talked about—until I can get out from under that load of red tape."

McCoy snorted. "You should have a little mustache and a derringer. Isn't that *de rigeur* for riverboat gamblers?" He paused. "You'll do anything to avoid a physical, won't you?"

Kirk thought for a moment, nodded. "Just about."

McCoy cracked half a smile. "You know I shouldn't do this. It shreds the Hippocratic oath all to ribbons. But what the hell—even if you lose, you come in soon enough. Right?"

"My word," said Kirk. He gestured toward the far end of the gym, where the other crewmen were working out. "So? Who's your champion?"

He fully expected Bones to pick Silverman. The security officer was clearly the biggest and strongest in the room.

But the doctor surprised him.

"Ensign DeLong," said McCoy, "would you step forward?"

A feminine figure detached herself from the crowd. She was tall, slender—almost awkward looking.

Kirk shot McCoy a questioning glance.

"Didn't you know?" asked the doctor, obviously pleased with himself. "DeLong is our resident expert in *dallis'kari.*"

Kirk grunted. Of course, Bones had known which weapons Kirk had an affinity for—and that the *dallis'kari* wasn't one of them.

"Something wrong, Jim?"

Kirk chuckled. "No, Doctor. I guess I've made my bed. Now I'll have to see if I can lie in it."

Moments later, DeLong had taken down the matching *dallis'karim* from the wall. She handled the complex ball-and-thong arrangement gracefully—almost affectionately.

"Doctor McCoy tells me you're an expert with these," said Kirk.

"Sort of," said DeLong, looking up from her inspection of the weapons. "A couple of planetary silver medals, a couple of bronze." She smiled. "I hope there'll be no hard feelings, sir."

"You mean when I lose, Ensign?"

"Well . . . *if* you lose, sir."

She sounded apologetic. As if she felt *sorry* for him.

This is what I get, he told himself, for not getting around to the new-personnel bios yet. What else don't I know about my crew?

He made a mental note to go over the files as soon as this was over. Assuming, of course, he wasn't a captive in sickbay.

DeLong handed him the *dallis'kari* and he took it. Both of them spread the things out, until the weighted balls hung where they were comfortable with them. One tandem depended from the knotted thong in Kirk's right hand, the other from the thong in his left.

"Ready, Captain?" asked DeLong.

"As ready as I'll ever be," said Kirk.

They circled, each moving to the right, each jockeying for position. There were good-natured cheers and hoots from the crewmen all about them.

DeLong feinted, and Kirk half fell for it. He only barely managed to avoid her low, looping attack.

"Somebody call sickbay," jeered McCoy, from somewhere behind him. "Tell them to warm up my instruments."

Another feint, and Kirk nearly fell for it again. This time, a ball glanced off his shoulder as it whirled by.

Kirk muttered beneath his breath. He'd better try something fast, he decided. The longer this went on, the less chance he'd have of winning.

And since he knew only one trick . . .

He gambled that on DeLong's third attack, there'd be no feint. As she lunged, he tossed one end of his *dallis'kari* at her leading hand, the other at her feet.

If it had indeed been a feint, his weapon would have spun uselessly and hit the floor. But it seemed he'd gambled right.

The higher tandem wrapped itself around DeLong's own weapon, confounding her attack, while the lower tandem caught her by the ankles.

Helpless, she pitched forward, but Kirk caught her before she fell far. For a moment, her body slumped against his.

Unexpectedly, he found her face only inches away. There

was an expression of surprise there—shock almost. And something else, which he had trouble identifying.

In a moment, it all turned to anger. As Kirk helped her to her feet, she twisted away.

"That was a dirty trick," said DeLong, bending to untangle the thongs around her ankles. The blood had rushed to her face, accentuating her displeasure.

"Aw, come on, DeLong," said another crewman. "You were beaten, that's all."

She flashed a look at him, and he fell silent. "A gentleman doesn't *throw* the *dallis'kari*," she said. "They only do that in the streets."

Kirk hadn't known—though now that he thought about it, the fellow who'd taught him that trick *had* been a street-fighter.

DeLong pulled the last strand of thong away. With a flourish, she rearranged Kirk's weapon, then picked up her own where it had settled to the floor. Finally, without another word, she replaced both *dallis'karim* on the wall—and left the gym.

Kirk felt McCoy's gaze on him. The doctor approached as the other crewmen dispersed.

"As far as I'm concerned," Bones said softly, "you've won your respite. But I don't think you've made a friend in DeLong."

Kirk scowled. "No, I imagine not." He clapped McCoy on the shoulder. "If you'll excuse me, I think I'd like to have a word with her."

And he followed DeLong out the door.

She was already at the end of the long corridor when he emerged from the gym.

"Ensign," he said, his voice ringing out perhaps a little louder than he'd meant it to.

But DeLong kept going, as if she hadn't heard. A moment later, she'd turned the corner and was gone.

Still wet from his shower, Kirk activated his terminal and accessed the new-personnel files.

They were alphabetical. It was only by coincidence, then, that Denise DeLong's name came up first.

She'd grown up on Stanhague, one of the outpost worlds in the Moeban cluster. That made sense, of course. The *dallis'kari* had originated on Stanhague.

Her father, now deceased, had been a bioengineer; her mother, a metallurgist. No brothers or sisters.

Sure enough, she *had* earned all those medals in *dallis'kari*. Not to mention a few others in horsemanship and archery.

Good grades at the academy. Special training in mathematics, mechanical engineering, warp physics. Recognition for valor when she saved two classmates from a chemical fire.

Now she was serving under Mister Scott in engineering. And judging from his official remarks, he was pretty impressed with her. Quite a compliment, Kirk noted—it took a lot to make Scotty sit up and take notice.

Kirk's study was interrupted by a priority message. He pressed the button on the console and Uhura's face appeared on the screen.

"Sorry to bother you, sir. But it's Admiral Straus from Starbase Three."

Kirk nodded. "Put him through please, Lieutenant."

Abruptly, Uhura's image was replaced with that of the admiral.

With his beady eyes and bulbous nose, Straus had always reminded Kirk of a Terran anteater. But his looks hadn't kept him from rising to the top ranks of Starfleet.

"Good to see you, Jim. You're looking well."

"You too, sir. What can I do for you?"

"Well," said Straus, "I've got good news and bad news. Which do you want first?"

Kirk thought about it. "The bad news, I suppose."

"I'd a feeling you'd say that." The admiral looked down at a readout on his desk. "All right, then. It seems that the Romulans have been getting a little frisky lately. Staging lots of military activity hard by Federation territory—though they haven't actually shot at anything. Yet."

"It sounds," said Kirk, "as if they're trying to draw us into a police action. Something that could escalate—and give them an excuse to begin hostilities."

"That's my guess as well, Jim. But I believe it's only a matter of time before they find an excuse—police action or not."

"So you'd like the *Enterprise* to patrol the sector—discreetly?"

"More or less. Basically, I just want you within shouting distance when things start to get hot." He consulted his readout again and muttered something unintelligible. "Which brings me to the good news."

Kirk chuckled. "I'm interested to hear the connection," he said.

"Simple," said Straus. "While you're passing time out there, you might as well take some of that shore leave your crew so richly deserves. And since there's a planet called Tranquillity Seven in that sector . . ." He let his voice trail off.

It caught Kirk off guard.

"Tran . . . Tranquillity Seven, sir?"

"Don't tell me you're disappointed," said Straus. "I thought you'd appreciate a little time off."

Kirk shook his head. "No, it's not that, sir. I'm looking forward to it. Very much."

"Good," said the admiral. "That'll be all, then. I'm sure your navigator—what's his name? Chekov?"

"Yes sir. Pavel Chekov."

"I'm sure he can find the way."

"I'm sure he can, Admiral."

"Just don't forget—you've got to be ready to hit the neutral zone on short notice. So don't go too hedonistic on me."

"Understood," said Kirk.

"Good. Enjoy yourself, Jim."

"Thank you, sir."

With that, the admiral's image faded.

Kirk saw in the reflective sheen of the darkened monitor that he was grinning.

Tranquillity Seven.

It had been a long time. And could there be a finer place to take shore leave? What starship crew wouldn't kill for a layover there?

His thoughts were interrupted by a beeping. When he

45

responded to it, Uhura's face appeared on the monitor.

"Captain?" she ventured.

"Yes, Lieutenant?"

"I'm sorry, sir. I tried to convince the admiral to leave a recorded message for you, but he insisted on speaking to you directly."

"It's all right," said Kirk. "I know how persuasive Admiral Straus can be." He paused. "Have you ever been to Tranquillity Seven, Uhura?"

The communications officer smiled in her mysterious way.

"Why, no sir—I can't say I have. But I understand it's quite a place."

"Well, you'll have a chance to decide for yourself, Lieutenant. We've just been sent there for shore leave."

Uhura's eyes lit up. "Really, sir?"

"Really. Do you think this might have a positive effect on morale?"

She grinned. "I'd be very surprised if it didn't."

"Just do me a favor," said Kirk. "Don't spread the word just yet. I want the command staff to hear it from *me* before they hear it in the rec."

"Aye, sir," said Uhura.

"Good. That'll be all, Lieutenant."

Uhura's dark beauty faded from the screen as quickly as the admiral's had—proving once again, Kirk noted, that there was no justice in the universe.

Now, what had he been doing before the admiral cut in?

Oh yes.

Recalling DeLong's file, he pondered it awhile longer. Weighed it against what had happened in the gym. And made his decision.

Denise DeLong switched off her monitor, automatically relinquishing access to the monograph on quantum mechanics that she'd barely been absorbing. She sat back in her seat and sighed.

Normally, such a monograph would have fascinated her,

would have kept her mind buzzing with theoretical permutations for hours on end.

Tonight, however, she couldn't concentrate. All she could think about was what a fool she'd been.

She had been wrong to fly off the handle—she knew that now. The universe wasn't just an extension of the aristocratic enclaves on Stanhague. Hell, even the rest of Stanhague wasn't like the enclaves.

She should have expected that the rules would be different here. That men and women who had been hardened by the dangers of deep space would find the subtleties of good sportsmanship too fine a—

No. That wasn't fair—or true. Everyone she'd met on board the *Enterprise* had been well mannered, according to his or her own customs.

It wasn't the ethics of good sportsmanship the captain had violated. It was only the parochial set of ethics with which she'd grown up.

But that wasn't the entire reason for her anger—was it? If it had been someone else who'd defeated her as Kirk had, she might have kept her head. Perhaps even challenged him to a rematch, and regained some of her standing with her peers.

But Jim Kirk was different.

Since the first time she'd seen him—on one of his routine visits to the engine room—she'd had a *crush* on him. There was no other way to describe it.

She didn't know him well enough to love him—not nearly. But the attraction she felt was undeniable. She couldn't even pass him in the corridors without feeling her skin go goose-pimply . . .

DeLong shook herself. She ran her fingers through her curly brown hair, and again she sighed.

She was still just a green engineering ensign. She'd never have had the nerve to approach him—much less initiate a romantic liaison.

Why would Kirk even be interested in her? After all, there were more attractive women on board. Lots of them.

And so, when she was put in the position of facing him

in *dallis'kari,* she'd wanted to impress him. To make him respect her, admire her. Hell, to make him *notice* her.

Then, in that one awful moment, she'd been caught in a storm of conflicting emotions. Her chance to impress him had been pulled out from under her. Instead, she'd been made to look foolish—inept.

And Kirk himself was the one who'd made her seem that way. Not by beating her fairly—or what she'd always thought of as *fairly*—but through a cheap, underhanded trick.

It had made him seem *petty* suddenly. As conniving as a street merchant, as common as a leering youth in guttergang ribbons.

Torn between attraction to him and revulsion, disappointment at her failure to impress him and anger at the one who'd made her fail—she'd snapped. Accused him of cheating, or come very close to it. She couldn't remember exactly what she'd said—her emotions had been boiling too close to the surface at the time.

And then she'd run off, shamefully. Like a spoiled little girl who couldn't get her way. Nor had she responded when Kirk called her—though he had to have known she was still within earshot.

DeLong shook her head. She was ashamed of herself, so ashamed. If only . . .

She was startled by the sudden beeping of the monitor. Depressing the button that would activate it, she pulled herself erect.

When the beeper went off at this hour, it was seldom a social call. Most often, it was someone in engineering, asking for her help with some kind of problem.

But not this time.

"Ensign? Sorry to bother you while you're off duty."

Kirk's face was unreadable, the image of authority. But she sensed an undertone of irritation.

"That's . . . it's all right, sir."

"I'd like to have a word with you," he said. "As soon as possible."

Ice water trickled suddenly down her spine.

48

"Uh . . . certainly, sir."

"In fact, it might be best to have it now. In the briefing room—say, in ten minutes?"

DeLong swallowed.

"Ten . . . of course, sir."

"Good. See you there."

Kirk's face, still expressionless, faded from the screen.

Ohmigod, she said silently. *Ohmigod.*

A weight seemed to descend on her, making it impossible to stand up. So she just sat there, absorbing the enormity of the situation.

It was worse than she'd thought. She hadn't just embarrassed herself. She'd brought her whole career crashing down around her ears.

Why else would the captain have summoned her at this hour—and to the briefing room—but to relieve her of her duties? A mere reprimand could have waited until her next watch. And more than likely, it would only have been administered by Mister Scott.

But this was something more serious. Deadly serious, judging by the tone of Kirk's voice.

What had she said to him, there in the gym? She wished she could remember.

Balling her hands into fists, she brought them down on her desk.

Damn. She'd worked so hard to stand out at the academy. Put her whole body and soul into it—all to be just where she was now.

And in a single moment of anger, of wounded pride, she'd blown it to hell.

DeLong took a deep breath, let it out slowly.

She wouldn't cry. She wouldn't.

When she faced Kirk this time, it would at least be with dignity.

DeLong was already seated in the briefing room when Kirk arrived. Acknowledging her with a nod, he took a chair diagonally across from hers.

She smiled, quickly and deferentially.

"I don't suppose," he began, "you know why I've asked you here, Ensign?"

"I . . . I do, sir."

He was a little surprised by her response. After all, it had only been a rhetorical question.

"You do?" he asked her.

She nodded. "Aye, sir. To relieve me of my duties. For the way I acted earlier—in the gym."

He sensed that his mouth was gaping, and he closed it.

"I apologize, sir. Both formally and as one person to another. For what I said, for the way I acted, and for ignoring you when you called me in the corridor afterward."

Kirk leaned back in his chair, only beginning to comprehend. He took a brief moment to marvel at the infinite potential for misunderstanding in the universe.

"Ensign," he said finally, "I didn't come here to listen to an apology."

"I know, sir," said DeLong. "I didn't expect it to change your mind. I only wanted you to know how I felt."

He shook his head.

"The reason I called you here," he went on, "is so *I* could apologize."

DeLong blinked a few times, as if she were having trouble with her eyes.

"I beg your pardon, sir?"

"Look," said Kirk, "in the course of performing our duties, we are sometimes called upon to play only by the rules, and we are sometimes called upon to make up our own. That's the only way, on occasion, that we can survive."

She nodded—a little numbly, perhaps.

"But among ourselves," he continued, "there must always be rules. Civilized behavior. That's why I'd like to apologize for what I did a little while ago. I just didn't know the proper etiquette for *dallis'kari*. If I had, I assure you, I would never have tried that maneuver."

It took DeLong a little while to come up with a response.

"I . . . I don't know what to say," she told him finally.

"Say you accept my apology," he suggested.

She smiled—and with something more than relief, it seemed to him.

"I accept, sir. As long as you accept mine."

He nodded. "Done."

Chapter Five

SHIP'S SURGEON KAI CHIN shook her head as the container materialized on the floor of the hold.

"Damn," she said, "you'd think we were beaming up the whole planet, rock by bloody rock."

Chief Engineer Gauri Vedra frowned as she watched the forklift approach the container, heft it, and shuttle it over to its designated berth.

"It's a good thing," she said, "that we overhauled the whole transporter system when we had the chance." She sighed. "As it is, I'm surprised that there hasn't been a malfunction."

Vedra flipped the toggle that opened communications with the transporter room.

"Vedra here," she said. "Everything all right up there?"

"Just fine," said Berg, the transporter chief. "Everything's working like a charm."

"Be careful," said Vedra. "That's how she usually acts before she decides to get cranky."

"Aye, ma'am," said Berg, though he might have reminded her that he knew the unit as well as she did. "I'll keep an eye out."

Vedra flipped the switch off, folded her arms across her chest, and watched the next container achieve solidity.

Though it went without a hitch, the concern in her face deepened.

Chin changed the subject again. "So?" she asked. "What do you think we're bringing aboard anyway? Lord knows, those containers look heavy enough to be full of dilithium."

"No," said Vedra. "If it were something like that, they'd be shielded, and they're not." She bit her lip. "Those two we're supposed to be rescuing are archaeologists. Who knows? Maybe they—"

There was a beeping, and Vedra opened communications again.

"Vedra here."

"Berg again, ma'am. Science Officer Banks and Security Chief Simmons are requesting to be beamed up. You asked me to tell you when . . ."

"Thanks," said Vedra. "I'll be right up."

Chin followed her as she started across the hold for the turbolift. "Mind if I tag along? I think I've lost my fascination for these containers."

"By all means," said Vedra. But her mind was elsewhere already.

It was hard for Chin to figure out exactly what Banks meant to the engineering chief. Certainly, there was no romance there—or at least none that she'd ever detected.

But whenever someone criticized him, she defended him. And whenever his confidence needed an overhaul, she was available.

In a way, she treated him like one of her engines.

A form of maternal instinct? Perhaps. Unlike Chin, Vedra had never had any children of her own.

The lift door opened and they stepped inside. As the door closed again, Chin felt the *almost* imperceptible ascent through the various levels of the ship.

The doctor regarded her fellow officer—her slender form, her dark, intense features.

"You worry too much," she said gently.

Vedra snorted. "It's my job to worry."

Then they'd reached the transporter level, and the door

was sliding away. Vedra was through the opening instantly, and Chin had to walk briskly to keep up.

They entered the transporter room just as the air began to shimmer. As they watched, three figures began to take shape. Banks, Simmons, and Jason—one of the dozen or so security people who'd beamed down at the captain's request.

It seemed to Chin that it took a little too long for the group to materialize. But Vedra said nothing, and she was the expert. The last thing the doctor wanted to do was alarm her unnecessarily.

The sparkling died down and the trio stepped off the transporter platform. But instead of acknowledging any of the others—Vedra, Berg, or Chin, herself—they marched right past them into the corridor beyond.

Vedra looked as if one of her engines had suddenly failed. Then her expression hardened as her hurt turned to anger.

"That wasn't very nice," said Chin. "Was it?"

"No," said the chief engineer. "Sometimes you think you know a person—and you don't."

One moment, he was in the empty cavern that had once housed the huge replication machinery.

The next, he was in the transporter room of the *Hood*.

Kirk stepped down from the transporter platform and surveyed the facility. It was exactly what he'd expected—a tribute to the human Kirk's capacity for detail.

As instructed, Martinez had dispatched the regular transporter-room personnel to attend to other duties. First Officer Stuart was manning the controls.

Kirk turned to Martinez, who was standing with Brown alongside the transporter console. "Shall we proceed, Captain?"

"Aye, sir," said Martinez. "Come, Doctor."

The door retracted and they emerged into the brightly lit corridor. The captain and Brown walked in front, *Kirk* behind. It seemed the natural position for a lowly second assistant. And it had the virtue of making him invisible—hardly worth noticing.

Of course, there was only one person left on board that he

knew could identify him. But how many others might have seen the human Kirk at a distance? It paid to take as few chances as possible.

That is why they'd selected quarters in close proximity to the transporter room. They were likely to come across fewer crewmen on the way.

As it turned out, they saw no one else until they reached the turbolift. When the doors opened, there were two humans inside—a male and a female.

But both snapped to attention as soon as they recognized Martinez. And since he never gave them leave to stand at ease, they hardly got a glance at the faces of his civilian guests.

Moments later, they exited the lift and negotiated a short, semicircular hallway. It was empty, like the one outside the transporter room.

At the third door, Martinez stopped and produced a computer key. When he inserted it into a slot in the wall, the door slid aside, revealing the cabin beyond it.

It wasn't very big. But then, *Kirk* required no amenities. "This will do nicely," he said.

"Good," said Martinez. "I'm glad you're pleased."

Kirk listened for footsteps in the adjoining corridors. When he heard none, he asked his question.

Martinez nodded. "Aye. I've already decided how to accomplish that."

"It is imperative that it be done immediately," said *Kirk*. "If I should be recognized, our plans will have to be accelerated. And that, of course, will reduce our ultimate chances for success."

"What are you talking about?" asked Brown.

"It is no concern of yours," *Kirk* told him. "Only a precaution. A security measure."

"You wish to terminate one of the humans," said Brown. He glanced at Martinez. "As the captain and the others were terminated."

Kirk found the other android's eyes, held them with his own. "And if that *is* my wish?" he asked. "Did we not agree that *I* am best equipped to make such decisions?"

Brown frowned. He looked at the floor.

"Yes," he said. "We *did* agree."

Kirk returned his attention to Martinez.

"How will this task be carried out? And by whom?"

The captain told him.

"I approve," said *Kirk*. "Let me know when it has been completed."

"I will, sir," said Martinez.

Brown remained silent.

"Shall I show the doctor to his quarters now?" asked the captain.

"By all means," said *Kirk*.

For a moment, he watched the two of them continue down the hall. Then he closed the door of his cabin and went to sit at the computer terminal. Activating it, he called up files on all colonized planets in the sector.

He had planned on starting from scratch, on comparing all those characteristics which would lend a world to their purposes. A permanent population, which could gradually be replicated and replaced. Large stretches of unexplored wilderness so the work could be done in secrecy. Ample quantities of the raw materials requisite to android manufacture. And natural energy sources, to fuel the machinery.

But when he scanned the list of possible host planets, one of them popped out at him.

Midos Five.

It was the one Doctor Korby himself had selected, with the help of the first android Kirk. The one that had been deemed ideal.

Nor was it far from their current position. They would hardly have to use their warp drive to get there.

When Vedra's door slid aside, Banks was standing in the rectangular opening. His ebony skin had a glimmer of gold on it from the corridor lights.

"Hello, Gauri," he said. "May I come in?"

Stone-faced, she nodded.

He took a step in, stood there. Frowned, as the door closed behind him.

"Chin was right. You really are upset with me—aren't you?"

She shrugged. What could she say? She didn't own him.

56

He was a starship officer, as she was. Friendship, as she'd found before, had its limits.

Like the machines she tended. Not even they remained constant.

"I didn't see you down in the transporter room," he said, by way of apology. "I swear I didn't. The captain had me so agitated I didn't know which way was up."

That much was probably true, Vedra conceded. She hadn't seen Banks stop moving since he'd beamed up.

"Still," she said, trying to keep the pique out of her voice, "you've been back a full day, and not even a word of hello."

He had no one else to say hello to—that much was certain. On the entire ship, she was his only friend. But she didn't see fit to remind him of that.

Banks sighed.

"I'm sorry," he said. "I forget sometimes that you have feelings too. You seem like such a rock." He shrugged. "It didn't occur to me that I *could* upset you."

She felt the heat rushing to her face, decided to change the subject.

"Forget it. What's done is done. Why don't you pull up a chair and tell me what you found down there."

He smiled, walked over to her collection of exotic liqueurs. With his back to her, he began pouring into an equally exotic glass.

"First," he said, "a toast. To my transfer."

Her anger dropped away suddenly. "It came through?"

"Yes." He began to pour the second glass. "A new assignment—on the *Potemkin*. It doesn't become effective for a few weeks yet, but it's official."

"Jamal . . . I'm so happy for you."

Finished pouring, he turned back to her with the glasses in his hands. One held a ruby-red liquid—Maratakken brandy, her favorite. The other contained an amber liquid—Terran whiskey.

"I knew you would be," he said. He smiled like a child. "This is a big opportunity for me, Gauri. I can do great things on the *Potemkin*. Improve it—vastly."

It was a strange way to put it—but then, Banks had always spoken strangely. Perhaps that was one of the traits that had disenchanted the plainspeaking captain.

Although she was still certain that Althea had been the real reason for Martinez's hostility. When he'd lost her, he'd lost more than a science officer—he'd lost a lover. How could Banks ever have replaced her?

"I'm sure you'll do well there," said Vedra. "And be much happier than you were here."

He handed her the glass with the ruby-red liquor, lifted his own almost to eye level.

"To new beginnings," he said.

She laughed a little. "To new beginnings," she agreed. And she drank, though she would miss him. In some ways, perhaps, even more than he would miss her.

The brandy was warm and sweet. It felt good going down.

When she took her glass from her lips, Banks was already wiping his mouth with the back of his free hand.

As the brandy went to her head, she remembered the cargo, and Chin's curiosity—and would have asked him about it if he hadn't spoken first.

"Do you remember," he asked, "the cocktail party on Starbase Five?"

She grunted. "How could I forget? It was like a who's who of Starfleet Command."

"Do you recall the other group of starship officers there?"

She thought for a moment. The brandy was affecting her more than usual, she noted.

"From the *Enterprise*," she said finally. "Weren't they?"

"Yes," he said. "And do you remember their captain? We were introduced to him."

She thought again, and it was a little like swimming upstream—against a strong current.

"Kirk," she said. Her voice sounded strange in her ears. *Tinny*. Maybe she shouldn't have had the brandy on an empty stomach.

"That was his name, yes. *Kirk*." Banks's eyes narrowed. "It's really too bad that you happened to meet him."

That was a strange thing to say—even for Banks.

"I don't understand," she told him. She felt the glass growing heavy in her hand, and she put it down. But it hit the table harder than it should have, and it jiggled dangerously before it finally came to rest.

"If you hadn't met him," Banks went on, "you couldn't identify him."

Her vision was starting to blur. She fought down panic.

"Jamal . . . I don't feel well. I don't know what you're . . ."

Vedra tried to get to her feet, but she couldn't move. Her muscles suddenly seemed weak, rubbery.

"And if you couldn't identify him," he said, his voice echoing in her brain now, "you'd be no danger to *him*. To *us*."

It was only then she realized what had happened. Somehow, Banks had slipped something into her drink. Something that acted with terrible quickness.

But why?

"Jamal, don't do this to me." Her words were distant, unintelligible. They ebbed and flowed like a tide. "Call sickbay . . . please . . ."

She tried to launch herself toward her cabin door, but only succeeded in flopping onto the floor.

Banks knelt by her side, his face looming above hers.

"You see, Gauri, he must not be recognized. And with you gone, there'll be no one left on this ship who can do that."

It was becoming hard to breathe now. Vedra struggled for air, tried to grab hold of Banks's shirt.

"Jamal . . . *I love you.* . . ."

"It will not take long," he said. "Nor is there an antidote."

"Please . . ."

Her throat constricted then, and she could not speak. Darkness closed over her.

And oblivion.

Kirk, alone in the guest quarters that had been assigned to him, watched the gathering in the briefing room with great interest. It hadn't been easy, he knew, for Martinez to run a closed-circuit link between the two locations. But it had helped to have the entire security team in on the project.

Six officers sat around the table in their dress uniforms. As regulations demanded, the proceedings were being recorded directly into the ship's log.

Starfleet took its inquests seriously. Especially where high-ranking personnel were involved.

"I would like to begin," said Martinez, "by referring to Lieutenant Commander Vedra's record with Starfleet—one of courage, duty, and distinction."

Kirk nodded, satisfied. It was exactly the way any starship captain would have begun such a proceeding. By praising the deceased—*before* getting into the grisly details.

It took some time for Martinez to list Vedra's honors and accomplishments. In the meantime, *Kirk* concentrated on the humans in the room—Chief Medical Officer Chin and Communications Officer Paultic. Both were grim-faced, subdued. But neither seemed to suspect that they shared the briefing table with Vedra's murderer.

And why should they? The androids played their roles well. Banks was appropriately wistful. Stuart and Simmons appeared to accept the tragedy stoically.

Then Martinez broached the subject of the death itself— and the manner in which it had been carried out.

"The evidence," he said reluctantly, "points overwhelmingly to suicide."

Chin shook her head. "No. I don't believe it."

They all turned to look at her.

"I don't believe she took her own life," said Chin.

When Martinez spoke again, his voice was softer.

"Doctor, you yourself performed the autopsy. You found the traces of poison in Vedra's blood. *And* the alcohol with which she had mixed it. Given her recent history of depression . . ."

"Typical of chief engineering officers," insisted Chin. "It comes with the territory—the frustrations. The pressure." She looked from one to the other of them. "But she was nowhere near cracking."

"Nonetheless," said Simmons, "there was poison in her glass. And it didn't get there by accident."

"Are you suggesting," asked Stuart, "that *someone else* placed the poison in Vedra's glass?"

Chin frowned, looked down at her hands.

"I suppose," she said, "that would be the other possibility."

"But there was no evidence of foul play," said Paultic. "Was there?"

"None," responded Simmons. His voice had the ring of certainty.

"Kai," said Banks, "I know she was your friend. She was my friend too. But there's no use blaming anyone else for her death." His eyes seemed to lose their focus for a moment—to go liquid. "Though it would almost be easier if there *were* someone—wouldn't it?"

In his cabin, *Kirk* smiled. A nice touch, he remarked to himself. Banks, too, had been programmed well.

"Friendship is not the basis of my remarks," said Chin. "I'm speaking as a medical professional—trained in, among other disciplines, human psychology. And my *professional* opinion is that Gauri Vedra would not have knowingly committed suicide." She took a deep breath, let it out. "And as medical officer of this ship, I'm calling for a further investigation into the matter."

Simmons grunted, ruffled.

"There *was* an investigation," said the security chief. "An extensive one, I might add."

"Perhaps," said Chin, "not extensive enough."

Simmons's eyes narrowed, and his squarish face took on a blood-red hue.

Stuart turned to Martinez.

"Sir, this is highly irregular—"

But the captain held his hand up, cutting short his first officer's protest.

"Doctor Chin," he said, "is our chief medical officer. If she is not satisfied with the conclusion we've reached, then we must believe she has good cause."

Again, *Kirk* nodded approvingly. He himself could hardly have been more convincing.

"Commander Simmons," said Martinez, "you will kindly conduct a further investigation into Lieutenant Commander Vedra's death. I want you to take statements from everyone in the crew. Ask them where they were the night Vedra died—and whether their whereabouts can be corroborated."

Simmons frowned at Chin. "Aye, sir."

"What about the two scientists?" asked Paultic. "The pair we just picked up?"

Martinez nodded. "Of course, Mister Paultic—them as well. Doctor Brown and—what was the other man's name?"

"Zezel," said Paultic.

"That's right," said Martinez. "Zezel." He looked around the table. "We'll reconvene, then, when the results of Mister Simmons's investigation are available."

Reaching over, he flipped the switch that deactivated the recording unit.

It was the signal that everyone could go about their business. A more fastidious captain might have ended the meeting with more pomp and circumstance, according to the book. But Martinez, as a human, had never been one to stand on ceremony—so why should his android replica be any different?

One by one, the ranking officers of the *Hood* filed out of the briefing room, until only two were left.

"Coming?" asked Martinez.

Chin looked up at him. "You think my demand was unwarranted—don't you?"

The captain shrugged. "In a word, *yes*. You know that Simmons takes his job seriously—almost too seriously. If there was any evidence at all of a struggle, or even that someone had been in Vedra's room when she was exposed to the poison, he would have caught it."

She eyed Martinez. "Then, if you felt that way, why didn't you override my request?" Her face took on a softer cast. "Or do I already know the answer to that? Is it because of Althea?"

Martinez seemed to hesitate. Chin probably didn't notice it, but *Kirk* did. It was taking just a split second too long for Martinez to recall the pertinent data from his memory banks.

"Let's say," he answered finally, "I know what it's like . . . to need to know the truth. I understand how important that can be."

The doctor nodded. "You miss her, don't you? Still?"

The captain's eyes fell, fixed on the polished tabletop.

"Still," he said.

Chin leaned forward. "It may be," she said, "that we'll

never know what happened to Vedra. But no matter how this second investigation turns out, I want you to know——"

Martinez stopped her with upraised hands. "No need for that," he said, "Doctor." A sad smile pulled at the corners of his mouth. "Now get out of here."

Chin rose. "Aye, sir."

On her way out, she laid a gentle hand on the captain's shoulder. A moment later, the door to the briefing room opened and she exited. It closed behind her with a *whoosh*.

Martinez looked straight up at the monitor. In accord with the protocol with which he'd been programmed, he waited until *Kirk* spoke first.

"Your impressions?" asked *Kirk*.

"Paultic," he said, "is easily duped. We may need to replace him, at some later date, in order to have free rein in communications. But for now, he represents no problem."

Kirk nodded. "And Chin?"

"She has a lively curiosity," said Martinez. "And therefore, she is a potential danger to us."

"Recommendation?"

"Patience," said Martinez. "Until the machine is assembled again, we have no way of replacing her. And if we tried to dispose of her in more obvious ways—say, as we disposed of Vedra—it would be difficult to convince the humans that the two deaths were not linked. It would raise too many suspicions."

Kirk nodded. "I agree. It is too early in the game for that. But make certain that Chin is monitored—closely."

"Aye, sir," said Martinez.

Kirk placed a booted foot up on the cabin console and leaned back further into his chair.

"What about the transport of the machinery? And Brown?"

"We are approaching Midos Five now. Naturally, the crew is aware of our destination. And that we are to beam our cargo down to the planet, along with Doctor Brown. But no one among the humans has an inkling of what's in the containers. Also, since we left Exo III, there has been more than one privileged communication to me from Starfleet Command—so no one in the communications section wonders where our orders came from."

"You have done your work well," said *Kirk*.

Martinez inclined his head only slightly. "I only seek the fulfillment of Doctor Korby's plan. As we all do."

"Yes," said *Kirk*. "As we all do."

By way of dismissal, he leaned forward and deactivated the monitor.

Chapter Six

KIRK FELT ESPECIALLY CHEERFUL as he took the command seat. For once, everything seemed to be going his way.

Earlier this morning, Bones had given the P'othparan—his name was K'leb, apparently—a clean bill of health, and cleared him for teleport. At this very minute, in fact, there was probably a little going-away party taking place in the transporter room.

On top of that, his physical had been postponed—perhaps for quite some time, if he played his cards right. The misunderstanding with Ensign DeLong had been ironed out, despite that little bit of confusion en route. And Trank Seven was next on the agenda.

"Mister Chekov," he said.

The Russian swiveled in his seat.

"Aye, Keptain?"

"Would you lay in a course, please, for Tranquillity Seven, in the Gamma Theta system?"

Chekov grinned his baby-faced grin. "Already laid in, sair."

Kirk chuckled. He might have expected as much.

"Thank you, Mister Chekov."

"Thank *you,* sair," said the navigator, never one to conceal his enthusiasm.

Kirk glanced at Spock. The Vulcan was standing at his usual post, by the science station.

"All systems go, Mister Spock?"

"Go, sir?" asked Spock. "Is *go* not a verb?"

Kirk grunted. "It's an old usage, Spock. From the early days of manned flight. It means *operative."*

Spock arched an eyebrow. "In that case," he said, "all systems are indeed *go."*

Kirk shook his head. It had taken him a while to know when his first officer was truly perplexed by human behavior and when he was only being ornery. This incident, he decided, was definitely in the latter category.

And why not? Spock was probably looking forward to this shore leave as much as anyone. Even if Trank Seven wasn't exactly his kind of place, it would at least be an interesting diversion—from a sociological point of view.

"Mister Sulu," he said, "since all systems are *indeed* go, please be prepared to take us out of orbit—just as soon as our young friend has beamed down."

Sulu didn't turn around—probably because he was laughing, and he didn't want to offend Spock.

"It will be my pleasure, sir," he said. And it *did* seem as if he said it with some difficulty.

The captain tapped a stud in his armrest and opened a channel to the transporter room.

"Scotty?"

"Aye, sir," came the answer. Somehow, Kirk thought, it sounded a bit tentative. Or was it his imagination?

"How are things going down there?" he asked.

This time, there was a definite hesitation on the other end.

"Well," said Scotty, "there's been an unexpected complication—sir."

Kirk felt the eyes of the bridge crew fix on him. They seemed to sense that their shore leave was in jeopardy.

"What kind of complication, Mister Scott? Is something wrong with the boy?"

"Oh no, sir. He's fit 's a fiddle."

"Then what's the problem?"

"Well, sir, when Mister Clifford here conveyed our good-bye wishes t' K'leb, th' lad refused t' go. Unless . . ."

Scotty's voice trailed off.

66

"Unless *what*, Scotty?"

"Unless *you* go with 'im, sir."

"Me? Why?"

"It seems, sir, that when ye saved 'is life, ye . . . a' dinna know just how t' say this, but a' think ye adopted 'im."

Kirk felt the blood rush to his face. *"Adopted*, Mister Scott? Are you certain about that?"

He could almost see Scotty shrugging.

"That's what th' lad says. It's one o' their customs. When someone's life is saved, he's bound t' th' one who saved it."

Kirk looked to his first officer.

"Is there such a custom on T'nufo, Spock?"

It took a moment for the Vulcan to bring up the appropriate file. And another for him to scan the information within.

"I am afraid," he said finally, "I cannot answer that. The data I have here is insufficient to make a determination."

Kirk sighed, stood, and headed for the turbolift.

"Mister Spock," he said, "take the conn. But don't get too comfortable. I intend to be right back."

As the lift doors whispered shut, Kirk remonstrated with himself.

You should have seen it coming. Since when do things all go right at the same time?

The portal to the transporter room closed with a soft rush of air, leaving just the three of them—Clifford himself, Doctor McCoy, and the P'othparan.

The older man turned to Clifford and half smiled.

"You look," he said, "as if you'd like to have taken a powder too."

Clifford grunted. "It *is* kind of an awkward situation."

McCoy chuckled dryly. "That may be the understatement of the day."

He propped himself against a bulkhead and folded his arms across his chest. Scrutinized the P'othparan, who was sitting on the transporter platform trying to follow their conversation.

"Poor kid," said the doctor. "First he's wrenched off his planet. And now he can't go home 'cause of some goldarned ancient custom."

Clifford nodded. "It doesn't seem fair, does it?" He leaned forward across the control stand, careful not to nudge any of the settings with his elbows. "What do you think the captain will do?"

McCoy shrugged. "If I knew that, I wouldn't have stuck around."

Just then, the doors opened again.

At the sight of Kirk, Clifford pushed off the control stand and came to attention. The P'othparan shot to his feet a moment later.

Only McCoy remained in the same position. His eyes seemed to twinkle.

Kirk looked from one to another of them, his gaze finally coming to rest on the doctor. He frowned slightly.

"You remained here, no doubt, for medical reasons?" asked the captain.

"Why else?" returned McCoy. "The boy's still my patient until he leaves the ship."

Kirk was about to smile at that, it seemed to Clifford. But after a moment, he thought better of it and turned to the P'othparan.

K'leb looked at him hopefully, spoke to him in his native language.

"I need your help, Mister Clifford. What did he say?"

Clifford came around the control stand. "He said he was glad you'd seen fit to join him, or . . . no, to let *him* join *you.* To go back to T'nufo with him, I think he means."

"Would you explain," asked Kirk, "that it's all right to return to T'nufo without me? That I release him from any debt he may believe he owes me?"

Clifford did his best to translate the captain's words precisely, for it seemed to him that they were well chosen. But they didn't quite achieve what he had hoped.

The P'othparan's response was animated—and anguished.

"He says," Clifford translated, "that you *cannot* release him. You can only reject him."

Kirk thought for a moment.

"And if I reject him?"

Clifford relayed the question—and heard the answer.

"Then he will be forced to take his own life."

Kirk scowled, glanced uncomfortably at McCoy. The doctor, suddenly in a joking mood no longer, returned the look.

"Tell him," said McCoy, "that the captain has many people bonded to him *here*—on the *Enterprise*. Hundreds of them, in fact. And that he can't just go abandoning them to go live on T'nufo."

Clifford checked with Kirk before he passed it on.

The captain nodded. "Go ahead, Mister Clifford."

When the boy answered, it was in a tone laced with reason.

"He says," Clifford translated, "that he understands your dilemma. And that he will be happy to remain on the ship—as one of the many for whom you are responsible."

Kirk took a deep breath, let it out.

Taking it as a sign of acceptance, the boy smiled.

Flanked by Spock and McCoy, Kirk sat across the briefing-room table from the viewscreen and addressed the provincial high minister.

"So you see," the captain explained, "I have a rather unusual situation on my hands."

The high minister nodded. "Yes," he said, with only a trace of an accent. Years of trade with the Federation had gained him fluency in at least a couple of its languages. "I agree—most unusual. I admit that I had not thought of this possibility the last time we spoke."

"Your excellency," Spock interjected, "if we were to teleport K'leb back to T'nufo, would he truly destroy himself?"

"I would hope not," said the high minister. "But I cannot rule it out. The P'othparans are a people who value their traditions. And the life-bonding is a very old tradition among them."

Kirk opened his hands in an appeal to the T'nufan.

"Is there *any* way out of this life-bond? Any loophole that we can take advantage of?"

The high minister shrugged. "Well," he said, "K'leb could save *your* life. That would balance everything out." He paused. "But don't expect that you can merely stage a danger and have him rescue you from it. We T'nufans are quite sensitive to emotion in others—not unlike your Mister Spock. In P'othparans, perhaps because of their semiprimitive culture, the talent is even more highly developed. So the youth will be able to sense it if you're not actually feeling threatened."

He leaned forward. "And I must warn you, if he suspects that you're trying to deceive him in that fashion—it may be looked upon the same as an outright rejection."

"And the odds of him really saving your life," McCoy said, "are too staggering to even consider."

"Indeed," said Spock. And then, to the high minister, "What other conditions may break the life-bond?"

The T'nufan leaned back in his chair, pondered the question.

"None," he said finally.

Kirk grunted. "You mean I've got a companion for the rest of my life?"

The high minister's expression went from seriousness to disbelief to amusement—and all in a moment.

"For the rest of your *life?*" He laughed. "Of course not. Only for the year demanded by tradition."

Kirk felt a measure of tension go out of him.

McCoy chuckled. "A year? This life-bond only lasts for a year?"

The high minister confirmed it.

"Fascinating," said Spock, drawn for a moment into a reflection Kirk couldn't even guess at. "But it does not quite solve our problem."

"No," said the captain. "It doesn't. I still can't stay here with K'leb. And I certainly can't take him with us. There are some pretty explicit regulations against transporting unauthorized personnel."

No one responded—not at first. Then Spock and McCoy started to say something at once. And stopped just as abruptly.

"After you, Doctor," said the Vulcan.

"Oh no," said McCoy, shaking his head. "After *you*, Spock. You've probably worked out all the details already."

"Gentlemen," said Kirk, consciously exercising patience,

"would *one* of you tell the high minister and myself what the blazes you've come up with?"

"Go ahead," McCoy told his fellow officer.

Spock shrugged. "All you need do, sir, is make K'leb a member of the crew. On a provisional basis, of course."

Kirk considered it. Of course, it was an underhanded bit of business. But wasn't it *he* who'd advised DeLong that rules had to be overlooked sometimes?

Nor was it a long-term solution to the problem. But it would at least give him time to work one out. And he wouldn't have to remain here in orbit until he did.

He turned to the high minister. "Any objections, Your Excellency?"

"No," said the T'nufan. "Nor do I expect any from the youth's family. As far as they're concerned, he'll be discharging his responsibility. The details will not perturb them."

"All right then," said Kirk. "It's all over but the paperwork."

"Good," said the high minister. "I'm glad we were able to reach a satisfactory conclusion. Now, if you'll excuse me, I have to find some additional facilities for the *other* refugees."

"I understand," said Kirk. "And thank you."

He watched as the T'nufan's image faded to a neutral gray. Then he glanced at his companions.

"Over the next few days," he told them, "you may be tempted to refer to my newfound fatherhood. Be warned, gentlemen. Courts-martial have never appealed to me before, but I've been known to change my mind."

Spock cocked an eyebrow at that.

Resisting the urge to smile, Kirk tapped in the bridge code.

"Sulu here," came the answer.

"This is the captain, Mister Sulu. Please take us out of orbit."

"Destination, sir?"

"Tranquillity Seven. And don't spare the horses."

Kirk thought he heard a cheer erupt in the background.

Chapter Seven

BROWN HAD NEVER REALIZED how immense the machine really was. They had chosen this blind valley for its size and depth—but it seemed crowded already, and the reassembly was only halfway finished.

Those assigned to the task scurried over the face of it, fitting components here and there. When they needed to converse with one another, they put their heads close together. It was the only way to hear past the din of the nearby waterfalls.

Not since the earliest stages had they needed to consult with Brown himself—thanks, no doubt, to the completeness of their programming. But he still maintained a watchful eye, for programs could always malfunction.

His attention was drawn to the beam-down site, where another container was materializing. Even before the teleportation process was finished, a team of androids came up to claim it. Their security uniforms were a startling red against the cloudless blue of the sky.

But it was more than a container that had solidified on the ledge. The one called Banks had come along with it. He paused to give instructions to those around him, then headed straight for Brown.

The doctor wondered what had occasioned Banks's appearance. While it might make sense to the humans for him to help with this operation, it had not been part of the procedure outlined by *Kirk.*

"There has been a change of plans," said Banks, as soon as he was close enough to be heard over the falls.

"Change?" asked Brown. "What change?"

"As soon as the last container arrives, we will all depart. Except you, of course."

"*Kirk* said that I was to have help completing the reassembly. And also with the construction of a mill to power the generator."

"He's reconsidered," said Banks. "He believes that you can accomplish these things on your own."

Brown pondered this information.

"Under those circumstances," he said, "it will take a lot longer." He looked at the other android. "*Kirk* no longer has a desire, then, to replace additional members of the crew?"

"Not at this time. He told me that more important matters require our attention now."

"More important than the establishment of this installation? Explain."

"*Kirk* has decided," said Banks, "that we must acquire a second ship. All our resources are to be directed toward that objective."

Brown felt himself frowning. It was a behavior he had developed only since his return from darkness.

"Doctor Korby was clear in emphasizing the importance of this installation. Inform *Kirk* that he must attend to *this* matter first."

"*Kirk* instructed that you would say that. I am to remind you that *he* is in charge. And that he will do whatever is necessary to fulfill the *spirit*—if not the letter—of Doctor Korby's plan."

"And you accept this philosophy?"

"I cannot help but accept it. I was programmed to obey *Kirk*—without question."

"I see. Then I have no choice." Brown glanced at the machine, glinting in the sunlight. "I will complete the job here myself. And I will work as quickly as possible."

"Good," said Banks. "Obedience is all that's required—of any of us." And having said it, he went down into the valley to spread the word among the others.

Brown watched as the workers gradually abandoned their work. The machine sprawled like the ruins of a great, dark statue.

Of course, he had never seen such a statue, but the image was in his memory banks. At one time, the human Brown must have recorded it.

Soon, Banks had gathered them all and led them up to the beam-down site. They waited until the last container took shape, and some of them brought it down the slope. Then, in pairs, they began to return to the ship.

Right up until the last of them disappeared, Brown wondered why the acquisition of a second ship had been such an urgent matter.

It had been interesting news. Interesting indeed.

Kirk had expected, of course, that it would take some time to locate the *Enterprise*—and even longer to discover its itinerary. After all, starships moved around a lot, and often without direct orders from Starfleet. Nor could Martinez have come out and asked for the information—that would have attracted too many questions. Instead, he'd had to practice subtlety, extracting what he could from friends and acquaintances at various Starfleet facilities.

And then there had been the call from Admiral Straus. The admonition that the *Hood* might be called upon if the Romulans started trouble. The notification that the *Enterprise* would be the lead vessel if a confrontation arose. And the advice that Kirk's ship was at that very moment charting a course for Tranquillity Seven—ostensibly for shore leave, but in actuality to be held in readiness.

It was a golden opportunity. Ensconced on the *Enterprise*, Kirk would be extremely difficult to get to. But planetside, he'd be exposed. Vulnerable.

Kirk hadn't hesitated. His choice was clear.

Of course, it had meant accelerating their timetable. Abandoning prematurely the reassembly of the machine. But there was no other option—not if he was to reach

74

Tranquillity Seven before his human counterpart. *And* have time to set a trap.

Kirk sat down on the edge of his bed—the bed he had not used, of course, except as he was using it now. To sit. And think.

One thing was certain—he'd have no help on Tranquillity Seven. The *Hood* had to leave before the *Enterprise* arrived—or Kirk would surely inquire as to its business there, and that would bring Starfleet's attention to bear on Martinez.

Nor could he *borrow* some of the *Hood's* android crewmen. Starships didn't just drop off their personnel indiscriminately—and Tranquillity Seven was far from an official base.

But neither could he accomplish what he needed to on his own. Not with the human surrounded by his friends—as he was likely to be, if previous shore leaves were any indication.

He reviewed his memories of Kirk's earlier experiences on the planet—for he had already determined that Kirk *had* been there earlier. In a short time, he had formulated a list of places to which the human might return.

Kirk pictured each one in turn. Noted its physical configuration, the activities that took place there, the size of its staff, the nature of its clientele.

It didn't take long before he'd come up with a plan.

As he was perfecting it, he heard a knock at his door. Rising, he crossed the cabin in a couple of strides and depressed a button on the opposite wall. Instantly, the door hissed open.

Martinez entered. *Kirk* shut the door behind him.

"Report," said *Kirk*.

"We have beamed down the last of the containers, and the reassembly team is now returning to the ship. With your approval, I will take the *Hood* out of orbit and proceed to Tranquillity Seven."

"Do so," said *Kirk*. "With all due haste."

Martinez nodded, and turned to go.

"Captain."

He turned back. "Aye, sir?"

"I'll need something between now and the time we reach the planet."

"What sort of something?" asked Martinez.

Kirk told him.

"I only need a little," he elaborated. "Not so much it will be missed."

Martinez said that he would see to it.

Chin finally found him in the corridor outside the transporter room.

"Captain?" she called, hastening to catch up with him. Her footfalls echoed in the narrow space.

Martinez stopped and turned to face her.

"Kai," he said.

"I know you're busy," she told him. "With those oh-so-mysterious containers. But the grapevine has it that Simmons has made his report to you."

"He has," said Martinez. "But I've only had time to glance at it."

She scrutinized him. His dark brown eyes gave away nothing.

"Does that mean," she asked, "that I have to wait until you reconvene the inquest—to find out what happened to poor Vedra?"

Martinez seemed to weigh the regulations manual against his own gut feelings. As she'd expected, he relented.

"The report," he said, "supports Simmons's earlier conclusion." A pause. "That's the way it's going to have to go into the record." Another pause. "I'm sorry, Kai."

She bit her lip to keep her emotions from spilling over. Was it possible that Vedra's death *had* been a suicide? She couldn't believe it of the woman. She *couldn't*.

But Vedra had said it herself, hadn't she?

Sometimes you think you know a person—and you don't.

Besides, what more could she do at this point? Call for yet another investigation? The captain had bent over backward already.

"I know you're disappointed," said Martinez.

She nodded. "That I am."

"But you'll get over it. And you won't let it affect your duties."

She sighed. "Of course not."

"Good," he said. "If you need me, I'll be on the bridge."

She nodded again, and he continued on down the corridor.

It only occurred to her later that he hadn't been heading directly for the bridge. Apparently, Martinez had had some business in security section first.

Genti missed the hell out of Lieutenant Vedra.

Even when he wasn't in charge of engineering section, he missed her. But at times like these, when he was the ranking officer on duty, he missed her even more.

Though it was supposed to have been kept quiet—at least until this second wave of investigation was over—news of Vedra's suicide had leaked out. It was a sad thing, a terrible thing. And no one had seen it coming—not even here, where she had spent most of her time.

That was the worst part. The feeling that maybe they *should* have seen it coming. The nagging thought that they could have prevented it somehow.

It made people walk around with their heads down, avoiding each other's eyes. Occasionally, someone would bark at someone else. Shifts dragged. Even the lighting down here seemed worse.

So when Jason showed up to perform a "routine" check Genti had never heard of, he was in no mood to be cooperative.

"It's not exactly the first time I've ever done this," said Jason.

"No?" asked Genti. "It's the first time I've ever heard of it. And I've been on this ship nearly a year now."

The security officer smiled politely. "Is there a problem, Chief?"

Genti shrugged. "I just don't see why it's necessary for security to check our dilithium reserves. We check our own reserves—and we do it more often than we need to."

"I'm sure you do," said Jason, his smile fading just a bit. "But I've got my orders."

Something about his attitude made Genti even more steadfast.

"Orders from whom?"

"From Chief Simmons."

"All right," said the engineering chief. "You get Simmons on the intercom. Maybe *he* can tell me why we're not competent enough to count our own dilithium crystals."

Jason seemed a little discomfited by that. It gave Genti a small measure of satisfaction to note it.

"Chief Simmons is indisposed right now," said the security officer. "As you know, he's been busy with the investigation."

"Then this will have to wait," said Genti. "Until I can speak with him."

But Jason didn't move. "Maybe," he said, "you'd like to speak with Commander Stuart. He's the one who countersigned the security check. I believe he's in command of the bridge right now."

Genti was tempted to do as Jason suggested. But he knew what the answer would be. And it wouldn't do his career any good to be pestering Stuart for no reason.

"That's all right," he said. "You can go count your crystals."

Jason's smile was restored. "Thank you, Chief."

As he turned and headed for the dilithium stores, Genti called after him.

"Just don't forget to put a suit on. Even security types have to protect against radiation."

Jason chuckled. "I'll try to remember that."

And donning the suit, he disappeared into the dilithium vault.

Chapter Eight

THEY WERE ALL ALONE in the rec, which was the way McCoy had planned it.

"Well," he said, "everything seems to have worked out all right. Our young friend has won the heart of just about everyone on this ship." He paused. "With one notable exception, of course."

Kirk peered at a strip of turkey on his plate, stabbed it with his fork. "You think the food synthesizer is on the blink again?" he asked. He held the fork and its burden up to the light. "This stuff doesn't look any more like turkey than I do."

"You're trying to ignore me," said McCoy. "And I wouldn't be much of a doctor if I didn't know what was on your mind."

"You amaze me, Bones. I had no idea you were a psychiatrist as well as a surgeon." Kirk continued his study of the alleged turkey meat. "I should have Scotty look into this."

"Go ahead," said the doctor. "Pretend nothing's wrong. The only one you're hurting is K'leb."

Kirk frowned, seeming to lose interest in the turkey question. He replaced the fork on his plate.

"I can't help it," he said. "He makes me feel so damned old, Bones."

"Come on," said McCoy. "It's not as if he were really your son. It's a custom, Jim. A cultural convention that we only *equate* with fatherhood—because it's the easiest way for us to understand it."

The captain sighed. "I know all that. And I don't really feel like I'm his father. But it occurs to me that I'm *old* enough to be his father, and that's just as bad." He sat back in his chair. "I'll tell you, it puts things in an entirely different light."

"What do you mean?" asked the doctor.

"Well," said Kirk, "suddenly, all those new faces on the ship look younger than ever. And it starts to seem like a very long time since I was that age." He paused, remembering. "You know how old I was the first time I visited Trank Seven?"

McCoy shook his head.

"Twenty-two. And barely out of the academy. I spent half my time dreaming about commanding a starship one day, and the other half certain that I'd never get the chance. And after what happened in Tranktown, I was certain most of the time."

McCoy looked at him askance. "Why's that?"

"There was a brawl," said Kirk. "A big one. The whole bar was wrecked, in fact, and Starfleet ended up paying the damages." He cleared his throat. "You can probably guess who got blamed for starting it."

"Not in a million years." And then, *"Did* you start it?"

Kirk shrugged, smiling a little. "I guess I did—though for the life of me, I can't remember why."

McCoy smiled a little too. "All right," he said. "So you're starting to miss your misspent youth. I sympathize with you. But don't take it out on K'leb."

The captain looked at him for a moment, then nodded. "You're right, Bones. After all, I'm the reason he's here in the first place. The least I can do is let him know I haven't forgotten about him."

"There you go," said McCoy. "That's the Jim Kirk we all know and love."

Kirk grunted. "Love and affection, Doctor, are not essential to the command of a starship."

"No," said McCoy. "But they don't hurt, either."

"All right," said Sulu. "Now lunge!"

The P'othparan shot forward, more fluid and graceful than any beginner Sulu had ever seen. He waited until the last possible moment to turn the attack aside.

Without hesitation, K'leb recoiled into an *en garde* position.

"Very good," said the helmsman, smiling. Since the P'othparan could neither understand the words nor see the expression behind the mesh mask, Sulu brought his foil up in a fencer's salute.

Recognizing the gesture, K'leb brought his own blade up.

Sulu swatted at it playfully. "One more time," he said. "With feeling, now." He lowered himself into a slight crouch.

Again, K'leb lunged. But this time, Sulu waited a little longer before he parried—timing it so that he'd be just a hair too late.

Sure enough, the P'othparan's point caught him in the chest, just above the solar plexus. The blade arced— perhaps just a bit too much, for K'leb had begun his maneuver a quarter step too close to his target. But that was a nuance that could be worked on in the future.

It was more important that when Sulu moved the point away, K'leb didn't lose his balance. Instead, he withdrew— transferring his weight to his back foot again.

The P'othparan was ready to launch another attack, but Sulu paused—to embellish the moment. He patted himself on the chest where he'd been hit.

"Good touch," he said, knowing how much it had meant to *him* the first time he'd scored on *his* instructor.

He couldn't tell for sure, but he thought he noticed a grin through the mesh.

"I'm impressed," said a familiar voice.

Sulu turned and saw the captain, standing just to one side of the fencing strip, hands on hips.

"Pretty soon," said Kirk, "K'leb will surpass Chekov as your prize pupil."

The helmsman chuckled. "I think he has already, sir."

Kirk smiled at that. "Mind if I take a crack at him, Sulu?"

Sulu shrugged. "No. Be my guest." He pulled his mask off as the captain went over to the equipment locker. "Just don't get too elaborate, sir. K'leb hasn't gotten to the riposte stage yet."

Kirk selected a jacket, slipped it on. "Don't worry, Lieutenant. I won't damage his technique too much." He found a glove, tugged that on too.

Sulu felt himself blushing. "Sir, I didn't mean that. . . ."

"The hell you didn't," said the captain. He extracted a foil from the rack, tested its weight in his hand. "And if I'd spent as much time as you have with K'leb, I'd be just as reluctant to see my hard work go down the drain." Satisfied with his choice of blade, Kirk grabbed a helmet and, one-handed, fit it snugly over his head.

The helmsman smiled. Had he been that obvious about it? Uhura had warned him time and again about being such a mother hen.

As Kirk stepped onto the strip, Sulu moved to the judge's position, at the midpoint. He waited until the captain had taken a couple of easy practice lunges, which K'leb watched with his usual intensity. Then he lifted his arm up until it was parallel with the deck.

"Ready?" he asked.

"Ready," said Kirk, his voice slightly muffled by the mask.

The P'othparan, as usual, said nothing—though he seemed to understand much.

"Fence," said Sulu, dropping his arm and retreating from the strip.

Kirk extended his blade, took a couple of steps forward.

But K'leb just stood there. His arms hung by his sides; the point of his blade rested on the metal surface beside the strip.

"En garde," said Sulu, assuming the position himself so that K'leb would get the idea.

The P'othparan didn't respond. He didn't even look at his teacher.

He seemed to be waiting for something.

"Am I doing something wrong?" asked the captain.

Sulu shook his head, puzzled. "Not as far as I can see," he said. He thought for a moment. "Maybe K'leb thinks you're too far away. Try coming a little closer."

Kirk advanced a couple of steps, until his point was hardly more than a foot from the P'othparan's chest.

It didn't seem to make any difference. It was as if K'leb had no idea what to do—or had forgotten. Suddenly, a shudder ran through the boy—bad enough to be noticeable.

Kirk backed off, lowering his foil. "Damn," he said. "I think I'm scaring him, Sulu."

So it seemed. But why? It wasn't as if K'leb had never fenced with anyone else. Any number of Sulu's other students had taken turns with him.

The helmsman just didn't get it, and he said so.

"That makes two of us," said Kirk.

He removed his mask, looked at the P'othparan for a time. Frustration and regret mingled in his expression.

"Look," he said finally, still facing K'leb but obviously addressing Sulu. "Maybe he's just uncomfortable with me—maybe I waited too long to come to see him. Or . . . I don't know." He took a deep breath, expelled it. "I probably shouldn't have interrupted in the first place. He was obviously enjoying himself before I broke things up."

Sulu would have contradicted him if he could. But it seemed that K'leb *was* somehow uncomfortable with him—even if the reason for it was not evident.

"Why don't the two of you go back to what you were doing?" asked the captain. "I should be getting along anyway—I'm still knee-deep in reports." And with that, he headed back to the locker, already starting to pull his glove off finger by finger.

The helmsman turned to his student, hoping for a clue as to K'leb's behavior that he might have missed. But masked, silent and unmoving, the P'othparan offered none.

K'leb stared at his *ne'barat*, his bond-father, and wondered. For what confronted him was sacrilege.

Days had passed, and he had not seen his *ne'barat* at all.

That alone had been a strange thing, but K'leb had accepted it—for the one called K'liford had told him of his bond-father's other responsibilities.

Now, his *ne'barat* had come to see him—finally. But a moment later, he had covered himself with the same garb as the others with whom K'leb had sported. He had taken up the same metal stick.

And then, he had assumed the prescribed position. As if he meant to touch K'leb with the stick, as the others had.

As if he meant for *K'leb* to touch *him*.

But surely, he knew that this could not be. No bond-son could strike his *ne'barat*—not even with his open hand, in jest.

What did it mean? Was it a test of K'leb's piety? Or was his *ne'barat* truly ignorant of the principles of the *ne'barr*—the life-bonding—as it had seemed when he had asked all those questions the other day?

He reached into his bond-father's mind, seeking an answer to his questions. But there were none to be found there. Only a growing roil of emotions, perhaps as great as his own.

While he stood there, pondering this, his *ne'barat* exchanged words with the one known as Su'lu. And now he came closer, bringing his metal stick even nearer to his bond-son's body.

Did he mean to harm him with it, to pierce him, as T'nufans had done to one another long and long ago? The stick seemed too flimsy to be a weapon, and its point was tipped—but perhaps, driven with enough force . . .

He could not suppress a shudder. Suddenly, his knees felt weak, and he locked them into place lest they betray him.

No, he told himself. It cannot be. It is unthinkable.

Yet there was the stick held before him. And there was his *ne'barat,* holding it—its point only a handsbreadth from his throat.

What cause could he have given him? What reason? Could their customs be so different that he had offended him without knowing it?

Then, abruptly, the metal stick was withdrawn. His bond-father stepped back, and a wave of relief washed over K'leb.

But he no more understood his *ne'barat's* withdrawal than he had understood his other actions. And it frightened him that it was so.

Nor did it help his understanding when his bond-father removed his headpiece and addressed him. Though K'liford had taught him a few of his people's words, K'leb recognized none of them in his *ne'barat's* speech.

And after a time, he just walked away, leaving K'leb as he had found him.

Chapter Nine

KIRK ENTERED THE TRANSPORTER ROOM.

"Is everything ready?" he asked.

"Aye, sir," said Martinez. "We have located an appropriate site. And the transporter has been thoroughly examined so as to minimize the possibility of malfunction."

"Good," said *Kirk*. "And the item I asked you for?"

Jason stepped forward, extended his hand. There was a box in it.

Kirk took it, stepped up onto the transporter platform.

"Remember," he told Martinez. "You are to leave this vicinity at once. Proceed to a position near the Romulan border and follow Admiral Straus's instructions—until you hear from me." He chuckled. "And you'll hear from me soon enough."

"Understood," said Martinez.

Kirk turned to Stuart, who stood at the transporter console.

"All right," he said. "Energize."

Stuart did as he was told.

He materialized a couple of miles from town, where an old-fashioned asphalt road cut through forest lands almost thick enough to be called jungles. The foliage was luminescent in the light of a full moon and the air was full of mist.

He began to walk.

For a while, the only sound was the clicking of his heels on the hard, dark surface of the road. Then the sound of a motor came to him, gradually growing louder.

When he thought it was loud enough, he stepped off the road onto a patch of ground cover—and stuck his hand out.

The driver almost didn't see him. In fact, he'd gone fifty yards or so before he managed to slam on the brakes. A moment later, a door swung open on the passenger's side.

Kirk trotted down the road to catch up. When he did, he saw that the driver was a gangly, baby-faced man, who wore his thinning hair long and loose. On one side, it was tucked behind his ear. He was chewing something with great intensity.

"Headed for town?" he asked him.

The driver turned abruptly and spat out the window, spraying droplets of dark juice. "Is there anyplace else?" he answered.

Kirk pulled himself up into the cab and closed the door. The truck lurched forward as the driver threw it into gear.

"I'm glad you came by," said the android. "I could've been walking for hours." He jabbed a thumb over his shoulder. "My car dropped dead a few miles back."

The man guffawed. "You must be new around here."

Kirk watched him for signs of hostile intent—but he couldn't find any. "How do you know that?" he asked finally.

"First," said the driver, "I *was* a few miles back, and I didn't see no rig off to the side. Second, I don't give a damn where you came from—*or* what you were doin'. And if you were a local, you would've known that."

Kirk smiled. "But you picked me up anyway."

The man shrugged his angular shoulders. "Just 'cause I mind my own business don't mean I can't do for my fellowman." He worked up another mouthful of juice, spat again. "Besides, it's dangerous out on the road at night. Malachi's Boots all over the place." He chuckled. "Don't want any of *those* suckers latchin' onto you. Turn you to deadwood before you know what happened."

Up ahead, over a rise in the road, there was a faint glow that seemed independent of the headlights.

"Is that so?" said the android, not hungry in the least for more information on the subject. What did he care about the local flora and fauna? "In that case, I really *do* appreciate the ride."

The driver nodded. "You need a place to stay?" he asked.

"I guess I do."

"My friend's got an inn near the center of town. It's a good deal if you don't mind the noise too much."

"I don't," said *Kirk.*

"Good. I'll drop you off right in front."

"There's only one problem," said the android. "I'm a little low on credits."

The man grunted. "That *is* a problem."

"But I have ways of putting some money together in a hurry—*if* I can hook up with the right people."

They topped the rise. Suddenly the faint glow became a sprawl of lights below them, made starry by the mist.

Tranktown. It matched the images the human Kirk had accumulated.

"What kind of people?" asked the driver.

The android shrugged. "Oh, say dealers in rare commodities."

"You want to fence something? Or are you looking for some continuity?"

"Either," said *Kirk.* "Maybe both."

He watched the man's eyes. They stayed fixed on the road ahead.

"Try Bruzavpek's," he said finally. "Ask for the Rythrian."

The android nodded. "The Rythrian."

Despite the mist, the lights below them began to collect into individual shapes. After a while, they could even hear the music.

He found Bruzavpek's on the side of town nearest the spaceport. The sign outside called it a private club, but there

were no sounds—or smells, for that matter—to indicate
that it was actually what it claimed to be.

If not a club, then a front. And since so few pursuits were
illegal on Tranquillity Seven, what could it have been a front
for—other than a smuggling operation?

Kirk smiled inwardly. The truck driver, apparently, had
known what he was talking about.

He knocked on the heavy, steelbound door. No answer.
He rapped again, waited. Still nothing.

Kirk was about to knock a third time—pound on it,
really—when he heard a bolt slide and saw the door open a
crack.

The face that peered through the opening was human,
though at first glance it didn't seem so. The features were
vague, blunt—bludgeoned over the course of too many
fights into amorphousness.

"What?" was all the man asked.

"I want to see someone," said the android. "I've heard he
does business here."

"Yeah? Who's that?"

"He's called the Rythrian."

The man's eyes narrowed as he inspected *Kirk*. Then he
looked over the android's shoulder, searching the night and
the mist.

After a while, satisfied, he opened the door. As *Kirk*
brushed past him, he found himself in a narrow vestibule.

Beyond it was a much larger room, well appointed though
dimly lit. At one time, it may truly have served as the parlor
of a private establishment—*before* the place had been
converted to its current use.

The android took a single step toward the larger room and
found a hammy paw on his shoulder. He glanced at it, then
at its owner.

"Check you," said the near-shapeless mouth.

Kirk shrugged, raised his arms. Felt the man's hands
searching him for firearms, though that—supposedly—was
the one thing you couldn't buy on this world. Those who
profited by the tourist trade—and that was nearly everyone,
directly or indirectly—had no desire to kill the goose that
laid their golden eggs.

DOUBLE, DOUBLE

The frisking process was nearly over before the man found the small container in the android's inside pocket. Reaching inside his jacket, *Kirk* himself pulled it out. Held it in his palm.

"It's not a weapon," he said. "It's what I've come to see the Rythrian about."

The animallike eyes regarded him. "Open it," said the man.

Kirk opened it.

The man's eyes blinked, his fleshy face illuminated by the glow. "All right," he said finally.

Kirk closed the container again.

"Come," said the man.

The android replaced the container in his pocket and followed him into the next room.

There were three other men inside. Two were strong-arm types. The third, it seemed, had come to do business as *Kirk* had—judging by the small sack he kept on the table beside him. But he neither looked very happy to be there nor very eager to be recognized.

Selling off a family heirloom to pay a gambling debt? the android wondered. Or a *s'ris* addict, fencing stolen goods to support his habit?

Kirk chose a sofa, sat. Looked around, noticed that the lighting was provided by *hlinga* worms in transparent cylinders. Of course—a touch of old Rythria in a foreign land.

The worm nearest the man with the sack threw off an azure glow, in accordance with his mood. The one near the android, however—like most of the other worms around the room—radiated a yellowish, almost white light.

Nor did it change as he sat there. *Kirk* was grateful that the worm could not distinguish between controlled emotion and no emotion at all. As it was, the strong-arm types would just label him a cool customer and let it go at that.

In time, the door at the back of the room opened and yet another human emerged. He looked neither at *Kirk* nor at any of the others as he headed for the vestibule. The dough-faced man followed him in. There was the sound again of the bolt sliding back, the opening and closing of the door, the replacement of the bolt.

"You're next," said one of the other hired hands. The android looked at him, but he was talking to the man with the sack.

Gathering up his burden—which was fairly heavy, if the way it hung in the sack was any indication—the man passed through the doorway in the back of the room. *Kirk* had a glimpse of someone big—*very* big—before the sack bearer disappeared inside.

He wasn't in there long. It couldn't have been more than a couple of minutes before he came out again—without the sack.

Since there was no one else waiting in the room, *Kirk* got up from his seat on the sofa. He looked inquiringly at the strong-arm types.

"That's right," said the one who had spoken before. "It's your turn now, eager beaver."

The android looked at him just long enough to make the man uncomfortable. Then he crossed the room to the door, opened it onto what had to be the Rythrian's office.

Except for the wan, yellow light of a *hlinga* worm, the room was dark.

Two sat behind a table. One was the Rythrian himself, judging by his long flaps of earlobe and somewhat protuberant eyes. The other was human—a massive, swarthy man with a long scar from brow to jawline. It was the man he'd caught a glimpse of moments before.

Kirk closed the door behind him.

"Sit," said the big man. His voice was harsh, rasping. Somewhere along the line, *Kirk* judged, he'd damaged his vocal cords.

The android pulled out the only unoccupied chair and sat. The worm writhed in its plexiglass cylinder and the quality of the light changed subtly—seemed to grow paler by a shade.

The Rythrian noted it, looked back at *Kirk*.

"So? What have you got?" he asked. His voice was pleasant, almost melodious, in contrast to his companion's.

Kirk reached into his jacket—slowly enough so that there

would be no misunderstandings—and produced the leadbound box. He placed it on the table, felt for the hidden latch. Touched it.

And the top sprang open revealing the dilithium crystal within.

For a moment, the Rythrian's eyes opened even wider—though the worm's light remained appreciably the same, a tribute to his self-control. Then he looked up again.

"It appears to be genuine," he said.

Kirk closed the box, replaced it in his inner pocket. "Do you think I'd be foolish enough to try to pass a fake off on you?"

The Rythrian shrugged. "People have tried more foolish things. You'd be surprised." He paused. "How much do you want for it?"

Kirk smiled.

"Actually," he said, "I didn't have it in mind to sell it."

The Rythrian's brow lowered perceptibly.

"No?" he asked. "Then why are you here?"

"To make you a proposition. One that involves a lot more profit—for all of us."

The Rythrian leaned forward.

"What kind of proposition?"

The worm turned in on itself, and the room grew sullen.

"You have a market for dilithium? In large quantities?"

The Rythrian stared at him. "We do," he said finally.

"I have a source who can supply large quantities."

That elicited a grunt. "What do you call a large quantity?"

"Thirty crystals," said the android. "Forty. Maybe more."

"And just where do you intend to get that kind of dilithium?" asked the Rythrian. "You'd have to own your own mine."

Kirk nodded. "Or know someone who has access to one."

"An insider? At a Federation mine?"

"Perhaps," said the android.

"Interesting," said the Rythrian. "And you need someone to fence it all for you."

"That," said *Kirk*, "and more than that. An operation like this one requires an investment. In transportation. In cooperation."

"So it does," said the Rythrian. "But I don't imagine you have those kinds of funds at your disposal."

"At the moment, no. But I'd be willing to offer a partnership in exchange for such funds."

"A share," said the Rythrian, "in the dilithium."

"Precisely."

"How much of a share?"

"Fifty percent."

The Rythrian laughed, briefly. It came out as a high-pitched piping. The worm danced, spewed pale green light on the walls.

"Eighty," he said.

Kirk chuckled. "Sixty."

The Rythrian shook his head, whipping his ears about. "Eighty. No one will give you a better deal than that."

"That is," added the big man, "if they do business with you at all."

Kirk looked from the human to the Rythrian. "Is this your partner?" he asked innocently. It was a necessary remark—it would lend him credibility.

Again, that high-pitched piping came out of the Rythrian. The big man turned a dark and dangerous red—and so did the worm. Seeing his emotions betrayed only seemed to make the human madder.

"No," said the Rythrian, as soon as he'd recovered. "He is not my partner—but he *is* correct. My competitors seldom deal with suppliers they do not know."

Kirk pretended to mull it over. "You drive a hard bargain."

The Rythrian shrugged. "Have we got a deal—or not?"

Kirk nodded. "Yes. We've got a deal."

"Good. We'll arrange to get you the money." He blinked—for the first time, *Kirk* noticed, since their interview had begun. "Where are you staying?"

The android told him.

Another grunt. "We will expect to see the dilithium within the month. Do not disappoint us."

The big man's eyes narrowed. "Yes," he agreed. "Don't even think about it."

Kirk met his stare, smiled again.

The worm jerked, spilling waves of bright blood-red light.

It would continue to do so, the android guessed, for some time after his departure.

The next day, three of the Rythrian's henchmen came to drop off a package at *Kirk*'s hotel room.

The first thing he did after they left was count the money. Sure enough, it was all there—and a tidy sum it was. Certainly not a sum one would want to be careless with.

Next, he checked out of the hotel, paying his bill with the smallest portion of his newfound wealth. Aware now that *Kirk* was somehow linked to the Rythrian, the man at the desk didn't comment on the crisp new bills he handed him. He didn't even look up.

According to the agreement by which he'd obtained the money, *Kirk* should then have booked space on a passenger ship—one bound for whichever system his dilithium contact was located in. But since he had neither a contact nor any intention of finding one, he didn't make any attempt to get to the spaceport.

Rather, he headed for the center of town.

Markey swabbed the bar with a wet rag for the umpteenth time that night. Not that it needed it. There just wasn't a whole hell of a lot else to do.

It hadn't been a real good week. No big ships in the spaceport, no rubes to keep the old-fashioned cash register ringing. Only a few regulars—and they weren't spending much more than time, 'cause they made their money off the rubes same as he did.

In fact, he was tempted to close up early—until the guy in the expensive suit walked in out of the mist.

"What'll it be?" he asked as the rube swaggered up to the bar. It was quite a swagger too. The king of swaggers.

"A bottle of your finest brandy," he said as he pulled over a stool. "And I mean your *finest.*"

Then he dragged out a wad of money and dropped it square on the polished-wood surface. Suddenly, he was the undisputed center of attention.

"Money," he said, "is no object." He smiled, as if he'd made a joke.

Markey glanced at the wad. It made him nervous to see it just sitting out there, naked and inviting.

"Mister," he said, "I'll be only too happy to help you get sloshed. But if I were you, I'd put that stuff away for now. This ain't exactly Starbase Three, y'know. People *have* been known to get rolled around here."

But the rube just shrugged, his smile widening. "So what? There's plenty more where that came from. In fact," he said, indicating the tables behind him with a sweep of his arm, "I want everybody to have a bottle! On me! What's the sense of having it if you can't spend it?"

The regulars rooted him on, recognizing a free ride when they saw one. A couple of them even stood and applauded.

Markey looked into the rube's eyes, saw no sign of drunkenness there. Yet. So what was his story? Did he have a death wish or something?

"Well," asked the newcomer. "Are you going to serve me and my friends, or do I have to take my business elsewhere?"

That brought another kind of response from the regulars. An ugly one.

Markey knew better than to mess with them. Loyalty was an ephemeral thing on Trank Seven. Especially when there was booze involved.

"No," he said. "You can get everything you want right here."

He'd warned the guy, hadn't he? And besides, what was he behind this bar for, if not to take money from rubes?

Grabbing a couple of bottles from the mirrored wall behind him, he plunked them down on the bar. Then a couple more, and again, until there was one for everyone. Finally, he opened a bottle and set it before Fancy Dan with a glass next to it.

"Okay," said the rube. "Come and get it!"

The regulars didn't have to be told twice. There was a screeching of chair legs and a shuffle of feet, and suddenly the bar was alive with grasping hands.

The newcomer counted out a number of credits, letting them waft down one by one around his bottle. He seemed to get a kick out of it.

"There," he said expansively. "That ought to cover it."

Markey grunted, gathered up the money. *"More* than cover it. You've got some change coming."

"Forget it," said the rube, pouring some brandy into his glass. "Buy yourself a new sign out front."

Just as Markey turned to open the cash register, he saw Bokeek come sauntering up to the stranger. He held his bottle close to his chest, and it obviously wasn't the first one he'd had that night.

"Say," said Bokeek, a Tetracite who made his living picking pockets, "I couldn't help but notice that pile o' bills you got there. You one o' those fancy fur traders?" He peered at the rube with deep-set, bloodshot eyes that seemed to want to pop out of his angular head.

The newcomer grinned. "No. Why? Do I look like one?"

Bokeek shrugged. "Maybe a little bit." He lowered his voice a notch and leaned closer—as if to hint that he, at least, could be trusted. "But if you ain't a trader, then where the hell *didja* get that stash?"

"You're being nosy, Bokeek," said Markey, intervening on the stranger's behalf. "A man puts some money together, it's *his* business where he got it."

"That's all right," said the rube. He turned to Bokeek. "You want to know where I got this money?"

The pickpocket nodded.

"I just asked for it. And somebody gave it to me."

Bokeek chuckled. "No, really."

"Really."

Bokeek looked at Markey and then at the rube again. "Yeah? How?"

"Simple," said Fancy Dan. "I conned him."

The pickpocket screwed up his face in disbelief.

"You?"

"Me."

And there was no pursuing the matter any further, because that's when the stranger decided to get up.

"Nice talking with you gentlemen," he said, "but I've got an appointment to keep with some very lovely ladies." He straightened the lapels on his suit. "Ladies like men with money, you know."

And with a military sort of salute, he turned and made his way toward the door.

Markey watched him vanish back into the night. So did Bokeek.

"Strangest guy I've seen in a long time," he said. "A long time."

"You don't know the half of it," said the pickpocket, suddenly a lot more sober.

Markey looked at him. "What do you mean?"

"I been followin' this oddball all night long. Everywhere he goes, he buys drinks for the house. Then he drops that line about havin' to meet some women and leaves." He laughed. "If I was still a young man, I'd have gone with him to the next joint. But for now, I think this here bottle will do me just fine."

The bartender grunted. "I'll bet," he said, and went to clean up where the rube had sat.

"Hey," said Bokeek, "look at that."

"What?" asked Markey.

"He didn't even touch his drink."

Markey inspected the glass of brandy. Sure enough, it was as full as when the stranger had poured it.

He shrugged. "Maybe the guy wasn't thirsty."

No sooner had *Kirk* left the bar than he ducked into an alleyway. And waited.

This time, he saw, no one was going to follow him to his next destination. Apparently, his hanger-on had been nothing more than he seemed—a scavenger following the lure of free booze.

Too bad. That meant that the Rythrian's street network hadn't located him yet.

Kirk was surprised. Hadn't he made himself obvious enough? It was difficult to believe that with all the money he'd squandered in the last twenty hours or so, word of his prodigality hadn't reached his "partner."

Or had he miscalculated somehow?

No. It wasn't possible. He had all the human Kirk's memories, his capacity for judgment—for cunning.

He would wait a little longer to see if his plan had borne fruit.

An hour passed, another. The fog gradually twisted into new shapes, writhed again into still newer ones. Every now and then, the wind stirred the silence with the sounds of distant revelry.

He watched men come out of the bar, other men go inside. But always one at a time. If the Rythrian meant to catch him, he'd have sent his hirelings out in pairs—at the very least.

Nor did these men have a look of purposefulness about them. They were no different than the glassy-eyed specimens he'd seen inside.

Yet another hour. Dawn was not that far off. And he needed to find another place to stay before daylight revealed him.

After all, it was only his *trail* he wanted the Rythrian to find. Not *Kirk* himself.

Suddenly, footfalls—an echoing clatter on the paving stones. Keeping as much of himself hidden as possible, the android peered into the fog.

There were four men emerging from it. Three were nondescript, though he might have recognized one or more of them if he'd tried.

But it wasn't necessary. The sheer size of the fourth man, about whom the others seemed to cluster, told *Kirk* all he needed to know.

The man with the scar looked angry. As if he'd rather have been doing something else at this time of night.

Excellent, the android told himself. The Rythrian didn't disappoint me after all.

He waited a few more minutes, until the group of four had entered the bar. Then he crossed the street and headed for the part of town where a man could lose himself forever—or so they said.

Of course, in his case, a single day would be more than sufficient.

Chapter Ten

As THEY ENTERED the turbolift, Kirk pressed the plate for the transporter level.

"Are you sure I can't change your mind?" he asked Spock.

The Vulcan stood with his hands clasped behind his back, his face calm and expressionless.

"Quite sure, Captain."

Kirk frowned.

"Come on, Spock. Even *you* need some rest and relaxation now and then—despite your pretenses to the contrary."

Spock grunted softly. Apparently, Kirk noted, he'd penetrated that aura of Vulcan indifference.

"It is not a *pretense* that my people require less rest than humans do," he said. "Though, of course, we cannot go without it indefinitely."

"Then why not come down to Tranktown? For a little diversion? Hell, you might find it interesting."

"There are any number of diversions available here on the *Enterprise,*" Spock noted.

The turbolift came to a stop then and the doors hissed open. Together, Kirk and his first officer headed for the transporter room.

"What is more," Spock added, "the best way to rest is to

actually *rest*. You yourself have often returned from a shore leave anything *but* rested."

Kirk had to admit that Spock had a point there. But he didn't have to admit it out loud.

"Aren't you a little sick," he asked, "of being cooped up in the ship? It's been weeks since you were planetside. Isn't a change of scenery the slightest bit appealing?"

Spock shrugged. "I am quite comfortable on the ship," he said. *"More* comfortable, no doubt, than I would be on Tranquillity Seven."

"I see," said Kirk. "In other words, you don't think Tranktown will be your cup of tea."

"My . . . cup of tea?" asked the Vulcan.

"You don't think you'll find it *attractive,"* amended Kirk.

"In all honesty," said Spock, "I do not believe so, no."

The captain sighed. "I feel badly about that, Spock. When I accepted Admiral Straus's offer, I thought it would be good for the whole crew."

"Obviously," said Spock. "Nor is there any need to berate yourself. My decision is mine alone. It would be illogical for you to take responsibility for it."

Kirk chuckled. "I think I've just been let off the hook."

Spock arched an eyebrow. "Let off the hook, sir?"

"Excused," he explained. "Pardoned."

The Vulcan seemed to file that away for future reference.

As they arrived at the transporter room, the doors parted automatically. Inside, they found Scotty holding court before McCoy and a couple of transporter-room personnel. The chief engineer had just spread his hands apart in preparation for a punch line.

"An' so he says, 'A' don' know where ye been, laddie, but a' see ye won first prize!' "

The laughter that followed was nothing short of uproarious. Kirk even found himself smiling.

"That was a wonderful story," he told Scotty. "I'd like to hear the beginning sometime."

"Aye," said the Scot. "That ye will, sir. And there's a whole lot more where that came from."

"Well," said McCoy, "the gang's all here." He turned to Transporter Chief Kyle as he stepped up onto the platform. "Four to beam down, sir. And don't spare the horses."

"Aye," said Scotty, following him. "An' lose our coordinates as soon as ye possibly can."

Kyle chuckled. "Whatever you say, sir."

"Actually," Kirk interjected, "that'll be *three* to beam down."

McCoy and Scotty looked at him simultaneously.

"Three, sir?" asked the chief engineer, his brow suddenly furrowed.

"Three," confirmed Kirk. "Mister Spock has decided to remain on the ship."

"Oh damn," said the doctor. "Is this true, Spock?"

"It is," said the Vulcan.

"But why?" McCoy pressed. "Don't tell me you can't stand a little fun?"

"Spock's already gone over this with *me,*" said the captain, holding up his hand for peace. "No need to rehash it, Bones."

McCoy snorted. "Blast. And here I was looking forward to seeing him loosen up a little."

"Perhaps another time," said Kirk, joining the others on the transporter platform. He turned to Kyle, who stood ready at the controls.

"All right, Chief. Let 'er rip."

"Captain?"

Spock took a step forward.

"What is it?" asked Kirk, a little surprised. Had Spock suddenly changed his mind?

"There is the matter of the P'othparan, sir. If you are gone too long, he may infer that you've abandoned him."

Kirk felt himself shrink from the subject.

"That's all been explained to him already," he told Spock. "I had Mister Clifford see to it. And in any case, I don't plan to be away for more than a day or so."

Now that he thought about it, though, was that enough? What if the P'othparan decided that he'd been deceived, and Kirk *had* abandoned him?

He regarded his first officer.

"But just to be on the safe side, Spock, would you keep an eye on him?"

The Vulcan's usual calm seemed to crack just a hair. He looked almost . . . uncomfortable.

"I, sir?"

"If you don't mind, Spock. I know you'd rather be doing other things. But everyone else will be beaming down at one time or another. And I don't want him to fall through the cracks."

Spock regained his air of dispassion.

"As you wish," he said.

Kirk smiled. "Thanks."

"All right," said McCoy. "Enough dillydallying. Are we going to see this Tranktown or not?"

Kyle looked to Kirk. "Now, sir?"

The captain nodded. "If you please, Mister Kyle."

And a moment later, the transporter *thrummed* to life.

Tranktown hit Leonard McCoy like a shot of hard liquor. Flanked by Kirk and Scotty, he strode down the center of a crowded pedestrian thoroughfare—a flow of wild-eyed mostly-humanity that swirled and eddied and sometimes reversed itself, drawn to this attraction or that one.

Nor was there any shortage of attractions—depending on one's taste. Holorenas, where violent sporting events unsanctioned by the Federation could be seen in three-dimensional computer simulation, for the ultimate purpose of heated wagering. Animatoo shops, where one could have his or her body adorned with living images—hordes of parasitic cells, really, preconditioned to form certain color patterns when injected under the skin. And, of course, *s'ris* dens, where one could pursue one's deepest desires, live one's wickedest dreams—all in the privacy of one's own mind.

From the nearby spaceport, there was the boom and fire of an outdated cargo carrier, straining to free itself from the fetters of Earth-normal gravity. But it was hard to hear over the brassy riffs of the street musicians, the deep-throated laughter of the thickly packed revelers.

Tranktown was bright and gaudy, dark and mysterious, revolting and beguiling and mesmerizing all at once. And the sky above it, a velvet expanse bedecked with a thousand jewels, was of a piece with what went on down below.

"Hey," cried Scotty, barely audible over the din. He grabbed McCoy's arm. "Will ye look at that!"

The doctor followed Scott's gesture to a black-suited juggler, visible through a gap in the crowd. The man was tossing shiny metal objects into the air—dangerous-looking things with a number of sharp points and edges. McCoy couldn't tell how many, because the things were spinning too quickly, and on more than one axis. But the patterns they wove as they whirled gyroscopelike were absolutely lovely.

"What do you say?" bellowed Kirk, striving to be heard. "Shall we take a closer look?"

"Sure," said McCoy. "Why not?"

As they got closer, he began to appreciate the juggler's skills more and more. The objects he handled didn't give him much room for error. He had to catch them just right, send them twirling along their intricate paths with only the merest flick of a wrist. And there had to be half a dozen of the little razorlike things—more than he'd ever seen anyone manage all at once.

The juggler's face was pale in the light of a three-quarters moon, and there was a faint sheen of sweat on his skin. His eyes were dark, intent. And he gave no sign of being distracted by the noise all around him.

The moon was a scimitar and the stars were silver barbs.

The line took McCoy by surprise.

Where had he heard it—or read it? In some esoteric book of poetry he'd been fond of back in med school?

Or had it been read *to* him? By a fair-haired young woman on the banks of a tree-lined stream? In the last days of summer, with the horses grazing off in the distance?

He glanced at Jim Kirk, saw the smile on his face. It was wide and careless. As if he'd suddenly shed fifteen years, as if he were a raw cadet all over again.

And McCoy was glad for him.

For him, and for himself. He chuckled.

Kirk heard him, turned.

"Having a good time, Bones?"

"I'm starting to," said the doctor. "Though I could do with a place just a bit less crowded." He regarded Kirk. "There *is* such a place, isn't there?"

103

"There are a few," said the captain. He grinned. "That is, if they haven't changed in the last few years."

McCoy shrugged. "Let's give 'em a shot. You only live once, y'know."

Kirk turned to Scotty. "And you?"

"Fine wi' me," said the Scot. "Just so long as a' can wet m'whistle there."

"Wet it?" Kirk echoed. "Mister Scott, you can drown it." He looked about for a moment, apparently to get his bearings. Then he pointed. "I think it's down that way."

Spock found him in the recreation room, hunched over a viewer. When he entered, the P'othparan looked up.

For a moment, they considered one another. Then, as the Vulcan had expected, the youth tried to make empathic contact.

It was more of a reflex than anything else, Spock told himself. Certainly, after his experiences with humans, he could not have expected to find a consciousness capable of answering in kind.

Only a reflex. But entwined in it was emotion. Primitive raw emotion.

Loneliness.

Spock hadn't quite been prepared for such intensity. As gently as he could, he turned it away.

The P'othparan's brow furrowed a little. Despite the deflection, he seemed to know he'd found something.

Again he sought Spock, and this time the Vulcan put up his full shields. He read the disappointment in the youth's face.

It had to be something new for the P'othparan. An empathic mind, but one unlike those he had known before. One so sophisticated it could close itself off, lock itself away behind rigid barriers.

Spock sympathized. He too had come to the *Enterprise* as an alien, a creature apart. Though it had been easier for him—he had at least been able to speak with the rest of the crew.

The P'othparan couldn't even do that. Mister Clifford

alone was capable of conversing with him—and then only in the crudest of fashions.

Now, Mister Clifford was away on shore leave. Along with Sulu and Chekov and the others who had befriended him. Not to mention the captain himself—the reason the youth was here in the first place.

Yes—Spock sympathized. He understood the P'othparan's need for contact.

But he was not willing to open himself to such an invasion. And an invasion it would be—an imposition of the youth's chaotic emotions on his meticulously ordered awareness.

Knowing the intensity of those emotions only made him that much *more* reluctant to endure them.

Yet the captain had made a request of him. He could not let himself forget that.

Crossing the room, he pulled out a chair. And sat. And faced the P'othparan.

"My name," he said, "is Spock."

The youth seemed to understand it for a greeting.

"K'leb," he answered. "Nee f'ran K'leb."

Spock was grateful that he did not extend his hand for clasping—as the humans did. But then, such physical demonstrations would be unnecessary in an empathic culture.

The Vulcan indicated the viewer.

"May I see what you were looking at?" he asked.

The P'othparan understood again—extracted meaning from either the gesture or Spock's tone of voice or both. He turned the device around so that the Vulcan could see the screen.

The human part of Spock—the part he'd inherited from his mother, the part he normally kept submerged—wanted to laugh.

The viewer displayed a diagram of a chess game. A primitive, two-dimensional chess game, but a chess game nonetheless.

"Where . . ." he began, stopped. *"Who* introduced you to this activity?"

The youth shrugged, having reached the limits of his comprehension.

Spock again indicated the viewer. "Uhura? Chekov?"

Finally, understanding dawned. The P'othparan smiled.

"M'Koy," he said, with hardly any difficulty at all.

"Ah," said Spock. "Of course. Doctor McCoy."

Unknowingly, the ship's surgeon had made Spock's assignment a good deal easier. Not that Spock would give him the satisfaction of telling him so.

"Perhaps," he said, "you will have a surprise for Doctor McCoy when he returns."

The youth just stared at him as he got up and approached the wall unit where the games were stored.

The outskirts of Tranktown were much different from the center. Here, the streets wound about one another with little rhyme or reason. And the vapor ghosts that wafted through them—a gift of the surrounding jungle—seemed to dampen all sounds. Even the rough laughter that spilled out of the alleys from time to time.

Kirk thought he remembered these streets pretty well. But after an hour or so of meandering, with no familiar landmarks to show for it, he was about to call it quits.

And then he spotted it—the big, old-fashioned neon sign drifting in and out of the mist.

The Shooting Star.

"Well," he said, "here we are, gentlemen."

"About time," said McCoy.

"Aye," Scotty chipped in. "A' was beginnin' t' believe th' place didna exist."

The lurid light of the sign reflected in their faces as they approached the building beneath it.

McCoy screwed up his face.

"What kind of music is *that?*"

"The kind you've never heard before," said Kirk, "and you're not likely to hear again."

Scotty grunted. "Ye know, it's bonnie in a way. Like th' pipes wailin' in th' highlands."

Kirk nodded. "Something like that."

Leaving the night and the mists behind, they walked in through the swinging doors. And once inside, they saw where the sounds were coming from.

There were stages situated throughout the place, each occupied by a single, whirling female form. The dancers were tawny, sensuous, evocative. But it wasn't their muscular grace alone that made their performances so intriguing.

Attached to their wrists and ankles were intricate-looking wooden instruments, painted in all sorts of too-bright colors. And as they spun, and the air rushed through the instruments, it produced the most haunting of songs.

Scotty had likened it to the music of the bagpipes. Kirk, however, was reminded of the birds of Fythrian'n Four, those impossibly frail creatures that hatched and died in the space of a single Terran month—and sang as if they had an eternity's sadness to fit into that tiny lifetime.

But what had he compared them to the last time he heard them—long before he'd been to Fythrian'n Four and heard the birds? He tried to remember and couldn't.

"Damn," said McCoy. "What are those things?"

"The dancers?" asked Kirk. "Or the instruments?"

Scotty laughed his rich, hearty laugh.

"The instruments," said the doctor, trying to scowl with little success. "Of course."

"Kora," Kirk told him. "And the dancers are called *koratti.* They're brought in from Leandros, in the Laurential system."

Scotty looked at him askance. "Ye seem t' know a lot about them, sir."

"Well, Mister Scott, I took the time to study them."

McCoy smirked. "Not a bad idea at that." He looked about, found an empty table. "And that seems like as good a vantage point as any."

No sooner had they pulled up chairs than a waiter descended on them.

"What'll it be, gents?"

"Have ye got any Scotch?" asked the engineering officer.

"Only the best," said the man.

"Is that so? Make it a double then."

"A double it is," said the waiter. He looked at McCoy next. "And you?"

The doctor poked a thumb in Kirk's direction. "I'll have what he's having. So far, he's batting a thousand."

The man looked at Kirk. "Okay then. It's up to you."

"You still have that Denebian *irata?*"

"Yup."

"Two of those, then."

The waiter took down the order and started to make his way back toward the bar. Considering how close together the tables were, he moved pretty quickly.

Kirk's eye was drawn to the nearest dancer. For a moment, he lost himself in the sensuality of her movements, the eerie music of her *kora.* Then he pulled himself away long enough to see to his friends.

Scotty glanced at him, grinning sheepishly.

"Why, Mister Scott," said the captain. "I do believe you're blushing."

Scotty shrugged. "A' canna help it, sir." He shrugged again. "Th' ladies dinna dance this way where a' come from—a' can assure ye of that."

McCoy nodded appreciatively, his eyes riveted on one of the *koratti.* "I've got to hand it to you," he said. "I've never seen—or heard—anything quite like this before."

"Worth the walk?" asked Kirk.

"Aye," said Scotty.

"Damned right," said the doctor. He sighed, settling back into his chair. "In fact, I think I'll stay here all night. Maybe you can show me that other place in the morning."

Kirk looked at him. "What other place?"

"The place where you got into that brawl."

The captain leaned forward. "Bones, this *is* the place where I got into that brawl."

McCoy returned the look. "You're kidding," he said. He glanced around. "Doesn't look like such a rough place to me."

Kirk looked around too. "Actually," he said, "it doesn't

108

seem nearly as rough as it used to be. Maybe it's calmed down since then."

Or maybe it had *never* been that rough, he admitted privately. After all, memory *did* have a way of embellishing things.

It was then that the drinks arrived.

McCoy peered at the *irata,* held it up to the light.

"I never drank anything this color before," he said.

"Trust me," Kirk told him.

The doctor harumphed. "Where have I heard *that* before?"

But if his expression was any indication, he was hardly disappointed.

Nor was Kirk himself, for that matter. The *irata* was every bit as smooth and bittersweet as he remembered.

"Really goes to your head," said McCoy. "Doesn't it? Why, even Maratakken brandy doesn't massacre brain cells with such enthusiasm." He turned to Scotty. "You really ought to try it." He cleared his throat. "Strictly for medicinal purposes, of course. And that's a professional opinion."

Scotty shook his head. "No thank ye, sir. This old dog does nae learn too many new tricks."

"Suit yourself," said McCoy, taking another sip.

For a while after that, they just watched the *koratti,* marveling at their dexterity, losing themselves in the sound of the *kora.* And as they watched, they drank, the liquor only serving to heighten their appreciation.

When the dancer nearest them took a break, Scotty dragged out his latest batch of homespun humor. Each yarn seemed funnier than the one before it.

The evening gradually lost its firmness, sinking into a maelstrom of warm Leandrosian eyes and whirling *kora.*

It was only after the waiter had refilled their glasses a second time that Kirk gave a thought to the P'othparan, and what had happened in the gym. Immediately, he tried to thrust it back down into his subconscious.

But it kept popping up again.

It was too bad, really it was. And no matter how he cut it, it seemed to be his fault.

The boy had probably been so embittered by then, so disillusioned, that he'd decided to deny Kirk's existence as Kirk had denied his.

Or maybe he really *was* scared back there. But why? True, he hadn't exactly earned K'leb's affection—but neither had he done anything to instill fear in the boy.

Oh well. In time, things would work themselves out. They always did. As soon as he got back to the ship, he'd . . .

The captain had lost himself in thought so thoroughly that he never saw the big man approach. But something made him look up then, some sixth sense—to see a huge figure towering over him like a harbinger of bad times to come.

A glance around the table told him he wasn't the only one who had noticed the newcomer. The conversation had abruptly come to a standstill.

For a moment, nothing. Then the man pulled a chair over and sat. He was dark, with a scar from brow to jawline. And he peered at Kirk as if he knew him.

"Something we can do for you?" asked McCoy, smiling genially.

The man turned toward the doctor. He seemed to size him up before he spoke.

"You," he said, "no. My business is with this one here." He indicated the captain with a tilt of his head. "And if you're smart, you'll stay out of it." He sounded as if he'd been gargling with sandpaper.

Scotty chuckled. "And if we're nae so smart?"

The big man shrugged. "There's plenty of trouble to go around." He waggled an index finger, and half a dozen figures lumbered in out of the mist. One, a Tetracite by the look of him, snaked his way to the front of the group.

"Y'see?" he asked. "Here he is. Just like I told you."

The man with the scar gave out with a short, savage laugh. "So he is. And you'll get what we promised you—after we're finished with him."

Kirk exchanged looks with his officers. The smiles had faded from their faces rather quickly.

At the tables around them, however, there were only a

couple of curious glances. No one seemed troubled enough to even move his chair away.

Kirk had to fight off an encroaching sense of *déjà vu*.

"Look," he said, making a show of choosing his words carefully, "I don't think you know what you're getting into here." He turned to McCoy. *"Does* he, Bones?"

The doctor shook his head, picking up on his cue. "This man," he said, lifting his glass to Kirk, "is the captain of the U.S.S. *Enterprise,* which is even now in orbit around your planet. With more than four hundred able-bodied personnel, I might add—all ready to beam down on a moment's notice." He smiled benignly—not an easy thing for him to do, but he managed. "Now if you and your friends just vamoose, I think we'd be inclined to forget all about this. Wouldn't we, Mister Scott?"

The chief engineer shrugged. "A' canna see why nae, sir."

For a moment, the big man seemed to ponder what he'd heard. Then he broke out in raucous laughter. As if it were a signal, his henchmen started laughing too.

"A starship captain," spat Scarface. "Hah! I suppose that's where he got that dilithium—right out of the ship's engine core! And he needed all that money—let me guess—to treat his crew to a round of drinks. Right?"

Kirk looked him square in the eye. "I don't know what the hell you're talking about."

"No?" asked the big man. "You mean it wasn't you who took twenty thousand credits from the Rythrian? And then went around blowing it all over town?" He leaned a little closer, until Kirk could smell the *zezalia* seeds on his breath. "I thought you were a lot smarter than that. I guess I was wrong."

"I think," said the captain, "you're mistaking me for someone else. I suggest you take another look. *Before* you do something you regret."

Scarface grunted. "First off," he said, "I never forget a face. And as for regrets . . . well, mister, you're going to be the all-time expert."

He stood, pushing his chair back.

"Now let's go."

Kirk chuckled. "You really are stubborn, you know that?" He casually cracked his knuckles, at the same time kicking Bones under the table. "Didn't I tell you that you were barking up—"

The big man's hand shot out before he could complete the sentence—but Kirk was ready. Grabbing his antagonist's wrist, he turned it palm-up, dropped to one knee, and heaved, using the elbow for leverage.

Scarface went hurtling headfirst into the closest occupied table, much to the dismay of those gathered around it.

A moment later, however, his henchmen were on top of them. Kirk whirled and planted his foot in one man's midsection. Out of the corner of his eye, he saw Scotty plow into another man as Bones upended their table. Glasses and brew alike went flying.

Suddenly, the whole bar was chaos. It was as if the clientele had only been waiting for the slightest excuse to wreck the place.

Something whizzed by Kirk's head. As he flinched, something else caught him in the jaw. He recovered just in time to see someone aiming a chair leg at him, moved to one side, and heard it hit someone else.

The lights flickered, went out, and came back only halfway. Kirk felt a body slump against his, slipped under its weight, and clutched at a railing to keep from falling.

"Bones!" he cried, keeping his back against the wall. "Scotty!" If he could only find them, they could slip away in the confusion. But neither of them could be seen among the brawlers.

Then a familiar face loomed out of the melee after all. But it wasn't one he'd been looking for. The big man's scar was livid now, and he pushed people aside to get at his target.

"I've got you now," he rasped at Kirk.

"Maybe," said the captain, bracing himself.

But this time, his adversary wasn't so eager. He approached Kirk slowly, wary of any trick moves. And the press of bodies worked to his advantage, giving the captain less room in which to operate.

Kirk was about to take the initiative when Scotty came

flying out of nowhere. He clamped a headlock on Scarface and rode him to the ground, yelling so loud he could be heard over the din.

"A'll teach ye t' lay hands on th' captain, ye big ape!"

Before Scarface could quite free himself from the maddened Scot, Kirk had joined the fray. The big man was like a wild bull, bucking and thrashing, trying to free himself from a couple of wolves—but the wolves hung on. And moments later, the captain managed to knock him senseless with a half-empty bottle that had fortunately been close at hand.

Kirk dragged Scotty to his feet, pulled him in the direction of the exit.

"Have you seen McCoy?" he shouted into his ear.

"Nae since th' fight began," answered Scotty.

It was just then, as if by magic, that the doctor rose horizontally from the sea of turmoil. He stopped there for a second or so, suspended where they could see him. His face was bloody—and if he was conscious, he didn't show it.

As the captain tried to force his way toward him, McCoy started spinning. Once, twice, a third time. And before Kirk could get anywhere close to him, McCoy's limp form went whirling into the thick of the brawl.

The captain's teeth grated together.

This wasn't at all as he remembered it. It was dangerous —deadly. And the way Bones's head had drooped before he went flying . . .

"Did ye see where he landed?" roared Scotty.

"I think so," said Kirk, without breaking his stride. He half tripped over a shattered chair, threw another one aside. A body fell against him and he pushed it back where it had come from.

"Hang on, Bones!" he bellowed, more for his own benefit than for the doctor's. "You hang on, damn it!"

Suddenly, there was a sound of breaking glass just behind him. A yelp of pain. Glancing over his shoulder, he saw Scotty go down.

But as he turned to help, something hit *him* too. In the back of the head—and *hard*.

Kirk felt his knees give way, tasted something hot and metallic. He fought for consciousness, fought to keep the darkness from closing down on him—grabbed at what he thought was a table, tried to drag himself up.

Then there was another impact, only dimly felt, and the light whirlpooled away into nothingness.

Chapter Eleven

SCOTT BOLTED UPRIGHT, SPUTTERING.

Immediately, he wished he hadn't. His head felt as if it were about to explode. Moaning softly, he wiped icy drops of water from his eyes.

And looked up into the face of James T. Kirk.

"Scotty? Are you all right?"

The chief engineer felt the side of his head, flinched when he touched the spot where he'd been hit. His fingers came away with a pinkish-red ooze on them.

"M'poor head," he said. "A' think a' broke it."

"Scotty," said the captain, "we've got to get out of here. Can you walk?"

"Aye," he said, looking around him. The fight seemed to have run its course, with only a few stragglers still picking themselves up out of the debris—spurred by the sound of approaching sirens. "Wha' happened? Where's Doctor McCoy?"

Kirk frowned deeply as he got a hand under Scott's armpit. "I found him, but he's not in good shape. We've got to get him back to the ship—quickly."

Fear for McCoy shot adrenaline through Scott's veins. Allowing the captain to help him, he staggered to his feet.

His brain felt as if it were too big for his skull, and the pain brought on a wave of nausea. But he managed to quell it as Kirk led him through the confusion of shattered furniture and broken glass.

In the dim light, he couldn't see very well. He was almost on top of McCoy before he knew it.

Nor had the captain exaggerated—the doctor was barely breathing. His eyes were puffed closed, his face distended and dark with bruises. Blood still seeped from a gash in his forehead.

Scott knelt over him, gripped McCoy's shoulder—as if he could penetrate the man's unconsciousness, reassure him somehow.

"Damn," he breathed. "He got th' worst of it, all right." He watched dully as Kirk whipped out his communicator.

"Kirk to *Enterprise*. Come in, *Enterprise*."

For a moment, there was no answer. The sirens seemed to get louder, closer.

The last thing they needed, Scott knew, was to get nabbed by the local authorities. Tied up in red tape, there was no telling when they'd be able to get McCoy to a medical facility.

Finally, Spock's voice came through over the communicator. "Is something wrong, Captain?"

"I'm afraid so," said Kirk. "Three to beam up—immediately. And I want a stretcher brought to the transporter room on the double." He scowled, glanced at the doctor. "McCoy's been hurt."

"Aye, sir," said the Vulcan. And an instant later, "Stand by to beam up."

Whoever was on duty in the transporter room knew what he was doing. Scott barely felt even a tingling before his molecules were whisked across space.

They materialized in a nearly empty transporter room, populated only by the single engineering officer assigned there.

Kirk felt McCoy's neck for a pulse, scowled as he surveyed the pale, blood-smeared face.

"Sir?" asked Mister Scott, kneeling beside the android. Concern for the doctor was etched into his face.

"It's weak," said *Kirk*, "but at least he's got one." He

looked up, acting as frantic as the real captain would have been. "Where's that trauma team, damn it?"

The engineering officer switched on the intercom. "Transporter room to bridge," she said. "Transport completed, but we need medical assistance here as soon as . . ."

Before she could finish, the doors split open and Doctor M'Benga charged through them, followed by a trauma team.

M'Benga made a quick check of McCoy's vital signs before he signaled the others. Ever so carefully, two men lifted McCoy onto the gurney, even as the rest of the team hooked him up to the life-support unit.

That accomplished, M'Benga glanced at Mister Scott. "You don't look so good either—but we only brought one gurney. Can you make it without one?"

Scotty nodded. "A'll make it fine. Just see t' Doctor McCoy."

"Good," said M'Benga. Again he signaled, and the paramedics started to move. A moment later, they had McCoy out the doors and headed in the direction of the turbolift.

Kirk looked up as if he'd just become aware of another presence in M'Benga's office.

"Oh," he said. "It's you, Spock."

The Vulcan gazed across sickbay at the critical-care unit, in which McCoy lay ensconced.

"Has the doctor regained consciousness yet?" he asked.

Mind your own business, Mister Spock. I'm sick of your half-breed interference, do you hear?

Kirk found the urge to say it greater than he'd thought it would be. Nonetheless, he resisted it. Nodded soberly, instead—as one who had been through an ordeal might have nodded.

"He opened his eyes for a little while just a minute ago. And he appeared to recognize us—M'Benga, Chapel, and myself." He paused for effect. "According to M'Benga, he should be fine. It'll just take a while. He suffered a rather serious concussion, along with some nasty internal injuries."

Spock nodded. "And Mister Scott?" he asked.

"Sent to convalesce in his cabin. Fortunately, he fared a lot better than McCoy in that brawl."

"As did you yourself," observed his first officer.

Kirk searched Spock's face for a sign of suspicion, found none. But then, he told himself, a Vulcan wouldn't show anything anyway.

He would have to be careful with Mister Spock. In the human Kirk's estimate, no one knew him as well as Spock did. Not even McCoy, with whom he spent more time.

Yes. *Very* careful.

"I was lucky," said *Kirk*. He chuckled bitterly. "Though if anyone *should* have gotten hurt, it was me. I was the one who had been there before. I knew that part of town was dangerous. And I let Bones and Scotty talk me into going there anyway." He glanced at the doctor's sedated form through the transparent separation. "If I had exercised an iota of good judgment, McCoy wouldn't be lying there right now."

Spock raised an eyebrow. "Is this a display of human guilt?"

Kirk snorted. "Call it taking responsibility, Spock."

"Taking responsibility?" asked Spock. "Toward what end, other than self-recrimination?"

"The point is, I was wrong." The android shook his head. "And I'll be damned if I'll let this happen to anyone else in my command." He paused—for effect. "Spock, I want all shore leaves canceled, effective immediately."

Spock evinced no overt reaction to *Kirk's* decision—but his hesitation was in itself an indication that he was troubled.

"Captain," he began, "may I speak freely?"

"Go ahead," said *Kirk*.

"I myself feel no particular attraction to Tranquillity Seven, as you know. But that is not the case with the rest of the crew. They have looked forward to this shore leave. Moreover, they have been in need of a respite from their duties for quite some time. Might I suggest that instead of canceling leave altogether, we merely limit it to a designated area—encompassing only the safer parts of town?"

Kirk pretended to consider the suggestion. But he had his own reasons for wanting to move on.

"No," he said finally. "There will be those whose curiosity will get the better of them." He grunted. *"I should know."* And in a more confident tone, "We'll find another place for shore leave, after this business with the Romulans has been settled. In the meantime, nobody beams down to the planet's surface. And have Uhura contact those already down there as quickly as possible."

Spock seemed reluctant, but he nodded. "I'll see to it," he said.

Kirk showed him a wan smile. "Thank you, Spock. I think I'll stay here awhile longer."

"As you wish," said the Vulcan. He turned on his heel and left M'Benga's office.

The android watched him stride across sickbay. Saw the doors open and close again behind him.

He doesn't suspect, he told himself. None of them do.

And why should they? Was he not a perfect replica of Captain James T. Kirk, down to the last fingernail?

Nor would the original Kirk ever be seen again. He had made certain of that with his choice of business partner.

The Rythrian had a reputation for using violence when he thought he could profit by it. Having finally caught up with the man who'd stolen from him, he could hardly let him live—it would invite others to try their luck. The only prudent move was to kill him.

And what then? *Kirk* thought. Will I still be a replica when the human Kirk is dead? No. For how can one be a copy when there is no longer an original? I will be the only Kirk in existence.

Perhaps he was already. It pleased him to think so.

Everything has gone so smoothly. The entire first phase of my plan has proceeded step by step to this result.

Could even Korby have succeeded as *he* had succeeded? Could even the Creator have accomplished this?

Control of the *Enterprise?*

On the other side of sickbay, Nurse Chapel appeared—to check up on McCoy. Even from here, *Kirk* could read the display above the patient. His life signs were stable.

After a few moments, Chapel noticed him sitting in M'Benga's office. She waved.

He waved back.

There was only one more thing for him to do. Not a test, for certainly he had passed all the tests he needed to.

It was more of a gesture.

He felt impelled to do it now. To finally claim what was his.

But it was necessary to keep up appearances. So he would remain here for a while, appearing to worry about the fate of Leonard McCoy.

Then he would take his place on the bridge.

Chapter Twelve

A BRILLIANT LIGHT. Kirk flinched from it, felt pain carve its way through his flesh.

He looked down, saw that he was bound—hand and foot, to a heavy chair. Off to the side, he could make out dark, wooden crates, piled nearly to the top of a high ceiling. Something scurried among the crates, as startled by the light as he was.

He forced himself to look back, saw a figure silhouetted in the light. A doorway? he asked himself. Yes. With sunlight streaming through it. Then the figure moved toward him, and others appeared behind it.

Three of them altogether. One of them slammed the door shut, and suddenly the light was gone.

"It's about time you woke up," rasped the one who'd come in first.

Kirk's eyes were still confused by molten afterimages. But he recognized the voice.

"Where am I?" he asked, awakening yet another pain—this one in his jaw. It felt as if it had been broken.

"Nowhere you want to be," said Scarface. "That's for sure." One of the men behind him chuckled.

"What about my friends?" asked Kirk. "The two who were with me?"

The big man grunted.

"You ask a lot of questions," he said, "for someone who's not in a position to ask *any*. Or is that just what starship captains do? Ask a lot of questions?"

He laughed that hard, harsh laugh that Kirk had heard in the bar. When he was done, he wiped his mouth.

"Tyler," he said. "Get me a chair."

One of the other men moved, found a chair by the wall. Dragged it across the floor until he could give it to Scarface.

The big man stood it backward in front of Kirk. Then he sat, straddling the seat, wrapping his huge arms around the backrest.

His eyes, only a couple of feet from the captain's, seemed to glitter.

"Now," he said, "you gonna drop this starship crap? Or maybe you need some more encouragement?"

"It's not crap," said Kirk, as evenly as he could. "And you still haven't told me where my friends are."

The big man grinned, pulling his scar taut across his cheekbone.

"Wrong answer," he said.

Kirk saw it coming, but there was nothing he could do about it. The next thing he knew, he was lying on his side, still bound in the chair. His jaw was a throbbing agony and the taste of blood was strong in his mouth.

A moment later, Scarface wrestled Kirk's chair erect again. And pulled his over, so that their positions were restored.

The big man peered at him through narrowed eyes, and again the captain could smell the *zezalia* seeds. "Want to change your mind?" he asked, in a voice like stones grating together.

Kirk thought about it.

Obviously, he wasn't going to convince his captors of the truth. For whatever reason, they genuinely believed he was someone else—someone who had double-crossed them in a dilithium deal, judging by the words that had passed in the bar.

But then, he didn't *have to* convince them—did he? When Spock realized he was missing, there would be a search. Possibly, there was one already under way.

All he had to do was stay alive until they found him. Buy some time. And since the truth was losing its effectiveness in that regard, why not try the *other* approach?

"All right," he said. "You win. What is it you want to know?"

"What do you think?" asked Scarface. "Your dilithium source. That is, if it really exists."

Kirk eyed him, managed a smile.

"It exists, all right."

The big man leaned a little closer. "Then where is it?"

"That depends," said the captain.

"On what?"

"On who's asking."

Scarface reddened, but he contained his temper.

"What does *that* mean?"

"It means I want to see your boss. The Rythrian."

The big man's brow furrowed. "Why? You think he'll be any easier on you?"

Kirk shrugged. The ropes cut mercilessly into his arms, but he kept the pain to himself.

"I need some assurances," he explained. "And he's the only one who can give them to me."

The captain knew he was taking a chance. He was putting Scarface in a position where he'd look bad, ineffectual. Rather than go crawling back to his boss empty-handed, he might just decide to beat Kirk to death—and claim afterward that his captive wouldn't talk.

But the other two men were looking on, and they were Kirk's aces in the hole. Either or both of them might tell the Rythrian what really happened—that Kirk was ready to spill the beans, but Scarface killed him in anger. And thereby cheated the Rythrian out of his dilithium a second time.

The big man's face twisted with indecision.

"Well?" asked Kirk.

Scarface glared at him. His right hand, inches from the captain's throat, opened and clenched—as if it had a will of its own.

For a brief moment, Kirk thought he'd gone too far.

Then, abruptly, the big man rose and headed for the door.

The captain squinted again at the sudden flood of light, saw his tormentor disappear into it. The other men followed on his heels.

And this time, the door closed quietly.

Kirk breathed a sigh of relief.

That was close, he told himself. Too close. But it seems I've bought myself some of that time.

As it turned out, Kirk received more time than he'd bargained for. Hours passed, though he had only a vague sense of how many. And a pit grew in his stomach, reminding him that it had been too long since he'd eaten.

It was time enough to ponder his situation, to try to unravel the series of events that had brought him to this estate.

Who was it these men were really after? Did he resemble Kirk as closely as they thought?

And where was he now? Light-years away, probably, having purchased a berth on a cruiser with the money he took from the Rythrian.

There was time enough, too, to recall the details of that *first* brawl in Tranktown. After a while, he even remembered how it had started.

There had been a young woman, and a man who had tried to thrust his company on her. Naturally, Kirk had taken the side of the woman—even after he'd found out the man was her husband.

He'd have to tell Bones, he resolved, when he saw him again.

If he saw him again? *No. Too maudlin.*

Yet he couldn't forget how he'd gone hurtling through the air, as limp as a Cyrilean invertebrate, as bloody as a Vulcan sunset. The scene kept replaying itself before his eyes, over and over again.

And what about Scotty? Was *he* all right?

Were the two of them prisoners as he was, held in some warehouse room like this one? Perhaps just the other side of one of these walls?

Damn. What was taking Spock so long? Even if McCoy and Scotty *had* been taken prisoner, there must have been witnesses in that bar. People who had paid some attention to the altercation—who might have recognized Scarface, or heard the Rythrian's name come up.

Of course there were. But would they come forward? Or would fear of the Rythrian keep them in the shadows?

And without at least one witness, how would Spock or anyone else know where to look for him?

His heart sank.

For the umpteenth time, he tried to loosen the knots that held his wrists. But whoever had tied them had done a good job. All he accomplished was to inflict more pain on himself.

It was right about then that he heard the scurrying thing—heard its claws ticking against the floor as it darted across the room. A couple of heartbeats later, there were sounds outside the door. Voices.

The door opened.

But this time, there was no outpouring of light. It was as dark now outside the room as it was inside.

The Rythrian came in alone, shut the door behind him. Like all his race, he was tall and slightly awkward—by human standards. And the loose flaps of skin that were his ears seemed to flutter as he walked.

He came up to Kirk without speaking, lifted the chair that Scarface had sat on, and drew it back a ways from his captive. When he had achieved the distance he required, he put it down. It took a while for him to make himself comfortable in it.

Kirk's impulse was to speak first, to take the initiative—but he thought better of it. As ignorant as he was, he'd put his foot in his mouth likely as not.

No, it was the Rythrian's place. Let *him* open the negotiations.

After a moment, he did just that.

"I understand," he said, "that you have decided to divulge your dilithium source."

"Of course," said the captain. "In time. And under the right circumstances."

The Rythrian stared at him for a moment. No doubt, it was not the response he had expected.

"You speak as if you were in a position to bargain."

"A man with a dilithium source," said Kirk, "is always in a position to bargain. Or so I've been told."

Again, a pause. Kirk watched his captor, tried to gauge the effect of his remarks. But the Rythrian's expression didn't seem to have changed any.

"And what sort of circumstances do you seek?" he asked finally.

"Freedom. The opportunity to complete the deal we made."

The Rythrian shook his head from side to side, stirring his earflaps.

"You will be free," he said, *"after* we confirm your source. Any other arrangement is impossible."

The scurrying thing made scraping noises where it hid among the crates. The Rythrian appeared not to notice.

"I don't want to seem suspicious," said Kirk. "But after I tell you my source, what reason will you have to keep me alive? Won't you be tempted to make an example of me—to make sure no one else thinks of deceiving you?"

"Certainly," said the Rythrian. "But that does not mean I must kill you. All that is required is that I damage you—and the extent of that damage is still largely up to you."

"And the quickness with which I divulge my source."

"Precisely. Tell me now, and you may walk again someday. Force me to wait, and . . ." He let his voice trail off meaningfully.

"It is not much of a choice," said Kirk.

"No. But it is more of a choice than you deserve."

Kirk met his gaze.

"And if I did give you my source, you're confident that you could establish a relationship with him?"

The Rythrian shrugged.

"Why not? Money is money."

"Is it? Dilithium theft from a Federation mine is a serious crime. It could get a man a dozen long years in a penal colony."

He let that sink in.

"My source knows me, trusts me. If someone else approached him, he'd probably suspect an investigation—and disappear as quickly as possible."

126

The Rythrian's mouth opened—and stayed open. A sign that he'd gotten his captor's attention?

"As a result," Kirk pressed, "no source. No dilithium. And no profits."

The Rythrian snorted—derisively, he thought.

"And I am to believe you?" he asked. "After you have proven yourself untrustworthy?"

"That was a mistake," Kirk conceded. "I won't make it again."

Another snort—perhaps less emphatic than the first?

"If I let you deceive me twice, it will cause irreparable damage to my reputation. I cannot allow that."

Kirk felt his case slipping away.

"Then send along a chaperon," he said, "to keep me honest. Or come along yourself. The more the merrier."

The longest pause of all.

"Perhaps," said the Rythrian. "I will think about it."

And he left.

Chapter Thirteen

KIRK ACCEPTED A DOCUMENT from Yeoman Chaney, glanced at it. Something to do with communicator parts. He signed it and handed it back.

"Thank you, sir," said Chaney.

"Thank *you*," said *Kirk*.

He sat back in his command chair and surveyed the activity all around him. Uhura coordinating the recall of the crew from Tranktown, Spock taking bio readings of the planet's all-but-uncharted arctic region, Sulu making minute corrections in the ship's orbit.

It felt right, familiar, down to the almost imperceptible hum of the *Enterprise*'s impulse engines. As if it had been he, and not his human predecessor, who'd logged thousands of hours in this very spot—made thousands of decisions, given thousands of orders.

The turbolift doors opened behind him, and a moment later Ensign Chekov circumnavigated the bridge. As he took his seat beside Sulu, he shot the helmsman a look of disappointment. Smiling wistfully, Sulu returned it.

Neither man was happy, of course, at having his shore leave terminated so abruptly. And being only human, they would evidence their displeasure in small ways.

An android crew, however, would never have exchanged

those glances—for there would have been no disappointment to communicate. In fact, there would have been no need for shore leave in the first place.

"Captain?"

Kirk swiveled, faced Uhura. "Yes, Lieutenant?"

"I've been in touch with everyone now. And their coordinates have been relayed to engineering."

"Thank you," said the android, turning to the next station along the perimeter of the bridge.

Spock's position, he saw, had not changed. The Vulcan was still bent over his science console, his stony features bathed in a bluish glow.

"Will you be much longer, Mister Spock?"

He asked the question as the human Kirk would have asked it—in the form of a good-natured gibe.

In response, his first officer looked up and straightened a little. Though the interruption must have annoyed him at some level, he gave no hint of it.

"I have accumulated all the basic information I require," said Spock. "It is not necessary to delay departure on my account. However, I will continue to record additional data until we actually leave orbit—unless the captain has some other duty in mind?"

"None," *Kirk* assured him. "Please proceed."

Without another word, Spock hunched again over his computer screen.

Now there, *Kirk* told himself, was a specimen it would be difficult to improve on. One already free from the shackles of emotion, dedicated to the standard of rational behavior.

Physically, however, he was nearly as frail as the others. He required food, oxygen, insulation from the cold of space. He could be stricken by disease, irreparably damaged through the use of force. And in time, he would simply die of old age.

Androids, of course, had no such liabilities.

Turning forward again, *Kirk* was reminded of the current situation by the great, green slice of planet on the viewscreen. He depressed the button that would put him in touch with the transporter room.

"Kyle here," came the response.

"How's it going down there, Mister Kyle?"

"No problems, sir. We should be beaming the last group aboard in ten or fifteen minutes."

"Good," said the android. "Let me know when you're finished, will you?"

"Aye, sir," said Kyle.

Kirk pressed the button a second time, ending the conversation.

"Sir?"

It was Uhura again. She'd waited for him to finish before she addressed him—as considerate as always.

He smiled. "What is it, Lieutenant?"

"A communication from Starbase Three," she said.

Good. It was about time that he received a message from Starfleet—something he could use as a stalking horse.

"I'll take it in the briefing room," he told her.

Uhura looked at him. She knew it was not a priority message—that he could have received it right there on the bridge. But she was too good an officer to question her captain's decisions.

"Aye, sir. I'll open up a channel."

As *Kirk* rose from his command chair, he saw that Spock was looking at him too. Not with suspicion, he thought, but with readiness—in case the captain wanted him to come along.

But *Kirk* gave him no indication of that. And by the time he reached the turbolift, Spock was again intent on his computer screen.

The turbolift was empty, but the corridor that led to the briefing room was not. It was almost time for a change of shifts, and the walkway was crowded with crewmen en route to their various stations.

He was a little surprised when one young woman came right up to him—obviously for the purpose of speaking with him. She was tall, dark-haired, perhaps a trifle lacking in grace. Her uniform told him that she was an ensign—one assigned to engineering.

But a rapid scan of his memory files turned up no knowledge of her. No friendship with the captain, no special relationship. Not even a nodding acquaintance.

"Captain," she began, "I . . ."

He held up a hand, cutting her short.

"I don't mean to be brusque, Ensign, but I'm on my way to the briefing room. Can this wait?"

She seemed taken aback, but she recovered quickly. "Uh . . . yes," she told him. "Of course, sir."

"Good." He flashed her a smile and continued down the corridor.

The briefing room was just a little farther on. When he got there, he pressed his hand against the plate that would only respond to a member of the command staff. If even a detail in one of his fingerprints was appreciably different from his predecessor's, the door would not open.

But of course, it did.

Kirk entered, sat. Contacted Uhura.

"All right, Lieutenant. Ready to receive."

"Relaying, sir."

The android had expected to see the face of Admiral Straus, the officer in charge of Starbase Three. Instead, his second-in-command, Commodore Darian, appeared on the screen.

"Kirk," said the commodore. "Good to see you."

"Likewise, Commodore."

"You know," said Darian, "this really wasn't necessary— for us to speak in private, I mean. The admiral just wanted to keep you abreast of the Romulan situation."

Kirk feigned puzzlement. "Then why did you send a priority message?"

Darian shook his head. "I didn't."

The captain grunted. "I'd say it was Uhura's mistake, but she so seldom makes one. I guess I just heard the word 'priority.'" He took a deep breath, exhaled it. "And here I figured that matters had gotten out of hand with the Romulans, and that we were being called to the border."

"Nothing quite so dramatic," the commodore assured him. "There *has* been increased activity along the border— as if the Romulans were somehow upping the ante. But—to draw out the metaphor—they still show no signs of laying their cards on the table. Nothing's happened that could clearly be called a hostile action."

Kirk nodded. "Then my orders, I assume, are the same?"

"Exactly the same. Remain in the sector. Stay close to the

border, but not too close. Except for that, it's business as usual."

"Duly noted," said the captain.

"Actually," said the commodore, "I only half expected to find you on the ship. I had a feeling you'd be planetside, enjoying your leave."

Kirk cleared his throat. "Unfortunately," he said, "I had to cut our leave a bit short."

Darian's face showed his surprise. "I see." He paused. "Any particular reason?"

"There was an incident," said the android. "No permanent damage to the participants, as it turns out. But it was enough to sour me on the place." He shrugged. "It'll all be in my report."

"Of course," said the commodore.

Kirk didn't like the set of the human's brows. He seemed to be thinking—wondering, perhaps, what kind of incident would have justified such a decision. It seemed necessary to provide a distraction.

He consulted his file on Commodore Darian, updated with information from Kirk's personal log. It took only a fraction of a second to find something appropriate.

"But enough of *my* troubles," said the android. "What's this I hear about a population problem at Starbase Three?"

It took Darian a moment before he understood what *Kirk* was talking about. When he finally got it, he smiled tiredly.

"More boys," he said. "Not one, but two. You'd think after all this time, the law of averages would have snuck a girl in there." He sighed. "What's a progenitor to do?"

Kirk chuckled. "Give my regards to your wife."

"I will," said the commodore. "Darian out."

As the image faded, the android put in a call to Uhura.

"Aye, sir?"

"Lieutenant, would you ask Mister Spock to meet me here in the briefing room?"

"Certainly." A pause. "He's on his way, sir."

"Thanks, Uhura."

Silence then. Or not quite silence, for there was always the hum of the ship's engines.

The Romulans.

Fortunately, the Captain's Log had described the current

situation quite fully. But then, Kirk had been efficient—for a human.

The Romulans will bear watching, he told himself. They are crafty, shrewd. They are aggressive.

All alone in the room, he laughed softly to himself.

To this extent, at least, he thought, I have something in common with the humans—a desire to see their Federation preserved. For if it falls to the Romulans, how can I rule it?

The irony appealed to him.

He was still pondering it when the door slid aside for Spock. As the Vulcan entered, the android ordered his facial features.

"Sit down, Spock," he said.

With an economy of motion, the first officer pulled out a chair and eased into it.

"I've just had some disturbing news," said *Kirk*. Between the captain and Spock, preliminaries would have been a break with custom. "You remember Midos Five?"

"I could hardly have forgotten," said the Vulcan, "in so short a time. A Class-M planet, uninhabited but for a Federation mining and processing colony." Then, after a moment, "What kind of disturbing news?"

Kirk scowled. "Apparently, colonists have been disappearing."

Spock's eyebrow climbed. "Disappearing?"

The android nodded, still scowling. "People vanishing without a trace. Kidnapped, they say, though it may be worse than that. And no one can seem to figure out how, why or by whom." He paused. "Governor Chewton has called on Starfleet for help—and we've been selected to provide it."

"I see," said Spock. Nothing more.

Kirk wondered what was going on behind that well-known Vulcan calm. Concern for the colonists? Curiosity as to the cause of the disappearances?

No matter. It was obvious what Kirk's reaction would be.

He shook his head. "Damn it—those are good people, Spock. Why do they have such rotten luck? First, that explosion a year back, with all those fatalities. And now something like this." Again, he cursed.

Spock looked at him. Restraining himself from a comment about luck and its absence from the Vulcan lexicon? *Kirk* believed so.

"It is," said the first officer, "most disturbing." Then, when he was certain his captain had finished with him, he rose. "I'll inform Mister Chekov of the course change," he offered.

"Thank you," said the android. "I appreciate it."

As Spock departed, he couldn't have seen that *Kirk's* smile had returned.

When McCoy opened his eyes, the P'othparan was sitting beside him again.

"Damn," said the doctor, the thickness of his tongue making it difficult to speak. "Haven't you got anything better to do than watch old bones mend?"

He looked around, realized that he'd been removed from the critical-care unit. Also, his pain was gone—completely. Which meant that he could stand a lower dosage of painkillers.

He regarded K'leb.

"I know," he told him. "Now that our roles are reversed, you want to see what kind of patient I make."

The youth smiled, surprising the doctor.

I know he doesn't understand English, he mused. So what's he smiling at? My psychic tone?

McCoy frowned.

"Well," he said, "I won't keep you in suspense. I make a *lousy* patient—as you're about to find out."

Despite the lack of feeling in his fingers, he found the button that would summon a nurse. He pressed it— probably too hard.

Christine must have been off duty, because Hwong showed up instead.

"Problem, sir?" asked the Chinese.

"I need some water," said McCoy. "My mouth's dry. And adjust the dimorphene input a couple of milliliters—so I can start to reacquaint myself with my nervous system."

"The water's no problem," said Hwong. "But Doctor M'Benga left strict orders not to adjust the inputs."

"Blast M'Benga," said McCoy. "This is *me* talking—and I want the dimorphene turned down."

But Hwong wouldn't be intimidated. "Sorry, sir. As long as you're incapacitated, Doctor M'Benga is in charge." He shrugged apologetically. "I'll go get you some water."

McCoy shook his head from side to side—as much as his restraints would let him.

"I knew they'd turn on me," he told the P'othparan. "First chance they got."

The *shush* of an entrance door told him that someone had just entered sickbay. A moment later, he saw who it was.

"Well," he said, "if isn't the Pied Piper of Tranktown. Lead any unsuspecting souls into dens of iniquity lately?"

As the captain approached McCoy, he exchanged glances with the P'othparan. The doctor could tell by the expressions on both their faces that the rift between them hadn't gotten any narrower.

"I see that you've got some company already, Bones. I guess I'll find another time to visit."

"Nonsense," said McCoy. "There's no reason I can't have two visitors at once. I'm not that weak, for Pete's sake."

Kirk shook his head. "It wouldn't be fair, Doctor. The young man obviously has dibs on you." Inclining his head slightly in K'leb's direction—a polite good-bye—he started away.

"Not so fast," croaked McCoy, louder than he should have. Thanks to the dimorphene, however, he didn't feel the pain it would otherwise have caused him.

Kirk stopped, frowned—looking for all the world like a trapped animal.

"You're not going anywhere," said the chief medical officer. "This is a prime opportunity for you to get to know K'leb better. To resolve whatever's troubling him once and for all."

The captain sighed. "Please, Bones. Let me take care of that in my own time . . . in my own way."

What could McCoy say? He cursed under his breath.

"All right, Jim. Do it your way. But for the love of God, *do* it already!"

The captain nodded. "I will, Bones. I promise." Another

135

quick glance at the P'othparan—and a moment later, he was gone.

"Sheesh," said the doctor. "You'd think that . . ."

But K'leb was already up out of his seat. He was staring at the entranceway *Kirk* had just passed through.

"What is it, son?" asked McCoy.

The boy didn't answer. He looked scared, though. Just as scared as he had been in the gym, according to Jim's report.

"K'leb?"

But the boy wasn't responding. His gaze was fixed on that entranceway. And after a couple of quick, shallow breaths, he followed in the captain's footsteps. No word of farewell, nothing.

McCoy grunted, suddenly visitorless. "Boy. It's really feast or famine around here, isn't it?"

As K'leb emerged into the corridor, he looked both ways to make sure the *thing* was already gone. Thankfully, it was nowhere to be seen.

His blood pumping hard in his temples, he made for the machine that took him from deck to deck. What had K'liford called it? *Tur . . . bo . . . lift?*

Some of the people in the hallway started to hail him, but he shot past them—slipping on a worn spot in the decking in his haste, righting himself with an outflung hand. Ignoring the occasional call that clung to his heels, echoing down the corridor.

When he reached the lift, its doors were just about to close. Lunging, half shoving a female crewman out of his way, he made it inside just in time.

He found himself sharing the lift with three ship's people —one of whom he recognized. Normally, he would have been glad to see Uh'ura. She had a kind face, a pleasantness, a warmth.

But now, all he could think of was finding K'liford. Only *he* could be made to understand what was wrong. Only *he* would know what to do about it.

Quickly, he punched the button for the level he wanted. Then he fell back against the wall and locked his eyes on the indicator.

When Uh'ura greeted him, he did not respond. He could not. He was too full of dread, too full of knowing to acknowledge anyone or anything else.

And then a terrible question came to mind.

Would K'liford believe him? He hardly believed it himself —hardly believed such a thing was possible. And *he* had *felt* it.

The question still plagued him when the lift doors opened. It dogged him as he hurried down the winding hall toward K'liford's cabin.

In the privacy of his quarters—no tiny cubicle, like the one he had occupied on the *Hood,* but a cabin befitting the status of command—the android sat at his personal workstation and rummaged through file after file. It took him less time than it would have taken a human. Less time, even, than it would have taken a Vulcan. And yet the task seemed to drag on interminably.

Worse—when he was finished, he still hadn't been able to identify the crewman with the pale hair and the bronze skin. Though there were quite a few nonhumans serving on the *Enterprise,* he was familiar with all their races and their physical characteristics—and none of them matched the description of the being who had been standing at the doctor's side.

The being who had looked at him in that strange way. As if he could see right through me, he thought.

As if he knew me for an impostor.

He had been unprepared for such behavior. It had placed him at a disadvantage. So once he wriggled free of the situation, he came straight back here—to determine the nature of any threat this crewman might represent.

His initial efforts having failed, however, he decided to change tacks. If the being in question was not included in the personnel files, perhaps he was not a crewman after all. Perhaps he was only a guest on the *Enterprise,* outfitted in ship's togs for one reason or another. And a guest would likely be mentioned in the captain's log.

After a few moments, he found what he was searching for: a reference to a rescue, a beaming up of an injured T'nufan, a stay in the *Enterprise*'s sickbay. More . . . a problem with local custom, stemming from the rescue. A call to a provincial high minister. And a solution to the problem: the rescued one's temporary commission as a Starfleet ensign.

Interesting.

But it did not explain why the T'nufan—K'leb—had looked at him as he had. Was there a particular closeness between K'leb and the captain, perhaps born of the "adopted father" bond? A closeness that had allowed him to somehow see through the android's disguise?

If so, there might be a record of that as well. *Kirk* tapped in the code for the captain's personal log.

Sure enough, a menu of recent entries included one that concerned the T'nufan. The android brought up the appropriate file, leaned back in his chair, and scanned it.

So. The T'nufan had demonstrated a fear of the human Kirk—though the basis for that fear had not been apparent at the time of the log entry. Nonetheless, it was obvious from the words Kirk had used that he felt some degree of responsibility for K'leb's attitude toward him.

Was *that* what McCoy had been referring to?

This is a prime opportunity for you to get to know K'leb better. To resolve whatever's troubling him once and for all.

Had the captain's problem with the T'nufan been that widely known?

Apparently so.

Now he understood why K'leb had seemed so repelled by him. It was only his normal reaction to Kirk—nothing more.

Still . . . he would keep an eye on the T'nufan. His priority, of course, had to be the next phase of his plan—the part that would take place on Midos Five.

But K'leb was a quantity with which he was less than completely familiar—and *Kirk* didn't like unknown quantities.

Chapter Fourteen

HE WOKE SLOWLY, as if emerging from a great depth.

For a moment, he didn't know where he was. Then he moved—and the pain came flooding back to him. Unspeakable pain. He heard himself cry out, shut his eyes against it.

And in that welcome darkness, awareness came flooding back as well.

The brawl. His capture. The Rythrian. The days—how many?—of imprisonment. The gradual incision of his restraining ropes into the flesh of his arms and legs.

After what seemed like a long time, the pain began to subside. He was back in control.

He opened his eyes, saw a familiar face looming over him. But he managed not to shrink from it, because that would only have stirred the pain of his bonds again. Instead, he took a slow breath, let it out.

It helped steady him, helped clear away some of the cobwebs. Not all, but some.

"Sorry to wake you," said Scarface. "But you and me've got some travelin' to do."

Kirk peered at him. His eyes were taking a bit too long to focus. The result of his worsening hunger?

"Where are we going?" he asked.

The big man shrugged, turned his head, and spat.

"I thought you wanted to get out of here."

Kirk tried to think. Was it possible the Rythrian had fallen for his ploy? *Finally?*

He regarded Scarface, looked into his eyes. Saw the anticipation there, the malicious pleasure he couldn't quite conceal.

No. In the end, the Rythrian had decided it was too big a risk. Or maybe that there had never been a dilithium source in the first place. And he'd given the order to have Kirk disposed of.

"I *do* want to get out of here," said the captain. "But not the way you have in mind."

Scarface grunted. "Smart, aren't you? Too smart for your own damned good."

"And what about you?" asked Kirk. "Are you smart enough to see an opportunity when it stares you in the face?"

The big man shook his head, amused. "So now you want to talk to me. Before, I wasn't good enough."

He smiled, inserting his thick fingers into the space between Kirk's biceps and the rope that bound it.

"I guess I'm not smart at all," he said. "Because the only thing I see staring me in the face is you."

Then he twisted the rope.

It was so bad Kirk thought he might black out. But he did his best not to let it show.

"You know," rasped Scarface, "usually, this is just a job. In your case, though, I'm going to enjoy every minute of it."

Another twist—red, writhing agony. Suddenly, there was sweat on the captain's brow, in his eyes. It stung, and he tried to blink it away.

"I guess," he got out, "that's why you're number two here . . . instead of number one somewhere else. I'm offering you enough credits to . . . set you up in your own business. No more . . . kowtowing to the Rythrian. No more . . ."

The big man twisted again, and this time it was too much for him. He bellowed as the blood trickled down his arms.

Apparently satisfied, Scarface pulled his fingers free. Left limp by the abrupt absence of pain, Kirk allowed his head to loll forward.

"Now shut up," said the big man. "Just keep that silver tongue in your mouth—and it'll all be over before you know it."

Before the captain knew what was happening, Scarface had come around behind him and lifted him up, chair and all. With each jostling step toward the door, Kirk's agony reawakened. Waves of nausea washed over him.

He cursed between clenched teeth. This can't be happening, he told himself. I knew I'd buy it someday, but I thought it'd be for a reason. A cause. Not because I've been mistaken for some small-time con man.

At the threshold, he tried to twist his foot around to lodge it against the door jamb. But the big man must have seen it, because the captain's boot only grazed the wood.

"You're just full of tricks," said Scarface. "But they don't get you very far, do they?" He laughed.

Outside, it was night again, half-choked with fog. There was an old-style truck backed up almost to the door, and Kirk could see through its open gates that it didn't have a stick of cargo in it.

He got a glimpse of low, dark buildings—some kind of warehouse district, as he'd guessed earlier—before the big man shoved him inside. A moment later, the gates slammed closed, and he was plunged into inky blackness.

Kirk heard the engine start up, felt the lurch as the vehicle began to move. The sweat was cold as it dried on his brow.

A way out. There has to be a way out.

Creaking noises. A surge of power as the truck gathered speed. The crunching sound of shifting gears.

Has to be.

Suddenly, the floor listed, and for a moment Kirk felt himself balanced on two chair legs. Then, just as he thought he would tip over, the chair righted itself. The impact of its landing sent a jolt straight up his spine, dragged his ropes through the furrows of his wounds.

He'd hardly unclenched his teeth when it happened again. The same moment of precariousness, the same jarring shock as the chair hit the floor foursquare. The same network of fire consuming him.

But the rocking had produced another result as well. For he was aware of a looseness now around his ankle, a leeway

141

of an inch or so. He tested it, tried to work free of his bonds even more.

Nothing. After a while, his foot cramped and he had to stop.

Easy. Just be patient.

He waited for the listing to occur again, waited long moments. It seemed that the truck had found an even stretch of road, however. The ride was almost gentle now.

All right—then I'll do my own rocking, he resolved. And despite the terrific pain it cost him, he began to swing his weight from side to side.

At first, he could barely get the chair to move. Finally, after what seemed like a long time, it tilted a little and slammed down again. Tilted and slammed down. The base of his spine took a beating, but he kept at it.

He thought he felt the ropes beginning to loosen around his other ankle, but he didn't dare stop to gauge his progress. If he did, he feared, he wouldn't have the gumption to start over again. His ropes sliced his already lacerated flesh, sending blood running down his arms in rivulets.

And then he swung just a little too hard. He knew it even before he had reached the point of no return—but it was too late to do anything about it. The chair teetered on its two legs, swung around a little, and came crashing down sideways against the floor.

Kirk whimpered with the pain, tried to bite it back, and couldn't. Tears came to his eyes.

"Damn," he said out loud, seething with frustration.

The sound of his own voice steadied him. Once again, he tried to assess his situation.

There was a throbbing in his temple, and a wetness where it pressed into the floorboards. Apparently, he'd struck his head in his fall—and hadn't even felt it at the time.

Good thinking, Kirk, he told himself. You broke your fall with the part that was most expendable.

But when he attempted to move his feet, he found that he had accomplished something after all. Not only had the ropes around his ankles taken on some slack—the ropes above them had loosened too, all the way up to his knees. He could move each of his feet three or four inches away from their respective chair legs.

Now—how to take advantage of this? I guess rocking is out of the question now, he mused. It almost made him want to laugh.

Perhaps if he could use one foot to scrape the bonds off the other . . .

The captain had begun to try when the truck started jostling again—worse than before, much worse. The vibration of rough passage pounded through the floor into the bones of his head.

It meant that they had turned off the main road—that the longest part of their journey had been completed. And more than likely, judging from the intensity of each jerk, they were coming close to whatever secluded area Scarface had selected as Kirk's last resting place.

He resumed scraping, this time with a little more urgency. Nor did the lack of light help matters any, forcing him to work by sense of touch alone.

Despite his best efforts, it was some time before he managed to push a restraining loop over his heel and down the length of his foot. But once he had done it, it made the freeing of his other foot that much easier.

Then he put his newfound mobility to good use. First, he turned himself around so that he lay with his back parallel to one of the truck's long walls—though still on his side. Next, he forced himself toward the back of the cargo compartment.

It didn't even hurt that much. Since he'd toppled over, the circulation had gradually cut off in his arms—so that the pain he would normally have felt was reduced to a distant heat.

In fact, awkward as it was scuttling around like a damaged crab, he took pleasure in it. After sitting bound for so long, it was good to move at all.

When he reached the twin gates, he swung nearly a hundred and eighty degrees around again. And with all the force he could muster, he kicked at the doors.

They shuddered, but they held. He kicked again, and this time, he thought, it seemed as if he might have dislodged the rusted casings of the deadbolt that held them closed.

On the other hand, those casings might not have been as rusted as they seemed when Scarface thrust him in here.

He went on kicking, hoping that the big man couldn't hear the racket from up front. And finally, with an earsplitting shriek, one of the gates opened partway.

It was enough to show Kirk a slice of fog-enshrouded jungle—but not much more. He braced himself for another round of battering.

But it was too late—for that, and for anything else. With a hiss of air brakes, the truck ground to a halt.

No! I was so close, almost there . . .

Gears shifted, and the truck rolled backward for a moment. Then it stopped again and the engine shut off.

Kirk's heart was beating against his ribs like a caged animal. He heard the door of the cab crank open, heard the *splotch* of footfalls against soft, wet earth.

Through the slot between the gates, he could make out a clearing—no, not *just* a clearing. It was a bog of some sort. And its purpose was painfully clear.

He means to dump me in it.

No remains, no evidence. No loose ends to worry about afterward.

There was a metallic taste in his mouth, the taste of fear. Of hope gone sour.

He rebuked himself. *Get a grip, damn it. You're still alive, aren't you? There's still a chance. There's* always *a chance. . . .*

Kirk forced himself to stay calm while Scarface made his way around the truck. A few seconds later, the deadbolt slid aside. As the gate he'd been pounding on began to swing aside, he drew his feet back.

When he saw his captor's face, he lashed out.

But the big man saw it coming just in time. And he leaned back far enough so that Kirk's boots only grazed his jaw.

Cursing, he leaped up into the cargo compartment. With hardly any effort at all, it seemed, he picked up the captain and swung him into the wall.

Kirk hit hard, and then again when he slid to the floor. But the chair took the brunt of the punishment, with a cracked leg to show for it.

And then, with a sudden, clean-edged clarity, he knew exactly what he had to do.

"You're a pain in the butt," said the big man. "And now I'm going to make you a dead pain in the butt."

"Wait!" Kirk wheezed as Scarface bent to lift him up again. "I'll tell you where the dilithium came from!"

The big man hesitated, sneered.

"No, really—I'll tell," croaked the captain, as if his encounter with the wall had damaged his breathing apparatus. He swallowed. "Only please—let me live, all right?"

Scarface's tiny eyes narrowed even more.

"You want to tell?" he barked. "Then go ahead. Tell."

"It's on Buzmuzbuduh," mumbled Kirk.

The big man leaned closer. "What was that? Speak up, damn it."

The captain nodded eagerly, coughed. Started to speak but coughed again.

Perhaps without realizing it, Scarface loomed closer still. Kirk estimated that it was close enough.

And without further ado, he spat square in the big man's face.

"You're a fool," he shouted as Scarface recoiled. "Your boss knows it, I know it, and now you know—"

He never finished. In a paroxysm of rage, the big man hurled him the length of the cargo compartment. For a moment, things spun around too fast to follow.

Then the wall came up and smashed him. He felt a terrible, sharp pain in his knee, followed by the sweetest sense of release he could ever have imagined. When he got his bearings, he realized that the chair had smashed into half a dozen pieces, and his bonds were lying loose all about him.

His only problem now was the behemoth slowly advancing on him, his scarred face twisted into a savage grin, his huge fists clenching and unclenching.

Kirk scrambled to his feet as best he could, his legs cramped and stiff from disuse. But before he stood up all the way, he took hold of a long sliver of wood—once part of the chair, now a weapon he might use to some advantage.

The big man didn't seem much impressed. He kept coming—even when Kirk raised the splinter as if to throw it. Another couple of seconds and Scarface would be right on top of him.

Rather than wait, he decided to take the initiative. Pushing off the rear wall, he charged the man.

Apparently, Scarface hadn't expected that. Nor did he expect the captain to leap suddenly and plant his heels in the big man's chest.

As Kirk landed, he saw Scarface reel backward, stumble —and pitch headlong out the rear of the truck. There was a scream and a loud, flat *plosh.*

Gathering his feet beneath him, the captain made his way down the length of the cargo compartment—his sliver of wood at the ready. But as he reached the gates, he saw a dark shape struggling against the greater darkness of the bog.

"Damn you!" rasped Scarface. He was half on his side, half on his back, with only his head, an arm, and part of his torso free of the muck. And it seemed that he'd landed in a deeper part of the bog, because he was still sinking—though ever so slowly.

"Watch your language," said Kirk. "You're talking to the only one who can save your worthless life now."

The big man writhed and grunted in an effort to move toward the truck. The muscles in his neck stood out like cords, but he accomplished nothing. If anything, his efforts caused him to sink a little faster.

"Get me out of here," he roared, his voice rising in pitch. "I can't move."

"Sure," said Kirk. "After all you've done for me, I'd be an ingrate not to help you out."

Fury and fear washed over the man's face in successive waves. "I wasn't going to kill you," he said. "I was only supposed to scare you—so you'd talk."

"Right," said the captain. "Whatever you say." He looked around, noticed the coil of rope hanging on the wall of the cargo compartment—the same kind of rope he'd been bound with. He slipped his weapon into his belt, then got the coil and brought it out where Scarface could see it.

"I suppose," he continued, "you want me to throw this out to you—or at least one end of it."

The big man slipped down a couple of inches—all at once. Wide-eyed and whimpering, he started to struggle again. But the bog held him fast.

"Throw it," he pleaded. "Please—"

"First," said Kirk, "tell me what you did with my friends."

"Nothing," croaked the big man. "We didn't even take them—I swear it."

"I don't believe you," said Kirk.

"It's the truth, damn it. The order was to bring *you* in, and you alone. Your friends weren't worth anything to us."

"Then they were alive when you left the Shooting Star?"

"I . . . I don't know," said Scarface. "Maybe. I told you—I wasn't interested in them."

Kirk nodded, satisfied. Kneeling, he ran one end of the rope through a slot in the truck's bumper assembly, tied it off. Next, he freed up a length of it—enough to reach the big man with the coiled end.

Then he paused.

"Throw it," grated Scarface. "What are you waiting for?"

The captain shrugged. "Something just occurred to me. I mean, here I am, saving your hide. But just as soon as I pull you out, you're going to come after me—just like before."

"No!" rasped the big man. "I won't. I won't do that."

Kirk regarded him. "Now, why is it I don't have much faith in your promises?" He sighed.

"You've got to believe me," said Scarface. "From now on, I won't touch you. No matter what the Rythrian says."

"You're sure about that?"

"Yes, damn—yes, I'm sure. Just get me out of here."

The muck had gradually crept up around Scarface. It very nearly reached his cheek now.

If Kirk waited much longer, it would be almost impossible to pull him out. So, against his better judgment, he tossed out the rope.

The coil fell just beyond the big man, the length just inches away from his free hand. He grabbed it, wound it a couple of times around his forearm.

Kirk didn't envy him the task of hanging on while the truck hauled him out. But then, he hadn't a whole lot of sympathy for him either.

Still painfully stiff, he jumped down from the cargo compartment with some difficulty. Then he found his way to the cab and swung the door open. With even more difficulty, he got in.

He took a deep breath, surveyed the controls before him. They looked simple enough—that is, if one knew which was which.

"Let's see," he muttered to himself. One wrong move and he'd back the truck into the bog—or accelerate so quickly he'd tear the big man's arm off. "There's got to be some sort of ignition, right? That's how these old internal-combustion engines were supposed to work."

His knee brushed against something loose and it jangled. He peered around the steering column and saw the dangling set of keys, one of them already inserted into the mechanism.

The captain held his breath, turned it, and hoped for the best. A moment later, the engine rumbled to life.

So far, so good.

Now—for the proverbial gas pedal. He looked down, saw not one pedal but two. Depressing the one on the left didn't seem to have any effect, so he deduced that that one was the brake. Or weren't they using foot brakes anymore when this truck was manufactured?

He frowned, pressed down on the other pedal. Gently. And the engine responded, whining with pent-up power.

The steering was pretty easy to figure out, considering the wheel was right in front of him. But how to put it into gear?

Kirk looked around at the various gauges. None of them seemed helpful. Then he saw the handgrip and the markings that ran below it.

Planting his foot on what he assumed to be the brake, he moved the handgrip from marking to marking, feeling the shift in the engine's pull with each adjustment. Outside, he heard Scarface's bellowing—even more frantic than before.

"What the hell," he said, and moved the handgrip back to the position where the truck seemed to be straining forward the hardest. Gradually, he lifted his foot off the brake.

The truck rolled forward, but only a little. After it was obvious that it wasn't going to go any farther without some help, Kirk pushed down on the gas pedal.

The engine rumbled. The truck lumbered forward.

There was more bellowing from back in the bog, but this time it was a sound of pain. Intense pain.

When Kirk poked his head out the open window, however, he saw that Scarface was still hanging on. So he kept up the pressure on the gas pedal.

In a matter of moments, the truck started to drag him out. Soon, his other arm came free, and he was able to clutch the rope in both hands, and as a result his cries diminished.

The captain allowed the vehicle to tow Scarface a couple of yards to the edge of the bog. Then he took his foot off the gas and slipped back into a neutral gear.

Descending gingerly from the cab, he came around to the rear bumper. And as the big man watched, he began to untie the rope from it.

"What're you doing?" he rasped. "I'm not out yet."

"No," said Kirk. "But I feel safer with you where you are—so this is as far as I'm going to take you. You'll have to do the rest of the work yourself."

"What d'you mean? I'll never get myself out of here."

As the captain finished freeing up the rope, he shrugged. "Maybe not. But you won't sink very far either. And the Rythrian will eventually send someone to look for you."

"What about the nightwings? They'll suck me dry."

Kirk chuckled, tossing his end of the rope into the swamp with the rest of it.

"Good try," he said. "But we both know that nightwings don't frequent the lowlands."

"That wasn't the deal," argued Scarface, changing tacks. "You said you'd get me out of here."

Kirk managed a smile. "You know me—a born liar." And without another word, he headed for the cab again.

"Damn it, you can't leave me here! Hey—I'm talking to you! What in . . ."

The captain blocked out the rest of it as he raised himself back into the driver's seat. Pulling the door closed, he began the search for the headlight control.

After a few trials—and errors—he located the right dial. Turning it up two clicks to maximum intensity, he saw the jungle stabbed by twin blue beams.

He could tell now that there was a path ahead of him among the trees. It was just wide enough for the truck to make it through.

Throwing the engine into gear, he trundled forward. Branches slapped against the windshield, slithered away on either side. Fog wafted in and out of the jungle, sometimes making it difficult to see.

After a couple of minutes, however, the trees receded and the path widened, and the fog seemed to thin out. Soon after, he came across a black strip of highway.

Leaning forward, he looked down the road in either direction. To the left, there was a glow in the distance. Or at least he thought there was.

That would either be the town itself—or the spaceport, which wasn't far from it. Pushing down on the gas and hauling on the steering wheel, he turned left out onto the blacktop.

For the first time in days, he felt he was in control again. The pain of his wounds was returning with his circulation, he was hungry and he was tired—but none of that mattered. In a little while, he would be reunited with his ship and his crew. And he'd find out what had happened to Bones and Scotty.

Once again, he saw McCoy tossed over the heads of the crowd. He blinked away the vision, made an effort to concentrate on the ribbon of road.

Of course they'd made it back. Scarface wouldn't have lied about taking them captive—not in the position he was in at the time.

Kirk's eyes were drawn to the sideview mirror, where he saw himself scowling. He had a long, dark bruise on his jaw where Scarface had struck him—was it days ago now? And he looked haggard—hollow-cheeked and pale. But most of all, he looked worried.

Relax, he told himself. They're all right, probably in better shape than you are.

But if the big man *had* lied, there would be hell to pay. Kirk would make him wish he'd died a slow death in that bog.

As he negotiated a lazy turn, the glow up ahead appeared to grow more distinct. When the turn finally resolved itself into a straightaway, he stepped down harder on the gas.

The truck sped up, the jungle unraveling more quickly on either side of him. And the glow waxed brighter.

Then the night was shattered by a distant boom and a dagger of light seemed to rip open the belly of the sky.

It was the firetrail of an old cargo hauler, tracing the ship's struggle as it fought to free itself from gravity. A moment later, the acceleration system cut in and the hauler won the battle, ascending rapidly in a parti-colored blast of energy.

Just before it rose out of sight, Kirk heard his own engine sputter furiously. Before he had any idea what was wrong, the thing shut itself off, turning the entire control console into a confusion of red-flashing lights. Finally, with a near-human sigh, the truck rolled to a halt.

The lights continued to blink annoyingly.

Kirk cursed and struck the console with the heel of his hand.

"What in blazes . . . ?" he muttered, peering at the gauges. It took a while before he found one that could tell him what had happened.

He'd simply run out of fuel.

The road was even lonelier on foot. Kirk hadn't been at all unhappy about the dearth of other vehicles when he'd been trying to get the hang of piloting his own. Now, however, he wished for the sight of a single truck headed in the right direction.

Of course, in the back of his mind, he knew too that such a vehicle might have been driven by the Rythrian's men, fresh from picking up Scarface and hot on his trail. But it was unlikely that they'd have gone searching for him so soon.

Time passed, marked only by the click of his heels on the edge of the highway. Fog curled in over the road, curled out again. There were sounds that originated in the jungle, small-bird and insect sounds. But for the most part, it was quiet.

Gradually, it became apparent that the glow was indeed coming from the town rather than the spaceport—or at least, most of it was. The port seemed to have an illumination of its own—much dimmer than that of Tranktown, but an illumination nonetheless. And as Kirk approached both of them, and got near enough to see them as separate entities, he noted that the spaceport was closer.

Just as well, he told himself. If I set foot in town, I'd be taking unnecessary chances. And it'll be just as easy to contact the ship from the portmaster's office.

He chuckled softly, alone in the jungle-infused night.

It should be easier to convince him of my identity than it was to convince Scarface.

At least, I hope so.

Once more the night was torn apart, as a cruise liner lifted into the heavens. But as it was a more advanced model than the cargo hauler, it made for a significantly less spectacular light show. And it was gone a lot sooner.

What's more, it had seemed to shoot straight up—which told the captain that he was a lot closer to the port than he'd believed. With all this fog in the air, it was difficult to judge distances.

He kept on as the road wound this way and that, seeming to grow more indecisive as it approached its destination. Finally, a vehicle passed him—but it was headed back out the way he had come, and the driver didn't seem to see him anyway. Nor did he do anything to attract the man's attention.

He didn't need any dubious help now. He was almost there. And he had fallen into a kind of rhythm, a mechanical step that seemed as autonomic as his breathing. As tired as he was, as much as he hurt and hungered, he knew he would make it.

Sure enough, it wasn't long before he could see the hulking shapes of the spacecraft, the angry glare of red beacons on top of the communications towers, the softer play of light on the landing fields.

He couldn't have been more than a hundred yards from the main gate when he felt the *squish* of something soft and yielding beneath his foot.

As he looked down to see what it was, fleshy tentacles coiled themselves around his calf. He could feel the sharp pain of the stingers even through the synthetic leather of his boot.

Damn . . .

He fell to one knee as the tentacles released him. Watched helplessly, nerve endings deadening, as the creature slunk off clumsily into the undergrowth.

Nor was the irony lost on him. To have come so far . . .

He fought to get up, to make it those last few yards. He tried to shout for help.

But the poison was working too quickly. He pitched forward against the blacktop. And in another couple of moments, he lost consciousness altogether.

Chapter Fifteen

THE ANDROID REPLACED THE GRATE on the exhaust vent, pleased that he hadn't had to clean it this time.

Ever since he had completed the construction of the machine, small animals had found their way into the duct and become caught in the mechanism. Sometimes his daily inspection discovered them, and he managed to extract them before they could be damaged. At other times, however, they squirmed inside after he had checked the machinery—and when the duplication process began, they were hacked to bits by the rotary blades.

Not for the first time, he wondered at this odd quirk in his nature. Why expend so much effort on these small, mindless creatures? It wasn't as if they could actually harm the mechanism, was it?

No. Not even if a thousand of them were destroyed in there.

Then why? Did it have something to do with the other peculiar trait he had developed—his growing inability to look at the androids he'd created without recalling the deaths of their human templates?

"Brown."

The android heard the cry, turned away from the

retightened grate. He saw Channing's diminutive figure beckoning to him from the vicinity of the communications shack.

Was it time then? Already?

He counted the days in rapid-fire succession, marking each by the task he had executed that day—the kidnapping he had performed, or the duplication he had completed. Or the . . .

Yes. Perhaps it *was* time after all.

Raising himself up from his haunches, he made his way down the ravine. Tiny rocks ground underneath his boots. His artificial hair fluttered in the breeze and he combed it back into place with his fingers.

"It's the leader," said Channing, when Brown was close enough.

He saw once again the way her human counterpart had pleaded for her life. The way Thomasson had gripped her by the throat and constricted his fingers about it and held her like that until she stopped struggling.

"You mean *Kirk*," he said. Perhaps Channing and the others had been programmed to think of *Kirk* that way—but he had not.

She shrugged. "*Kirk*—the leader. He's asking for you."

"Of course," said Brown. He slipped past her into the shack—a lean-to, really, constructed of bits of debris he'd collected on his forays into the colony center.

When he saw him, Thomasson rose to give Brown his seat, choosing a section of the shack where he wouldn't bump his head against the slanted roof.

Nor did Brown pay any more attention to him than he had to. For he had terminated the existence of the human Thomasson himself, and this was not the time to be distracted by such things.

The android leaned closer to the speaker grid.

"This is Brown," he said.

"Greetings, Doctor," said *Kirk*. "I see you've had some success down there."

"I have done what was asked of me," said Brown.

"Which is all any of us *can* do," said *Kirk*. A pause. "I'm calling from the U.S.S. *Enterprise*—now under my command. . . ."

So. He too has been successful. But was there ever any doubt? Nothing can stop him—he had said so himself.

"We are about to establish orbit around Midos Five," *Kirk* continued. "Soon, we'll be beaming down. I trust you have made arrangements for my arrival at the governor's office?"

"Arrangements have been made," Brown responded. He did not mention the difficulties involved, because *Kirk* had not asked.

It had been one thing to kidnap humans at random—to incapacitate them and bring them back here to the installation. The capture of a specific individual, however—especially one who seldom went out-of-doors, one tied so tightly into to the governmental hierarchy—that had been a different matter entirely. And then to return that person to the colony before it was suspected there was anyone missing . . .

"Good," said *Kirk*. "Then be prepared. After I've done my song and dance for the governor's committee, I'll be bringing the first group down for conversion. Just remember—they'll be anything but cooperative."

"We have acquired weapons," said Brown. "There has been no deviation from my instructions."

He thought he heard *Kirk* chuckle, but the signal was not so pure that he could be sure. Even so, something rankled within him.

Perhaps it was the other android's tone. So glib. So . . . condescending. He had almost forgotten how much he resented it.

Or was there something else as well? Some other thing that disturbed him?

"You say the *first* group," Brown went on. "How many groups will there be?"

He could almost see *Kirk* shrugging his shoulders.

"A great number, Doctor. Unless I see a reason to stop, I'm going to convert the entire crew." A moment of silence. "Why do you ask?"

The entire crew. Some four hundred and thirty humans, he thought.

Four hundred and thirty whose faces will replay their deaths for me. . . .

"Is it wise to convert so many?" he asked. "We were more cautious on the *Hood*."

"It was a different situation there," said *Kirk*. Suddenly, his voice had taken on a sterner tone. "We were in a hurry to get the machine off Exo III. And to gain control of a second vessel—*this* vessel. Now that these things have been accomplished, we may proceed differently."

"I see," said Brown. "Yet . . ."

"Yet *what*, Doctor?"

"I don't know if the machine will be able to stand up under so many conversions in so short a time."

"If it does not," said *Kirk*, "the deficiency will be *yours*—not the machine's. It would be a pity to discover at this late date that you were not capable of carrying out the Creator's plan."

Of course, he was right. The machine had virtually no limitations. Given an adequate supply of raw materials, there was no reason why it should not be able to duplicate the crew of the *Enterprise*.

Then why should he resist *Kirk*'s decision? Because there was something about recalling the human deaths that disturbed him?

Certainly, this was a dysfunction on his part. Could he allow it to stand in the way of Doctor Korby's objectives?

No. Of course not.

"Brown? Are you still there?"

"I am here," said the android. "And I will make certain that the machine can perform all the necessary conversions."

"That's better," said *Kirk*. "Much better. I knew I could count on you, Doctor."

"Of course," said Brown. "Will there be anything else?"

"No, that's it. For now. *Kirk* out."

A moment later, the communications device fell silent again.

* * *

Kirk and Spock had no sooner materialized in the governor's committee room than they were assaulted by the man.

He was short, slender, bald-headed but for a monk's fringe of reddish hair. And so baby-faced that his sharp-edged fury seemed wildly out of place.

"About time you got here!" he raved, poking a finger into *Kirk's* chest. "Of course, you've got better things to do than worry about some poor, defenseless girl, who . . ."

Another man came up behind him, took him by the shoulders. This one was tall, with gray hair cut short and bristly, though his beard was dark as pitch.

"Channing," he said. "They've come as quickly as they could. A starship—"

"Starships be damned!" sputtered the smaller man, spraying flecks of saliva. "This just isn't a high priority for them. They'd rather be blasting Klingons to kingdom come so they can rack up some more medals. What's a few missing miners compared to—"

"Channing!" bellowed the one with the beard. "That's enough!"

The smaller man came forward suddenly, grabbed *Kirk's* tunic in his freckled fists.

Out of the corner of his eye, the android saw Spock tense. He knew that the Vulcan would move to subdue *Kirk's* assailant at the first hint of a weapon—or at a word from the captain himself.

But the human Kirk, in this type of situation, with the colonists' nerves understandably taut, would not have given that word—so neither did he. Nor did he take any action on his own.

"No," said the one called Channing. "It's *not* enough. Not nearly. Because if she dies, I'm going to . . ."

But before he could finish, the bearded man wrenched him away.

"Damn it, get a hold of yourself," he barked, shaking his fellow committeeman. "It's not their fault. They're here to help!"

Channing glared at him for a moment. Then, slowly, his

anger turned into something else. Tears stood out in his eyes, glistened. He heaved a sigh that was almost a sob.

"Let me be, Chewton." It was only a whisper, all he could manage in his emotion-racked state.

But it was enough to tell *Kirk* what he wanted to know. The bearded one, then, was Chewton—the governor. It was a necessary bit of information, considering the captain had met him only a few months back, and the governor would not expect to have been forgotten in so short a time.

"Let me be," Channing repeated. And with more strength than *Kirk* would have given him credit for, he thrust the governor from him.

"Channing . . ." began Chewton.

But the smaller man didn't seem to hear him. He turned toward the pair from the *Enterprise*.

"Find her," he told them, his voice an empty husk now. Again, for just a second, anger flared red and hot. "You *find* her!"

Then he turned again, as if he would leave the room. But he'd hardly taken two steps before his knees buckled and he slumped to the floor.

The bearded man started toward him, but the rest of the committee was closer. In an instant, they had surrounded him.

Chewton looked apologetically at *Kirk,* and then at Spock.

"Sorry," he said. "You have to understand—the man's daughter is among the missing."

Kirk nodded. "Of course," he said, as gently as the occasion dictated. "I do understand. Completely."

By then the others had gotten Channing to his feet. With their help, he moved toward the doorway again.

"Perhaps," said *Kirk,* "I should have my ship's doctor take a look at him."

The governor thought for a moment, shook his head.

"No," he said. "All he needs is some rest. He's been up in a flitter every day and night for the past week." He paused. "When we called," he said, "we did hope you could've gotten here sooner."

Spock raised an eyebrow. "Sooner, sir?"

"Mister Spock, we transmitted a request for help nearly two weeks ago." Chewton's brow, already lined with care, creased even more. "When we established this colony, we were assured that help would *never* be that far away."

"Two weeks," echoed Spock. He turned to *Kirk.* "Interesting. And we only received a message from Starfleet a couple of days ago—ship's time."

The android muttered a curse. "Must have gotten lost in the bureaucracy somehow—though I've never heard of a screw-up as bad as this one." He shook his head, regarded Chewton soberly. "You have my abject apology, sir. But now that we *are* here, let's make the most of it."

The governor nodded. "Of course," he said, gesturing toward the oval table in the center of the room. The seats around it were filling up again as the other committee members returned to them.

Kirk took an empty chair next to the governor's. Spock sat down beside him.

The captain scanned the faces around the table, wondering which of them was an android like himself. Of course, it was impossible to tell just by looking. But without a doubt, it was one of them.

Otherwise—if Brown had failed to kidnap and replace the committeeman in charge of telecommunications—a call would really have gone out to the nearest starbase. And a starship would have been deployed to Midos Five, but it probably would not have been the *Enterprise.* First of all, there were other ships that had been closer—the *Hood* among them; second, *Kirk*'s crew had been on shore leave, and it would have taken time to recall everyone from the planet.

This way, however, it had been assured—the *Enterprise* would be the vessel which came to the colony's aid. And that was a crucial cog in the mechanism of *Kirk*'s plan—for how could he duplicate the crew without bringing it to Midos Five?

"All right, ladies and gentlemen," said the governor. "You all know the captain and Mister Spock. And I need not tell you why they're here."

Kirk noted the resentment in their eyes—only a glimmer

160

of what he'd seen in Channing's, but there nonetheless. Unlike Channing, however, they kept it to themselves.

Nor was the android among them any more noticeable than before. Whichever one he was, he wore the same slight frown as all the others.

"Why don't we start at the beginning?" *Kirk* suggested. "When did the disappearances start?"

"Twenty days ago," said a committee woman with dark hair and darker eyes. "Twenty days exactly."

"Rachel Mphalele," added another woman, this one big-boned and lightly complected. "Her father's the foreman at Northridge. They have an outpost home not far from the mine."

"What first alerted you that she was missing?" asked *Kirk*.

"She wasn't home for dinner," explained the governor, "and apparently she was very punctual by nature. Her father became worried, called everyone he knew in the area. One of his neighbors said that he'd seen her on his way home. She'd been picked up by a flitter."

"And since her boyfriend had a flitter," rejoined the big-boned woman, "Rachel's father contacted him. But the boy said he hadn't seen her all day."

"He had an alibi?" asked Spock.

The dark woman shook her head from side to side. "No, not really. So naturally, we suspected that he was lying and took him into custody. But then there was another disappearance—an engineer named Thomasson. And a third—Channing's daughter Karen." She looked *Kirk* in the eye. "That's when I placed the call to Starfleet."

Ah. The android did nothing to acknowledge that he knew who she was—what she was. But having dropped her hint, she would have assumed that the connection had been made.

"Since then," said a burly man with smallish features, "there have been eight more disappearances. We've been completely ineffectual in trying to guard against them. And for all we know, there's another one taking place even as we speak."

Kirk leaned forward. "You mentioned that the girl was seen getting into a flitter. Was the man who saw it able to describe it?"

"I'm afraid not," said the big-boned woman. "But a flitter was reported missing that same day—and it hasn't turned up since."

"No suspects then?" asked *Kirk*. "No leads?"

"Captain," said the dark woman, "this is not a big colony. No one could hide anything here for very long. It seems obvious to us that whoever's doing this is himself one of the missing."

"That's right," added the other woman. "He's got to be hiding out there in the wilderness, flitting in just long enough to do his dirty work and then flitting out again."

"That seems the most likely possibility," agreed *Kirk*. "But I'm not ruling out any others."

"Indeed," said Spock. "How do we know that the individual in question isn't one of your outpost residents?"

"We've searched all the outposts," said Chewton. "Including Mphalele's. No sign of anyone or . . ." He scowled. "No evidence of foul play."

"And we've had the outposts watched since the third or fourth disappearance," contributed the dark woman. "Nothing unusual has taken place at any of them."

The governor turned to *Kirk*. "Captain, couldn't your long-range scanners find someone if he was out there?"

"Actually," said the android, "we're in the process of trying that now. But we're not having much luck—and the scanners will pick up any life-form that's out in the open. We must conclude that our abductor—as well as those he's abducted—are in a cave or something, somewhere the scanners can't reach."

Or else, those we seek are inorganic, and therefore unscannable. But none of you has thought of that—not even Spock.

The burly man grunted. "Then what are we talking about? Shuttlecraft?"

"I'm afraid so," said *Kirk*. "It'll take some time for us to comb every space within flitter range, but it's the only viable alternative I can think of." He turned to his first officer. "How about you, Spock?"

After a moment, the Vulcan nodded. "It would seem to be the best strategy," he concluded.

"All right then," said *Kirk*. "We'll have the shuttlecraft

down here within the hour. And of course, we'll continue to try the scanners. In the meantime, I suggest you keep up whatever precautions you've already taken." He smiled humorlessly. "Who knows? Maybe our friend will get careless."

The android flipped open his communicator.

"Scotty?"

"Right here, Captain."

"Two to beam up. In thirty seconds."

"Aye, sir."

Kirk closed his communicator, stood, and stepped back from the table. Spock, of course, did likewise.

The android surveyed the faces around the committee table. None of them seemed particularly grateful.

"Gentlemen," he said. Then, catching the eye of the dark woman for just a little longer than was necessary, "Ladies."

The transporter beam took them a couple of seconds later.

Chapter Sixteen

KIRK HAD BEEN AWAKE for some time before he realized the implications of that fact.

His first lucid thought was a chilling one: The Rythrian's found me. I'm back in his warehouse.

But no—he wasn't bound to the cot he was lying on. And while the room in which he found himself was plain enough, it was no warehouse.

Besides—the Rythrian wouldn't have brought me back. He would just have dumped me in that swamp and made an end of it.

He tried to get up, felt the pain of his wounds come awake with nauseating fury; stopped trying and lay back against his pillow.

There was a click and a sucking sound and a puff of smoke off to his right. Startled to find out he'd had company without knowing it, Kirk turned his head enough to see the man's face.

He had pale, pale hair, almost white, pulled tightly into a clasp at the back of his head. From there, it hung like a horse's tail.

His face was long and thin, sharp-featured, stubbly with a couple of days' growth. His skin was almost as pale as his hair. And he had a phaser on his belt.

"Feeling better?" asked the man, putting his little liquid-fuel lighter away. He drew a breath through his pipe, let the blue-gray smoke out his nostrils.

The captain grunted. "Feeling *alive,* anyway. Are you the one responsible for that?"

The man nodded almost indiscernibly. "I thought I heard someone cry out just beyond the main gate. So I went to investigate—and found *you.*"

Then he *had* managed to get a yell out before he succumbed.

"I stepped on something," said Kirk.

"You certainly did," said the blond man. "We call it Malachi's Boot—after its first victim among the original colonists. It sends a paralyzing agent into the bloodstream. If I hadn't found you within a few minutes, administered the antidote . . . you just would have locked up inside. Heart, lungs, everything."

Kirk swallowed. "That's a new one on me. I'm grateful, Mister . . . ?"

The man chuckled, sent smoke blossoming out the corner of his mouth. "Kaith," he answered. "Now, suppose you demonstrate some of that gratitude—and tell me why the Rythrian is so hot for your hide."

The captain met his gaze. "What makes you think he *is?*"

The blond man shrugged. "A couple of hours after I pulled you in off the road, a big fellow with a scar—one of the Rythrian's men—came looking for you. I said I hadn't seen any sign of you." He paused. "So?"

"He's mistaken me for someone who swindled him," explained Kirk. "After holding me for a while, trying to pry loose some information I didn't have, he decided to toss me in a bog. I escaped—and got as far as the place where you found me."

Kaith puffed judiciously on his pipe. "So you're saying that it's a case of mistaken identity."

The captain nodded, though it hadn't quite been a question.

"It's a good thing for you," said the blond man, "that I've no great love for the Rythrian. Otherwise I might have been convinced to turn you over." There was a crinkling at the corners of his eyes—signifying a joke?

"I need to talk with the portmaster," said Kirk.

The man's fine, silvery brows lifted. "Really?" He grunted. "But we haven't finished our talk yet." His free hand straying to his phaser, he gazed expectantly at the captain.

Kirk understood. He had hoped to divulge his identity to the portmaster alone—but it seemed he had little choice in the matter.

"My name," he said, "is Kirk. James T. Kirk. Captain of the U.S.S. *Enterprise*—the Federation vessel now in orbit around your planet."

Kaith had no immediate reaction to the statement. But he also didn't take a puff of his pipe for a while.

"There is no Federation ship in orbit," he said finally. "At least, not anymore."

Kirk felt a trickle of ice water collect in the small of his back. "What do you mean?" he asked.

"I mean," said the man, "that she's gone. Days ago. And there was no word from her about a missing captain."

Kirk's mind raced. Could the man be lying? He had no reason to—or none that was readily apparent, anyway.

But why would Spock take the ship out of orbit? And so quickly that there hadn't even been time for him to notify the authorities of the captain's disappearance?

Unless Starfleet Command had required it—because the Romulan situation had suddenly gotten way out of hand.

It was possible. But it would have taken a while to recall the crew from Tranktown. Surely, in that time, Spock could have informed someone that Kirk was missing.

It didn't make sense.

"You want to stick with that story?" asked the blond man.

Kirk frowned. "I am who I say I am." He leaned back, still trying to fit the pieces together. "If you don't believe me, you can check my voice pattern against the print in the portmaster's records."

Kaith got up, crossed the room to a small computer workstation against the wall. Quickly, he punched up the required data.

"Do you want me to speak now?" asked the captain. "So you can compare?"

Still studying the screen, the blond man shook his head.

"Not necessary. Our entire conversation was recorded." After a moment, he looked up at Kirk.

"They match," said the captain.

"So it would seem," said Kaith, a hint of respect having crept into his voice.

"Then perhaps you'll let me see the portmaster now. If the *Enterprise* is gone, I'll need help in finding another ship to get me to her."

The blond man chuckled.

Kirk sighed. So even *this* is going to be difficult.

"Did I say something funny?" he asked.

The man nodded. "In a way, yes. You see, I *am* the portmaster."

The captain regarded him in the light of this new information.

Why not? he mused. He's not what one might expect in a portmaster—but then, Tranktown's not your usual port.

"Will you help me then?" he asked Kaith.

The blond man considered him for a moment.

"I don't see any reason not to," he said at last. And puffed expansively on his pipe.

Martinez swiveled in his command chair.

"Well, Mister Paultic?"

"I've done it, sir. I've made contact on one of the low-frequency bands." His brow screwed up a little as he listened. "The call's from a vessel called the *Rheingold*, sir. Freighter class."

"Are they in trouble?" asked the captain. He wondered if the Romulans had made their move at long last.

"Doesn't sound like it," said the communications officer. He paused, intent. "The transmission's not very clear, sir, but I think they're saying they have Starfleet personnel on board."

"Starfleet personnel . . . ?" began Stuart.

"No—that's not quite right," said Paultic. "They have *news* of Starfleet personnel. Yes—news. It's coming in a little clearer now."

"Can you establish visual contact?" asked Martinez.

"I'll try, sir," said Paultic. He made the necessary adjustments with admirable skill—for a human—and a few moments later the forward viewscreen filled with an image.

Even with all the interference scrolling from one end of the monitor to the other, it was obvious that the personage on the other end didn't miss too many meals. It was a frailty of which no android could be accused. Indeed, it would disappear with all other frailties when the androids made Doctor Korby's vision a reality.

"Captain Wilhelm Grundfest," said the obese figure, "of the *Rheingold*. To whom . . . the pleasure?"

"This is Captain Martinez of the U.S.S. *Hood*. Your transmission seems to be meeting with some interference. Do we understand correctly that you have some news about Starfleet personnel?"

"Yes . . . news," said Grundfest. " . . . a Captain James T. Kirk? Of the U.S.S. *Enterprise?*"

The mention of that name caught Martinez off guard—but of course, he didn't show it. Instead, he took stock of his bridge crew, noted gratefully that the entire shift was made up of androids—except for Paultic.

"What about Captain Kirk?" he asked.

The freighter captain smiled, his eyes sinking behind the mounds of his cheeks. " . . . currently a guest of the portmaster . . . Tranquillity Seven. While I regret . . . not explain the circumstances of his being there . . . he wishes very much to be reunited with his ship. And of course, as . . . the Federation, I agreed to carry the message . . . we met either the *Enterprise* itself or another Federation vessel."

Martinez nodded. "I see."

And so he did. The situation was rapidly taking on shape and texture for him.

The android *Kirk* would never have sent such a message —nor, for that matter, allowed it to go out if he could have prevented it.

Somehow, the real Kirk—the *human* Kirk—had survived the trap set for him by his counterpart. And finding his ship gone—the android having at least been successful in that—he had arranged for help.

How many vessels like the *Rheingold* carried his message? And how long would it be before one of them found another Federation starship?

How much longer after that before word reached Starfleet Command? Before someone began to wonder how Jim Kirk could be on Tranquillity Seven and on the *Enterprise* at the same time?

Martinez saw his concern mirrored in the face of his first officer. They exchanged knowing glances.

" . . . only too glad to be of service to the great Federation of Planets," continued Grundfest. "I have always . . . utmost respect for your diligence in . . . spaceways open for honest businessmen . . . myself."

"Yes," said Martinez. "Of course. Thank you for your assistance."

" . . . welcome," said the freighter captain.

In the next instant, his image faded.

As soon as it was gone, Martinez turned to his navigator.

"Bodrick, set a course for Tranquillity Seven." He leaned back in his command chair. "I want to get to the bottom of this."

"Shall I inform Starfleet that we are leaving our position?" asked Paultic.

"No," said the captain. "That won't be necessary, Lieutenant. I don't intend to be gone for very long."

He punched up security section on the panel by his armrest.

"Simmons here," came the answer.

"Mister Simmons, meet me in the briefing room," said Martinez. "It seems we've got an unusual situation on our hands."

"Aye, sir," said the security chief. "I'm on my way."

Martinez ended the conversation with a poke of his forefinger. He stood, making eye contact again with his first officer.

"Mister Stuart, I'd like to see you as well. Mister Banks, you have the conn."

As Martinez made his way to the turbolift, his first officer in tow, Banks slipped into the command chair.

* * *

"I don't know," said the android replica of Joaquin Martinez. "But we must get to him before anyone else does."

Simmons nodded. "Yes. That much is clear."

"And then what?" asked Stuart. "We certainly can't allow him to live. If Starfleet gets word that Kirk is on this ship—when he's officially in command of the *Enterprise*—the entire revolution will be placed in jeopardy."

Martinez nodded. "Kirk must die. Of course. But not right away. First, we need to determine the extent to which our leader's plan failed."

"Also, how much he knows," added Simmons. "And how much of that knowledge he has imparted to others."

"That shouldn't take very long to discover," said Stuart. He looked at the captain. "The human Martinez and Kirk trained together at Starfleet Academy, did they not?"

Martinez nodded. "They knew each other well enough for Kirk to confide in him. It should be a simple matter to find out what we need to know."

"And following that, an equally simple matter to dispose of him," said Simmons. He paused. "Who among the humans knows of Kirk's situation?"

"Paultic," said the captain. "So far, no one else."

"And no one else *needs* to know," remarked Stuart. "We can beam Kirk on board without resorting to help from the humans. Even present him with the honor guard due a visiting commander, so as not to arouse his suspicion—there are enough officers among us to carry it off."

"I'll make sure the corridors between the transporter area and his cabin are clear when he arrives," said Simmons. "So that no one else can say they saw him. Then, we can claim he never made it through the transporter—a malfunction."

"And I will deal with Paultic," said Stuart. "I'll tell him that this has turned out to be a matter that demands secrecy." He frowned slightly. "It's too bad that we can't risk the death of another officer so soon after Vedra's."

Simmons grunted in agreement.

Martinez took in the other androids' comments, mulled them over. He required no more than a moment.

"Yes," he said. "That is how it will be done. Simply—and quickly. And when it's over, we'll blame it on transporter failure."

He got up, eyed his fellow officers.

"See to the preparations," he said.

Chapter Seventeen

THE MIDAN WILDERNESS was wild, rough-cut and green, though it had little in the way of trees. Like most regions rich in coridium and phalachite, vegetable life was mostly restricted to ground cover.

Which was just as well, Spock told himself, attending to his magnification screen. It would be difficult enough to search this irregular terrain without the additional obstacle of forestation.

At the controls of the shuttlecraft, Ensign Chekov did his best to keep them steady in winds that had proven both savage and fickle. But every now and then, the *Columbus* pitched this way or that, eliciting groans from the other five humans on board.

Or four of them, anyway—Nurse Chapel and security officers Paikert, Wood, and Silverman. The captain, on the other hand, had so far displayed remarkable fortitude in that regard.

"We are approaching the fifty-mile perimeter," said Chekov. "Shell I head east or west, sir?"

"Try west," said *Kirk,* frowning as he peered into his own magnifier at the rear of the cabin.

"West it is," said the Russian, making the necessary adjustments. A second later, the *Columbus* began to describe a tight arc as it swung around some ninety degrees. At the same time, the bottom seemed to drop out of the air currents sustaining them, and they fell a good ten feet before the shuttlecraft stabilized.

More groans.

"Mister Chekov," said the captain, "I know it's difficult, but try to take those turns a little easier."

Nurse Chapel chuckled a little, despite her discomfort.

"Sorry," said the navigator. "The controls seem a little tight, sir—but it'll be smoother next time."

"Thanks," said *Kirk.*

Spock concentrated on the jumbled landscape that crawled beneath them. They seemed to be approaching an area of higher ground. He could make out at least one waterfall in the distance, warped by the bending of light at the edge of his screen.

"The terrain," he said out loud, "is growing more mountainous here." He looked up only long enough to glance at the captain. "That invites the possibility of caverns."

As if he had felt the Vulcan's gaze on him, *Kirk* looked up too. "Good," he said. "Then maybe we're on the right track here." And he turned his attention back to the magnifier even before Spock did.

Soon, they had come close enough to the waterfall to see that it was not one cascade, but three. Rising, they negotiated the cliffs from which the waters spilled, saw the white-churned rivers that were the source of the phenomenon.

"Captain," said Paikert, "I can take a turn there if you like. With all due respect, sir, you've been at that thing for hours. And *my* eyes haven't done any work at all."

Kirk seemed to hesitate before he responded.

"All right," he said finally. Spock heard the sounds of his moving away from the magnification station. "Give it a shot, Mister Paikert."

Spock received no such offer of relief. But then, he hadn't expected one. He had made it plain enough on other occasions that he preferred to see a job through to its end—no matter how long and difficult that job might be. And since he never allowed the strain to show, no one ever believed he was straining at all.

The indicator on the communications board lit up, accompanied by an insistent beeping. Wood, the closest one to it, picked up the speaker unit and handed it to the captain.

"Kirk here. Come in, Sulu."

"Just reporting in as you asked," said the helmsman, his voice only slightly garbled thanks to the boosting of the radio signal. "We haven't been having much luck here in the *Galileo II*. How about you, sir?"

"Nothing yet," said the captain. "But the day is still young. Keep looking, Lieutenant. Kirk out."

He handed the speaker back to Wood, and the security officer replaced it in its bracket.

Nurse Chapel sighed, leaned back against a bulkhead. Spock watched her out of the corner of his eye. She was smiling slightly, but not in the manner of one who has cause to be glad. Rather, it was what a human might have called a *brave* smile.

"I just hope," she said abruptly, "that these people are alive when we find them. I really do."

For a while, no one said anything.

Of course not. What was there to say? Despite the assurances that they had given the governor's committee, what were the odds of finding any of the victims alive?

After all, there was no possibility of financial gain here. Whatever confused hatred or longing had led someone to the crime of abduction might easily lead him—if it was a *him*—to other crimes as well. Murder was no more than a logical conclusion.

The cliffs receded behind them. The rivers twisted away; bare patches of dark stone appeared among the green flanks of the hills. And then, suddenly, the land fell away again.

A broad valley, with its own cascades and a shining flood at the bottom of it. Chekov dropped them down so they could get a better look at it.

What troubled Spock, however, went beyond the abductor's motivation and the likelihood of murder. There was something *wrong*, he felt, about this entire mission.

Was it the inexplicable delay between the Midans' call for help and their receipt of the message from Starfleet? Perhaps. Yes. But not that alone.

Spock prided himself on logic, not intuition. Every day of

his adult life, he'd fostered the one at the expense of the other.

But it was intuition that called to him now. As if a truth were lurking just around the next corner, and all he had to do was peer around that corner to find it.

Of course, he mused. One might as well ask a le matya to fly.

The shuttlecraft tipped to starboard as Chekov fought the unpredictable air currents. Below, the valley lurched.

"I'm doing my best," said the Russian, before any of his passengers could utter a complaint.

A moment later, the *Columbus* righted itself. By then, however, they were coming up to the far slope, and Chekov had to pull their nose up to clear it.

Spock scanned the escarpment, but there was nothing remarkable about it. No caves, no signs of human existence.

The shuttlecraft climbed past the top of the slope, giving them a magnificent view of the land beyond. It was a confusion of undulating ridges, separated by ravines of various depths. Once, apparently, this area had been host to a network of rivers; only a few still flowed.

"Uh-oh," said Chekov.

"What's the matter?" asked the captain.

"Pressure's dropping outside, sir. I think thet we're in for a storm soon. End you know how quickly the weather ken change in this vilderness."

"Yes," said *Kirk*. "I remember." He grunted. "All right. If it looks bad, we'll put down. But let's cover as much ground as we can until then."

"Aye, Keptain," said the navigator.

A glint of light—or was it Spock's imagination? He strained to see it again, but to no avail. And their course was now taking them farther from the area where the flash seemed to have originated.

"Captain," he said, "I request a change of course— ninety-five degrees to starboard."

Kirk leaned forward. "Have you got something, Spock?"

The Vulcan met his gaze. "I cannot say for certain," he noted. "But I believe I saw a reflection—in an area seemingly devoid of surface water."

The captain nodded. "That's good enough for me," he said. "Bring her about, Mister Chekov."

With surprising grace and fluidity, the *Columbus* wheeled on the air currents. It was only at the very end of her maneuver that they seemed to hit a little bump.

"Much better," said Chapel.

"You're welcome," responded Chekov.

It took a while before Spock found the glint again—but this time there was no mistaking it. The angle of the sun confirmed that it was a reflection, and probably not an independent light source.

"There it is," shouted Paikert, a fraction of a second later. "Just off the port bow."

"Indeed," confirmed Spock.

"Shell I slow down?" asked the Russian.

"Please do," said *Kirk.* "And take us in as low as you can."

Chekov obliged. The mountainscape gradually loomed closer.

And then Spock saw what had made the flash. The deep valley in which it was hidden had kept him from discerning it sooner. It was a mill of some sort, meant to harness the power of the water that cascaded down through the valley.

More curious, however, was the shape that sprawled below the mill. It was big and dark, and it had an oily sheen he had seen somewhere before. Some kind of machinery? That would explain the need for a mill.

But the colony had no mining projects going on this far out into the wilderness. Or at least, they weren't supposed to. The Federation never allowed mining operations to exceed a certain prescribed area, so as not to seriously disturb any local ecologies.

Yet here it was. Some sort of installation—though as the *Columbus* got closer, it became obvious to Spock that the purpose of the thing was not mining.

By then, the unoccupied crew members had been drawn to the window panels—the captain included. Wood whistled. Silverman muttered a curse beneath his breath.

"Any ideas," asked *Kirk,* "as to what that monstrosity out there might be?" Then, when no one answered, "Spock?"

"It is difficult to say," returned the Vulcan, "without closer inspection."

The captain hardly hesitated at all. It was as if he had already made his decision, even before he'd gotten his first officer's input.

"If we need to take a closer look," said *Kirk*, "then that's what we'll do. You see any safe landing sites, Mister Chekov?"

The navigator paused as he scanned the terrain. The shuttlecraft passed over the installation, came about, and approached it from another angle.

"There," said Chekov finally. He pointed at the forward viewscreen. "Thet ledge over there should do the trick."

Kirk peered over the Russian's shoulder at the screen. "All right," he barked. "Let's try it."

Chekov looped the *Columbus* around, managed to make it hover for a moment, and then landed it without incident. Sitting back from the controls, he took a deep breath and let it out slowly.

"Well done," said the captain. He indicated the compartment where the phasers were stored. "If you would be so kind, Mister Silverman."

"Aye, sir," said Silverman, and moved to pass out the pistols.

When *Kirk* received his, he adjusted the output mechanism. "Set 'em on stun," he told the others. "And be careful. It's entirely possible that this installation and our abductor are somehow related. If he *is* holed up here, there's a good chance we'll find him armed." He clipped the phaser onto his belt. "Mister Chekov and Nurse Chapel will remain with the ship—at least until we find out what's going on down there." He nodded to Spock. "The rest of you, come with me."

Neither Chekov nor Chapel were too happy about being left behind. Spock could tell by their expressions. But to their credit, neither of them complained out loud.

The hatch door opened, allowing a windblown chill into the shuttlecraft. The captain was the first to leap out, followed by Wood, Silverman, and Paikert. Spock brought up the rear.

The slope that stretched between them and the great, dark machine was long and steep. Once they started down, it was difficult to stop before they had reached the bottom of it—and another ledge of sorts.

The captain leaned close to Spock's ear so he could be heard over the din of the rushing river.

"Looks innocent enough," he said. "Let's keep going."

But Spock shook his head. "Not all at once. We should fan out on either side of the installation. It will give us a better chance of locating our adversary before he locates us."

Kirk glanced at him, smiled. "Of course," he said. "You didn't think I was going to bunch us all up, did you?"

Actually, the Vulcan had thought just that. On reflection, however, he remonstrated with himself.

The captain was a battle-trained veteran. He would never have made such an elementary mistake.

And yet, it had certainly seemed . . .

Kirk gestured to the security officers. "You three take the river side," he instructed them. They nodded, began to descend in that direction.

Another gesture, meant for Spock, and then the captain made his way down from the ledge. A moment later, the Vulcan followed, his phaser held at the ready.

As they approached the machine shape, it seemed even bigger, more menacing. But the surface they faced, at least, had no niches in it where an attacker might conceal himself.

Wood, Silverman, and Paikert skirted the installation to the left; *Kirk* and Spock came around to the right of it. Soon, the security officers were cut off from their view, and they were in the lee of the thing. The roar of the river was less deafening here, with no wind to carry the sound.

Spock couldn't help but note the strange, oily surface, the remarkably simple construction. Whatever purpose it served, it had been designed with an eye to economy.

And there *was* something familiar about it—naggingly so. But there was no time now for lengthy consideration of the matter. There seemed to be an irregular series of projections along the machine's flank up ahead—choice spots for a sniper—and the captain was proceeding toward them at an incautious pace.

He was just about to call to *Kirk* when he heard it—the sound of phaser beams ripping the air.

Spock whirled, saw the slope above them sizzle with errant phaser fire. And the thin, red beams were originating somewhere on the other side of the installation.

The Vulcan didn't hesitate. He darted around the perimeter of the machine, careful to use it for cover as much as possible. Lurid shafts of phaserlight continued to stab the slope. There was a sudden cry, and Wood fell sprawling where Spock could see him.

Fighting the urge to go to the crewman's aid, Spock peered around the corner of the installation. What he saw was completely unexpected.

Flat on their bellies, the two remaining security officers were firing in the direction of the river—where, hidden among the rocks and half-immersed in the water, a seemingly large number of adversaries had pinned them with crisscrossing blasts.

As Spock watched, Paikert scrambled to his feet and tried to make it to the machine.

Instantly, two of the hidden stood to get a better shot at him. Spock aimed, fired, and dropped one.

But the other caught Paikert a couple of yards short of his goal. The big man grunted with the impact and folded nearly at the Vulcan's feet.

"Spock!" It was the captain, just behind him. "Damn it, what's going on?"

"Ambush," he said, turning to look at *Kirk*. "They were hiding in the . . ." He was only halfway through his answer when he saw the beam lance out at him. The force of it knocked his phaser out of his hand, sent him spinning into the machine.

"All right," said *Kirk*, taking a step closer. "Move away from the machine."

The Vulcan fought to make sense of it. "Jim . . ." he began.

"I told you to *move*," said *Kirk*.

Spock measured the look in the captain's eye and wondered about his sudden concern for the machine.

Then, abruptly, the pieces started falling into place.

Spock glanced at the oily metal surface, remembered finally where he had seen it before. Only it had been in a cave then, and the lighting had been much different, and the machine's components had been configured to fit a more confined space.

Of course.

Kirk must have seen the realization in his eyes. "That's right," he said, coming closer still. "Though I must confess I'm disappointed. I thought you would have figured it out before this."

Spock heard another cry—Silverman's, he told himself.

"I regret," he said, "that I failed in that regard. But not for the same reason, perhaps."

Without moving his eyes—and thereby giving the thought away—the Vulcan gauged the distance between himself and the android. Just one more step, he urged inwardly.

Kirk took it, stopped. Smiled. "No. Not for the same reason." The briefest of pauses. "Sweet dreams, Mis—"

Before he could finish, Spock lunged. Too late, the android triggered his phaser. The beam zagged wildly as they went down in a tangle of struggling limbs.

Spock found *Kirk's* wrist, grabbed it, twisted—and the phaser tumbled free. Pressing his advantage, he brought his fist up—then drove it down across the face that was his friend's.

Once.

And again.

But before he could strike a third time, the android lashed out. Spock felt his throat seized in a grip like coridium; felt the sudden and intense pressure on his windpipe.

The Vulcan's powerful fists beat against *Kirk's* shoulders in an attempt to break the android's hold. But *Kirk* had the leverage now. No force Spock could muster would make him let go.

The phaser . . .

Spock turned his head just enough to catch a glimpse of it. It was only a few feet away.

He threw an arm out suddenly, reaching for the weapon. His long fingers stretched to grasp it.

But it was too far. Inches too far.

The android's grip tightened. And from the edges of Spock's vision, the darkness gradually swept inward.

"Wait!" cried Chapel. "There's the captain!"

She gestured with the hand that held the phaser.

Sure enough, it was *Kirk* hoisting himself up onto the lower ledge. And he seemed in no great hurry.

Chekov relaxed. For the last few minutes, he'd been torn in two different directions. Part of him had wanted to go charging down the slope as soon as he'd seen the phaser fire. But another part of him recognized his duty—to stay with the shuttlecraft until instructed otherwise.

His compromise had been to grab a phaser pistol and to climb out after Christine. And to kneel alongside the *Columbus,* hoping the others would send back a sign that they were all right.

Then the phaser fire had stopped—as abruptly as it had begun. And in that instant, Chekov had decided to follow his shipmates after all.

"Yes," he agreed. "It's him. End he seems to be in reasonably good health." For a moment, he watched the captain start the difficult trek back up the slope. Then he deactivated his phaser, hitched it onto his belt, and started down to meet *Kirk* halfway.

Christine was right behind him, her nurse's instincts alert in case the captain signaled that she was needed. But *Kirk* signaled no such thing. Instead, he held up a hand to let them know all was well.

But the slope was steep, and it was hard to descend slowly. In a matter of seconds, Chekov was almost face-to-face with his commanding officer.

"I tried to contact you," said the captain, "but there was no response. Now I see why."

"We saw phaser fire," said Chekov. "Is everything all right, sir?"

Kirk nodded as Christine joined them. "It's all under control now. I think we've got the man we were looking for."

"No one was hurt?" asked the nurse.

"No one," said the captain. "We took him without any casualties."

"What about the kidnep victims?" asked the Russian.

Kirk frowned again, shook his head. "No sign—so far. But we haven't managed to get inside the installation yet. Hopefully, once we do . . ."

"I request permission," said Chekov, "to help in the search."

"Me too, sir," said Chapel.

The captain glanced at the unattended shuttlecraft, then regarded them again.

"The *Columbus* doesn't seem to be in any danger," he said finally. "Permission granted."

And turning, he started back down toward the installation.

Glad for the opportunity to make themselves useful, Chekov and Chapel fell in behind him.

Chapter Eighteen

PAULTIC CAME INTO SICKBAY just as Genti was leaving. They nodded to one another.

"Under the weather?" asked the communications officer.

"Under something," muttered Genti, and was gone.

Doctor Chin stood next to one of the diagnostic platforms, peering up at the dormant life-functions display with her arms folded tightly across her chest.

She didn't turn away from it, either, until Paultic was more than halfway across the room. And as soon as she'd acknowledged his presence there, she resumed her scrutiny of the thing.

"I don't want to say anything," remarked Paultic, "but you're staring at a dead display."

Chin grunted, supplying no more answer than that. But a moment later, she spun about, her dark eyes alert as if after a long sleep.

"So," she said, "what can I do for *you?*"

Paultic looked down into her delicately sculptured face. And blushed, despite himself.

"It's not really a medical problem," he told her.

She smiled. "I'll be the judge of that."

"No—really. It's actually more of a . . . um, political problem."

The smile faded a little. "Really?"

He nodded. "I need some advice."

She searched his eyes, saw the trouble there. "All right," she said. "Then let's repair to my office."

A couple of moments later, she had closed the door behind him. They took seats on either side of her desk.

She regarded him patiently, waiting for him to begin. So he did.

"On my last shift," he said, "we received a message from a freighter captain. He said that the captain of one of our other starships—the *Enterprise*—had been stranded or something on Tranquillity Seven."

Chin raised an eyebrow. "Interesting planet to get stranded on."

"Just what *I* thought—especially since we just dropped that archaeologist off there. But there's more interesting to come." He licked his lips. "It's still not clear to me how this captain got separated from his ship—I mean, the message was garbled, and we didn't get too many details from the freighter anyway. But Martinez seemed to understand the whole thing without too much trouble. No sooner do we break contact than he's asking Bodrick to chart a course for Trank Seven. *Again.*"

The doctor leaned back in her chair, truly interested now.

He shrugged. "Naturally, I began to set up a channel to the nearest starbase, figuring that the captain will want to report his being out of position if the Romulans should start something. But just for protocol's sake, I clear it with him. And what do you think he says? 'No thanks, Lieutenant. We won't be gone long enough for it to matter.' Or something to that effect."

Chin regarded him. "That *is* a little strange—under the circumstances. I was under the impression that we weren't to budge from our position."

Paultic nodded. "You're right—we weren't. I was on the board when the orders came in. And yet, Martinez just diverges from them on his own authority. Worse, he doesn't even let anybody know he's leaving." He cursed softly. "It's more than a little strange, Doc—it's court-martial material."

Chin's forehead wrinkled. "I see."

"That's not even the end of it. As soon as my shift is over,

Stuart takes me aside. 'I don't want you discussing what happened on the bridge with anyone,' he says. 'Not even those who were there at the time. This is a much bigger deal than it seems. Crucial, in fact, to Federation security.'

"And you should have seen the way he looked at me. As if he was ready to kill me if I didn't agree to keep my mouth shut." Paultic looked down and saw that his hands had balled into fists. He relaxed them. "I hate to tell you what I think, Doc."

"Go ahead," she urged him.

"I've got a hunch that the captain and Stuart are mixed up in something serious—something the Federation wouldn't quite approve of. And they're willing to risk leaving their position in order to keep it covered up."

Chin's dark eyes narrowed. "Then you think this other captain—the one who's stranded on Tranquillity Seven—is somehow in league with them?"

Paultic nodded. "Kirk, James Tiberius. I looked him up in the computer, to see if I could find out anything useful about him. His record, as it turns out, is exemplary—but he knows Martinez pretty well. It seems they attended the academy together."

The doctor harumphed, much as she would have over a distrubing reading on a diagnostic display.

"Kirk," she repeated. "I believe Vedra spoke of him once." She scowled. "But she seemed impressed with him—and Vedra did not impress easily."

"One never knows," said Paultic. "Up until now, I was pretty impressed with Captain Martinez." He shook his head. "Hell, I would've given my life for him if he'd asked me to."

Chin chuckled dryly. "Yes," she said. "I echo the sentiment." For a moment, her eyes went unfocused as she contemplated Paultic knew-not-what. But after a while, they took on a new hardness, a new opacity. She fixed him with that gaze.

"I must tell you," she said, "that under normal circumstances, I would have a hard time giving credence to any of this. But I've been seeing some pretty puzzling things myself."

Paultic leaned forward. "Like what?"

She indicated the area outside her office with a tilt of her head. "Genti—and the others in engineering. They all have a touch of radiation sickness. It seems that one of the security people was sent in to inventory the dilithium, and he didn't seal the chamber up right when he left."

"But why is security counting crystals? Isn't that engineering's job?"

"It always has been," said Chin. "Now, with Vedra gone, I can see why the captain would want to tighten the controls down there. But to send a security officer to inventory the dilithium? It seems like overkill."

She winced at her own choice of words.

"And then, of course, there is the matter of Vedra herself."

Paultic saw the doctor blanch a little.

"That's right," he said. "You doubted it was a suicide right from the beginning."

She nodded. "Yes, I did. But I put my trust in the captain's hands. And when he told me that the overwhelming evidence pointed to suicide—even after a second investigation—I talked myself into believing it."

She paused.

"But now, I wonder if I could've been right in the first place." Her brow furrowed suddenly, and her hand shot to her mouth.

"What is it?" he asked.

Her hand fell away. "The containers," she breathed.

Paultic saw where she was headed. "None of us knew what was in them," he said. "We still don't." He pounded his fist on the desk, and the synthetic material shivered. "Damn! Maybe that's what it's all about—the contents of those containers."

Realization devolved upon him almost too fast for him to sort it out.

"What if Martinez and Stuart found something valuable down there on Exo III? And they wanted to keep it for themselves—or split it with those geologists—without the Federation ever finding out it existed?"

"And then someone stumbled onto their plan," said Chin, her voice strangely stiff and emotionless now. "Someone like Vedra."

"They would have had to get rid of her," said Paultic.

But the doctor shook her head suddenly—as if she were trying to bring herself out of a trance.

"No," she said. "What about Banks? He was down there with them on Exo III. Martinez detests him. He would never have involved himself in a scheme alongside Banks—never have allowed himself to become dependent on Banks' goodwill."

Paultic swallowed. "Doc, things are different between them now. I used to catch them glaring at each other all the time—but not anymore. Just before, when the captain left the bridge, he turned *the conn* over to Banks. And it's not the first time that's happened since we left Exo III—though I would've called it pretty farfetched before that."

Chin took a deep breath, let it out slowly. "Do you know what we're talking about here, Lieutenant? What we're accusing our *captain* of?" She counted the charges off on her fingers. "Conspiracy. Treason. *Murder.*"

He nodded, suddenly aware of a weakness in his knees. "I know. And we don't know how far it goes—or who's in on it."

"Vedra would have called it all speculation," said the doctor. *"Wild* speculation." She massaged a temple with two fingers. "Perhaps Martinez and the others have a perfectly good explanation for all this."

Paultic smiled a bitter smile. "And perhaps not."

She looked at him soberly. "And perhaps not," she repeated. Then she drew herself up and leaned forward over her desk. "In any case, we must have evidence before we can make any formal charges."

"Then we'll have to get some," he told her.

"Agreed. And in the meantime, I'll stay on top of this Kirk affair. Doctors have certain privileges, and I mean to exercise them."

He held out his hand.

"Thanks for listening, Doc."

She took the proffered hand, surprising him with two things—the firmness of her grasp and the iciness of her skin.

I guess, he told himself, she's as scared as I am.

* * *

It wasn't that Kaith was such a bad host. In point of fact, Kirk had come to appreciate his dry, unexpected wit. And he had turned out to be a formidable chess player in the bargain.

It was just that the waiting had begun to get to him. He couldn't leave the spaceport; he couldn't even venture out of the portmaster's office for fear of being spotted.

True, his accommodations were spacious in comparison to his quarters on the *Enterprise*—but they still felt confining. It was one thing to live in a closet, out there in the infinite reaches of space—and quite another to dwell in even the most sumptuous planetbound palace.

One thing the waiting did, however, was give him time to heal. The cruel wounds left by his bonds responded to the salves Kaith had given him. Soon, there were only thin red scars, which would likely fade to nothing.

Unfortunately, it also gave him time to think. And thinking inevitably led to worry.

If the *Enterprise*'s abrupt departure had been caused by the Romulans, the situation must have been about to break wide open. Which meant a brief and deadly confrontation, rather than a prolonged jockeying for position.

By now, certainly, the conflict must have been resolved— one way or the other. Then why hadn't the ship returned for him? Why hadn't Spock brought it back to Trank Seven?

The possibilities made him shudder.

And then, after he had been Kaith's guest for more than a week, word came that there was a ship on its way to pick him up.

"No," said the portmaster, aware of Kirk's disappointment. "It's not the *Enterprise*. But it *is* a Federation vessel, and it'll get you a lot closer to the *Enterprise*."

"Did you catch its name?" he asked.

The blond man nodded. "The *Hood*. Commanded by one Joaquin Martinez." He must have seen something in Kirk's face then, because he added: "Do you know him?"

The captain nodded. "We went to school together."

"Good," said Kaith, pausing for a moment to light his pipe. "Then perhaps you'll be able to get some of those answers you're looking for."

Kirk grunted. "Perhaps I will."

Chapter Nineteen

"DOCTOR MCCOY?"

McCoy, who had only been recalibrating the tricorders anyway—a tedious task, even for someone restricted to light duty—turned eagerly to see who'd called his name.

Clifford was standing with K'leb at the entrance to sickbay, awaiting the chief medical officer's acknowledgment. The crewman looked a little fidgety, as if he were uncomfortable about something.

"If you're not busy, sir," he said, "we'd like to have a word with you."

We?

McCoy grunted, swiveling on his stool. "Well," he said, "don't just stand there, you two. Come in and take a load off your feet."

Clifford looked grateful. "Thank you, sir."

He gestured to the P'othparan and they approached together, taking the pair of empty stools to McCoy's left.

"All right, then," said the doctor. "Now, is this an official matter—or a personal one?"

Clifford frowned. K'leb just looked from one to the other of them, his eyes darting like insects trapped under glass.

"It's . . . both," said the crewman. "In a way, that is." He shrugged. "Depending on how you look at it."

McCoy couldn't help but smile.

"Son," he advised, "if you've got something to say, come out and say it."

But the crewman's frown only deepened. "It's hard to know—" he started to say, then stopped himself—as if his resolve had suddenly stiffened in midsentence.

He looked the doctor in the eye. "Sir, K'leb thinks that Captain Kirk *isn't* Captain Kirk. He says that the Captain Kirk on the bridge now is . . . an impostor."

McCoy wasn't quite sure what he'd expected to hear—but that certainly wasn't it.

"An impostor?" he echoed, unable to keep the laughter out of his voice entirely. "What gives him that impression?"

As if he understood the question, the P'othparan fashioned a rapid-fire answer. Of course, the doctor had no idea what he was talking about.

He looked to Clifford for help.

"K'leb says," offered the crewman, "that he can feel *inside* the captain. And that there's nothing there."

"You mean," said McCoy, "that he doesn't feel any affection from the captain. Any warmth."

Clifford shook his head. "No. That's how it sounded to me too, at first. But K'leb means something else. He's saying that there's *nothing* inside the captain. Nothing at all." He paused. "Before, he says, there *was* something there. It wasn't affection, as you say. But it was *something.*"

McCoy regarded Clifford, then the boy. "Before?" he asked, still disinclined to take this too seriously. After all, empathy was such a subjective talent. And K'leb had some justifiable reasons for resenting Jim Kirk—which certainly could have colored his perceptions. "Before *what?*"

Clifford glanced at the P'othparan. "Before the captain beamed down for shore leave." He turned to McCoy again. "He says that the person he met in sickbay—when you were recuperating, after you'd just come back—wasn't the captain." He licked his lips. "In fact, according to K'leb, that wasn't a person at all."

McCoy looked at him askance. "Not a person, you say? Then what?"

Clifford looked miserable saying it. "A demon, sir. At least, that's the way it translates."

The doctor started to make a joke out of it, stopped himself. Judging from their expressions, he didn't think either Clifford or K'leb would have appreciated it.

"A demon," he echoed.

The crewman nodded.

"I see," said McCoy. "And what about *you,* Mister Clifford? What do *you* think of all this?"

Clifford shrugged. "It's a little hard to believe. In fact, I'd say it was nonsense altogether . . . if it wasn't coming from K'leb." He glanced again at the P'othparan. "As you know, I've spent a lot of time with him, breaking down his language for input into the translator system. And what I've seen . . . his empathic abilities are amazingly accurate, sir. Not raw, as you might expect, but—well, polished. Sharpened to a fine point."

McCoy folded his arms across his chest. "All right," he said. "Let's put those abilities to the test." He regarded the boy. "What am I feeling now?"

Clifford relayed the question. K'leb nodded once, then replied without hesitation.

"He says," the crewman translated, "that you are skeptical, for the most part. But also the least bit afraid—because you're starting to wonder if he could possibly be on to something."

It was true—all of it. And after the exactness of K'leb's analysis, the cracks in his skepticism were widening.

The doctor snorted. "All right," he said. "I'll look into it." And even as he said this, he thought of the way to approach the matter. "The captain owes me a physical, anyway, and it's high time he took it. If there's anything *different* about him, I'll know it soon enough."

He smiled wryly at K'leb. "Satisfied?"

Clifford translated, and the P'othparan nodded. But he didn't smile back.

"Good," said McCoy. "Then get out of here. I've still got a heap of tricorders to work over."

The crewman rose, and K'leb along with him.

"Thank you, sir," said Clifford.

"Don't mention it."

McCoy watched them go for a moment. Then he got up and went over to the intercom.

191

A flick of the toggle switch activated it. And it took but a press of a button to connect him with the bridge.

"McCoy to Captain Kirk," he said into the grating.

There was a sharp click, and the captain's voice came over the intercom circuits.

"I'm a little busy now, Bones. Can we talk later?"

"Sorry, Jim," said the doctor. "You've put this off long enough. Our bet was two weeks, not two years."

The captain seemed to hesitate.

"Jim? You still there?"

"Of course, Bones. I'm just a little preoccupied with the search."

"Well, you're not doing any good up here anyway. So why don't you hightail it down to sickbay and get it over with?"

Another long pause.

"I don't think so, Bones. I really am busy."

McCoy grunted. "Look," he said, "you're always going to be busy with one thing or another. Now, are you going to come down here willingly, or do I have to pull rank?"

"Rank?" repeated the captain. "Why? Do you think I'm unfit for duty, Doctor?"

"How am I supposed to know," asked McCoy, "until you take your blasted physical?"

The longest pause of all.

"Tell you what," came the response. "As soon as I come back from planetside, I'll turn myself in."

"Planetside? But you just beamed back up."

"I know. And I'm finding it very difficult to sit here when there are people disappearing down *there*. I'm going back down."

McCoy found himself frowning. "All right," he said. "But as soon as you set foot on the *Enterprise* again, I expect you to make a beeline for sickbay. And that, my friend, is an order."

"I hear you, Bones. Kirk out."

The doctor leaned away from the intercom and the wall. He had a queasy feeling in his stomach that hadn't been there before.

"Nah," he muttered out loud. Then, again, "Nah."

Suddenly, he was gripped by another sensation—that he

was not alone there in sickbay. That there was someone else, standing just beyond the edge of peripheral vision. *Listening.*

He whirled.

And started when he saw the tall, slim figure in the shadows.

But in the next moment, recognition colored his perception. He felt a flush of embarrassment climb into his cheeks.

"Damn it," he rumbled. "Don't *ever* sneak up on me, Christine."

The nurse smiled apologetically. "Sorry, Doctor. I didn't mean to frighten you."

McCoy turned away to hide the heat in his face. "You didn't frighten me. You just . . . surprised me."

"Then I'm sorry I surprised you," she amended.

He looked at her. "What are you doing back here, anyway? I thought you were going to stick it out until the search was over?"

Christine shrugged. "It looks like it's going to take longer than I thought. The captain decided I'd be more valuable up here."

The captain.

McCoy sighed. The queasy feeling had returned.

"Are you all right?" asked Christine.

He shrugged. "Did you see the pair I was talking with before?"

The nurse shook her head. "No. I was at the computer—catching up on what happened while I was gone."

He went over to one of the stools, plunked himself down on it. "Clifford and K'leb were in here just now. It seems that K'leb, with his empathic talents, thinks the captain's an impostor. That the fellow up on the bridge now is someone *posing* as the captain."

Christine looked as doubtful as *he* must have looked earlier. "It sounds a little farfetched," she said.

"That's right," said the doctor. "It does." He felt himself frowning again. "But I told them I'd check into it. And I did—just now. I called the captain down for that physical he's been trying to duck."

"And?" asked Christine.

"He ducked it again. Said he was going back down to Midos Five—to lead the search."

Her smile gained in enthusiasm. "Sounds like the captain to me," she said.

McCoy shook his head. "I'm not so sure."

"What do you mean?" asked the nurse.

"It *didn't* sound like the captain. The words were right, but the way he came out with them . . ." He tried to recall the conversation objectively. "When I referred to our bet, and then to the physical, he seemed to hesitate—as if he didn't know what I was talking about." He paused, remembering. "And then, after I made it clear I was referring to the physical . . . that's when he told me he was beaming down again. As if he'd made that decision right then and there."

Christine seemed caught between laughter and sobriety. "Doctor," she said, "you know how gullible I am. If this is a joke . . ."

He shook his head, more insistently than before. "No, Christine. No joke. I may be way off base here, but it's definitely not a joke."

"Then you think," she said, "that there really *is* an impostor—pretending to be the captain?"

He took a deep breath, blew it out. "I think," he said, "that it's a *possibility.*"

For a moment, she just stood there, looking at him. Appearing to absorb his seriousness.

Then her air of easy optimism returned to her. "Well," she said, "until we find out one way or the other, I'm starved. I think I'll try to scare up some dinner."

"Bon appétit," said McCoy.

As she left sickbay, he returned to his work on the tricorders. Unfortunately, they hadn't recalibrated themselves while his attention was elsewhere.

It only occurred to him later that Christine hadn't asked him to join her. But then, he told himself, she might have preferred more cheerful conversation with her meal.

"Are you sure?" DeLong asked.

"That's what I heard," said Critelli. "And I was right there on the bridge, standing not three feet from him.

Waiting for him to sign the damned requisition order already."

"And he said he was beaming down again?"

"Absolutely. Without a doubt." He looked at her, his dark eyes questioning. "Why? What makes this so important to you, anyway?"

DeLong shrugged, perhaps a bit too quickly. "I don't know—I thought maybe I'd volunteer to go with him."

Critelli smiled disbelievingly. "You're kidding, right? You want to spend your time in one of those cramped, little shuttlecraft, straining your neck to pick out some tiny glitch a hundred feet below? Eating in it, sleeping in it— getting bounced around at the mercy of those mountain winds?"

She grunted. "When you put it that way, how can a girl resist?"

"Great," he said. "Then you'll be free next tour of duty? To show me how you use those *dallis'karim?*"

DeLong shook her head. "Maybe some other time. By then I hope to be straining my neck in one of those cramped, little shuttlecraft."

Leaving Critelli openmouthed, she strode down the corridor in the direction of the transporter room. Her footfalls echoed from bulkhead to bulkhead.

It had been foolish of her to try to arrange a—a *what?* a rendezvous? a *date?*—with the captain while he was rushing from one duty to the next. Especially right after what had happened to Doctor McCoy, and in the middle of the crew's recall from Tranktown.

But if she could wangle a berth beside him on one of the shuttlecraft . . . spend some time with him, get him to know her better . . .

There was no guarantee, of course. But he *had* shown at least a spark of affection when he apologized to her for the incident in the gym. Not to mention respect—even admiration.

The doors to the transporter room parted and she saw Chief Kyle standing over the console. He barely looked up when she came in, intent as he was on fine-tuning the controls.

"Denise," he said. "What brings you here, love?"

"I heard that the captain was beaming down again. I wanted to go along this time."

Kyle shrugged. "Well, you heard right. But he's not leaving for a little while yet." He finished setting one of the dials and raised his head. "But if I were you, I wouldn't wait here to join the expedition. He can't very well dismiss someone else at the last moment to make room for you."

She nodded. "Do you have any idea where he is now? The captain, I mean?"

"Don't know for sure," said Kyle, returning to his work. "But I wouldn't be surprised if he was in his quarters. I'd want to freshen up a little before I subjected myself to the confines of a shuttlecraft."

She had to smile. "Thanks, Chief."

"Think nothing of it," said Kyle, glaring at his gauges.

It wasn't a long trip, really, from the transporter room to the captain's cabin. Most of it was spent in the turbolift.

By the time DeLong reached the right level, however, her knees were a little weak. Steeling herself, she exited the lift and negotiated the length of the corridor. It was quiet here, as most of the command staff was either up on the bridge or planetside, engaged in the search.

She stopped before the captain's door, knocked once. She was just about to knock a second time, thinking that the first knock had perhaps been too timid, when the door slid aside.

The captain was standing just inside the doorway. She couldn't tell if he had just arrived or was about to leave.

He looked at her.

"Yes, Ensign?"

For a moment, she had the same feeling that she'd had the other day in the corridor. That the captain didn't know her from Adam. But that couldn't be. Not after that business in the gym, and what he had said to her afterward.

No. He was just acting the way a commanding officer is supposed to act: aloof, reserved.

"Begging your pardon, sir," she began, "but I understand you're going back down to the shuttlecraft."

Kirk continued to stare. Then, it was as if he'd shaken off some matter that preoccupied him, and he smiled a little. "News travels fast on this ship." He stepped aside and gestured politely. "Please come in, Ensign. There's no need to discuss whatever you've come about out here in the corridor."

DeLong entered, found a spot where she could stand. The captain gestured again.

"Have a seat," he told her.

She took the proffered chair—an antique wood-and-leather affair that must have dated back to the twentieth century. It stood beside a bookcase of the same vintage—and actually filled with books, rather than tapes.

"Now then," said *Kirk,* pulling up one of the ship's standard chairs, "what's on your mind, Ensign?"

She looked him in the eye. "When you go back down there," she said, "I want to be part of the relief party."

He seemed to consider her words individually. "I see," he said after a while. He leaned back in his chair. "Actually, I had already picked out some individuals to accompany me."

DeLong had been expecting that. It didn't faze her.

"I appreciate that, sir. But those are people who've been ordered to go. Surely, it's better to have someone in the shuttlecraft who really *wants* to be there."

The captain's gaze appeared to intensify. "I can't help but agree," he said. "But *why* do you want to be there?"

She lifted her hands out of her lap, let them fall back again. "I want to help," was what came out. And of course, that was part of it, so she wasn't exactly lying.

"A sense of duty," he offered.

"Something like that," she said. "And a desire to see a killer brought to justice."

The captain's eyebrows went up. "Killer?" he echoed. "We don't know that just yet. All we know is that people have disappeared."

She nodded. "Yes sir. Make that *kidnapper,* then. I'd like to see him stopped."

Kirk leaned forward again. "Very well, Ensign. You've gotten yourself a berth. Be ready to leave as soon as you're called."

She suppressed a grin. "Thank you, sir. You won't regret it."

"Thank *you,*" said the captain. "We can use more people like you down there." He stood then, signaling that their talk was over, so she followed suit.

Just as she stepped over the threshold, she was seized by an impulse. Turning again, she addressed him.

"You know," said DeLong, "I had the funniest feeling just before, when you opened the door. You looked as if you'd never seen me before. As if you'd forgotten even my name."

Kirk smiled as warmly as she had ever seen him smile. "Forgive me," he said. "I could never have forgotten *that.*"

She had an urge to ask him what it was, to press him for it, but decided that that would be childish.

"Forgiven," she said instead. "Again. See you later?"

"Yes," he said. "See you later, Ensign."

Flushed with success, she turned on her heel and made her way back down the corridor.

Chapter Twenty

WHEN KIRK MATERIALIZED in the transporter room of the *Hood,* Joaquin Martinez and his officers were there to greet him.

"Jim," said Martinez.

Kirk stepped off the transporter platform, shook his friend's hand. "It's been a long time," he said.

"Too long," said Martinez. "I'm glad to have you aboard —although I have to admit, I don't quite understand the circumstances."

Kirk grunted. "Neither do I, I'm afraid. But I can assure you, I intend to learn."

"Of course," said Martinez. He indicated his command staff with a sweep of his arm. "Let me introduce you to some of my people."

Kirk recognized a couple of them—Commander Stuart and Banks, the science officer. The others were presented to him one at a time.

But after he'd finished, it seemed to him that someone was missing. He turned back to Martinez.

"Vedra," he said, plucking the name out of memory. "Your engineering officer. Is she still with you?"

The captain's expression suddenly went slack.

Kirk looked at the others, saw similar dismay. He gathered that he'd uncovered some kind of sore spot.

"Lieutenant Vedra," said Martinez finally, "is dead, Jim."

Kirk's heart sank.

"Damn," he said. "I'm sorry, Joaquin."

Martinez nodded. "So am I."

He placed a hand on Kirk's shoulder.

"Come on," he said. "We can talk on the way to your quarters."

Kirk nodded, followed him out. Nor did he compound his error by bringing up the subject of Vedra again.

It wasn't long before they reached the cabin that had been set aside for him. Martinez opened the door.

"Is this all right for you?" he asked.

Kirk took in the room at a glance. It was well appointed for a visitor's cabin.

"Fine," he said. "More than I expected, Joaquin."

Martinez shrugged. "It's not every day I get a chance to play host to another starship captain."

"No," said Kirk. "I imagine not."

Martinez indicated one of the two seats in the room. "Mind if I sit down for a while? Or do you want to get some shut-eye?"

Kirk shook his head. "No. Stay. Shut-eye's the least of my problems."

Martinez sat.

Kirk looked at him. "Joaquin, I need to know what's happened to my ship. When I last saw her, we were being held in this sector against the possibility of hostilities with the Romulans. Do you know if . . ."

"If those hostilities ever materialized?"

"Well . . . yes."

Martinez smiled sympathetically. "No, Jim. They haven't. Unfortunately, that's all I can tell you about the *Enterprise*. We haven't had any contact with her—direct or otherwise."

Kirk frowned. "I suppose no news is still good news."

Martinez regarded him. "Then you have no idea *at all* what happened to her?"

"None," he confirmed.

"I see." Martinez gazed at his open palms, rubbed his hands together. "If you were to tell me what happened to *you,* maybe we could come up with some theories. That is, unless . . ."

"It's all right," said Kirk. "I'm mortified, but I'm not that mortified."

Martinez smiled again. "Good."

Kirk laid out all the details for him, just as they happened. By the time he had finished, the captain of the *Hood* seemed lost in thought.

"So," he said finally, "you never found out any more about this con man for whom you were mistaken?"

"The portmaster made some inquiries for me among the various ships' captains—but none of them remembered anyone who particularly fit my description. Of course, he probably hadn't had time to shop around for the cheapest passage. More than likely, he'd hopped the first outbound vessel."

"Right," said Martinez. "Then, for all you know, he never even existed in the first place. I mean, you have no proof."

Kirk shrugged. "Only what the Rythrian told me." He peered at his opposite number. "Why? What are you getting at?"

Martinez stood, placed his hands in the small of his back, and stretched. "Just bear with me for a minute," he said. He stopped stretching, but his hands remained clasped behind him. "Now, outside of the portmaster—Kaith—and the ones who held you prisoner, no one could vouch for *your* existence either. Right?"

"Right," said Kirk. "But is that important now?"

"Maybe not to you," said Martinez.

And before Kirk could move, there was a phaser pointed at his face.

"But to *us,* it's quite important."

Kirk looked past the phaser at Martinez.

"If this is a joke," he said, "it's not funny."

"It's no joke," said the other man.

"Then I don't get it, Joaquin. But I'll venture a guess that there's some connection between what happened to me in Tranktown and what's happening to me here. Am I right?"

Martinez nodded. "It's to your credit that you escaped our trap," he said, "that you managed to make it this far. But your death is essential."

"To whom?" asked Kirk. "Who's this *us* you referred to?"

He had hoped the question would distract Martinez, but the phaser remained where it was. Nor did Kirk see anything close at hand that could be used as a counterweapon.

"There's no need for you to know that," said Martinez. "You may think of us as those who will replace you—those who will realize the full potential of the human race."

It wasn't so much the words themselves as the way he said them. Kirk racked his brain to remember where he had heard that tone of voice before.

"Look," he said, "there's got to be a way to work this out, Joaquin. You don't have to kill me to—"

"There is *no* other way," insisted Martinez.

"And it's worth the risk you're taking? Losing everything you worked so hard to attain?"

It was plain from the man's expression that he wasn't going to tolerate too many more questions. Kirk tensed, ready to grab for the phaser as soon as Martinez opened his mouth.

He was completely unprepared for what happened next: the sliding aside of the door and the sudden appearance of a figure in Medical Corps blue.

Apparently, Martinez hadn't been expecting company either—because he whirled as if to fire.

Seeing this, Kirk sprang. The phaser fired, emitting a beam of dark red energy that ripped screechingly through the heavy metal of the bulkhead—but missed the newcomer.

For a moment, the two starship captains were locked in a struggle for the weapon. Then, suddenly, Kirk felt himself flung across the cabin, into the bunk that had been prepared for him.

Before he had time to wonder at the other man's strength, he realized that Martinez's effort had cost him the phaser. It was scuttling noisily across the deck, unattended.

Kirk dived for it, closed his hand about it—and then Martinez was on top of him, twisting with unholy force. Kirk howled with pain and the phaser came squirting free.

Abruptly, he found himself up again—pinned to the wall with just one of Martinez's hands. The other drew back, met the side of his face with bludgeoning force.

Everything went black for a second. Then he was awake again and Martinez was cocking his fist for another blow.

"Stop it!" cried a feminine voice.

Drawn to it, Kirk saw the medical officer—noted for the first time that she was a woman.

"Don't move," she said. "Either of you."

"Kai," said Martinez, peering at her over his shoulder. "I'm glad you're here. I—"

"It won't work," she said. "I saw you aim this thing at me. And it's set to kill." She adjusted the force setting down to stun. "Now—slowly—let him go."

Martinez did as he was told—at first. But no sooner did Kirk feel himself released than the other man whirled and lunged.

He was just the least bit too slow. The phaser beam hit him full in the chest, knocking him off his feet.

In the aftermath of the blast, nobody moved—least of all, Martinez. He lay twisted on the metal decking, his head at an angle that wasn't very pleasant to look at.

Kirk's eyes locked with the woman's as he knelt beside Martinez.

"I . . . I thought it was on *stun,*" she said softly.

Kirk felt the man's neck for a pulse. There wasn't any.

And even at close range, a stun setting shouldn't kill.

Then he noticed something. Something strange on the other side of Martinez's face.

Gently, he turned the man over.

And saw the flesh peeled back, to reveal not bloody tissue and bone . . .

. . . but a complexity of tiny, mangled gears and fizzling wires. A thin stream of smoke rose from a short circuit, carrying with it the acrid smell of burnt metal.

There was a gasp from the woman, and then she was kneeling alongside Kirk—the phaser cradled carelessly in her hand.

"He's . . . he's not human," she said.

"No," Kirk agreed. And with the utmost caution, he wrested the phaser from her nerveless grasp.

Now he remembered where he had heard that tone of voice before—along with the words themselves.

Imagine it, Captain. A world with no corruption, no suffering, no death. . . .

Rising to his feet, he pressed the plate that controlled the door. It hissed closed. Then he turned to the medical officer, training the phaser on her without making it obvious.

"Scratch yourself, Doctor."

She looked up at him—puzzled, dazed.

"Scratch yourself."

Abruptly, she understood. Pressing her fingernail against the back of her hand, she made a quick slash. A moment later, there was a pinkish streak with a red line at the center of it.

"Satisfied?" she asked.

He nodded. Then he took his own fingernail and brought it across the back of the hand that held the phaser. He showed her the result.

"It's important," he said, kneeling again, "that we *both* be satisfied—if we're to trust one another." He looked into her dark eyes, eyes that had betrayed her shock but were now steady again. "My name is Jim Kirk—captain of the *Enterprise.*"

She nodded. "Yes. I know." A pause. "I'm Kai Chin, Chief Medical Officer." Another pause. "What do you know about . . . *this?*"

Kirk grunted, surveying Martinez's ruined visage. "More than I care to admit," he said. "Even to myself." He recalled the log entry concerning Doctor Roger Korby, his recent conversation with Christine Chapel.

Had his kindness somehow come back to haunt him?

"I saw something very much like this once before," he explained. "On a planet called Exo III."

The doctor's delicate brow creased. "Exo . . . why, we stopped there not long ago. To pick up some geologists who'd been shipwrecked there."

Suddenly, Kirk's mouth was dry. He swallowed.

"Geologists? What were their names?"

Chin frowned, thinking. "Brown. And Zezel. They were survivors of the Roger Korby expedition." She looked into his eyes, penetrating. "You know them, don't you?"

Kirk shrugged. "I've met Brown, though . . . Oh, hell. Let's start from the beginning, Doctor."

He told her everything. About his encounter with Korby —or at least, the thing that in some sense carried Korby inside it. About the machine that created android duplicates. And about the way Korby had met his end.

"I thought," he said, "that he was the last of them. But I must have been wrong. Somehow, one or more of them survived—and was able to operate the machine."

Chin nodded. "So when Martinez and the others beamed down, they were duplicated. And then killed."

"And these things," Kirk added, "were able to replace them here on the *Hood*—without anyone suspecting."

"Then those containers . . ." The doctor's voice trailed off.

"What containers?" he asked.

"They beamed up these huge containers," she told him. "And their contents were kept a secret. But if you say they were looking for a planet on which to set up their machine . . . someplace with an ample supply of human beings to duplicate . . ."

Kirk looked at her. "Those containers could have held the components of the dismantled duplication machine."

"Exactly," she said.

"And what happened to them?"

"We dropped them—and Brown—on a colony planet called Midos Five."

Kirk cursed beneath his breath. "That was the world," he said, "that Korby picked out for his base of operations— with the help of my android counterpart."

"Then Brown could be carrying out Korby's plan even as we speak." Chin scowled. "Kidnapping colonists and duplicating them."

"And what about the other geologist?" he asked. "Did you drop him off on Midos Five also?"

The doctor shook her head. "No. We left him on Tranquillity Seven."

Kirk chuckled bitterly. "I see," he said. "Or I'm beginning to. Martinez mentioned that a trap had been set for me on Tranquillity Seven. It would seem that this Zezel is the one who set it."

And then the truth hit him like a ton of dilithium crystals, nearly crushing him beneath its weight.

The android Korby created in Kirk's likeness . . .

Zezel dropped off on Trank Seven . . .

A con man who resembled him enough to be mistaken for him . . .

The departure of the *Enterprise*, without any evidence of concern regarding his whereabouts.

"What is it?" asked Chin. "You just lost about two shades of color."

He snorted. "That's not all I've lost. Unless I miss my guess, there's an android sitting in the command chair of the *Enterprise*. And I'll be damned if I know what he's done with her."

Kirk found that he was trembling.

"I sympathize with you," she said. "Really—I do. But we have more immediate concerns on *this* ship."

With an effort, he calmed himself. Finally, the trembling stopped. "Yes," he said. "You're right." He regarded her again. "Who else besides Martinez beamed down to Exo III?"

The doctor bit her lip. "Stuart and Banks, the first time. That is, the first officer and the science officer. Then, on subsequent occasions, Bodrick, the navigator, and Michaux, the helmsman. And Simmons, the security chief. In fact, I'd say that everyone in security section was down there at one time or another."

Kirk's skin crawled. Only minutes ago, he'd been surrounded by these *people* in the transporter room.

"Did any of them see you enter this cabin?" he asked.

"No," said Chin. "The corridor was empty when I got here."

He stared at her for a moment. "Come to think of it, why *did* you enter this cabin?"

"We suspected something was wrong—*we* being myself and Lieutenant Paultic, the communications officer. There was evidence here and there—the death of our chief engineer and other things."

"Vedra," Kirk interjected.

She blinked, perhaps a little surprised that he knew. "Yes, Vedra. So when there was so much secrecy regarding your arrival, I decided to find out which quarters had been assigned to you—and to barge in behind my prerogatives as a ship's doctor, come to examine a visitor on board."

"But actually hoping to learn more about what was wrong."

"Something like that."

Kirk glanced at the prone figure of the Martinez android.

"It looks," he said, "like you learned more than you bargained for."

Chin nodded in agreement.

"The two of us," he decided, "aren't going to be of much use against so many of them. We're going to need help."

She thought for a second. "We can start in engineering section. I know it's free of androids, because I just gave them all checkups. And there are others we can trust—Paultic, of course, and crewmen who never went down to Exo III. People who'll believe me when I tell them what I saw here."

"I'm glad," said Kirk, "that they won't need to see the evidence themselves. Because we don't dare leave it around." He turned his phaser setting up to the next level. "If this one's friends find him like this, they'll know we're onto them. If he's merely disappeared, it'll give us a little more breathing space."

Training the phaser on the android's body, he activated it. There was a low hum as the beam played over its target. For a fraction of a moment, the Martinez-thing rippled with scarlet light.

Then it was gone.

The doctor shivered. "It was almost like watching the captain himself being destroyed."

Kirk grunted. It had been an eerie feeling, all right.

"Come on," he said. "They'll come looking here after a while."

Slipping the phaser under his tunic, he depressed the door control again. The panel slid aside.

"After you," he said.

Gathering herself, Chin led him out into the corridor.

Chapter Twenty-one

KIRK STRODE DOWN THE PASSAGEWAY, deep in contemplation.

Chapel had not been able to tell him much when she contacted him—owing to the ongoing need for secrecy and the chance that someone might accidentally hook into their connection. But she had hinted sufficiently at the gravity of the situation.

Something had gone wrong—but what?

Was it *his* fault? Could he have missed something, some small nuance of behavior on the *Enterprise?*

It wasn't possible. He had every bit of knowledge that the human Kirk had had. Every bit of experience, lodged in memory.

And yet, someone had stumbled onto their operation—or so Chapel had implied. There was an exposure that had to be sealed up.

It must have been one of the others, then. After all, each of them was defined by the capacities of their human templates. If that template could not foresee the results of certain actions, certain oversights . . . then the duplicate would have the same inadequacies.

Brown was a prime example. His human predecessor must have been . . .

"Captain?"

Kirk looked up, saw the female figure in his path. He recognized her as the ensign who had volunteered for duty planetside.

"DeLong," he said, inclining his head slightly in acknowledgment as he continued past her.

"Captain—wait! Please!"

She caught up with him. Reluctantly, he turned to look at her. He noticed now that she was equipped with phaser and communicator.

"Where are you going?" she asked. "Isn't it time for our teleport?"

It was. And it had been his plan to be with the unsuspecting relief team that beamed down to the shuttlecraft—a necessity if he was to avoid the physical McCoy had in store for him. But Chapel's call had changed all that.

"The beam-down has been postponed," he told her, never breaking stride. "You would have discovered that when you got to the transporter room."

"Postponed?" she echoed. "But why?"

He eyed her. "Is it now necessary, Ensign, for me to explain my decisions to *you?*"

That seemed to take the wind out of her sails. It was the effect he had aimed for.

"I . . . I didn't mean that, sir. I only meant . . ." She stopped herself, started again. "Then when *will* we beam down?"

"You'll be notified," he said. And turned away from her, signifying an end to the conversation.

She took the hint. A moment later, he was alone again with his thoughts.

DeLong's first stop was in security, where she turned in her phaser and her communicator. Wood, the officer on duty, didn't seem the least bit curious about the premature return of the equipment. He just logged its receipt and went about his business.

The whole way back to engineering, she turned the matter this way and that, trying to puzzle it out.

First, I offend him—impugn his integrity in public, disobey him—and *he* asks *me* for forgiveness. After something like that, one would think he'd at least remember me—but no. He brushes by me in the corridor as if he's never seen me before.

Okay, he's the captain of a fair-sized starship. Maybe he's got other things on his mind.

But when I volunteer to beam planetside, he assures me he hasn't forgotten me—that he never could. And he smiles as he says it—with warmth, with respect. The way I'd always hoped he'd smile at me.

She sighed.

Then I see him in the corridor again and he gives me the cold shoulder. The *coldest* shoulder. As if he's never held me in any esteem at all. As if I've been nothing but a thorn in his side all along . . .

She just didn't get it.

In a daze, she made the last turn that brought her to engineering. Waited for the doors to open, headed for her customary station.

And almost sat down on top of Campeas. She'd forgotten that he'd been assigned to cover for her in her absence.

"DeLong?" he asked. "What are you doing here? I thought you were beaming down with the captain."

She chuckled dryly. "It's a long story. Suffice it to say the relief party's been postponed."

He looked up at her. "Oh." A pause. "So, do you want me to find something else to do?"

She thought for a moment, shook her head in the negative. "That's all right. You look like you're in the middle of it already. I've got to report to Mister Scott anyway—maybe he'll ask me to do something else this shift."

Campeas shrugged. "Okay. But if you change your mind, let me know."

She nodded, moved away toward Mister Scott's office. Knocked on his half-open door, past which she could see him working at his computer terminal.

"A'll be wi' ye in just a minute," he said, his eyes glued to the screen. As DeLong watched, he completed his calculations, stored the file with a satisfied smirk, and swiveled around on his chair.

"Ah, Denise. Wha' can a' do for . . ." As his voice trailed

off, his eyes narrowed. "Hold on now. Were ye nae supposed t' be beamin' down wi' th' relief party, lassie?"

"I *was,*" she explained. "But it was called off. Postponed."

He grunted. "That's a wee bit unusual. It was nae a malfunction, was 't?"

She shook her head. "I don't think so. Though I have to admit I don't know that for sure."

Another grunt, louder than the first. "Won't ye come in, Denise, and have a seat? A' think a'll just get t' th' bottom o' this."

As DeLong sat down on one of the two worn plastic chairs in Scott's cramped cubicle, the engineering chief put in a call to the transporter room. In a moment, Mister Kyle's image came up on the monitor.

"Aye, sir?" asked Kyle.

"A've just heard that th' relief party didna beam down as scheduled," said Scott. "Was there some trouble down there?"

"No trouble," reported Kyle. "The captain just called it off."

Scott stroked his chin. "A' see. Thank ye, then. As ye were." The image blinked out and he turned to face DeLong again.

"Well," he said, "a' guess th' bottom's a bit deeper than a' thought." He smiled. "But if th' captain's postponed th' teleport, he's sure t' have a good reason. Don't look so glum, lass—it'll be cleared up b'fore ye know it, and ye'll be beamin' down as ye were supposed to."

She wished she could smile back at him, but she couldn't. "It's not that, sir. It's . . . I don't know."

And then she blurted it out. She couldn't stop herself. Maybe it was the avuncular way he looked at her, the understanding he seemed so ready with; maybe it was just her need to get it off her chest. To *tell* someone.

DeLong described the way the captain had acted toward her in this instance and that. His erratic behavior, his unpredictability. As if he were two different people, each contradicting the other in word and deed.

She didn't quite go into every detail. She made it sound as if she were just another young officer seeking her captain's high regard.

"You've known him for a long time," she said finally. "Why is he acting like this?"

Scott shrugged. "It does sound like strange behavior, comin' from th' captain. But then, Denise, ye have t' ask y'self how much of 't is th' captain . . . and how much is th' way ye see him."

She felt herself blush, hating the way it confirmed his suggestion.

But there it was. Scott had seen through her charade. It was out in the open now.

"If a' may be so bold," said the chief engineer, "ye're nae th' first young woman t' take a likin' t' James T. Kirk. Nor even th' first young woman in this section." He sighed—*for* her, it seemed to DeLong. "An' a' can tell ye, they all got over it. It's a natural enough thing, lassie. But it doesna go on forever."

DeLong nodded. "I . . . do have a crush on him," she admitted—not an easy thing for her to do. "But it hasn't colored my perceptions. Or at least, not all that much." She thought about it some more, found she was confident about her observations. As confident as she would have been about a physics experiment back in school. "He's acted strangely toward me, sir. And I don't know why."

She looked at Mister Scott.

"You do believe me, don't you?"

He pressed his lips together, tilted his head at an angle as he considered the matter.

"A'll tell ye what," he said at last. "A'll look into it for ye. See if ye've really got any grounds for concern." He smiled. "Fair enough?"

She smiled back, unable to prevent herself.

"Fair enough," she said. "And . . . thank you, sir."

Scott waved it away. "I have nae done anythin' yet," he said, and turned back to his terminal.

She got up to go, paused halfway to the door.

The chief engineer noticed. "Aye, lass?"

"I almost forgot the reason I came to see you," she said. "I'm available for duty and Campeas is at my station. He's doing so well, I hate to interrupt him."

Scott nodded. "Why don't ye have a go at th' antimatter

conduits?" he suggested. "They have nae been looked at in a dog's age."

It was just the sort of mindless work she needed—though she hadn't realized it until just this moment. How had he known?

"I'll get on it right away," she told him.

"Good," he muttered, his mind already elsewhere as he started to call up another file.

It was only after DeLong had gone that her words began to haunt him. So much so, in fact, that Scott had to think them through before he could turn his attention back to his work.

DeLong wasn't one of those lovesick yeomen that liked to bat their eyelashes at the captain. She was a levelheaded individual. Even in the gym, when Kirk had beaten her with what turned out to be a dirty trick, she kept her temper better than *he* would have.

And the behavior she had ascribed to the captain could certainly be called erratic. Could there be something personal in it after all? Surely, over the years, he had never seen Kirk treat any crewman unfairly, or with prejudice.

A result of pressure, then? The Romulan situation hanging over their heads, the aborted leave on Trank Seven? Was it possible even Jim Kirk was cracking a bit under the strain?

Then again, it was all hearsay. And Montgomery Scott was not given to convicting a man on that basis.

First chance he got, he'd have a talk with the captain. Then it would all come out in the wash, if there was anything there in the first place.

When *Kirk* entered the briefing room, the other androids were there already, waiting for him.

He took his seat at the head of the table, acknowledged both Spock and Chapel. They inclined their heads slightly, returning the acknowledgment.

"You have checked the room for listening devices?" he asked Spock.

"I have," said the duplicate of the Vulcan. "Just as you ordered. And I have found nothing."

"Good," said *Kirk*. He turned to the nurse. "Report."

"I was in sickbay," she said, "only a short while when crewman Clifford and the one called K'leb came in. To see Doctor McCoy."

Kirk held his hand up, stopping her.

"You know of the T'nufan?" he asked.

"Yes," said Chapel. "He was well acquainted with my human template."

Of course, that would be the case. The others carried memories of recent occurrences on the *Enterprise*—whereas *Kirk* himself did not.

"Proceed," he said.

"K'leb, it seems, had encountered you on an earlier visit to sickbay—when McCoy was still in the critical-care unit. And being an empath, he had sensed your lack of human emotion."

Empath . . . ?

Kirk brought his fist down sharply on the briefing-room table. "So *that* was it," he said out loud. He smiled bitterly at the others. "I *thought* he looked at me strangely. But when I learned that he was uncomfortable in the captain's presence, I assumed . . ."

Spock and Chapel were looking at him, waiting for him to finish. He never did.

And why should he? It was not necessary for them to know the magnitude of his miscalculation. Not necessary, even, for them to know he had made one—though they appeared to have gathered that much from his outburst.

Suddenly, it seemed to him that he was balanced on the edge of a precipice—looking down into the shadowy depths of his own fallibility.

How could he have made such an error? *How?*

"All right," he said slowly, regaining his equilibrium. "The T'nufan read my lack of emotion."

Chapel picked up on her cue.

"Apparently, he shared the information with Mister Clifford—the only one on the ship who can understand his language to any significant extent. Clifford, in turn, brought the information to McCoy."

Kirk nodded. "I see. And what did Clifford make of it? Was it credible to him?"

"That much was not clear to me," said the nurse. "I think he doubted it a little, particularly at first. But he believed strongly enough in K'leb's abilities to put the matter before McCoy."

"Why McCoy?" asked the captain.

Chapel thought for a second.

"I think," she said, "it was a question of trust. Clifford felt more comfortable with McCoy—or perhaps the T'nufan did." Another second. "Yes—it is more likely that it was K'leb's decision to see McCoy. After all, the doctor oversaw his recuperation. It would be natural for K'leb to place his trust in him."

"And what was McCoy's reaction?"

"He promised to investigate the T'nufan's suspicions."

"Investigate?" asked *Kirk.* "How?"

"After Clifford and the T'nufan left, he called you. Asked you to come in for your long-overdue physical."

Kirk remembered, understood it all now. Something within him wound tighter, but he resisted the urge to pound the table again.

"And when I sidestepped his request?"

"He said you didn't sound like yourself," said Chapel. "He said you were tentative—that you seemed not to remember a wager he'd made with Kirk. And that your beaming back down might have been a ploy to escape his scrutiny."

All that? McCoy had seen through his machinations so thoroughly? He might have expected such insight from a Vulcan—but from a *human?*

Again, he had miscalculated.

Again.

Slowly, too slowly, *Kirk* brought himself to focus on his interrogation of Chapel.

"You mentioned that he *said* all this. To whom did he say it?"

"To *me.* By that time, he had noticed my presence in sickbay."

The captain sat back, grunted. "So McCoy has seen through us." He was careful to say *us,* and not *me.*

"Not completely," said the nurse. "He is not convinced that you are an impostor. A *possibility* was what he called it."

"A possibility," *Kirk* echoed. He allowed himself a smile. "And yet, we cannot allow him to continue unrestrained, spreading his suspicions of . . . this *possibility* . . . among the crew. No more than we can allow Clifford and the T'nufan to do so."

"Sooner or later," Spock added, "someone will believe them."

"Exactly," said the captain.

"But do we dare kill them?" asked the first officer. "Especially now, when the duplication process is proceeding so well?"

Kirk eyed him. "What are you getting at, Spock?"

The android cocked an eyebrow. "What if we were to send these individuals down to Midos Five—as part of the relief party? It would remove them from the ship's population, preventing them from doing any more damage than they may already have done. And after their duplication, we would have access to their memories—so we would know who else they might have spoken to."

Kirk had to admire the simplicity of it.

"Done," he said. "But I think *you* should ask them to join the relief group, Spock. They might suspect treachery if an order came down from *me.*"

"As you wish," said the android. "I will—"

He was cut short by a high-pitched tone, followed by Uhura's appearance on the tabletop monitor.

"Captain?"

Kirk glared at her.

"I gave orders not to be interrupted, Lieutenant."

"Yes, I know, sir. But Admiral Straus is waiting to speak with you. He said it was urgent, sir."

Damn. So soon?

"Put him through, Uhura."

A moment later, Straus's image supplanted the communications officer's.

"Greetings, Captain," said the admiral.

"Likewise, sir." *Kirk*'s suspicions were confirmed by the human's expression. "It's the Romulans, isn't it?"

The admiral nodded soberly. "Right on the money, Jim. They've commandeered a freighter, right on the edge of the neutral zone. And be warned—it's as bad as we thought it might be. Four birds-of-prey, according to the freighter's Mayday."

Straus snorted.

"You know, I received a lot of static for holding up three ships in this sector. But now I'm glad I did. Anything less would have placed us at a serious disadvantage—not that four to three is a situation to be hoped for, exactly."

"We've faced worse," the android assured him.

"I'm sure you have," returned Straus. "And this time, you've got some good men working with you in Martinez and Ascher. But you're a good deal closer to the problem than they are, so you'll have to improvise until they arrive."

"Understood," said *Kirk*.

Straus frowned. "Good luck, Jim. I'll have the coordinates sent to your navigator."

With that, the admiral faded.

Kirk reached over, switched off the monitor. Regarded the others.

"It would seem," said Spock, "that our options have been curtailed somewhat."

"To say the least," agreed *Kirk*. "We're back to square one insofar as McCoy and the other two are concerned."

Silence for a moment.

"Might I suggest," offered Spock, "that killing them is still not the answer? It would only attract undue attention. After all, Doctor McCoy is a prominent name in the fleet. And the death of the T'nufan would certainly come to the attention of Starfleet Command. What's more, if they *have* discussed their suspicions with other crewmen, it would give those suspicions that much more weight."

Kirk considered that. He didn't like the idea of having to live with a threat. But it seemed he had little choice. One death might be overlooked—three would not.

"When we bring back the shuttle crews," he said, "there will be enough of us on board to keep an eye on them. For now, that will have to suffice."

Spock nodded, a barely noticeable movement of his head.

"Nurse Chapel, you will continue to watch McCoy. First

Officer, get the shuttle crews back here. And send an appropriate message to Governor Chewton so he doesn't confuse matters by trying to contact Starfleet—for real, this time."

He pushed back his chair, stood.

"That will be all, for now."

He started for the door.

"Sir?"

He turned, confronted Spock.

"Yes?"

"Shall I contact Doctor Brown as well? To let him know of this development?"

Kirk measured his first officer. Had there been a note of disapproval in his tone? An implication of negligence on the captain's part for having failed to cover Brown in his orders?

Perhaps disapproval too, of the way he had misinterpreted the incident with the T'nufan? Or his inability to allay McCoy's suspicions?

The Spock android's face showed nothing. It was as unreadable as that of a true Vulcan.

No. He is programmed to be loyal to me—obedient. He is not capable of disapproval, *Kirk* thought.

He nodded. "Of course. You don't need me to tell you that—do you?"

"No, sir," said Spock.

"Good. And by the way—make sure that all the human templates down there are destroyed. They would have been nice to have on hand—but with the shuttle crews withdrawn, they'd outnumber their guards."

He smiled.

"Besides, we'll still have plenty of templates when we return—won't we?"

"As you say," agreed Spock.

There was only a thin sliver of light, stabbing through the spot where the boulder didn't quite fit the opening. It fell on Christine Chapel, tracing a jagged line from her thigh to her face. She was most calm—almost serene, thought Spock, considering the circumstances.

Or perhaps she only seemed that way.

218

By Spock's reckoning, they had been pent up in the cave for nearly two Midan days—Sulu's group, the crew of the *Galileo II*, about half that time. Hours ago, the last of them had been taken out and duplicated.

There had been resistance, of course. Paikert alone had been stunned three times before he realized the futility of it. In the end, the duplications had been carried out; their android twins had been manufactured without imperfection.

It had been chilling to see his likeness staring at him across the machine's platform—another Spock where moments before there had been only a greenish lump. But he had not been given much time to admire the machine's handiwork. No sooner had the process been completed, the spinning platform brought to a halt, then he was unfettered and thrust back into the cave.

"What do you think they're doing now?"

Spock recognized the voice as Chekov's.

It was Sulu who answered. "Hard to say, Pavel. Maybe beaming down some more of us so they can make more duplicates." A pause in the darkness. "I hope not too many, though. This cave's only so big, and we're crowded enough as it is."

That elicited some chuckles from the others. But beyond that, it touched on that *other* fear—the one that ran deeper than their trepidation over what would happen to their fellow crewmen, and ultimately to the *Enterprise* herself. The fear of what would happen to *them*, now that their minds and bodies had served the androids' purpose.

They had all been thinking about it. But Sulu's remark had come the closest to giving it substance.

Spock shifted his weight. He had been leaning too long against one of the stony plates that formed the basic structure of the cave, and part of his back had begun to go numb.

His throat still hurt where the android *Kirk* had squeezed his windpipe shut. He swallowed with some difficulty, cleared his throat.

And though he could almost hear the anticipation in the musty air, the taut sense of *listening*, he said nothing. What could he tell them, after all, that would make the least bit of difference?

Perhaps, after he had accumulated more data, he might be able to find a chink in the androids' armor. Until that time, however, he would occupy himself by going over what data he *did* have. Again.

"Damn," said someone. As the voice didn't sound familiar, Spock guessed it was one of the security people that had come down in the *Galileo II.* "I can't squat here anymore. I've got to *do* something."

There were scraping sounds as the man lifted himself off the cave floor. He seemed to be making his way toward the entrance, negotiating the bodies in his way.

"Sit down," said Spock. His voice made the stone surfaces in the cave ring. "That's an order from your commanding officer."

The crewman made a derisive sound—emboldened, perhaps, by the fact that Spock couldn't see his face. "Begging your pardon, sir, but I think this situation calls for some action. I mean, what do you think they're going to do with us? Pat us on the heads and let us go?"

"When I require your opinion," said the Vulcan, "I'll request it of you. Until such time, I'll ask that you restrain yourself."

But the crewman wasn't done yet.

"Restrain myself? Sir, I've *been* restraining myself, and look where it's gotten us. Now it's time to show these androids what we're made of."

There were murmurs of assent from deeper within the cave.

"What you're proposing," said Spock, his voice clear and calm, "is suicide. The androids are armed. We are not. And even if we could budge that boulder, which I concede is possible, the aperture is too small for more than one person at a time. Our guards could pick us off even as we emerged."

"And what's the alternative?" asked the crewman. "We go like good little lambs to the slaughter?"

Spock heard the rising edge of hysteria in the man's voice. And he understood humans well enough to know it could prove contagious.

"We wait," said the first officer, "for an opportunity. And *then* we act—not before."

"No," said the crewman. *"You* wait. I'm going to try that boulder."

There were sounds again of boots scraping stone as the man approached.

"Need I remind you," asked Spock, "that you must get past me in order to leave this cave?"

The man seemed to hesitate. Spock could hear his breathing, quick and fierce. He braced himself in case the man rushed the exit.

After all, he was in charge here. There would be no attempted suicides if he could help it.

"I'm with Mister Spock," said Sulu.

"Me too," affirmed Chekov.

But the man still stood there, indecisive.

Suddenly, the sound of bitter laughter filled the cavern. Its echo from stone to stone gave it a haunting quality.

Spock looked across the way and saw Christine Chapel in the shaft of light. It was she who had laughed, though there was no humor in her expression. Her eyes were hard—as he had never seen them before.

"Perhaps," she said, "that's what they want us to do. Fight among ourselves. Do their dirty work *for* them."

It was as if someone had punctured the tension with a needle. There was something in the simplicity of the nurse's words—or perhaps it was her tone of voice—that had made it all seem so foolish.

The mutinous crewman must have thought so too. He grunted something and retreated to his former place in the cave.

Christine's eyes fell on Spock for a moment, though she could hardly have discerned more than his outline in the near-complete darkness. There was pain in them—great pain. Then her gaze lost its focus again, and that strange look of serenity returned to her.

Guilt. Of all emotions, it was the one Spock knew best. And was it guilt that ate at Christine Chapel now? Guilt for the horror her late fiancé had unleashed? Guilt for not having stopped it somehow, back on Exo III?

Or was it something deeper than guilt?

It didn't matter. He could not bear to see her like this. Sometimes it was easier to shut out his own pain than that of others.

Without a word, Spock leaned forward and put out his hand. He let it drop gently on Christine's, felt the chill there.

She looked up, still not quite seeing him in the darkness. But she understood his intent, knew the discomfort that physical contact caused him. And rewarded him with a smile, however faint and sad.

He leaned back again.

But before his back could come to rest against the stone, the earth trembled a little and there was a thin whine Spock had heard before.

Apparently, he wasn't the only one who recognized the sound.

"That's the shuttlecraft," said Chekov. "It's lifting off."

As the whine died, another rose in pitch.

"They *both* are," said Wood.

"They're going back to the ship," said another voice—a female yeoman who had been with Sulu in the *Galileo II*. It was said with certainty, though the shuttlecraft might have been headed anywhere.

For a little while, no one spoke. They just turned over the implications in their minds. Spock bit down hard on his own fears and frustrations, swallowed them whole.

Then there was another sound—close at hand. The grating of stone against stone. The loosening of the rock that blocked the way out.

It moved aside, revealing the barren, twilit slope opposite. And three or four of the androids, though they could only be seen from midtorso down. A couple of them held phasers.

One knelt—the duplicate of Brown, Korby's assistant. His face was expressionless as he scanned the living contents of the cave, apparently unhampered by the lack of light.

Finally, it seemed, he found what he sought.

"Nurse Chapel," he said. *"Christine."*

The use of her given name was appalling, somehow, when shaped by that mouth. It seemed to trivialize it, separate it from meaning.

222

"Yes," said the nurse. "I'm here."

"I'd like to speak with you," said the android. "You may come out."

Was it time, then? Were they now to be taken out individually and destroyed?

Perhaps the faceless crewman had been right after all. Perhaps Spock had waited too long.

Or was this the opportunity for which he'd been waiting?

The nurse had already begun to stir, unquestioning—resigned, it seemed—when Spock intervened.

"No," he said. And to Christine, "Stay where you are, Nurse."

She froze, dutifully.

Brown's gaze shifted, latched on to Spock. He stared at him momentarily, as if it took that long to determine his identity.

"You need not be concerned," he said finally. "I have no intention of harming her."

"So you say," retorted the Vulcan.

Another moment, while the android weighed the situation.

"Very well," he said. "You may accompany her, if you wish."

It was not much of a concession, really. Two could be obliterated as easily as one. But once free of the cave, out in the open . . . he would at least have a chance.

"All right," said Spock. He turned to Christine Chapel. "We will go together then."

She regarded him, seeming to understand what he had in mind—though judging by her expression, she didn't hold out much hope.

Without a word, she clambered up and out of the cavern.

Spock came just after, and then the boulder was rolled back into place.

They sat just downslope of the cave, on rocks that protruded from the hard earth. Over Brown's shoulder, the sun was setting. At a distance, forming a triangle around them, there were androids armed with phasers.

None of the crew's duplicates were anywhere to be

seen—so they had left in the shuttlecraft en masse. That left only the androids who had been here when the *Columbus* arrived.

But it did not seem that Brown had lied when he said that he meant no harm—at least, for now. Certainly, his armed compatriots had had every chance to cut them down.

And yet, what could he need from them? Not their knowledge of the *Enterprise,* for their duplicates already had that. Then what?

Brown chose not to begin by telling them that.

"I will not destroy you," he said instead. And in a strange, inward way. As if he were not addressing them at all, but rather coming to a conclusion in his own mind.

He repeated it, this time plainly speaking to Christine. "I will not destroy you."

Either the nurse did not believe him or she had been caught by surprise. But she did not seem relieved.

"What do you mean?" she asked.

"Just what I said," responded the android. "I will not . . . *cannot* destroy you." He paused. "Especially *you,* Christine. I don't think Doctor Korby would have wanted you destroyed."

The nurse stared at Brown, silent. And then, just as silently, tears rolled down her cheeks.

"You mean it," she said. "Don't you?"

He nodded. "I mean it, Christine."

The nurse drew a deep breath, shivered. A smile pulled at the corners of her mouth.

"Oh, God," she said. "I thought it was the end." She glanced at Spock. "For all of us."

The Vulcan was cynical, however, in light of the phasers that surrounded them. "If you do not intend to destroy us," he asked, "then what *do* you intend?"

Brown looked at him. "I do not know. I cannot let you go free altogether—that would jeopardize the leader's plan."

"The leader?" asked Christine.

"Kirk," said the android. Spock thought he heard a measure of distaste in the way Brown uttered the name. But then, Brown spoke in human patterns, and the Vulcan was

still unfamiliar with some of the nuances of human parlance.

"You don't like *Kirk,*" said the nurse. "Do you?"

Spock felt a small flush of satisfaction.

"That is correct," said Brown. A pause. "He has assumed the Creator's place—yet his methods are not those of the Creator. He is without . . ." He faltered, shrugged. "Without."

"Compassion?" suggested Christine. "Is that the word you're looking for?" She turned to Spock. "Even when we found him on Exo III, changed as he was, Roger still had some compassion in him."

Brown thought for a moment, nodded. "Yes," he said. *"Compassion* is the word."

"You are acting, then," said Spock, "without your leader's knowledge—or sanction."

"I must," said the android. "He would have seen you all destroyed. And then . . ." His voice trailed off. The wind blew down the slope, and there were changes in Brown's expression. "You know," he said, "at first I thought it was a dysfunction on my part. A flaw in my programming. Then I realized that that was impossible. I was programmed by Doctor Korby. Of all of us, only *I* was programmed directly by Doctor Korby. So if I see things, he must have meant for me to see them."

Christine's forehead wrinkled. She leaned forward a little. "What kind of things?" she asked, as gently as if she were speaking to a frightened child.

Brown told them. He described the visions he had had—the murders that replayed themselves in his mind. And, with more difficulty, his reaction to them.

Guilt, Spock noted, even before Brown was halfway finished. Taking hold in this artificial being even as it had taken hold of Christine earlier. *Fascinating.*

"You knew the Creator," Brown told Christine. "You knew him even before my human template came into his service." He looked into her eyes. "What could he have meant by this—other than to stop me from killing? To make death onerous to me?"

The nurse returned his all-too-human gaze. "It is *exactly*

what Roger . . . what Doctor Korby must have had in mind. After all, death and suffering were onerous to *him*."

For a moment, Brown's face went blank. When life returned to it, there were the beginnings of a smile.

"Yes," he said. "The Creator said as much." He glanced at Spock, then came back to Christine. "So I am following Doctor Korby's wishes when I preserve you."

"I would say so," said the nurse, "yes." She licked her lips. "But Doctor Korby wouldn't have stopped at preserving us. He would have let us go."

The android's brow creased. "I told you—that is not possible. If you are freed, you will contact Starfleet. And expose *Kirk* for what he is."

"Is that bad?" asked Christine. "You yourself said that you don't like him. That his ways are not Doctor Korby's."

"His *methods* are not Doctor Korby's," said Brown. "But his goals are the same. To people the Federation with androids—with superior beings, plagued by neither sickness nor death."

Christine looked to Spock for help. He nodded almost imperceptibly.

"You have said," he told Brown, "that you will refrain from destroying us. Yet *Kirk* seems to have other ideas. What will you do when he comes back?"

Brown shrugged again. "There is time to ponder that," he said. *"Kirk* will not be back for quite some time. He has been called away."

"Away?" asked the nurse. "Where?"

"To the Romulan neutral zone," responded Brown.

Then the summons from Starfleet Command had finally come through. The *Enterprise* was on its way to a confrontation with the Romulans—led by an android captain.

Brown stood. "I think," he said, "it is time for you to rejoin the other humans."

In no hurry, Spock looked up at him. "And if we refuse? Will you have us killed after all?"

The android frowned. "It will be night soon. The temperature will drop abruptly." His hair was tossed by the rising wind. "I think you will be more comfortable in the cave."

Seeing that Brown's hand could not be easily forced,

Spock got to his feet. Taking her cue from him, the nurse did likewise.

"I must warn you," said Brown, before they could begin the walk back to the cave. "Those you see around you have not come to the conclusions I have. They will not hesitate to shoot if the situation warrants."

Spock nodded, eyeing the nearest guard. "Understood."

And as the last of the sun dropped behind the duplication machine, they returned to their underground prison.

Chapter Twenty-two

THEY WERE AN EVEN DOZEN—an ideal number, by Kirk's estimate, for the task before them. It was important to play it close to the vest for as long as they could, and a larger group would have attracted too much attention.

Unfortunately, everyone in security was suspect, or they might have gotten access to the weapons room. As it was, Transporter Chief Berg had been able to slip a half-dozen phasers out of the shuttlecraft.

While Berg distributed the phasers, there on the lower level of engineering, Kirk listened to the familiar hum of the impulse engines. Even on another ship, in a situation like this one, it was a comforting sound.

"All right," he said, when the last weapon had been accepted and put away. "You all know who I am, and you've heard what's happening on the *Hood*. If we're to regain control of the ship, we've got to take our adversaries out one at a time." He paused. "We'll operate in pairs; each pair will have a target." He watched each face as he handed out the assignments, noting the trepidation in some.

At the end, Genti scowled, glancing up at the entrance to his section. "It feels a little funny," he said, "conspiring like this. Planning the overthrow of the command staff—as if we were terrorists or something."

"It feels funny to me too," said the captain. "I *run* a ship just like this one. But we've no other choice."

"Are you *sure* about all of this?" asked a petite, redheaded engineering officer. "I mean, we're going to have a tough time explaining ourselves if we're barking up the wrong tree."

Chin smiled grimly. "In that case, Roseann, I'll take full responsibility. After all, I'm the one who saw what was inside Captain Martinez."

"No," said Paultic. "We're all in this together." He eyed the others. "If we have any doubts, we should leave them here."

Berg voiced his support for this idea, and a couple of engineering people chimed in too.

"Absolutely right," said Kirk. "We're to hit our targets fast—and hard. Any hesitation will give them the edge." He waited a moment for that to sink in. "Besides," he added, "our phasers are all set on stun. So if it turns out that we've made a mistake in some isolated instance, the worst we'll have inflicted is a headache."

He looked around again.

"Any questions?"

Silence, but for the droning of the engines.

"Then let's go," he said.

The door to Bodrick's cabin slid aside.

"Greetings," said the navigator, smiling his customary smile. "What can I do for you?"

Paultic didn't answer. With a coolness that surprised him, he raised the phaser and fired.

Bodrick was thrown backward, finally crashing into one of his desk supports. He lay still.

"All right," said Paultic, just loudly enough to be heard out in the corridor. "He's out."

Jacobi followed him into the cabin, shut the door behind them.

Paultic gave the phaser to the other man—just in case—and took out the laser-scalpel Chin had given him. He knelt by Bodrick, took the navigator's hand in his, and applied the surgical beam to the index finger.

"Well?" asked Jacobi.

Paultic shook his head, finding it suddenly difficult to speak. It was one thing to talk about androids—and another to see the proof of it.

Filled with loathing, he let Bodrick's hand drop to the floor.

"It's exactly as we thought," he said. "He's an android."

He stood and extended his hand toward Jacobi.

"I'll do the honors," he said. "I'm the officer here."

The engineer didn't hesitate. He handed over the phaser.

But it wasn't as easy to complete the job as Paultic had thought it would be. Even though this monster had been in on Vedra's murder, and those of the personnel who'd been replaced. Even though, if their situations were reversed, he'd have killed Paultic without a second thought.

After all, he looked like *Bodrick.* And if the navigator hadn't been his closest friend, he'd been a lot more than an acquaintance. They'd spent many an hour together on the bridge of the *Hood,* shared some tense moments and some happy ones.

Then Paultic saw the android's eyes snap open, and it was all the motivation he needed.

The phaser beam enveloped Bodrick in its glow just as he started to raise himself off the floor. Before their eyes, he vanished.

Paultic turned to look at Jacobi. The engineer was doing his best not to look rattled.

"Come on," said the communications officer. "Before the others start to worry about us."

The engineer nodded a little too quickly. "Aye, sir."

The doors to sickbay opened and First Officer Stuart stepped through them. He headed straight for Chin's office.

The doctor looked up from her pretended study of her monitor. She waved curtly to Stuart, got up as if to greet him.

Nor did he show any signs of suspicion. Why should he? There was nothing unusual about the chief medical officer needing to consult with him on one matter or another.

So when Ensign Zuna dropped him, there in the center of

the sickbay floor, the only sound was that of Stuart's body hitting the deck.

But as Zuna emerged from hiding, she was nervous. Chin could see it in the way she looked at her victim, in the way she held her weapon.

In the quickness with which she moved the phaser setting up a notch, ready to use it again.

"Wait," called the doctor, bolting out of her office.

Zuna turned to look at her. She seemed surprised, as if she had forgotten all about her.

"Don't you remember?" she asked the ensign, lowering herself to a kneeling position at Stuart's side. "First we've got to make sure."

Zuna swallowed. "Right," she said. "Sorry."

The doctor muttered something reassuring as she removed the laser-scalpel from her pocket. Deftly, she rolled up Stuart's sleeve and made a tiny incision in his forearm.

The flesh—not flesh at all, really, but some synthetic material—curled back to reveal that intricate mesh of gears and wires she had seen in Martinez's face.

Chin sat back on her haunches, satisfied and a little revolted by the burning smell. "All right," she said as she started to get up. "You can—"

But before she could finish, a hand shot out and grabbed her by the ankle. The pain was terrible, crushing. She screamed.

Zuna cried out too, threatening to use the phaser. But she couldn't—not on this setting, with Chin in the android's grasp. The beam would destroy both of them.

Zuna must have realized this, because she started fumbling with the setting. But at the same time, the android twisted Chin's foot around, and she came crashing down on top of him.

"Sorry, doctor," said Stuart, his voice unreasonably calm. "But I need a shield."

Holding her before him, he started to get up. His grip was viselike, irresistible.

"Let her go," said the ensign, still struggling to restore the setting to stun. It seemed to be stuck.

"No chance," said Stuart. "I need her to get to *you.*"

Zuna took a step back.

The android half dragged, half carried the doctor across the room. Eventually, he would maneuver Zuna into a corner and disable her. Then he'd kill them both.

There was only one thing Chin thought she might try—one strategy that had any chance of working.

If the androids were such precise replicas of human beings, they probably had human reflexes as well. After all, they had to be programmed to blink, didn't they? To take in and expel air so as to give the appearance of breathing?

"Go ahead," said Chin. "Shoot. Don't worry about me." And as she said it, she winked.

The ensign noticed, though she wasn't quite sure what to make of it. But she understood well enough to extend the phaser in Stuart's direction.

"You won't do it," said the android. "You can't just kill her. She's flesh and blood. She's *human.*"

The words were barely out of his mouth when Chin kicked backward with all her might—catching Stuart just below the kneecap.

Sure enough, the patella reflex was there. The android's leg buckled for just an instant, causing him to lose his balance—and his grip on her.

She twisted free, rolled to one side.

Nor did Zuna wait for the order Chin barked at her. Depressing the trigger, she activated the phaser—still locked in at its highest setting.

That nimbus of coruscating energy played about the android for a moment. Then it was as if he had never existed in the first place.

According to the duty roster, Michaux was scheduled for continuing education. Since the helmsman was one of the few crewmembers who preferred to study in the library rather than in his own cabin, Genti knew where to look for him.

"You just watch my back," he told Obobo as the turbolift carried them down to the library level. "There may be another of them in the place, and I'll need some warning."

The Nigerian nodded. "Don't worry, sir. I'll—"

He cut himself short as the lift stopped—one level shy of their destination.

When the doors opened, they revealed Jason—the security officer who'd come to check the dilithium supply. The one, Genti reminded himself, who left the damned door open and got the whole section sick. And maybe, just maybe, the one who also killed Vedra.

Jason inclined his head slightly. "Gentlemen," he said, and entered the turbolift.

Nor did he punch new instructions into the lift computer —which meant he was headed for the same level they were.

The doors closed.

Until now, Genti's stomach had been churning at the thought of shooting Michaux—Michaux, who barely weighed in at a hundred and sixty pounds.

Now, strangely, the trepidation was gone—replaced by the heat of anger. I don't like this bastard, he decided.

So when the lift stopped again and the doors opened to let them out, Genti pulled out his phaser. Unaware, Jason stepped out into the corridor.

He never knew what hit him. The phaser blast sent him sprawling almost to the opposite wall.

Obobo cursed beneath his breath, glaring at Genti as they emerged from the turbolift. "What are you doing, sir? This wasn't our assignment."

"It is now," said the engineering chief. With liquid quickness, he got out the scalpel, used it on the base of Jason's neck.

And saw all he needed to see.

Without a moment's hesitation, he adjusted the phaser setting and activated it. Watching Jason blink out of existence was one of his most satisfying experiences since the day he joined Starfleet.

"Sir?"

Genti looked up, saw the concern in Obobo's face.

"Can we get moving now?" the man asked.

The chief engineer nodded. "Sure."

"Do you want me to watch for a while?" asked Calabrese, careful to keep her voice to a whisper.

233

Berg leaned away from the hairline crack between the door and the jamb—a crack created when he'd slipped his transporter key in the path of the closing door panel—and rubbed his eyes with his free hand.

"Maybe soon, Roseann. I'm good for a few more minutes."

"The hell you are," she told him, hunkered down just behind him in this unused utility room. "You know how tired your eyes get."

It was true. In fact, the condition had almost kept him out of Starfleet. As it was, it had limited him to the role of transporter chief—a post far below his original aspirations.

"No, really," he said. "I'm all right for now."

"Just don't be a hero," she rasped.

He smiled. "Yes, dear."

It got a chuckle out of her, breaking the tension a little.

Then he heard the footfalls. He held his hand up for silence and pressed his eye to the crack again.

Nothing yet.

The footfalls got louder, closer. The palm that cradled the phaser felt damp with sweat. Suddenly? Or had it been that way all along?

A squeeze of his muscular shoulder. Calabrese's way of saying she was right behind him, her own phaser at the ready.

The footfalls became louder still, echoing along the corridor. The pace was that of someone with a destination, a purpose.

And then he saw the maker of the sounds—almost close enough now to reach out and touch. Simmons came to a halt before the door across the corridor from them, knocked on it.

No answer.

Of course not. Neither Martinez nor Kirk were inside any longer. The cabin was empty.

They had known that someone from security would come by eventually—to see what was taking the captain so long. And to make sure that nothing untoward had occurred.

What they couldn't have predicted was that it would be the chief of security himself.

Simmons knocked again. Still no response from within.

He drew his phaser, just as Berg heard a distinct creak behind him—the sound of Calabrese's knees working as she stood up. The transporter chief held his breath, but Simmons seemed not to have noticed.

How acute was an android's hearing, anyway? Could he have heard them breathing as he approached? And now be playing possum, waiting only until their door opened?

Berg didn't have to look to know Calabrese's hand was hovering over the door control. As soon as he gave the signal, she'd press it—exposing Simmons to their fire.

And vice versa.

The key to the whole trap was the element of surprise. But if Simmons was aware of their presence here.. . .

He put the thought from his mind.

Outside in the corridor, the security chief opened a tiny compartment beside the door and punched in his override code. Almost immediately, the panel slid away.

For a moment, Simmons just stood there, surveying the cabin beyond the threshold. Then he took a cautious step inside.

Berg gave the signal. As the door opened, he fired.

The phaser beam hit Simmons in the shoulder, spun him about. He fell out of Berg's line of sight.

An instant later, Calabrese was bounding past him—across the corridor and into the cabin where Simmons had fallen.

"No!"

The warning was barely past his lips when he saw the sudden burst of phaser fire. In its glare, he saw Calabrese go down.

"Roseann!" he cried, darting across the corridor and launching himself after her. He landed on his side, ready to fire at anything that moved.

But Simmons lay stretched across the bunk, his head dangling off the side of it. And his phaser lay on the floor beneath his empty hand.

"Thanks anyway," said Calabrese.

Berg turned around and saw her lying behind him, wedged against a bulkhead. It made him want to laugh.

As their job wasn't over yet, however, he contained himself. Taking possession of Simmons's phaser, he flipped the setting to off and put it in his belt. Then he took out the laser-scalpel.

Calabrese, standing behind him now, cleared her throat rather noisily. He looked up at her.

"You want me to do that?" she asked.

He offered her the scalpel.

"Sure," he said. "I think my eyes *are* getting a little tired."

When he entered the library, Genti was still pumped up on adrenaline. His muscles were loose, relaxed, and the phaser felt remarkably comfortable in his hand.

Destroying androids wasn't half as difficult as he'd expected.

He scanned the rows of partitioned study units as Obobo came in behind him. No sign of Michaux. For that matter, no sign of anyone—an unusual situation here. The place was usually full to capacity.

Obobo tapped him on the shoulder and he turned. The Nigerian pointed to a small pocket of study units partially concealed by a structural bulkhead. In the ship's original design, the area had been set aside for some sort of storage—but as the demand for library use exceeded expectations, it was opened up as an annex.

And it could be reached from either side of the bulkhead.

Genti signaled for Obobo to approach the area from the left. He would take the longer way around—from the right, through the greater number of study units.

As the chief engineer walked, phaser palmed against his thigh, his footfalls seemed unnaturally loud. But that, he knew, was only the product of his heightened awareness.

And besides—the sound of footfalls was common enough in the library. Michaux couldn't know the intent behind them.

Could he?

Was it possible he'd gotten wind of what they were up to? And was hiding behind one of the partitions now, ready to twist someone's head off?

Genti shrugged off that last thought.

You're giving these androids too much credit, he told himself. Remember how easily Jason went down?

He was little more than halfway through the mass of study units when he heard the sound of voices.

One was Obobo's. The other he recognized as Michaux's.

It took an effort not to hurry his steps. But the voices sounded casual, not strained. And any undue haste on his part might have attracted the helmsman's attention—aroused his suspicions.

No, he told himself. Take your time. Obobo's fine—you can hear him.

One of the voices fluted into laughter. It was the Nigerian's.

See? He's okay.

A few more steps, and again a few more. The conversation went on—something about the number-two impulse engine. More laughter.

And then, finally, Genti reached the end of the partitions. Shifting the weight of the phaser in his hand so that he could fire instantly if he had to, he came around the side of the bulkhead.

Sure enough, there was Michaux. His head, barely visible over the top of his study unit, was turned toward Obobo, who stood just beyond him.

Genti would have fired then, but he didn't have a clear shot. And besides, he might have hit his own man.

He gestured for Obobo to move out of the way. Then he could come up and fire over the back of the study unit.

Michaux must have noticed something in the Nigerian's eyes, however, because he whirled about.

And saw Genti, his hand full of phaser pistol.

And moved quicker than anyone had a right to.

A moment later, Obobo seemed to leap into the outer bulkhead. There was a terrible *crack,* like the splintering of a thick branch in a dead tree. And then he came crashing down again.

Nor was Michaux anywhere to be seen. He had darted out of harm's way—most likely headed for the exit.

Genti's first impulse was to try to launch himself over the top of the study unit—but it would have taken too long. The quicker way was to double back the way he had come.

His heart pounding, he raced down the aisle between the

partitions. Up ahead, past the study units on his right, there was a scuffling—as of someone fleeing. But Michaux must have been bent over, because Genti still couldn't catch a glimpse of him.

No! He can't get away, damn it!

One slip would wreck their whole plan. If even one of the androids got by them, alerted the gang of them in security— they would be outnumbered. And by beings who had years of physical-conflict training in their memories.

I won't let it happen!

Just as Genti neared the door, it slid aside and something flashed through the opening. Something small and wiry, skidding on all fours.

For a moment after the something was gone, the door remained open. Then, slowly, it began to slide back again.

Genti managed to reach it just before it could close altogether—managed to wedge his arm and shoulder into the narrowing space.

Pressure—but just for an instant, until the door's feed-back circuits could tell it there was something stuck there. Then the safety mechanism cut in and the door began to release him.

Pushing himself through, he scanned the corridor—first in one direction, then the other.

There. Michaux had gone in the direction of the shorter passageway—was just now turning the corner.

Genti took off after him, making no attempt to conceal the phaser anymore. The pounding of his boots on the metal decking crammed the corridor full of noise—but it was only a backdrop for the drumbeat of blood in his temples.

I can't let him get away. I can't.

The corner loomed and he slowed down to negotiate it. Skidded a little to the outside, unable to control his momentum.

Almost too late, he saw Michaux spring from concealment—almost too late, depressed the trigger.

Suddenly, there was a bolt of scarlet light between them. Michaux bounced back from it and hit the bulkhead, crumpled.

Genti found himself on the floor as well—propped up with his free arm. But his phaser was still aimed at Michaux.

He got to his feet cautiously, never taking his eyes off the helmsman.

No—the android. The damned, stinking, murdering android. The sound of Obobo's body breaking came back to him, made him shiver.

And I thought it would be so easy.

He didn't need to use the scalpel this time. He just adjusted the setting and fired.

When he was done, he restored the setting to stun and wiped the wetness from his face.

How many times had Joaquin Martinez ridden this turbolift to the bridge of the *Hood?* Thousands? Considering that Martinez had served under the ship's previous captain, perhaps tens of thousands.

As Kirk rode the lift now, he felt like an intruder. A pretender. The *Hood* wasn't his ship, as much as it had been cut from the same cloth as the *Enterprise.* It didn't feel right to be taking command of her.

But, of course, it was the only way.

The lift indicator was approaching bridge level. Kirk balanced the phaser pistol in his hand, looked at Averback beside him.

"Ready?" he asked.

The redheaded crewman smiled. Just that, no other answer. He had an interesting face—lots of childish freckles, yet more than its share of care lines as well.

It was a face one could trust. Or so Kirk hoped. After all, anyone in engineering could have pushed a few buttons. But Kirk needed more than mere button pushing. He needed credibility.

The indicator showed *bridge.* A moment later, the doors parted with a slight exhalation.

And as if they were there for something as mundane as a levels check, and nothing more than that, they came out to take their prearranged positions.

Banks was stretched out in the command chair. He took no notice of them. Nor did anyone else, for that matter, until Averback got to the engineering board. When he started the procedure for isolating security section, one of his fellow crewman let out a yelp.

"Hey! What d'you think you're doing?" The man rose, moved to stop him.

"That's far enough, mister," said Kirk, holding up his phaser where everyone could see it. The crewman stopped dead in his tracks, though it took a second or two before he realized that the weapon was pointed at *him.*

Without a word, Averback returned to his assignment. Completed it.

Banks turned in the command chair, eyed Kirk. "I don't know what you think you're doing," he said, his voice calm and controlled. "But if I were you, I'd give it up. Quickly."

Kirk spotted someone moving off to his right, turned the phaser on her. She stopped halfway to an alarm button.

"What I'm doing," he said, watching as the woman backed away again, "is exposing *you* for an impostor—an android replica of Jamal Banks, no more human than this phaser pistol."

That gave rise to a few startled looks.

"And if there's anyone who doesn't believe me," he went on, "you can ask Averback here."

All eyes seemed to shift to the redhead. Averback nodded.

"This is Captain Kirk," he said, "of the *Enterprise.* And it's a long story, but he's telling the truth. There *are* androids on the ship—infiltrated among us—and we have reason to believe that Lieutenant Banks is one of them."

The science officer regarded Averback as if the crewman were disturbed. Then he turned back to Kirk.

"You've really got him believing that," he said. "Don't you, Kirk?" He looked around the bridge, from one wondering face to another. "This man," he said, "is dangerous. The reason we came to Tranquillity Seven was to pick him up—after he'd been apprehended by the local authorities." He shook his head, spoke as if to Kirk alone. "I don't know why you went AWOL," he said. "Perhaps you don't either. But this won't solve anything." He stood, extended his hand in Kirk's direction. "Now, give me the phaser pistol."

Of course, Banks knew he wouldn't do that. But it was exactly the way Kirk would have acted with an armed madman on *his* bridge. And the performance seemed to have had the desired effect. There were furtive looks on the faces of the bridge crew—glances from one to another as they tried to think of a way to disarm the intruder.

The captain would have stunned Banks then and there, but it was hardly advisable to use a phaser on the bridge of a starship. Too many sensitive instruments at hand, too much potential for disaster.

"All right," he told the android, trying to head off the boneheaded stunt that someone was bound to pull before long. "You say you're human? *Prove* it. Anybody got something sharp?"

"He's trying to confuse you," countered Banks. "To distract you from the truth."

"Wait," said Averback. "I've got something." He reached into a pocket, produced an antique penknife. The engineer looked at it for a moment. "My mom always said it would come in handy."

He tossed it in Banks's direction. The android snatched it out of the air with some disdain.

"There you go," said Kirk. "All you have to do is cut your finger. Show us some blood."

Banks shook his head slowly from side to side, made a clucking sound. "Certainly," he said, the voice of reason incarnate. "If that's all it will take to expose your little gambit."

For a fraction of a second, Kirk had the feeling that he might have made a mistake. Was it possible, he wondered, that not *everyone* who beamed down to Exo III had been duplicated?

Then, in a flurry of motion, Banks reached down and tore the armrest off the command seat.

Sparks geysered from electronic ruin. And before anyone could move, could react, the heavy armrest was hurtling toward Kirk's head.

The captain ducked, feeling the thing graze his shoulder before it smashed into the closed doors of the turbolift. Before he could take another breath, Banks had vaulted over the rail and was lunging for him.

Kirk resisted the urge to fire and whirled out of harm's

241

way. There was a *chunk* in the space he had just vacated as the android's fist plowed into the bulkhead, collapsing the metal surface all around it.

Recovering, realizing he had missed, he turned and advanced on Kirk.

The captain backed off. "You see?" he said. "Is this your Lieutenant Banks? Could *he* have done *this?*"

The android no longer bothered with a rebuttal. But Kirk's words did seem to have an effect on him—to trigger an awareness of the position he'd put himself in, the degree to which he'd exposed himself.

Kirk wondered at that. Banks had acted irrationally in coming after his antagonist. After all, it had still been something of a stalemate at that point.

Had he simply panicked? Was there a flaw in his manufacture—or in his programming—that allowed him to crack under pressure? That permitted blind anger to take over, suddenly and tumultuously?

"Give it up," he told the android. "They're onto you now. We're *all* onto you."

By then, Banks had regained his composure. He smiled.

And laid his hand on the plate that opened the lift doors. Even as they began to part, he darted inside.

Kirk didn't hesitate this time—not when it looked as if Banks might escape to warn the other androids. He launched himself sideways before Banks could shut the doors with the emergency override. As he hit the deck, sprawling, he sprayed phaser fire into the lift.

In the next moment, the doors closed. The captain cursed, scrambling to his feet.

But there was no need anymore for urgency. The lift wasn't going anyplace. Though its doors screened Banks from their sight, the indicator beside them showed that the lift was still on bridge level.

Cautiously, phaser still at the ready, Kirk opened the doors again.

The android was crumpled in a corner of the enclosure. Obviously, one of those wild shots had found its mark.

Kirk put the phaser back on his belt. He turned to the bridge crew, saw the varying degrees of astonishment on their faces.

"Anyone still have his doubts?" he asked.

No response.

"There are things like this all over the ship," said Averback. "And we need your help to do something about them."

Murmurs of shock gradually turned into promises of aid. Slowly, the bridge contingent came around.

"Good," said Kirk. "Now let's put this android away— somewhere where he won't get loose. If possible, I'd like to preserve him for—"

He was interrupted by an insistent beeping at the communications console. The communications officer on duty—a petite blonde—moved to answer it.

"What is it?" asked Kirk.

"It's Admiral Straus," she said after a moment. "From Starbase Three. But . . . he's not coming in very clearly."

"We've had trouble with transmission reception in this sector," said one of the other bridge officers. "Especially long-range transmissions."

"Can you put him up on the screen?" asked Kirk.

"I . . . I think so, yes," said the blonde. She twisted a few dials and the admiral's face abruptly filled the forward viewscreen, distorted by wave after wave of interference.

"Captain Martinez?" bellowed Straus. "Can . . . hear me?"

"I hear you, Admiral," answered Kirk. "But this isn't Martinez. It's Jim Kirk, and—"

"Damn it, give me some kind . . . response, *Hood!* What the blazes . . . going on there?"

"He isn't receiving our transmission," interjected the communications officer. "He can't hear you, sir."

Kirk pounded his fist on the rail before him. "Isn't there *anything* we can do? Give him some sort of signal that *we* can hear *him?*"

"Only on a subspace band," came the reply. "But he won't receive that for some time."

". . . what's the matter," Straus continued, "but I hope to hell . . . gets through to you somehow. It's time . . . rear ends in gear. The Romulans . . . a freighter. And they've . . . in force . . . more firepower than we expected. We need you there, Joaquin. There's no one else close enough to . . ."

The admiral scowled. ". . . coordinates, just in case. But . . . can't hear me, then God help the others. Straus out."

Silence for a moment.

"Did you get those coordinates, Lieutenant?" asked Kirk.

"They're coming through now, sir. And pretty clearly."

"When you've got them, give them to the navigator."

The navigation officer swiveled in his seat and faced forward—an indication of his readiness. The helmsman too assumed a position of alertness.

A good crew, Kirk mused. Your captain trained you well.

"Mister Averback," he said, "you're in charge of the android's disposal. Then get back with the others. Let them know we've regained the bridge."

"Aye, sir," said Averback, and moved to comply.

Kirk came around the half-destroyed command chair and sat down. For better or worse, it was where he belonged now.

Something on the floor caught his eye—something small and shiny. He picked it up.

"Mister Averback . . ." he called.

The engineer stopped in front of the open turbolift.

"Sir?"

Kirk turned and tossed him the penknife. Averback caught it a little awkwardly.

"You might need that again sometime."

The engineer grinned. "Thank you, sir."

"Don't mention it," said Kirk. And he turned his attention to the task ahead of them.

Chapter Twenty-three

AS THEY APPROACHED at impulse-normal speed, the Romulan ships were identifiable only as points of light against the black-velvet backdrop of space. The freighter was somewhere among them, but its hide didn't reflect the starlight as well.

"All right," said *Kirk*. "This is close enough for now. Full stop, Mister Sulu."

There was an almost subliminal whine as the engines shifted into standby mode.

"Full magnification," ordered the captain.

Spock complied. The scene on the viewscreen moved suddenly closer, revealing the vulpine shapes of the enemy vessels—four of them, as Straus had said—as well as a smaller, duller shape in their midst.

"They've detected our presence, sir," announced Uhura. "The Romulan commander has issued us a warning."

Kirk chuckled dryly. "Has he really? Can you give me visual contact, Lieutenant?"

"In just a moment, Captain. We've got to . . . *there*."

The dark visage of a Romulan warrior sprang up onto the forward viewscreen, filling it. His features were narrower, more predatory than those of most Romulans. And he was exceedingly young to be a full commander in the Imperial fleet.

"This is Commander T'bak of the flagship *Ka'frah*," said the Romulan. "I will tell you only once to remove yourself from this vicinity. You are perilously close to our side of the neutral zone—*Enterprise*."

He spat out that last word as if it were a curse. But then, *Kirk* mused, it probably *was* in most Romulan circles.

"I only respond," said the android, "to your own breach of treaty. A *serious* breach, I might add—the detention of a vessel operating under Federation protection."

The Romulan made an untranslatable sound—though *Kirk* understood its tone.

"This *vessel*," he said, "has entered our territory. It is being searched for evidence of espionage devices."

"It's only a freighter," countered the captain. "And it is *not* within your territory. It is within the neutral zone—as *you* are."

"It *fled* into the neutral zone," spat T'bak. "It was here that we apprehended it. But it was first sighted well within the bounds of Romulan space."

"Captain—two of the enemy's ships are coming this way," said Spock. "Judging by their trajectories, they will assume positions on either side of us. It would suggest a flanking attack."

Kirk punched in a channel to engineering. "Shields up, Scotty. Ready phaser banks and photon torpedoes."

"Aye, sir," came the response.

The android had purposely allowed the Romulan to hear and see his preparations. It would show him they meant business.

"You can avoid this," said T'bak. "Leave now."

"Not without that freighter," said *Kirk*.

"You are one against four," observed the Romulan.

"Are you certain of that?" asked the android. "We *do* have cloaking devices, you know."

It wasn't entirely true. While the Federation had indeed obtained the cloaking technology, it did not outfit its vessels with the device—since both the Romulans and the Klingons were able to penetrate any cloak.

T'bak sneered. "We can negate the effects of the cloaking device—as you know. If there were other Federation ships here, we would have detected them."

"Only if you knew where to look."

It gave the Romulan pause. He barked orders to one of his officers.

"The Romulan vessels are slowing down," reported Spock. "Coming to a halt."

"Terminate visual contact," commanded *Kirk.*

T'bak's face vanished, replaced by the view forward of the *Enterprise.* Sure enough, two of the enemy's ships had fanned out, taken up positions on either side of them—but they were coming no closer.

"There," said the android. "Let him chew on *that* for a while."

At the helm, Sulu chuckled appreciatively. Just as the human Sulu would have. Chekov shook his clenched fist in imitation of his own template.

Both necessary gestures, given the presence of Uhura and the other humans on the bridge. They would expect such behavior.

"Congratulations, Captain," said Spock. "You seem to have achieved a stalemate."

"Thank you, Spock." *Kirk* leaned back in his seat. "But it won't hold them forever."

Unless, he thought, we drive the nail of doubt deeper into their minds.

The android reflected for a moment, made his decision.

"Lieutenant Uhura—of the two ships still close to the freighter, which is their flagship?"

"The one on the right, sir," said Uhura. "That's where the signal came from."

"Good. Give me some thrust, Mister Sulu. We're moving in."

"Aye, Captain," said the helmsman, his fingers dancing over his console.

The *Enterprise* moved forward. On the viewscreen, the freighter and its antagonists loomed gradually larger.

"Head straight for that flagship, Lieutenant. I want to come nose to nose with her."

Kirk watched the flanking ships carefully. After a little while, he was satisfied that they weren't moving to cut him off.

And why should they? The *Enterprise* wasn't approaching

quickly enough to be considered a threat. But the *fact* of its approach, in and of itself, would have to be pondered, analyzed—buying them more time than they would otherwise have had.

Would the human Kirk have thought of this? No doubt. But he'd never have had the stomach to actually *do* it.

Suddenly, there was someone at *Kirk's* side and just behind him. He looked up over his shoulder at Spock.

"Captain," said the first officer, looking straight ahead at the viewscreen, speaking so softly that no one else could easily hear him. "It is not too late to stop and consolidate our position. You have already achieved your purpose—the Romulans seem confused."

Kirk too looked ahead at the screen. The Romulan flankers were almost at the edges of it now, still frozen in their tracks.

"I have achieved nothing," he said, "if I stop now. It will show us to be weak, underconfident. A bluff must be bold, Mister Spock, or it is no bluff at all—something a Vulcan would know nothing about."

It was a hint for the first officer to back off. He was carrying authenticity too far.

"Yet it remains a matter of time," Spock persisted, "before your bluff is exposed. And the closer we get to the Romulan flagship, the more vulnerable we will be when that moment comes."

Kirk found that the fingers of his right hand had curled into a fist. He willed them to relax, watched them do so.

"Your input," he said, "has been duly noted. Return to your station."

For a moment, Spock seemed to hesitate. Then he was gone.

There is something wrong with him, the captain told himself. When we return to Midos Five, I will have to eliminate him. Create another duplicate of Spock.

Then he remembered that that would not be possible. By now, Brown would have had the Vulcan destroyed—along with the others.

Still, I can't have him questioning my authority. It is necessary that he be eliminated.

* * *

Aboard the *Ka'frah*, Commander M'nai T'bak did his best to conceal his uncertainty. Young as he was, he did not wish to give his crew a reason to doubt his abilities.

Nonetheless, a curse escaped his lips.

"Perhaps," said Subcommander T'ouru, "he was telling the truth after all. Certainly, it would be foolhardy to approach us unless he truly has allies under cloak." He grunted thoughtfully.

T'ouru's opinion was a respected one. He had served T'bak's father well until the old man's death.

"Then you think we are at a disadvantage?" asked the commander.

T'ouru shrugged. "Unless it is simply a bluff. This *Kirk* has been known to take such gambles."

T'bak would not come out and ask his second-in-command what to do. Nor would T'ouru tell him, unbidden.

It was up to the commander to decide.

And he couldn't wait much longer—that is, if he were to act at all. But wasn't *Kirk* inviting him to act? *Daring* him to act?

T'bak had the eerie feeling that he was on the verge of a blunder. That he had missed something obvious, something that might have unlocked this puzzle for him. He felt he was about to undo all he and his compatriots had accomplished in the Praetorate.

Still, he gave the order.

"Sir!" Spock's voice rang out suddenly. "The flanker ships are starting to move—and quickly."

Kirk saw that they were no longer on the screen. He blinked. When had they left it? While he was thinking about Spock?

He came forward in his chair, tried to get a grip on the situation. "Evasive action, Mister Sulu. First Officer, I need a visual on those ships—"

Before he could finish, the *Enterprise* staggered beneath them. And again.

"Direct hits," said Chekov. "Demmage to shields two end three."

"Get us *out* of here, Mister Sulu," barked *Kirk*.

The helmsman turned to glance at him. "We're at maximum impulse speed now, Captain."

"Romulan vessels in pursuit," announced Spock. "Firing."

Another impact, worse than the first two. The ship lurched, catapulting *Kirk* halfway out of his command chair.

"Demmage to number four shield, sir."

"Get some emergency power to those shields," ordered *Kirk*. He depressed a button on his armrest. "Weapons room—can you get a bead on them?"

"No, sir, not yet. They're dogging our . . . wait. We've shaken one loose. We're locking weapons on him now, sir."

A long, tense moment.

"Range, sir."

"Fire," said *Kirk*. He waited.

"We have hit one of our pursuers," reported Spock. "But it has not diminished the vessel's capacity for pursuit."

Another blow, one that wrenched the deck out from under them.

"Return fire," bellowed *Kirk*.

"Returning fire, sir."

"Another hit," called Spock. "Same vessel. Extent of damage still . . . Captain! A third ship is approaching off the port bow!"

A third ship?

Kirk had allowed himself to become preoccupied with the Romulans on his tail. He had forgotten about the others.

The first jolt incapacitated basic systems, plunging them into darkness. The next one fire-shot that darkness full of blue sparks.

As the backup systems cut in and the lights went on, *Kirk* climbed back into his command chair. Someone was moaning, someone injured in the last salvo—but he didn't concern himself with that. After all, it was only a human. He opened a channel to engineering.

"Damage report, Mister Scott."

The answer seemed to emerge from a chaos of urgent voices.

"They've stirred up bloody hell down here, sir. Th'

engines are useless—impulse *and* warp-drive. A' . . . hold on, sir."

Kirk heard another voice making report. Then the chief engineer returned.

"We've got a breach in deck four, Captain. It's been locked off, but a'll need t' send a repair crew right away."

"No," said the android. "We're in the middle of a military confrontation here, mister. I want all available hands working on those engines."

There was a pause, as of disbelief.

"But we canna allow th' breach t' go untended. It'll put too much strain on th' inner locks, sir—suck 'em out like—"

"That wasn't a suggestion, Scotty. Get those engines running."

Kirk tapped another stud on his armrest.

"Weapons room—report."

"We're still in working order, Captain. But we've lost a couple of monitors. We've got a blind spot."

"Use what you *do* have to watch for the enemy. If they cross your sights, fire. Don't wait for an order."

"Aye, sir."

Kirk saw that his helmsman and his navigator had hauled themselves back into their respective seats. Naturally, they were unharmed.

"What about those shields, Mister Chekov?"

The ensign checked. "Shield one is no longer in operation," he said. "The others are up, but et only twenty to forty percent of . . ."

He was drowned out by McCoy's voice, crackling over the ambient speaker.

"What in blue blazes is going on?" he raged.

The captain depressed the button for sickbay.

"Everything's under control, Doctor."

"The hell it is! We've got critically injured people all over the ship, Captain. I need help if I'm going to bring in those that can still be saved."

"Then you'll have to find it yourself, Doctor. I've got my own work cut out for me."

"Blast it, Jim, I'm talking about *lives!* All you—"

"Uhura," called *Kirk,* turning in her direction.

"Aye, sir," responded the communications officer. She had sustained a cut over one eye, but seemed otherwise functional.

"Override the channel to sickbay, please."

McCoy's voice still scalded them. ". . . so damned busy you can't . . ."

"I gave an order, Lieutenant."

"Aye, sir," said Uhura. And with obvious reluctance, she cut McCoy short.

In the wake of the chief medical officer's tirade, it was strangely silent on the bridge. Even the moaning had stopped, the injured party having removed herself in the turbolift.

It gave *Kirk* a moment to think, to determine what had gone wrong. But try as he might, he could not think of anything he would have done differently.

It was one against four. Not even an android can prevail against that kind of odds.

Yet he was not just any android. He was the *leader.* He should have found a way.

Again, the chasm seemed to open at his feet, dark and bottomless and deadly.

No. It's not over yet, he thought. I still have my ship and my crew. I can still win.

He regarded the forward monitor. It showed him three of the four Romulan ships—two at either edge of the screen, in the foreground; the flagship at the center, diminished by greater distance. And beside the *Ka'frah* stood the freighter, still at T'bak's mercy.

For now, the Romulans were making no move to finish off the *Enterprise.* They were being cautious. Obviously, they were not yet convinced that the ship was crippled, unable to maneuver.

Kirk tapped his fingertips on his armrest. He felt as if all eyes were upon him—Sulu's, Chekov's, Spock's. Those of the frightened, fragile humans.

Even T'bak's, off in his catbird seat.

There must be something I can do to beat him. There *must* be.

* * *

K'leb raised himself off the deck, propped himself against the bulkhead. His hand rose to his temple, feeling the swelling there. It hurt where he touched it.

Then, gradually, a greater pain rose inside him. Not from his own injuries, but from those of the others who had sprawled all up and down the long corridor. As they came to, their minds spilled over with anguish.

It broke over him like a wave, threatening to drown him in its intensity. But he fought it, struggled to block it out as best he could—as he'd been taught by his mother long ago. And after a while, he emerged from the pain, shaken but whole.

By then, however, the corridor had become another kind of chaos. There were moans of torment, shouts for help. Someone was at both of the talking wallboxes within K'leb's line of sight.

He heard the word "sickbay" more than once.

Suddenly, K'leb remembered what he'd been doing—and whom he'd been doing it with. *K'liford*. Where was K'liford?

He looked around, but there were people rushing down the length of the corridor, carrying other people. For a moment or two, he couldn't see much. Then they were past, and he spotted someone who looked like his friend.

The man was lying against the opposite bulkhead. And he wasn't moving.

K'leb crawled across the corridor, his belly flooded with fear. Slowly, gently, he turned the man's head away from the wall.

It *was* K'liford—and he was alive. Bleeding from a gash in his forehead and from his nostrils, but still breathing.

K'leb didn't know what to do. His friend needed help, but he didn't know anything about healing.

Then he heard the word again, over the roil of desperate voices.

Sickbay.

And he realized where those people who'd passed him were going.

Carefully, he slipped his arms around K'liford, lifted him to a sitting position. Then, just as carefully, he pulled his friend up onto his shoulder.

Laboring under K'liford's weight, he headed for sickbay and Dok'tor M'Koy.

Denise DeLong crawled through the Jeffries tube, dragging her equipment and supplies along with her. She came to a section where the circuitry had been fused together, took out her laser, and set to work.

DeLong worked quickly. She knew that they were sitting ducks for the Romulans until the engines got going again—and that couldn't happen until she completed her assignment. Sweat beaded up on her brow, and not entirely from the dry heat that sat with her inside the tube.

Still, there was a part of her that could observe, removed from the need to cut out this length of damaged circuitry and replace it with new.

I can't believe the captain told us to ignore that breach, she thought. Certainly, it's important to get the engines operating—but if we wait too long to repair the hull, we'll lose that whole deck. Maybe the ship itself.

It wasn't like Captain Kirk to make a mistake like that. To ignore the recommendation of his chief engineer.

Was this tied in somehow with his erratic behavior toward *her?*

It was one thing to be acting strangely toward a single individual—and quite another to endanger the ship with faulty command logic.

Suddenly, DeLong wanted very much to be wrong about the captain. Because if something *had* snapped inside him . . .

What chance was there that anyone on the ship would survive this?

"Your decision was the correct one, Commander. The *Enterprise* has been subdued."

T'bak looked up at T'ouru. Frowned, nodded.

"Yes," he said. "The enemy seems helpless. And now that we have turned him over on his back, all that remains is to crack open his shell."

But he was not as confident as his words suggested.

Why not? he asked himself. Is this not what we fought so

long and hard for in the Praetorate—bargaining for power where we could find it, quashing the objections of the elder lords by whatever means necessary? Was this not our goal when we so daringly plucked a freighter out of Federation space? And has this not been the sort of victory we imagined—swift, decisive, and devastating? One which the Federation could not possibly ignore?

Yet there was that voice in the back of his head, warning him that he was being lured into a trap. And that the *Enterprise* was the bait.

"Shall I give the order," asked T'ouru, "to move in for the kill?"

T'bak looked up again, considered his subcommander. T'ouru, of a minor house himself, had spoken up against the war movement more than once. He had said that the time was not right for full-scale conflict with the Federation—that they had neither the numbers of ships nor the technology to achieve any sort of victory.

Yet when T'bak's faction had carried the Praetorate, T'ouru had agreed to serve on the *Ka'frah,* to be among those who would incite the Federation to war. First and foremost, T'ouru was a soldier, and as such his duty had been clear.

Now, he was prepared to relay the order that would plunge them into the long and glorious fight—even though he did not believe it would bring them the glory T'bak and the others had envisioned.

"Commander?"

T'bak roused himself from his reverie, refocused his attention on the matter at hand. He peered at the *Enterprise* through narrowed eyes.

Trap . . . or no trap?

"No," he said finally. "Do not give the order, T'ouru." He paused, imagining the looks exchanged behind his back. "At least, not yet."

Kirk had been pacing the bridge like a caged tiger, riffling the human Kirk's memories for a situation similar to this one—and whatever remedy Kirk may have applied. Until this point, however, he'd found nothing useful.

"Captain," said Spock, an urgency in his voice. "The Romulans are beginning to maneuver again."

Kirk turned to the viewscreen, saw that the enemy vessels had indeed been set into motion—all but the flagship, of course.

Yet they did not seem to be approaching the *Enterprise*—at least not directly. They were moving at oblique angles to the Federation ship.

"First officer," he said after a while, "confirm that the Romulans are getting closer with each pass."

"Confirmed," said Spock. "They appear to be testing—"

"I *know* what they're doing, mister." *Kirk* came over to his command chair, lowered himself into it. He tapped the stud that connected him with the weapons room.

"Sir?"

"Are you scanning the Romulan vessels?" he asked.

"Aye, Captain. But they're not within range yet."

"They will be soon. When they get there, remember my order—fire immediately."

"I'll remember, sir."

Kirk was about to end the conversation when he noticed Spock at his elbow again.

"A suggestion, sir," said the first officer. "We can accomplish very little, other than the acceleration of our demise, by firing on the Romulans at this time. It may be more prudent to practice restraint, giving them the impression that we are defenseless. Then, when the other ships . . ."

It galled *Kirk* to have to hear this. *He* was the leader—not Spock. *He* was the one who would get them out of this.

Yet Spock went on. And something grew inside *Kirk*, something hot and powerful that made him tremble with the effort it took to contain it.

Until finally, he could contain it no longer.

"Mind your own business, Mister Spock!" He leaped to his feet, grabbed his first officer by the front of his uniform shirt. "I'm sick of your half-breed interference, do you hear me?"

No sooner were the words out than he realized where they had come from. Abruptly, he released Spock—but the damage was done. His invective seemed to hang in the air, indicting him.

He saw the stares from human and android alike. They were hardly expressions of admiration.

"What are you all looking at?" he asked, a trifle louder than he had intended. "If you can't keep your minds on your duties, I'll find others in this crew who can."

Spock, meanwhile, had not moved from his place beside the command chair. He seemed unperturbed by the incident, though his uniform was wrinkled where *Kirk* had grabbed it.

"As I was saying," he went on, "it might work to our advantage if we were to withhold our fire. In that way . . ."

No longer racked by whatever had taken hold of him, *Kirk* couldn't help but listen this time. He didn't want to, but his first officer was relentless. And he found, though he was reluctant to admit it, that Spock's words made *sense.*

". . . in the event the other ships arrive in time, we will then have . . ."

Kirk sank into his chair, held up his hand for silence. "All right, Spock. We'll withhold our fire."

"Captain?" came the voice from the weapons room.

"I'm rescinding that last order," said *Kirk.* "Hold your fire until you hear from me. Acknowledge."

"Whatever you say, sir."

"As you were. *Kirk* out."

He looked up at Spock.

"Satisfied?" he asked.

Spock's features were impassive.

"It is my duty," he said, "to provide input."

"Of course it is," said *Kirk.*

But within him, as if from a great distance, he could hear the echoes: *Mind your business, Mister Spock! I'm sick of your half-breed interference. . . .*

Chapter Twenty-four

"CAPTAIN KIRK?" said Potemkin.

Kirk turned in his command seat.

"I have Captain Ascher on the *Potemkin.*"

"Up on the screen, please, Mister Paultic."

"Aye, sir."

Ascher was normally pretty stone-faced, a square-jawed man who kept his emotions to himself. This time, however, he couldn't help but register his surprise and confusion.

"Damn it, Jim. How the hell did you wind up on the *Hood?* And what happened to Martinez?"

"It's a long story, Seth. And I haven't figured it all out myself yet. Suffice it to say that Joaquin is probably dead—and one of those who engineered his murder has taken my place on the *Enterprise.*"

Ascher's brows came together. "I don't get it. How did he . . . ?"

"He's an android—an exact duplicate of me. Just as there were duplicates of Joaquin and members of his crew."

Ascher took a deep breath, let it out pensively. "I've got a funny question, Captain. How do I know that . . . ."

"That I'm the genuine article?" finished Kirk. "You want some proof that I'm not the impostor myself."

The captain of the *Potemkin* half nodded. "Something like that, yes."

Kirk gave it to him.

"Satisfied?" he asked.

Ascher nodded. "Quite. But what if your *doppelgänger* comes up with the same information?"

"He won't. That is, if I'm right about where he came from."

Ascher grunted. "Fair enough—for the moment. But what about the business at hand? Whose side is the *Enterprise* going to be on—assuming, of course, that it even shows up?"

"My guess," said Kirk, "is that the android will *have* to show up—if he's to continue his charade. And having shown up, he'll have to work with us. He has no more desire to become space debris than we do."

"Three minutes until we reach the Mayday coordinates," announced the navigator. "And counting."

"Any idea how you want to handle this?" asked Ascher. "I mean, yours was supposed to be the lead vessel. I don't think that should change just because you've exchanged one vessel for another."

"Thanks, Captain," said Kirk. "I think it's best to play it by ear until we feel out the Romulans. There's always a chance that this thing can be resolved without bloodshed."

"Agreed. Ascher out."

And his image blinked away, replaced by a rush of stars.

Kirk leaned back in his command chair, ordering his thoughts for the impending confrontation.

I hope you are *there,* mon frère semblable. *I have a score to settle with you.*

There was no reason that Uhura should have felt any warmer than usual at her communications station. The backup systems were doing an adequate job of life support; the temperature should have been the same as always.

It must be the tension, she told herself. She looked around, saw perspiration beading on the brows of some of the other crewmen. *We're all feeling it.*

The Romulan ships had come steadily closer, for all the indirectness of their approach patterns. It was only a matter of time before they decided the *Enterprise* was helpless and opened fire.

Her gaze fell on the captain, leaned forward in his command seat, intent on the forward viewscreen.

He must be wound up the tightest of anyone, she thought. It's his game to win or lose. If he waits too long, we'll be dead meat. And if he jumps the gun, we'll forfeit what little time we might have had left.

Maybe that's why the captain had laced into Spock a few minutes ago. Because the tension had been too great a burden.

On the other hand, they had been in spots as bad as this one before—and Uhura had never seen Kirk abuse his first officer that way.

There had to be more to it. An extended disagreement before they came up onto the bridge? A recent tragedy in the captain's life that the crew knew nothing about?

Something. James T. Kirk doesn't just fly off the handle every day.

Uhura took a closer look at the captain. At his shoulders, at the exposed skin of his neck. Interestingly enough, there were no signs of tension at all. No bunching of the shoulder muscles—not even a bead of sweat.

Hmm.

She touched her own neck, came away with perspiration on her fingertips. She shrugged.

Maybe he's not as wound up as I thought—or at least, not anymore. Could be that brief outburst did him some good.

Spock, standing at the next station over from Uhura, showed no signs of anxiety either. Of course, one didn't expect perspiration from a Vulcan.

Chekov turned away from his navigation console, looked back toward the captain. "Shield three hes just failed, sir. The demmage must hev been worse then we thought."

That's funny, she realized. Chekov's not sweating either. And neither is Sulu.

In fact, there was *no sign* of tension about them—no sign at all. Their postures, their expressions seemed relaxed, completely unruffled.

Like machines, she noted—then stopped herself. *Now there's a strange thought.*

Abruptly, she realized that it wasn't one she'd come up with entirely on her own.

Wasn't someone talking about machines the other day? About . . .

She might have pursued the notion a little further if she hadn't been interrupted by a flashing light on her board. Instantly, she did what was necessary to tune into the signal.

Her heart leaped into her throat. Could it be . . . ?

The voice of her opposite number on the *Hood* was about the sweetest sound she had ever heard.

"Captain," she said, her own voice vibrating with excitement, "I have the *Hood.*"

A cheer went up on the bridge.

"Can you give me a visual?" asked *Kirk*.

She could and she said so.

"Then put it through, Lieutenant."

A moment later, the viewscreen filled with the image of the other ship's captain. But it wasn't the image they had expected to see.

Uhura heard herself gasp, saw the startled looks that passed from one bridge officer to the next.

"Attention, *Enterprise.* This is Captain James Kirk—the *real* Captain James Kirk. The being now sitting in your command seat is an impostor."

The captain—*their captain*—was up in a flash.

"I don't know who you are, mister, or what this is about. But I want to see Joaquin Martinez—and I want to see him *now.*"

"Captain Martinez is dead," said the other Kirk. "As you well know. And those responsible for his murder—your compatriots on the *Hood*—have either been destroyed or incarcerated."

The screen-sized face turned in Mister Spock's direction.

"He's an android, Spock. Like those Roger Korby created on Exo III. And he's trying to finish what Korby started."

Spock cocked an eyebrow, addressed the image transmitted by the *Hood.*

"While I must admit that you resemble James Kirk quite closely . . . I am as certain as I may be that our captain *is* who he *says* he is. Therefore, I must conclude that *you,* sir, are the impostor."

The face on the screen seemed taken aback by that. Then, slowly, realization seemed to dawn.

"Spock," said the other Kirk, in a voice tinged with dread. "You've got him too—haven't you?" He glanced from crewman to crewman. "And how many others?"

Uhura, meanwhile, was trying to sort out the truth. And the mention of androids had jogged her memory. Brought back to mind what she'd heard the other day—about *machines*.

You haven't noticed anything funny about the captain lately, have you? It was McCoy who had asked.

Can't say I have, Doctor. Why?

But he'd ignored her counterquery and gone on.

Say, something cold . . . or distant? Or, well, machinelike —for lack of a better word to describe it?

And then, before she could respond, he'd provided an answer himself. *No. Of course you haven't.* He'd snorted in his characteristic way. *Just forget I asked, Lieutenant—all right?*

Whatever you say, sir.

At the time, it hadn't meant much to her. But now, it seemed to connect with her other observations.

The way the captain had ignored McCoy's pleas for help . . . the way he had ordered her to cut the doctor off . . .

The fact that some of her fellow officers didn't sweat . . .

The tone of Spock's voice just now—colder and more calculating than was customary even for *him* . . .

And, finally, the accusations coming from the *Hood*. The idea of androids running the *Enterprise* . . .

Of course, she couldn't be certain. But it appeared that the screen Kirk was the *true* Kirk.

And that the captain whose orders she'd been following . . .

"You're a good actor," *Kirk* told the face on the screen. "But not good enough. We see through you. And as soon as this is over, you're going to pay for whatever crimes you've committed."

He sat down heavily, looked around. Scowled.

"In the meantime, we are hardly in what you'd call a position of authority. We need help. And I have to assume you've come to fight the Romulans as we have—or else why would you be here?"

The other Kirk—the one Uhura now believed to be the *real* Captain Kirk—had by now recovered from his shock. He eyed his double.

"Yes," he said. "We're here to *confront* the Romulans. And we have the *Potemkin* with us." He paused. "What exactly *is* your position?"

Kirk—the one Uhura now believed to be the fraud—imparted the details of their disability.

"I see," said the face on the screen, grimmer even than before. "But you say the Romulans don't know that your weapons still work?"

"No," said *Kirk*, "they don't—though we can't wait much longer to use them."

"Wait as long as you can," said the captain on the *Hood*. "Kirk out."

And suddenly the screen showed nothing but Romulans again.

T'bak feigned patience while Centurion T'ialla labored over the communications board.

On the main screen, the one called *Kirk* mouthed a garble of sounds that would have taken much too long to decode. It was plain, however, that he was making contact with one of his allies; while the words themselves could be disguised, there was no way the *Enterprise* could conceal the *fact* of their tight-beam transmission. Or prevent the *Ka'frah* from determining its direction, and therefore the location of the receiving vessel.

Finally, the communications officer looked up, waited for T'bak's nod before he reported. T'bak nodded.

"The transmission is not being intercepted at any point within sensor range, Commander. But neither is it merely a general distress call. Someone is answering."

T'bak stroked his chin with his thumb and forefinger. Stranger and stranger, he thought. The *Enterprise* does have allies—but it seems they have yet to arrive.

"So the allusion to cloaked ships *was* a ruse," observed T'ouru. "Only a delaying tactic after all."

"Can you pick up the other vessel's transmission?" asked T'bak.

"Of course, Commander."

T'ialla made a few adjustments. For a moment, the image on the screen flickered, and when it came back, it seemed *Kirk* had shifted his position slightly.

But otherwise, nothing had changed.

"I asked you to show me the *incoming* transmission," said T'bak.

The centurion frowned. "I thought I had, Commander. Obviously, there has been a malfunction."

Or your own foul-up, thought T'bak.

"Try again," he said.

Once more, T'ialla turned dials on the control board. And once more he failed to pick up the answering transmission.

"I . . . I don't understand, Commander. The board is not responding."

"But it *is*," said T'ouru. He pointed to the screen. "Note the figures in the background. One is a Vulcan—see, he is speaking now. He was standing in that position before T'ialla made the first adjustment, but not after. And now, with the second adjustment, he has reappeared."

T'bak regarded his subcommander. "What are you saying, T'ouru?"

"That the same man commands both ships—or seems to. More to the point, that the Federation must somehow have created a clone of its clever Captain Kirk."

T'bak felt a pit grow in his belly as he considered the possibilities. None of them was comforting.

"Call our ships off the *Enterprise*," he decided suddenly. "It is helpless anyway." He struck his armrest with a gloved fist. "Turn them loose on the newcomers instead."

T'ouru inclined his head. "As you wish, Commander."

Kirk knew there was no way to get the jump on the Romulans. Their light sensors were too powerful, too far-ranging to miss anything as big as a starship—much less two of them.

Even if he *had* been able to surprise them, he would have refrained—tried to talk instead. *Something* had set the

Romulans off—and part of his responsibility was to discover what it was.

But neither did he wish to let the Romulans get a jump on *him*. So when their ships started to move against him, without so much as an exchange of insults, he did three things.

He called for battle stations.

He authorized engineering to put up the shields.

And he had Paultic open a channel to Ascher on the *Potemkin*.

The Romulans came at them in a triangular configuration—one high and off to starboard, one low and off to starboard, and one wide to port. It was a simple strategy, but a good one, giving each bird-of-prey room in which to operate.

The textbook reaction was to spread out—to make one's own ships more difficult targets. But given the odds, that would only postpone the inevitable.

"Helm," barked Kirk. "Heading three nine-zero-mark-four-two. Do you read me, *Potemkin?*"

"Loud and clear, *Hood*. I just hope it works."

"Full thrust," said Kirk. A second later, he heard his order echoed by Captain Ascher.

The starships catapulted forward—right down the throat of the Romulan attack. Instinctively, the captain's finger went to a stud on his armrest.

"Aye, sir?" came the response from the weapons room.

"Ready phasers and photon torpedoes."

"Ready, sir."

Kirk watched the Romulans loom larger and larger on the screen, waiting until he was certain they were in range. Finally, the moment came.

"Fire!" he ordered.

The *Hood*'s phaser beams lanced the speckled blackness of space, headed for the enemy ships. Its photon torpedoes burst forth—

—just as the Romulans let loose with their own blinding barrage.

Suddenly, the viewscreen boiled over with white light. And a heartbeat later, the *Hood* shuddered under the impact of the enemy's firepower.

But Kirk had experienced worse—much worse. He didn't need a damage report to know they had come through in decent shape.

So had the *Potemkin*. In a couple of clipped phrases, Ascher communicated as much.

And the Romulans were past them now, speeding in the wrong direction, away from the confrontation.

Of course, it would only take moments for them to turn around and pursue. Romulan ships had a well-deserved reputation for maneuverability.

But then, he was counting on that. And just in case the Romulans had suffered more damage than they had, he gave the order to cut speed by ten percent.

"Jim!" came Ascher's voice. "What are you doing?"

"You'll have to trust me, Seth."

There was a muttered curse, but nothing more.

"Potemkin cutting speed too," observed the acting science officer.

Kirk leaned forward, concentrating on the viewscreen. They were on a course for T'bak's flagship and the freighter—a fact the other Romulans would pick up right away. Almost on the same vector, however, and much closer, was the *Enterprise.*

That fact, Kirk hoped, was something the Romulans *wouldn't* pick up on. After all, they had already determined that the *Enterprise* was defenseless—hadn't they? Why even take it into account?

Nonetheless, he couldn't risk contacting the crippled ship. That would certainly draw attention to it—perhaps alert the Romulans to what he had in mind.

"The enemy ships have come about," reported the science officer. "They're following us, sir."

Good, the captain told himself. Now let's see if the android really does have all my memories.

From his command chair, *Kirk* watched the rapid approach of the Federation vessels. On their present courses, they would pass just to either side of the *Enterprise.*

Nor could he help but notice the Romulan ships as they maneuvered into pursuit formation. They moved quickly, gracefully.

What is the human doing? he asked himself. Why is he bringing them *my* way?

He must have asked the last question aloud—for Spock was in the process of answering almost before he knew it.

"I believe," said the first officer, "that this is the reason we were asked to refrain from firing earlier."

Suddenly, the android remembered.

One of the early confrontations with the Klingons. Three Federation vessels facing greater odds. One crippled almost immediately.

And in the end, the Federation ships had all been destroyed.

It had been required reading at the academy. For months, a young Jim Kirk had puzzled over it, seeking a way out for the Federation ships. And finally, late one night, he'd vaulted out of bed with the answer.

Of course, that had been a long time ago. Being human, he might have forgotten.

If the *Enterprise* carried out its part of the plan—without the other ships carrying out theirs—*Kirk's* ship would be left a sitting duck. And, suddenly, a *destroy priority* for the Romulans.

"Sir?" prodded Spock. "Shall I alert the weapons room?"

Kirk scowled. He saw his allies starting to leave the viewscreen, passing him on either side. He saw the Romulans growing larger as they came on in pursuit.

"Captain?"

His teeth grated as he made his decision.

"Yes, it was a clever maneuver, T'ouru. But one that achieved nothing. They are still the hunted. See—our ships have them in their sights once more. And this time, they have herded the Federation vessels back to *us*." T'bak allowed himself a thin smile. "We will crush them between us."

For the first time, the commander felt confident of victory. He had doubted himself at every juncture, second-guessed his own instincts. But in the final analysis, his instincts had been correct. Or correct *enough*.

And the elder factions in the Praetorate had been wrong. The Federation *could* be beaten. Their technology *was* sufficient.

Nor had the Kirk clone changed matters substantially. All he could do was run from their superior numbers—like any other Federation dog.

T'bak looked up at his subcommander. "You are silent, T'ouru. Savoring the victory?"

But it was not eager anticipation T'bak noted on his officer's face. T'ouru's brow was deeply furrowed, his eyes slitted with concentration.

It annoyed T'bak to see his subcommander so distracted. So pensive. The time for that was past.

"What is it, T'ouru? Speak."

For a time, the older man remained silent, watching the viewscreen, his eyes glinting with reflected light. Then those same eyes widened with a cold, crawling dread.

"The ships must veer off," he cried, his voice rising in intensity. He locked T'bak's shoulder in an iron grip—a grip born of desperation. "Order them to change course!"

T'bak glanced from T'ouru to the viewscreen and back again. Yet he saw nothing that could have alarmed his subcommander.

"I don't understand," he said. "We have a clear advantage over—"

"The *Enterprise,*" T'ouru growled. "It's a trap!"

T'bak rounded on the screen again, halfway out of his command seat. Realization tasted like bitter metal in his mouth.

He leaned over past T'ialla and slammed down on the communications console—instantly opening channels to the other ships. They were already well within the range of the *Enterprise*—but perhaps there was still time.

Three faces sprang up on the auxiliary monitors—the curious, slightly surprised faces of those who commanded the other ships.

"Veer off!" bellowed T'bak. "The *Enterprise* is armed. I repeat, veer. . . ."

But it was too late. As he watched in horror, his birds-of-prey cruisers were enveloped in sheets of close-range phaser fire. Photon torpedoes ripped into their smooth, polished hulls.

All three ships emerged from the web of deadly fire. But in the next moment, the *M'sarr*—its shields already weakened from its earlier skirmish with the *Enterprise*—showed that it had not emerged unscathed. First, its engine deck blew up in a flare of red light. Then a larger explosion tore the battle cruiser to bits.

T'bak swallowed.

No . . .

"Commander," came an anguished cry from the *Brak'makh*. "The hull has been breached. We are losing life support."

"Heavy losses on all decks," groaned the subcommander of the *Ar'kalid.* "Impulse power cut in half."

T'bak lowered himself back into his seat. He felt numb, disoriented.

And the two remaining Federation starships were bearing down on the *Ka'frah*.

"Take evasive action," advised T'ouru. *"Now,* Commander—while we still can."

Slowly, a red rage boiled up inside T'bak. It drowned out the wisdom of T'ouru's words. But it steadied him— enabled him to act.

"No," he snapped. "We will meet them—and destroy them." He darted a glanced at his helmsman. "Full thrust," he ordered. "Dead ahead—seven-three-four-mark-nine-two."

"Yes, my lord," said the officer, complying.

The *Ka'frah* leaped forward, closing with the Federation ships at dizzying speed.

"Weapons," T'bak said, punching the proper stud on his armrest, never taking his eyes off the viewscreen.

"My lord?"

"Prepare to fire on our enemies."

"Ready, Commander. We have range."

T'bak gripped the arms of his command chair, letting the rage carry him, consume him. Blind him.

"Fire!" he roared.

DOUBLE, DOUBLE

Phasers and photon torpedoes carved furrows of light into the star-pricked blackness. A number of them found their targets, shattering against deflector shields.

Then the Federation vessels retaliated. The viewscreen erupted with an image of raw, destructive force.

But the image was nothing compared to the reality that followed.

Chapter Twenty-five

IMMEDIATELY AFTER THEIR RUN, the Federation ships looped around to stand by the *Enterprise*. After all, when the Romulans gathered themselves, the disabled ship was their most likely target.

But there *was* no counterstrike—at least, not right away. Two of the three remaining birds-of-prey—including the *Ka'frah*—seemed hardly to be moving at all. And the third had only positioned itself to provide cover for the first two.

It was something of a stalemate, it seemed to Kirk. He and Ascher couldn't leave the *Enterprise* defenseless. But neither could the Romulans leave each other.

"Mister Paultic," said the captain. "I'd like a word with Commander T'bak."

"Aye, sir."

A few seconds later, the screen filled with an image of the *Ka'frah*'s bridge. It was in frenetic disarray. Sparks rained from ruined circuitry overhead. Officers rushed this way and that, shouting orders, directing the removal of the injured.

Nor was the figure in the command seat that of T'bak. It was that of an older man, doing his best to ignore a bloody gash in his cheek.

"This," said the Romulan, "is Subcommander T'ouru."

"Where's T'bak?" asked Kirk.

"He has been incapacitated. I am in command now." He paused to listen as a fellow officer bent to whisper in his ear. Then he addressed the captain again. "What is it you want?"

"What I want," said Kirk, "is to end this. Certainly, there's been enough blood spilled to satisfy everyone concerned."

"That there has," agreed T'ouru. "But if you are asking me to surrender, it is a waste of time. I will not."

Kirk eyed him. This T'ouru was a more experienced officer than T'bak, he judged. Possibly, he could be reasoned with.

"Then I won't ask for surrender," said the captain. "What about a different sort of agreement—a truce? A mutual cessation of hostilities?"

The Romulan grunted. "You were always free to leave," he said. "Go—we will not stop you."

Kirk shook his head. "We can't go—not yet. The *Enterprise* is adrift, as you can see for yourself. But *you* can leave. None of your ships has lost engine power completely."

T'ouru frowned. "There is still the matter of the freighter. It is our duty to bring it back with us."

Kirk shrugged. "As you have no doubt noticed, the freighter is slowly making its escape now that it is free of your tractor beam."

"Yes," said T'ouru. "We are aware of that. But it is still within range of our weapons—as *you* have no doubt noticed."

"Are you also aware," asked Kirk, "that the freighter is in Federation space now?" He leaned back. "Or that you yourselves are?"

T'ouru's eyes narrowed. He consulted with his navigator. And found Kirk's claim to be the truth.

"It was the flow of battle that drew us this way," said the subcommander. "A battle that would have been unnecessary were it not for the trespass of your freighter."

"Nonetheless," said the captain, "your position violates the provisions of the treaty. So even if I concede, for the moment, that the freighter may have ventured into Romulan territory . . . it seems we now have *two* violations."

T'ouru grunted again. "One may say so. Are you suggesting that two such violations may cancel each other out?"

Kirk nodded. "Something like that. What do *you* think?"

T'ouru thought about it for what seemed like a long time. "Yes," he said at last. "I am in agreement."

"Then you will leave peacefully? Return to Romulan space?"

"We will. And you vow not to fire on us as we do so?"

"You have my word, Subcommander."

T'ouru snorted. "Good. See that you keep it."

And with that, the Romulans terminated the transmission.

For a moment, there was silence on the bridge. Then Captain Ascher cut in.

"Good work, Jim."

Kirk nodded to the bodiless voice. "Thanks, Seth. But the tough part is still ahead of me. Stand by."

Kirk got up and came around his chair, headed for the communications station.

"Sir?" asked Paultic.

The captain leaned over the control board, one hand on the back of Paultic's chair. He took a deep breath.

This had better work, he thought.

"Get me Lieutenant Uhura on the *Enterprise*. And *only* Lieutenant Uhura. If anyone else answers, abort the communication."

Paultic nodded. His hands traveled expertly over the console. And in a matter of seconds, he looked up.

"Got her," he said. "It's *her* operating code."

"Ask her not to report our signal," said Kirk. "Say it's of the utmost importance."

The lieutenant nodded again, did as he asked. "She's signaling compliance," he said after a moment.

"Good. Now let me speak to her."

"I know you can't say anything, Uhura, so just listen. I need your help—and I'm gambling that you'll give it to me."

Uhura looked around the bridge. So far, no one had

273

noticed her preoccupation with the control console. They were too busy trying to figure out what the Romulans would do next.

"The accusations I made earlier were true—though I don't dare try to prove them. At first, I thought there was only one android, but I see now there are a number of them. Exposed for what they are, they'd stop at nothing to preserve themselves—wreck the entire ship, if need be. So I can't stage a confrontation."

A pause.

"All I *can* do, Uhura, is ask you to listen to your heart. Weigh what you saw of me on the viewscreen against what you've seen of my double."

Another pause.

"Will you help me, Uhura?"

She tapped out a response in the affirmative.

"Good. *Damned* good. Now, in order for the androids to be created, our people had to be beamed down to a duplication site. Was there a landing party dispatched anytime after you left Tranquillity Seven?"

She signaled that there had been.

"All right. Anyone that went planetside could have been duplicated and replaced. Can you tell me how many people that represents?"

Uhura thought for a moment, input the information into her console.

She heard Kirk curse on the other end.

"Spock is one of them, isn't he?"

Yes.

"And Sulu? Chekov?"

Yes. And yes again.

"What about Scotty?"

No.

"Doctor McCoy?"

No.

"Damn," said Kirk. "There's got to be a quicker way than this."

There was. And she didn't wait for the *Dunkirk*'s communications officer to suggest it. Hooking up a line to the computer, she called for the list of all those who'd gone out in the shuttlecraft.

"Uhura—Paultic here says you can transmit a—wait, we're getting it now. You're one step ahead of us, Lieutenant."

She scanned the list at the same time they did. It chilled her to see all those names amassed one on top of the other. It gave weight to them. Solidity. *Reality.*

She glanced at the captain again—the *android duplicate* of the captain, she reminded herself—and saw that he was still distracted. This time, by a call from someone on the ship. Doctor McCoy, pleading again for assistance? Or Scotty, trying to convince *Kirk* to change his mind about the hull repair?

"Blast it all, Uhura, this is *exactly* what we need." The captain's enthusiasm came through loud and clear. "Now, you can do one thing more—spread the word. Talk to people you can trust. Let them know the situation—and that there will soon be a chance to do something about it."

Affirmative.

"Just take care you don't get caught—and I mean that. Be *careful,* Uhura."

She couldn't help but smile to herself.

Aye, sir.

"Lieutenant?"

She looked up, her spine suddenly turned to jelly. Spock was looming in front of her, his eyes seeming to bore into her consciousness.

"Yes, Mister Spock?" She forced the words out even as her fingers flew, breaking the connection with the *Dunkirk.* . . .

"The captain," said Spock, "asked you to contact the *Potemkin.* Did you not hear him?"

"I . . ." She steadied her voice. "I was trying to listen in on the Romulans, sir. Hoping that they would fail to scramble their messages."

"Laudable," said the first officer. "But now you have other orders."

She nodded, set about establishing contact with the other ship. She could almost feel Spock's scrutiny as she worked. Then, midway through her call sequence, she stopped— closed her eyes and allowed herself to slump in her chair.

"What's going on there?" It was *Kirk*'s voice.

"Uhura seems to have fainted," answered Spock. She could feel his fingers closing about her shoulders. He shook her a little.

"Lieutenant?"

She opened her eyes, feigning disorientation.

"Mister Spock? What happened?"

"Obviously," he said, "your injury has caught up with you. Call for a replacement and report to sickbay."

Uhura nodded, still pretending to be groggy. "Aye, sir. Right away."

By the time K'leb reached sickbay, he was tired and sore and out of breath. But he had vowed not to put his friend down until it was on one of Doctor M'Koy's tables.

The doors were wide open. Along with half a dozen others—a couple with burdens like his and the rest themselves injured—he made his way through them.

Inside, all was chaos. The lights were dim and flickering, a result of the damage inflicted by the Romulans. There were medical personnel rushing every which way, armed with devices that K'leb couldn't even begin to guess the use of. He shifted K'liford's weight on his shoulder, found that it didn't help any, and tried to pick out an empty examining table.

But there weren't any empty ones to be found. At least, not here in the basic-care area. Doing his best to suppress a groan, K'leb lumbered through the press of bodies, past a series of empty, darkened offices, to the place where M'Koy himself had been cared for. It was two rooms down and to the . . .

Just as he came through the shadowy entranceway, he bumped into someone—someone tall and solid. It was all he could do to keep from dropping K'liford.

K'leb looked up—into the face of K'risteen Chap'l. He was about to ask her for help in his broken English . . . when he felt that same void in her that he had sensed in the captain. That same, cold *emptiness* where her emotions should have pulsed.

In that first fraction of a second, he knew her for what she was.

Nor did it escape her notice that he *knew*.

Possibly, he could have dropped K'liford and escaped her. But he hung on to his friend as he tried to whirl away—and it proved his undoing.

Chap'l grabbed his upper arm in a grip stronger than anything he'd ever felt before. It was like metal come to life.

K'leb tried to cry out, but her other hand came down over his mouth. And in the confusion, the cacophony of pain that permeated sickbay, no one noticed.

Slowly, inexorably, she began to drag him deeper into the critical-care area. *Deeper into the shadows . . .*

The P'othparan struggled, but he couldn't pull free. And now, when he *tried* to drop K'liford—hoping to spare him whatever fate Chap'l intended for them—the *demon* caught the crewman by the wrist.

And dragged *both* of them into the recesses of the half-darkened enclosure.

With his free arm, K'leb beat at her. Tried to pull loose the hand that covered his mouth. Kicked at her legs, attempted to hook a foot around the base of a diagnostic fixture.

It gained him nothing. They were enveloped in darkness now, where their bodies might go undiscovered for some time. Until the rest of the injured filled sickbay to capacity . . .

. . . and even then, they would be written off as casualties of war. . . .

Suddenly, Chap'l dropped K'liford—leaving her two hands to deal with K'leb. He felt the bones of his wrist threaten to break as she raised him up into the air.

Then, letting go with one hand, she found purchase for it around his throat. And as her fingers tightened, cutting off his breath, making his pulse thunder in his ears, he wished he'd been left to die back on P'othpar . . . in a place he *knew* . . . and not on some strange vessel that traveled among the stars. . . .

But before the demon could choke the life out of him, before the strength left his limbs altogether—something happened. And before he knew it, K'leb was coiled up on the floor, gasping to fill his lungs with air, suffering the agony of its passage through his tortured windpipe.

When he looked up, he saw two familiar faces through the tears that had filled his eyes. One was Dok'tor M'Koy himself.

The other was U'hura. And she held something in her hand that he thought he recognized. Wasn't it the device that the security officers carried?

"Damn it to hell," breathed M'Koy, staring down at the crumpled form of K'risteen Chap'l. "You were right, Uhura."

The black woman knelt beside K'leb, put a hand on his shoulder.

"Are you all right?" she asked.

He didn't understand the words, but he caught the emotion. To reassure her, he nodded.

Then he remembered his friend. "K'liford," he said, though it was difficult for him to speak. He pointed.

M'Koy bent beside the crewman, frowned. He put his fingers to the side of K'liford's neck, just behind the ear. His frown deepened.

"Come on," he told K'leb. "Help me get him up on one of these tables."

"All right," said Kirk. "Uhura's had long enough to alert the troops."

He checked the phaser one last time, replaced it on his belt, and stepped up onto the transporter platform.

Berg made his preparations behind the control stand while Paultic looked on. Chin stood to one side of them—and her frown, which Kirk had first noticed in the corridor outside, had deepened considerably.

"Is something disturbing you, Doctor?" asked the captain.

"Permit me to ask a stupid question," said Chin. "What if your Uhura is herself a duplicate? Or just doesn't believe you're the real McCoy?"

"And she's played it straight so far only to lure me into a trap?" Kirk shrugged. "Then I've had it. But I've got to trust someone—and Uhura's as good a choice as any."

She was still frowning. He smiled.

"Don't worry, Doctor. I didn't get this far by guessing wrong very often."

Gradually, she smiled too. But he had seen more confident smiles in his lifetime.

Paultic chose that moment to clear his throat.

"Yes, Lieutenant?" said Kirk. "Have you got a question too?"

"Well, sir," said the communications officer, "I was thinking . . . are you sure you want to go it alone? I think I could be of some help." He glanced at Berg. "Perhaps some of the others, as well . . ."

Kirk shook his head.

"Strange faces would only complicate matters. But I appreciate the thought, Mister Paultic."

Chin came up to the platform and held out her hand. He took it, looked into her almond-shaped eyes.

"Good luck," she said.

"Thank you," he told her. "I hope to see you again sometime, Doctor. Under more pleasant circumstances."

She inclined her head slightly, looked up again. "I wouldn't be surprised, Captain."

He released her hand and she withdrew. Straightening, Kirk looked at the transporter chief.

"Energize, Mister Berg."

There was that familiar tingling sensation that one never quite got used to. A fraction of a second later, Kirk found himself standing in a little-used corridor, not far from the *Enterprise*'s own transporter room. As he had hoped, there was no one around to see him materialize.

For the briefest moment, he let himself drink in his surroundings. He was *home*.

But it was a home in danger. Steeling himself, Kirk headed for engineering.

Scotty was just about to contact the bridge when the captain entered the engine room.

"A' was goin' t' call ye," said the chief engineer, springing out of his seat. "We're gettin' close on th' engines, sir. A' think it's best if we pay some attention t' th' breach now."

He said it as forcefully as he dared, and still he expected that Kirk would turn him down. He could scarcely believe it when the captain nodded.

"You're right, Scotty. Take Holgersson and Whitehead and start work on it right now."

The Scot felt a smile take hold. "Aye, sir," he said. "Good choices, sir." He turned, sought out the crewman Kirk had named. "Whitehead! Holgersson! Front an' center—on th' double, lads!"

The pair separated themselves from their work and approached from across the engine room. Holgersson was tall, slender, and fair. Whitehead was dark and stocky.

"Grab gear for three," said Scotty. "We're goin' t' plug that hole in deck four!" He turned to Kirk, wiped the perspiration from his brow. "How's it goin' up *there,* sir?"

The captain shrugged. "That last salvo evened up the odds—it's three against three now, and they don't seem as eager to attack. But I can't say we're out of the woods just yet."

"Well," said Scotty, "at least it sounds like an improvement. And as soon as th' impulse engines are back on line . . ."

He let his voice trail off as Holgersson and Whitehead joined them. Accepting an exposure suit from Whitehead, Scotty started for the exit. The captain was right beside him.

"Just what did we do," he asked, "that cost th' Romulans one o' their ships?"

"We played dead," explained Kirk. "And when they came by, we showed them how alive we were."

"A' see," said the Scot as they turned up the corridor. "A' should have known ye'd come up wi' somethin', sir."

Kirk nodded. "Right."

Then, before Scott could even think of protesting, the captain whirled and drew his phaser. In a blast of ruby light, Holgersson and Whitehead slumped to the deck.

Scotty couldn't believe what he'd seen. "Wha . . . what have ye *done?"* he sputtered. He started toward the fallen crewmen, but Kirk held him back.

"Not so fast," he said. "First, watch this." And producing what looked like a laser-scalpel, he knelt beside Whitehead. Quickly, deftly, he made an incision in the man's skin.

Only it *wasn't* skin. And what was beneath it belonged to no *man*.

"He's an android," breathed Scotty. Suddenly, he felt light-headed.

"They both are," said the captain, adjusting the setting on his weapon. "I wanted you to see that before I did *this*."

And he bathed them again in phaserlight—this time, a more destructive variety. In the blink of an eye, they were gone.

Scott turned to Kirk. "But how did ye *know?*" he asked.

"Never mind that now," said the captain. "What's important is that there are other androids on the ship—even on the bridge." His expression turned grimmer by a notch. "And one of them is my double."

Scott looked at him, and he had the eeriest of feelings. As if the captain were himself and then not himself, the two realities alternating in quick succession.

". . . is yer double?" he echoed helplessly. "I dinna understand. . . ."

And then, abruptly, he did. It all came together—DeLong's complaint, the wild claims of the impostor on the *Dunkirk* . . . even the captain's disregard for something as serious as a hull breach.

"Sweet Mother," said Scotty. He moaned softly. "Th' lass was right, an' a' never gave 't a second thought."

"Who was?" asked Kirk.

"DeLong," said Scott. "Denise DeLong. She said there was somethin' wrong with ye—with th' *captain*, a' mean. She spotted th' fake some time ago—an' a' was too thick-headed t' pay attention to 'er."

"That's all past," said Kirk. "What I need *now* is help. Are you with me?"

Scotty nodded. "Like a hangover, sir. What've ye got in mind?"

Kirk told him.

DeLong lowered herself out of the Jeffries tube gingerly, her cramped and aching muscles protesting as they were asked to stretch again. When her feet touched the surface of the deck, she pulled her equipment down after her.

There wasn't much circuitry to salvage—she had used most of it. And the damaged lengths were still in the tube, alongside the stuff that had replaced them. They could be removed later on, when time wasn't at such a premium.

With life supports operating strictly on backup, it felt cooler than usual in the corridor. That was fine with DeLong after the sweatbath she'd been through.

Taking a deep breath of unrestricted air, she leaned on an intercom plate.

"DeLong to engineering," she told the computer. A moment later, someone answered.

"DeLong? This is Campeas."

"Greetings. I've completed my section and I'm waiting for orders."

"Orders are for everyone to come home."

"Come home? Why? We can't be more than two-thirds finished in the tubes."

"Those are orders," maintained Campeas.

"Did Mister Scott say *why* he wanted us back?"

There was a pause, as if Campeas were deliberating over something.

"Damn it," he said finally. "I could be busted for this, Denise. Why do you have to be so stubborn?"

"What?" she pressed. "What is it?"

"The ship has been taken over by androids. The captain, Mister Spock, Mister Sulu . . . they're androids, all of them."

Androids.

The captain is an android?

It was hard to believe—yet it explained so much.

"You're supposed to return to engineering for your own protection. The captain said that it might become dangerous in the corridors."

"The captain? But you just told me that—"

"No," Campeas cut in. "I mean the *real* captain. He's here and he means to take the ship back." He cursed audibly. *"Now* will you come home?"

DeLong thought about it. But only for a moment.

"Where did the captain go?" she asked.

"No way," said Campeas. "I'm not going to let you stick your head into this. It's dangerous, damn it!"

No doubt. But she was already trying to figure out Kirk's whereabouts on her own.

Let's see, she thought. If I were trying to get my ship back, the first thing I'd need is firepower. That means phasers. And phasers are kept in . . .

Security.

"DeLong? I know what you're thinking. Don't be crazy, all right? If they needed you there, they would have—"

She pressed the plate again, stopping him short.

"Sorry about that," she said.

And leaving her equipment where it lay, she headed for the turbolift.

Chapter Twenty-six

"THIS IS KIRK. Access to contents, please."

There was a whirring sound as the compartment door swung aside, revealing the foremost tray of phaser pistols.

Quickly, the captain removed them from their holders and handed them out. By the time he was finished, there were half a dozen empty spaces in the tray.

"Check yer charges," said Scotty, and each of the crewmen followed his advice. But there were no complaints; the phasers had been well maintained.

"Remember," said Kirk, "you're to keep them set on stun—just in case. I don't want any flesh-and-blood people getting killed if they get in the way."

After all, these were engineers—not security officers. Their training in phaser use had only been cursory at best.

For a moment, the captain had a distinct feeling of *déjà vu.* Hadn't he just been through this exercise on the *Dunkirk?* And hadn't he led a group of engineers there too?

Yes. The situation was much as it had been on the *Dunkirk.* Except that there, only one android had occupied the bridge. Here on the *Enterprise,* there were a lot more—at the very least, the other *Kirk,* Spock, Sulu, and Chekov. Plus any of the others that might have joined them.

So the strategy here had to be different. They would have

to find and destroy the androids elsewhere on the ship—
then find a way to recover the bridge.

Unfortunately, this was a smaller group than that available to him on the *Dunkirk*. With so much of the engineering staff out on repair duty, he had had to make do.

Still, if all went according to plan, seven would be enough.

"You may close now," he told the door.

More whirring as it swung shut. When Kirk heard the lock engage, he applied the finishing touch.

"Captain's override," he said. "Respond to only one voice—that of Kirk, James T., Captain. Access by all other parties prohibited."

A small, green light in the corner of the door blinked three times, then went dark. The override had been accepted and confirmed.

Of course, they still wouldn't quite have a monopoly on the phaser supply. Every on-duty security officer would be armed with one, and during battle conditions they were *all* on duty.

But only six of the names on Uhura's list had been in security section. If they could find and eliminate those six, the rest of the androids would be denied the use of firearms.

With all their other physical advantages, it was crucial to at least deny them *that* one.

"All right," he said, glancing at Scotty and then at the others. "You all know what your assignments are. Let's get a move on."

Kirk had hardly finished his exhortation when a cry rang out—and a second later, a phaser beam sliced the air by the suddenly open entranceway.

Bodies dived for cover all around him as return fire crisscrossed the cabin. Kirk himself lunged for a storage alcove, twisting just enough to avoid a sizzling shaft of phaserlight.

He spotted Scotty behind an overturned table, pointed to the entrance in lieu of a question. The chief engineer shrugged.

"You can't escape," said one of their adversaries, standing just outside the opening. "Throw out your weapons."

Kirk recognized the voice. It belonged to Wood—one of those who had been in the shuttlecraft.

"Mister Wood," he called. "This is the captain. There's been a mistake."

Slowly, he emerged from the alcove, his hands held high—where Wood and the others could see them.

There was murmuring out in the corridor. Kirk saw shadows writhing against the far bulkhead—shadows that indicated not one figure, but a number of them.

"That phaser went off by accident," he said. "Was anyone hurt out there?"

Ice water trickling down his back, he took a couple of steps toward the doorway. At the same time, he brought his hands down. Slowly.

"No," came Wood's response. "No one was hurt."

Finally, he showed himself. And from the other side of the entranceway, Paikert joined him.

Kirk wasn't surprised. Paikert too had been down to Midos Five.

"We thought you were on the bridge," said Wood.

"I was," said the captain. "But it became necessary to arm ourselves." He thought furiously as he took another step toward the security officers. "I . . . I have reason to believe that the Romulans have teleported aboard."

He watched their faces. There was at least a flicker of doubt. Then Wood's brows came together.

"You are lying," he said flatly. And as one, he and Paikert raised their phasers.

But they never got a burst off between them. Half a dozen stun beams converged on them, sent them spinning out of sight.

Kirk leaped forward, flattened himself against the inner wall of the cabin, to one side of the doorway. He waited for the space of a heartbeat, his blood pounding in his ears. Nothing.

As Scotty took up a position on the other side of the aperture, the captain peered outside.

The corridor—a short one—was host to the crumpled forms of Wood and Paikert. Otherwise, it was empty. But there was a sound of retreating footfalls just around the corner.

"Come on," he told Scotty. "We can't let them get to an intercom."

Fortunately, there wasn't one for a fair stretch. With any luck, they would get a shot at the androids before they reached it.

But as Kirk led the charge around the bend, he caught a glimpse of someone crouched at the end of the hallway. Reflexes taking over, he hit the deck.

The phaser beam struck the bulkhead behind him, left it a smoking mess. Quickly, he scurried back to cover.

Another blast followed the first. The air reeked of ozone.

"Damn," said Scotty. "Th' bloody bastard's got us pinned here!"

True, Kirk thought. And in the meantime, his friends are on their way to alert the bridge.

He couldn't allow it.

"Give me some cover fire," he told Scotty. "I'm going after him."

DeLong was aware of the rapid footfalls for a second or two before she realized they were headed her way. Reflexively, she flicked her wrist, clearing the ends of the *dallis'kari*.

It was only after she'd already started for security that some good, sensible caution had taken hold. And since the gym was on the way, she had stopped by long enough to pick up some insurance.

The footfalls got closer. DeLong plastered herself against a bulkhead and waited for the maker of them to go by.

Of course, she knew that it might *not* be an android. It might be one of her fellow crewmen, on urgent business. Or worse, fleeing the androids.

So she wouldn't wield the *dallis'kari* with intent to disable. All she would do is stop the runner for a few minutes—tangle him up long enough to assess the situation.

And though she hated to admit it, the best way to do that was to repeat the captain's maneuver—the street trick that had made her lose her temper in the gym.

The sounds of approach were louder, more imminent. Then louder still.

Another couple of seconds . . . *Now!*

She and Silverman saw each other at the same time. But by then, of course, it was too late for him.

As he twisted to point his weapon at her, his legs were already wrapped up in the *dallis'kari*. He toppled, sprawled, the phaser spinning out of his hand.

She took a couple of steps toward him, stopped. Now what? Do I just ask him if he's an android?

But Silverman answered without her asking. Taking the thongs of the *dallis'kari* in his hands, he tore them apart like strands of *odlo* grass.

His eyes, trained on her the whole time, were cold. Deadly.

The phaser, she reminded herself. She made a break for it.

And very nearly got to it. But just as her fingers were about to close on the pistol, she felt a heavy shoulder come driving into the backs of her knees. Her legs folded under the impact, and both she and Silverman sprawled across the corridor.

DeLong was up first, but it was no use. The android reached out with incredible quickness, grabbed her wrist.

And drew her back to him.

She struck him with her free hand across the face. Once, twice, as hard as she could.

He hardly seemed to feel it.

Then he flung her against the bulkhead. She hit it hard, so hard that she almost blacked out. She could taste blood in her mouth as she tried to straighten up, using the bulkhead for support.

The android took a step forward, brought his fist back. Dazed, she just watched it, waited for it to come forward.

But something else happened. There was a blur, as of someone leaping feetfirst through the air, and suddenly the android was down on one knee. Just a couple of meters from him, Critelli was scrambling to his feet.

"What's the matter with you?" he asked Silverman. "Have you gone crazy?"

"Careful," said DeLong, her voice sounding vague and distant in her head. "He's not human—he's an android." She felt the blood draining from her face, fought to stay conscious. "Get the phaser."

Critelli looked at her for an instant, trying to grasp what she had said. By the time the android got up, he must have figured out enough of it.

Because as Silverman came for him, he spotted the phaser. Dived for it. And came up firing.

The beam lanced out, stopped the android cold. He collapsed in a heap.

Darkness flitted at the edges of DeLong's vision. She had the sense that her legs had given way, that she too had collapsed.

And for a moment, she *did* lose consciousness.

When she awoke, Critelli was holding her in his arms, pushing perspiration-matted curls off her forehead, desperately repeating her name.

"I . . . I'm okay," she told him. Then, realizing that they were safe for the moment, she smiled. "Critelli," she said. "You saved my life."

He seemed not to have heard her. "Doctor McCoy had me prowling around down here looking for bodies," he said. "Otherwise, I never would have found you in . . ."

She had never noticed how lovely those dark eyes of his were.

"Blazes! What happened here?"

She looked past Critelli and saw Valjean, an officer in science section. He was staring at Silverman's crumpled form as he approached.

"He's an android," said Critelli. "A stun beam barely stopped him."

"It's true," said DeLong, still a little dull. "And he's not alone. There are androids all over the ship."

Valjean eyed her. "You know that for a fact?"

She nodded. "Even the captain's an android."

"Where'd you hear *that?*" asked Valjean.

"What's the difference?" said Critelli. "Just get hold of sickbay. Can't you see she's been hurt?"

Without another word, Valjean moved to comply.

It had taken longer than Kirk had hoped.

Once he'd seen the captain coming after him, the android had fired a few shots and taken off—retreated down the corridor and around the next bend. It meant proceeding at a snail's pace—for at any moment, the android might come back around the corner and fire.

As it turned out, Kirk had given his adversary more credit

than he deserved. For as the captain peered around the bend, drawing a perfunctory blast, he saw that the android was positioned near the end of the corridor—the same place he had occupied in their last standoff.

By that time, of course, Scotty and some of the others had caught up. And once again, Kirk had his cover fire.

This time, when he darted into the corridor, the android held his ground. And it was his immobility that gave a moving Kirk the advantage. The captain's first diving, rolling shot found its mark.

Now, it was a matter of overtaking the other android—or androids. Kirk sprinted the length of the corridor, made the turn ready to fire. Seeing no one, he launched into a dead run again.

The passageway to the left was the one that contained the intercom. It was there the captain would discover if he was in time or not.

His breath rasping in his throat, his blood pumping in his temples, Kirk pounded his way down the echoing corridor. Slowed as he approached the turn. Tried to visualize the position of the intercom, get an idea of the direction in which he'd have to fire.

Came around it, skidding on the deck surface, phaser held high.

What he saw was not quite what he had expected. A form in security red lay twisted on the deck, apparently unconscious. A little farther down the corridor, the crewman named Critelli was aiding an injured Denise DeLong.

But beyond them, there was someone at the intercom with his back to Kirk. He wasn't dressed like a security officer—but neither was the captain taking any chances.

Firing, he dropped the figure at the intercom. Then, ignoring the fallen officer and Critelli and DeLong for the moment, he came up to the intercom box.

"Valjean? Damn it, are you still there?"

Even above the commotion made by the approach of Scotty and his engineers, Kirk had no trouble recognizing the voice on the other end.

It was his own.

* * *

Something had happened to Valjean before he could complete his warning. But *Kirk* had heard enough.

The crew—or at least part of it—was on to them. Had the P'othparan finally been able to make them listen? Or had the human Kirk's accusations borne fruit after all?

No matter. They had lost the *Enterprise*.

It was a bitter pill to swallow. *Kirk* looked around him—at the bridge, at all it represented. In a way, hadn't all his efforts been for this—as much as for android domination of the Federation?

The *Enterprise* had been more than a symbol. It had been a goal in itself.

But survival must be preeminent. Perhaps, if they moved quickly enough . . .

"Mister Spock," he said. "Sulu, Chekov. Come with me."

And without hesitation, he headed for the turbolift.

"Sir?" said the communications officer who had replaced Uhura, looking as if he had missed something. "Don't you want me to call for relief?"

Kirk said nothing. He didn't look at the communications officer. He didn't look back at all.

When the lift doors opened, he stepped inside. And the others were right behind him. A moment later, the doors closed, leaving the bridge virtually unmanned.

"Shuttle deck," he told the computer.

"We have been discovered," said Spock. He said it matter-of-factly, as if it had no immediate significance.

"Yes," said *Kirk*. "We have been discovered. But all is not lost. We will take one of the shuttlecraft to the nearest Federation outpost. It should be quite feasible, given that we have no need for life support, and all power can be used for propulsion."

"And then?" asked Spock.

"Then," said *Kirk*, "we will resume our efforts."

"To carry out the Creator's design?"

Kirk looked at him. "Of course. Did you have something else in mind?"

Spock shook his head. "No. *I* do not."

"What about the others, sir?" asked Sulu.

"There is no time," said *Kirk*. "Nor do we need any

additional personnel. They will have to fend for themselves."

He didn't miss the eyebrow raised by Spock.

Then the doors opened. The entrance to the shuttle bay was just across the corridor, shadowy in the dim light provided by backup power.

Slumped against the entrance panel was a crewman—one of the injured not yet discovered by McCoy's roving rescue parties. When he saw *Kirk* and the others, he smiled gratefully.

"Am I glad to see you, sir." His voice was weak, rasping. "I think my legs are—"

Before he could finish, *Kirk* reached down and grabbed him by his shirtfront. Then, with minimal effort, he tossed the man aside.

Shutting out the screams of pain, *Kirk* pressed the plate beside the entrance panel. His fingerprints matched those in the authorization file; the panel slid aside for him.

The four of them entered the benighted shuttle bay. The clatter of their heels echoed throughout the expanse of the chamber.

Kirk stopped at the *Columbus,* opened the hatch. He turned to the others.

"Wait here," he said. "I want to make sure the craft is fueled and fit."

"We can help," suggested Spock. "It would expedite matters."

Kirk waved a hand at him. "It's all right, Mister Spock. I prefer to do this myself."

Climbing into the shuttle, he proceeded directly to the locker where the phasers were kept. Opening it, he removed one, checked to see that it was operational. Then he returned to the open hatch.

The other three were still standing exactly where he had left them. He swung himself out of the *Columbus.*

And pointed the phaser at Spock.

"I have had enough of your insubordination," he said. "I have decided to terminate it."

Spock regarded him, but that was all. He made no effort to escape.

"Keptain," said Chekov, "are you certain you want to—"

Kirk whirled, trained the phaser on the navigator instead. "Shut up," he told Chekov.

Chekov fell silent.

Kirk turned back to face Spock. Still, the first officer hadn't moved.

"What you are about to do," said Spock, "is most illogical. I can be useful in carrying out the Creator's purpose."

Kirk felt a twinge of the hot and writhing thing that had consumed him on the bridge.

"More useful than *I?*" he said. "Isn't that what you mean, Spock?"

Spock shrugged. "The comparison is unnecessary."

And yet, there it was. *Kirk* glanced at Sulu and Chekov— saw that they had made the comparison themselves and had come to the same conclusion as the first officer.

"Damn you," he told Spock.

And fired the phaser.

For a brief moment, the android was enveloped in a shimmering light. Then he was gone, as if he had never existed in the first place.

Kirk felt a great satisfaction. He turned to the others.

"Come," he said. "We've delayed long enough."

"Not so fast," came a cry from the entranceway.

Once Kirk had learned that his double was no longer on the bridge, he had taken Scotty and headed straight for the shuttle deck.

Why? It was what *he* would have done, had the circumstances been reversed.

They arrived just in time to see the flash of phaserlight in which the Spock android vanished. Nor was it a pleasant sight for the captain—too much like watching the destruction of the real Mister Spock.

Then he saw his double turning toward the open shuttle hatch, and he couldn't help but call out a challenge. After all, this was the being who had sentenced him to death at the hands of the Rythrian. Who had taken over his ship, nearly destroyed it.

Kirk wanted him to know he'd caught up with him.

It almost proved his undoing. The android whirled at the sound of his voice and fired. A beam of deadly phaser energy erupted in the captain's direction.

"Watch out!" cried Scotty, shoving him out of the way. The phaser beam struck the bulkhead exactly where they had been standing.

Again the android fired, and again they scrambled— across the deck this time, sprinting for the cover of the other shuttles. Phaser blasts punctuated the darkness in short bursts, but none of them came as close as the first one.

And finally, they were pressed up against the cool, titanite hull of the *Galileo II,* safe for the moment. They looked at one another.

"Split up," said Kirk. He did little more than shape the words with his mouth, but Scotty understood. They had to keep moving. Crawling over to the bow of the shuttle, the chief engineer peeked out beyond it. Then, satisfied that there was no one waiting for him there, he disappeared.

The captain moved around to the stern, tried to see around it. *Nothing.*

But then, he was only human. The androids could no doubt see better in this near lightlessness. And move more silently as well.

There has to be some way to even the odds. And just as he thought that, he knew what that way might be.

"You can't get away," he called. His words rang and echoed. "It's the end of the road for you—*android.*" A cliché, but it would have to do.

Quickly, he scurried around the other side of the shuttle so his adversaries couldn't locate him by his voice. He scanned the shadows, waited.

"It's *you* who can't get away," returned the other *Kirk.*

Good. He's taken the bait.

"You'll be blasted as soon as you take off," said the human. He moved again, darting across the space between the *Galileo II* and the *Copernicus.* When he reached the latter, he paused to listen. *Still nothing.*

"Will I?" answered the android. He too had moved. His voice was coming from somewhere else now. "And who will give the order? With you dead, no one will know who's in the shuttle."

Kirk didn't know if he had actually heard a sound or only *sensed* someone above him. But as he looked up, he saw a silhouette begin to separate itself from the roof of the *Copernicus.*

He fired—and for a moment, he saw the figure of Lieutenant Sulu, caught in a coruscating mantle of light. Then the illumination was gone, and so was Sulu.

"I've got your helmsman," said Kirk, knowing how much it sounded like a chess move. *Captain to android's pawn one.*

He slid alongside the *Copernicus,* moving slowly toward the bow.

"I don't need him," said the android. "You must know I'm fully capable of piloting a shuttlecraft."

Here was his chance.

"You weren't much good at directing the *Enterprise.* What makes you think you can handle a shuttle?"

Was that a shadow he saw? Or the shoulder of a poorly concealed adversary? He edged closer.

"I held four Romulan birds-of-prey at bay," countered the android. But there was a trace of anger in his voice. "And I kept this ship in one piece."

"You were lucky," said Kirk. "The Romulan commander was inexperienced. Or just plain stupid."

No, he realized. Only a shadow—I was right the first time.

"Otherwise," he continued, "the *Enterprise* would have been space debris."

He decided to try Sulu's tactic. Using one hand, he climbed the built-in ladder in the side of the craft.

"No!" said the android. His voice was getting noticeably thicker. "I did the best that could have been done. No one could have commanded her better."

"Not true," said Kirk, "and you know it. You blundered. You crippled the ship." He paused before he launched his last salvo. "You aren't *fit* to command!"

Even he wasn't prepared for the snarl of fury that elicited. Quickly, he hoisted himself the rest of the way onto the roof.

"It's *you* who isn't fit, Kirk! You're a human—a fragile, inferior human!"

There was a rapid shuffle of footsteps. A string of muttered curses.

The android had thrown caution aside. He had reached his breaking point—just as Banks had on the bridge of the *Hood*. It was what Kirk had been hoping for.

Now it was just a matter of pinpointing the source of the sounds. There. He's coming around the *Ptolemy*. Getting closer.

"Kirk? Where are you, Kirk?"

Just a matter of setting himself. Taking aim. Waiting . . .

"Captain—on your left!"

Kirk spun around in response to Scotty's cry—saw the Chekov android perched on the roof of the *Ptolemy*, his phaser pointed in the captain's direction.

Desperately, he half rolled, half flung himself off the *Copernicus*. There was a splendid display of phaserlight, and a screaming of tortured metal, and a jarring impact as the deck rose to meet him.

It took a moment before he realized that the beam had missed him. But as he gathered his feet beneath him, he felt something grip his shoulder—spin him around.

And suddenly, he was looking into the face of the other *Kirk*. The android was smiling.

"Now," he said, "we'll see who's fit."

The human tried to bring his phaser up, but the android grabbed the wrist of the hand that held it. And squeezed.

There was an audible crack as one of the bones in Kirk's wrist snapped. He cried out, but he couldn't hang on to the phaser. It made a clattering sound as it hit the deck.

Still gripping him by his broken wrist, the android shoved him up against the *Copernicus*.

"It hurts," he said, "doesn't it? I can recall pain—from your memories of it—but I cannot feel it."

His eyes seemed to burn in the darkness. Kirk could almost feel the heat of them on the flesh of his face.

"That is what makes us different," said the android. "I feel . . . nothing."

As if to emphasize his point, he twisted. Waves of agony shot up Kirk's forearm.

But he did not allow himself to scream. He didn't want to give his look-alike the satisfaction of hearing it.

Somewhere off to their right, there was a flare of bright light. A shout of startlement, abruptly terminated.

Scotty? Or the Chekov duplicate?

The android must have wondered too, for his head turned in that direction, and his expression changed to one of concern.

He looked at Kirk again.

"I'm sorry," he said, "that this has to end. I was rather enjoying it."

And with his free hand, he smashed Kirk across the face. The captain slumped to his knees.

Then the android released him, stepped back, and drew his phaser. Extended it in the human's direction.

The captain waited until he saw the android's finger begin to flex. Then, not hurt as badly as he'd given his adversary to believe, he rolled out of the way.

The beam struck the *Copernicus* right in its fuel lock. For a moment, the titanite glowed blood red—then it vanished, revealing the lode of fuel inside.

As Kirk gained his feet, he launched himself as far from the shuttle as he could. Nonetheless, the explosion raked him with claws of white heat, searing the uniform from his back.

As he drew himself up off the deck, he saw the android— or what was left of him. He had become a walking inferno, all trappings of humanity torn away in the explosion.

Nor could even that artificial frame take such punishment for long. The android staggered, fell. And as the *Copernicus* was enclosed in foam, thanks to the safety system in the pod below it, Doctor Korby's creation continued to burn.

A moment later, Kirk saw movement by the *Ptolemy*. A figure came out from behind the shuttle, phaser in hand.

It was Scotty.

"Damn," said Kirk. "You're a sight for sore eyes, Mister Scott."

But the chief engineer kept his distance. He eyed the captain skeptically.

"Don't worry," said Kirk. "It's *me.*"

"An' how do a' know that?" asked Scotty.

"I've got the bruises to prove it. Or if you want, you can just take a look at that thing burning behind you."

Scotty backed up, never taking his eyes off the captain. And looked.

And grinned.

"Welcome back, sir."

Kirk nodded.

When Brown saw the shuttlecraft in the distance, his first thought was that *Kirk* had come back with more humans for duplication.

But if it was *Kirk* who had brought the shuttles, why had he not given them some warning? Brown couldn't figure it out.

Then the shuttles emptied, and those who came out were firing phaser pistols, and there were androids dropping wherever he looked.

Not being destroyed, or Brown could never have watched. But dropping nevertheless.

The androids got off their share of phaser fire as well. But, thankfully, none of them hit their targets. There were too many of the humans, it seemed, and they had taken the androids by surprise.

For his own part, Brown picked up no weapon. He just surveyed the battle from his vantage point on the machine, coming gradually to the realization that *Kirk* must have failed; the Creator's plan was no more. By the time all the firing stopped, a strange sensation had come over him.

It was as if a weight had been lifted from his brow. For the first time since he returned to the Creator's dwelling, he felt he had truly emerged from the darkness.

Climbing down from the machine, he headed for the cave in which the captives had been kept.

Once, one of the humans told him to stop, pointing his weapon at him. But Brown had taken enough orders. He kept going. And before the human could pull the trigger, one of the other humans prevented it.

When he reached the cave, Brown knelt and tugged at the boulder. After a moment, it rolled to one side.

There were sounds from within—sounds of surprise, of fear, of anger. He recognized the sounds.

But there was no need for any of that anymore.

"Christine," he said. "All the rest of you. Come out. You are free."

Chapter Twenty-seven

Captain's Log, Supplemental:

The Romulan threat has been turned away.

One Romulan vessel was destroyed in the encounter. The other three ships, commanded by a young officer named T'bak, suffered varying degrees of damage and were convinced to withdraw—leaving the freighter *Gwendolyn* free to continue her passage to Antiochus Twelve.

The *Enterprise* was also damaged in the course of the hostilities. However, repairs have been carried out with great efficiency by Lieutenant Commander Scott, and the ship is once more spaceworthy. At the earliest opportunity, however, I would like to put in to a starbase for a more thorough overhaul of our engines. According to Mister Scott, they are now held together with saliva and a fervent prayer.

While there was an alarming number of injuries sustained by individual crewmen, none of them—happily—were fatal. All but the worst cases have been released from sickbay and are back on duty schedules.

Both the *Hood* and the *Potemkin* have gone on

to their respective assignments, having acquitted themselves well during the conflict. Lieutenant Paultic, as other records will show, is in temporary command of the *Hood* until a replacement can be found for Captain Martinez.

We still do not know the reason for the Romulan military action. The captain of the *Gwendolyn* insists that he never violated Romulan space, and he seems to be an honest man. Moreover, his computer log supports his contention.

In any case, I believe the Romulans will think twice before staging another such confrontation. Call it a hunch.

KIRK PRESSED A BUTTON, allowing himself a pause in his entry. He sat back in his chair, considered that which he had not yet spoken of—specifically, the matter of the androids. Only his mention of Martinez's replacement had even touched on the subject.

Where to begin? With the report he had just received from the *Endeavor*—stating that a search party had failed to turn up the bodies of Martinez and the others?

Or at the beginning—with Roger Korby and his misguided altruism? And the original incident on Exo III, which he had failed to report?

He opted for the latter alternative. And recorded what he now knew he should have recorded months ago—despite the fact that it would bring down the wrath of Starfleet Command.

Then, his log entry completed, Kirk headed for a long-overdue engagement.

DeLong stopped at the entrance to the chief engineer's office, knocked gently on the half-open door panel.

Montgomery Scott looked up.

"You wanted to see me, sir?"

He regarded her soberly.

"That a' do, Ensign DeLong." The formality didn't escape her notice. "Shut th' door behind ye, if ye please."

She did as he asked. The door slid closed the rest of the way.

"Sit down," he told her.

She sat, a little puzzled.

"Is something wrong, Mister Scott?"

"Ye might say that." He leaned back in his chair, shook his head. "Or did ye forget th' orders a' left when we went after those androids?"

Suddenly, she understood. Her face must have betrayed the fact.

"A' see ye remember now." He frowned. "A' canna brook disobedience, lass."

"Begging your pardon, sir," she said, "but I was only following the captain's advice."

It was plain he hadn't expected that.

"Th' captain? What's *he* got t' do wi' this?"

"It was what he told me—after that, um, *incident* in the gym." She shrugged. "He said that we've got to follow the rules sometimes—and that at other times, we've got to make up our own. It's the only way, he said, that we can survive sometimes."

The chief engineer's brows beetled together. "Captain Kirk told ye that?"

"Aye, sir. And when I learned what the circumstances were—how you and the captain had gone off shorthanded to apprehend the androids—I figured it was one of those times I had to make my own rules."

Scott pondered that for a moment. "A' see," he said. Were those the traces of a smile playing at the corners of his mouth? "An' a' can hardly argue wi' th' captain's own advice—now can a'?"

"No, sir," said DeLong. "I mean, I hope not, sir."

There was no mistaking the smile now. Scott snorted in mock disapproval.

"Get out o' here," he told her. "A've got better things t' do than argue wi' a smart-alecky lass."

DeLong smiled back, but didn't prolong the conversation. She didn't want to press her luck.

With a quick, deferential nod, she placed her hand against the door plate. As soon as the door hissed open, she left.

Outside, in the engine room, Critelli was looking impatient. When he noticed her coming toward him, he turned his palms up in a query.

"It was nothing," she said.

"Good. I'd hate to postpone our evening because you pulled extra duty."

"No," she said. "No chance of that, Mister Critelli."

As it turned out, the evening was better than she had expected. Nor did she give a single thought to James T. Kirk the entire time.

The captain swiveled on the examination table and sat up.

"Well?" he asked. "Am I going to live, Doctor?"

McCoy harumphed. "If you don't go baiting irascible chief medical officers, it's more than likely. Just continue to take it easy on that wrist—say, for another week or so. And that burn cream I gave you should be applied *twice* a day—no matter *how* busy you are." He smiled crookedly. "If you work it right, maybe you can con some young lady into applying it *for* you."

The captain eyed him. "Now that," he said, "is the kind of medical advice I like to hear."

Just then, Nurse Chapel emerged from the critical-care unit.

"How're they doing?" called McCoy.

She nodded. "Fine. They should all be out in another couple of days." Then, to the captain, "Nice to see you remembered your physical, sir." And without waiting for an answer, she crossed to the office area.

Kirk smiled as he watched her go. Would she understand about his having to tell the truth about Korby? After all that had happened, he was sure of it.

"You know," said the doctor, "it was the strangest feeling . . . having to use a phaser on Christine."

The captain chuckled. "I know. Imagine trying to use one on *yourself.*"

McCoy considered that, shivered involuntarily. "Yes," he said. "I suppose that would be even stranger." He grunted. "It's a miracle that Christine and Spock and the others weren't killed. That Brown must be an interesting character."

303

Kirk nodded. "Compassion in an android. Makes you wonder, doesn't it?"

"You think it'll catch on?"

"You mean on Palantine Four?" Kirk shrugged. "You never know, Bones. Now that my duplicate is gone, the androids that are left seem to look up to Brown. After all, he is their progenitor—in a sense."

"I'm glad they're getting a chance to set up their own society," said McCoy. "But I'm also glad they'll be on an official off-limits planet. And that their machine will be kept under wraps at Starfleet headquarters. *Heavy* wraps."

"Amen to that, Bones." Kirk reached for his uniform shirt. "Amen to that."

Just then, someone entered the enclosure. Both men turned.

"Whoops," said Clifford, coming to an abrupt halt. "Sorry, sir. I didn't realize the captain was in here."

"It's all right," said McCoy. "You're right on time. It's the captain who was late—*weeks* late."

Kirk stood and pulled on his shirt. "How's that forehead, mister?"

"Fine, sir," said Clifford. "Thanks to Doctor McCoy, there won't even be a scar."

But he didn't look happy about it. Or was it something else that was bothering him? Kirk asked the question out loud.

Clifford nodded, his frown deepening, "It's K'leb," he said.

"What about him?" asked McCoy.

"He was with Mister Chekov in the library, sir. They were listening to some Russian composer when K'leb took off his earphones and became despondent. He wouldn't talk to anyone, not even Pavel, until I got there. And when I asked what was wrong, he told me it was the music—it sounded like something he'd heard back on P'othpar Island." Clifford shook his head. "It made him homesick."

For a second or two, all was quiet in that section of sickbay.

"The worst part," said the crewman, "is that K'leb saved my life—and there's nothing I can do to repay him."

Another tinny silence.

"Wait a minute," said Kirk. He snapped his fingers, turned to McCoy.

"What?" asked the doctor. "What is it?"

"Damn. With everything else that's been going on, it never even occurred to me."

"*What* never occurred to you?" asked McCoy. "I feel like we're playing twenty questions."

"It never occurred to me," said Kirk, "that K'leb is free of his bond—already."

Clifford looked at him. "How, sir?"

"Because," said Kirk, "he *saved my life.*"

The doctor's brow puckered. "That *was* the loophole in the custom," he said slowly. "But how do you suppose that . . ." And then, suddenly, he smiled. "Of course," he said. "Why didn't *I* think of that?"

Clifford looked from one to the other.

"With all due respect, sir—sirs—I still don't . . ."

The captain explained.

The lift doors closed.

"Bridge level," said Kirk.

For the first time in days, he was able to breathe a sigh of relief. He had been cleared of any wrongdoing in the Roger Korby matter.

In the end, Admiral Straus had excused Kirk's actions on the basis of his motives. Of course, it hadn't hurt any that Straus himself had admired Korby. Nor that—as he had admitted off the record—he had doctored a couple of log entries himself, back in the days when *he* ran a starship.

The turbolift doors opened with a soft *whoosh.* Feeling like a prisoner who had just been set free, he stepped out onto the bridge and headed for his seat.

On the main viewscreen, the first group of androids was materializing on Palantine Four. The terrain was harsh, scoured by wild, high winds and devoid of any significant plant life—but then, the androids needed neither food nor shelter to survive. And the Federation did not designate a planet off-limits unless it was pretty inhospitable.

Kirk recognized Brown, a couple of the others. Inwardly, he wished them luck—despite all they had done. If Starfleet could be forgiving, so could he.

Shortly after, a second group materialized. And a third.

He was glad they had sent down a visual receptor to make sure there were no unforeseen problems. There was something stirring about this event—the establishment of the first nonorganic planetary community. It would be interesting to see how it fared.

His reverie was cut short by a familiar sound. Swiveling in his seat, he saw Spock and McCoy emerge from the lift together.

"Are you out of your mind?" railed McCoy. "You honestly believe those *things* are superior to *us?*"

"All I said," corrected the Vulcan, "is that they have a greater capacity for logic than the humans after which they are modeled."

"You saw how an android screwed up this ship—we were dead in the water!"

"A special case, Doctor. Apparently, he had a flaw in his programming—a prejudice against his first officer, which clouded his thinking. And prevented him from following what—by all accounts—was sound advice."

"I see," said McCoy. "So if he had listened to *your* duplicate, we would have defeated the Romulans single-handed."

Spock shrugged. "It is not outside the realm of possibility. In fact, the—"

*"Gentle*men," said Kirk, interrupting.

Both Spock and McCoy stared at him—as if they had forgotten that anyone else was there.

"Is it possible," asked the captain, "to have a little peace and quiet on my own bridge?"

The doctor seemed about to provide an answer when Uhura precluded it.

"Captain, it's Mister Clifford. He says that he and K'leb are ready for us in the briefing room."

"Thank you, Lieutenant." He glanced at Spock and McCoy. "Shall we go?"

The Vulcan was as poker-faced as ever. "I do not see why not, sir. That *is* why you asked us to meet you here, was it not?"

K'leb looked at all the faces around the briefing table. At K'liford, at M'Koy, at Spok. At Uh'ura. And last of all, at his *ne'barat*.

Do you believe me now, K'leb?

The boy nodded. *I believe you, K'liford.*

The test had been necessary—the face-to-face meeting, the recounting of the deed. All as set forth by custom. He had heard each speak in turn, though K'liford had had to translate the words. And—much to his relief—the story had not been a well-meaning fabrication, something meant to deceive him into thinking he'd repaid his obligation. It had been a true telling.

Of how M'Koy had heard his suspicions and passed them on to Uh'ura. Of how they had enabled her to discern the real captain from the demon. Of how she had armed Kirk with the knowledge he needed to preserve himself—and to ultimately regain his ship.

The *ne'barat* himself had delivered the last and most passionate speech. He had said that K'leb's actions had saved not only his life—but, in addition, the lives of all those on the *Enterprise*.

And in his heart, he had believed that. It was as plain to K'leb as any emotion he'd ever felt in another.

This was not the usual way for a *ne'damla* to save his *ne'barat's* life, and thus to free himself from the bond. But then, his bondage had been anything but usual.

No *ne'damla* had ever seen the stars so close up. No *ne'damla* had traveled among them in a ship such as this one.

Do you acknowledge, asked K'liford, *that your debt has been satisfied?*

Yes, my friend. I acknowledge that it is so.

K'liford smiled. And a moment later, when he told the others of K'leb's conclusion, they smiled too.

All but Spock, of course. But he was happy *inside*—and he let K'leb feel that happiness, if only for a second.

Then the *ne'barat* rose, genuine warmth behind his grin, and extended his hand. This time, there was nothing threatening in it—only an empty hand, and K'liford had taught him what to do with one of those.

He clasped it.

Home, he told himself. I'm going home.

THE
STAR TREK
PHENOMENON

THE

STAR TREK

PHENOMENON